MW00935975

Praise for VIper .... ui Sangue Series

"Outlaw vampire bikers. The women who tame them. What's not to love? Patricia Rasey's new series Sons of Sangue is hot!"

—*Monette Michaels, author of Security Specialists International series*

"I picked up Viper: Sons of Sangue by Patricia A. Rasey. Needless to say, I was a goner from the first scene... a very hotttt one at that. Not only do we have extremely attractive Vampires, but these Vampires are in a motorcycle gang. BRILLIANT."

—*Kimberly Rocha 5 Stars for Goodreads and Book Obsessed Chicks*

"I was hooked from the very beginning with the opening scene of the book, all the way to the very end. She mixed in all the things I think makes an incredible story. A great plot. Hot men. Danger. And incredible sex with said hot man. By the end of the story Miss Rasey had me thinking about the next book, then the one after that and so on. I sincerely hope she has already started on Viper's twin Kaleb's story, because I can only imagine it is going to be another great, steamy read."

—*Michelle Boone 5 Stars, guest reviewer for Book Obsessed Chicks*

Viper
Sons of Sangue

Patricia A. Rasey

Patricia A. Rasey
patricia@patriciarasey.com
www.PatriciaRasey.com

Publisher's Note: This is a work of fiction. Names, characters, places, and incidents are a product of the author's imagination. Locales and public names are sometimes used for atmospheric purposes. Any resemblance to actual people, living or dead, or to businesses, companies, events, institutions, or locales is completely coincidental.

Book Layout ©2013 BookDesignTemplates.com

Ordering Information:
Quantity sales. Special discounts are available on quantity purchases by corporations, associations, and others. For details, contact the email address above.

Viper: Sons of Sangue / Patricia A. Rasey – 1st ed.
ISBN-13: 978-1490991689

Dedication

To Lara Adrian, who pushed me to write a story about vampires and mentioned the one idea she knew I'd fall in love with: Vampire Bikers. Thanks for a friendship that's lasted a lifetime!

To my Beta Readers: Barb Auzins, Becky Heath and Suzi Behar for giving me their honest opinions, and being there for me throughout the book.

To my editor, Blair Bancroft, for helping make Viper a better story. I appreciate your hard work, insight and expertise.

To my Readers, you have my gratitude. Without you, I would have no one to tell my stories to. Thank you for reading them!

And to my husband Mark, who has been by my side through thick and thin. I love you!

In Loving Memory of Georgie Davis, who believed in my writing and was always waiting for the next book. Rest in peace! You will be missed.

PROLOGUE

AGAINST THE WALL, JEANS SLUNG LOW ON LEAN HIPS, HIS MO-torcycle vest hiding a well-muscled ass, he slid smoothly in and out. The blonde's back rode up the tiled wall with each thrust. Soft moans echoed off the bathroom ceramic tiles. Not his ... just hers. He made no sound at all, which added to the eroticism as Cara watched the carnal scene play out before her. The woman's legs wrapped his trim waist, her toes curling in open-toed sandals. Ash-blonde hair laid in disarray, hiding her facial features, all but her candy-apple red lipstick, the entire scene reflected in the mirror across from them.

Cara's heart damn near stopped as he tipped the blonde's chin with the pad of his thumb. His deep-red tongue snaked out, licking the pulse visible beneath her pale white skin. His nostrils flared, his mouth opened and teeth pierced flesh, causing Cara to gasp and give up her position. The blonde, lost in ecstasy, barely glanced her way. It was the tightening of the leg muscles above his ass that gave away she had heard.

But him ... he raised his dark shaggy mane of jet hair and turned toward her. His obsidian like gaze locked with hers, holding her feet fast to the white tiled floor. She couldn't run if she wanted to. Elon-gated canine teeth dripped blood as he growled with menace. Her heart stopped dead for what felt like an eternity and light-

1

2 | PATRICIA A. RASEY

headedness threatened to make her world go black. His second growl sent Cara into action as she swung the bathroom door wide and fled the room.

His name spilling off the blonde's red lips was the last thing she heard before the door swung shut.

Kane.

CHAPTER ONE

H IS THIGHS HUGGED THE WORN, BROWN LEATHER SEAT OF HIS Harley Davidson CVO Fat Bob as he leaned into the corner at seventy-miles-per-hour. Rubber tread ate up the asphalt and blurred the yellow lines beneath him. The wind rustled his dark hair as the Twin Cam Screamin' Eagle 110 engine took the blacktop with ease. He loved the freedom of the open road. His black-leather motorcycle cut, flapped behind him, something he was rarely without. The jackets were referred to as cuts due to their sleeves being removed, giving them a vest-like appearance. He wore his with pride like the rest of his brothers.

Kane pulled back the handle grip, gassing the engine. His bike hit ninety on the straightaway. His leather chaps beat against his denim clad legs in the cool breeze that came off the Siuslaw River, though he felt none of it. Low-hanging fog rolled in from the heavy cold air settling into the valley, blanketing the ground and hampering visibility. Normally, he might have taken a bit more precaution on the hairy road conditions, but not today. Too much weighed on his mind and speed seemed to clear it. Besides, he knew these roads like the back of his hand.

The town of Pleasant, Oregon, had seen bloodshed as of late, or rather blood drainage. Two bodies had been found dumped in the Siuslaw National Forest, void of blood, and the law wanted answers.

They had a blackguard on their hands, a nasty piece of work. They couldn't afford one of them running loose, murdering innocents. The OMC, or rather Outlaw Motorcycle Club, had been questioned. Every one of his brothers. They were outlaws, one-percenters as the American Motorcycle Association had coined all outlaw bikers, therefore dangerous in the eyes of the law. Forget the fact they had protected the little town for decades because of their presence.

No one dared intrude on their territory … not without repercussions. The OMC had its own form of justice. Swift and severe. When they found this miscreant, he'd be dealt with, but not by any court of law. Kane gassed the bike and buried the needle of the speedometer, feeling the liquid adrenaline course through his veins like a junky injecting heroine. Bikers were born to the road. It wasn't a lifestyle choice, it was an identity. Most didn't accept them, let alone understand them. They lived an existence outside of the law.

He wore the president patch on his left breast. His twin, Kaleb, sat at his right hand, sporting the vice president patch. They were the oldest of the Sons of Sangue and the closest direct descendants of Vlad III himself, better known as Vlad Dracula or Vlad Tepes. They weren't braggarts by any means, not with the man's blackened history, just merely a fact of how they came into existence. Kane respected his position as president, even reveled in it, but some days it weighed on his shoulders … like with these recent murders. He needed to take care of business and fast before the cops focused solely on the club or discovered their secret.

And if that weren't enough, keeping the VP in order proved to be a challenge at times, he thought with a harrumph. Just the thought of his twin brother left him grumbling beneath his breath. Reckless is what he was. Hell, he only arrived in this world minutes before Kaleb, but by the way his brother acted, you would think years separated them. Kaleb could be downright foolhardy, leaving him the sole director of the Sons most days.

Kane slowed his bike to a stop, his thighs holding it upright. He turned the key off, cutting the rumble of the bike short as he sniffed the air. His keen sense picked up the metallic tang of fresh blood. Just the scent had his fangs aching as they elongated from his gums. Hunger gnawed deep in his gut, as if he needed a reminder of what he was. He hadn't fed in three nights, at least nothing of real substance. He could consume regular food when the need arose for him to fit into normal society, but it held no nutritional value for his kind. Without blood, they'd age rapidly and die.

He unsnapped his skull cap, half helmet, hung it on the rubber grip of his handle bar, and turned his head to see if he could track the whereabouts of the scent. Kicking down the centerstand on his Harley, he swung a leg over the brown leather seat, and headed for the woods. He leapt effortlessly over the twelve-foot deep ditch, his black boots crunching on the fallen pine needles and debris as he landed. Kane ducked his six-foot-four inch frame under low hanging branches of the darkening woods. He didn't need sunlight to see; his eyes were as good as night-vision goggles. Critters scurried for cover and birds took flight as a predator entered their sanctuary.

Stopping momentarily, Kane raised his nose and sniffed the air again. The scent was ten times stronger than where he left his bike.

Human blood.

He followed a small trail that led deeper into the trees, stepping over fallen brush and limbs, skirting large Sitka spruces. About a football field from the road, Kane stopped next to a small mound of dirt.

A very shallow grave.

One that was meant to be found.

Kane walked an arc around it, noting a red-tipped nail poking through the debris. He knew he should call the cops, not taint the crime scene due to his curiosity. Hell, they already suspected the Sons knew something about the previous crimes. He certainly didn't need to give them evidence pointing right to their door. But if Kane could find clues as to who might be feeding off the humans and dumping their remains, he stood a much better chance of catching this son of a bitch before they did. Not likely the sheriff, Oregon State Police or their FSD, Forensic Services Division, would share any information with him. Besides, what would they do? Arrest him? Put him behind bars? Kane thought with a snort. There wasn't a prison built that could hold his kind.

With the toe of his boot, he moved the finger, further exposing the hand. Kane hunkered down and brushed away some of the dirt and leaves when his keen sense of hearing picked up the sound of someone approaching. He felt the presence of his twin long before he stood mere feet away. Kane didn't bother to acknowledge Kaleb as he continued to uncover the body.

Kaleb looked over Kane's shoulder. "What the fuck? We got another drainage?"

Kane brushed the dirt from his hands on the seat of his jeans as he stood to face Kaleb. Another scent hung in the air, one he couldn't quite put a finger on. The promise of the oncoming rain, mixed with the heavy scent of dirt, tainted the air enough that he couldn't get a handle on the smell. Possibly that of the perpetrator, indicating a fresh kill.

"What the hell do you think?"

"This is the third body in Pleasant … our town, Viper. You think whoever is responsible is sending us some kind of message?"

"It's starting to look that way."

"Then this fuck is pissing on us. We got to do something. Show this fuck he can't shit in our territory."

Kane nodded slowly. Anyone knew that to disrespect an MC's territory in such a manner would start an all-out war. The question was who would be stupid enough?

"What the hell do you think they want?" He voiced his frustration aloud, not that he expected an answer from Kaleb. "We should call the sheriff."

"Jesus, Viper. You know they'll try and lay this one on our doorstep again. They don't trust us. I say we get rid of the evidence. Incinerate it. No body, no evidence of foul play."

"You got some fucked-up desire to go to battle with the locals, Hawk?" Kane faced his twin full on, fists on hips. "If this one follows the last two cases, the sheriff's office has already been tipped off. It's not likely they'll be far behind. We get rid of the body and they'll be all over us. We fought too hard to co-exist. We keep trouble outside the limits; they turn a blind eye when it comes to us and our activities. We get rid of this body and that tenuous truce will end."

Kaleb indicated the dirt mound with the tip of his chin. "So what the hell are you doing? Doesn't look like you're waiting for the cops to me."

He turned his back on Kaleb, knelt before the body and ignored his twin. He didn't need to answer to anyone, leastwise Kaleb. Although he knew his twin was correct, that he shouldn't be disturbing the evidence, he had to see if this victim followed the previous profiles. As he brushed more dirt away from the face, he revealed matted, long ash-blonde hair, red lipstick smudged across a pale white cheek, neck slit ear to ear.

Son of a bitch. Lightning lit the sky, eerily illuminating the face he had just uncovered, followed by a crack of thunder. Kane hardened his jaw, hearing Kaleb's answering whistle. Not only was she the same description as the last two victims, she was Kane's current—scratch that, he'd now be needing to find a new one—blood donor.

This shit just got personal.

"DETECTIVE BRAHNAM?" DISPATCHER Reeves poked his head into her office.

Cara glanced up from the file she perused. The dispatcher's brown hair appeared lightly streaked with blond in the fluorescent lighting as it fell over his darker brows, making him look even younger than his twenty-two years, fresh out of the academy and new to their force. He had an enthusiasm for the job that Cara could appreciate.

"We got an anonymous call again. Phone number traces back to a cell, just like last time. Looks like we might have another dumped body."

Her breath caught. Adrenaline coursed through her veins. Not another murder. They still had to figure out what the hell had happened to the last two victims. Throat slit, that part they understood. But nearly every ounce of blood had been drained from both women, that part they didn't. Both bodies showed very few signs of postmortem lividity, the settling of the remaining blood to the lower regions of the body. There hadn't been much blood left to settle. No rope burns could be found to indicate if the bodies had been hung upside down and bled out. In theory, if the throat had been sliced, the body then moved and dumped, a small amount of blood would still remain in the body, more than had been left it both victims combined. The medical examiner had said, "It's the damnedest thing."

Cara had her own theories, but she didn't dare voice them. They'd undoubtedly take her away in a straightjacket. Ten years ago she had been a witness to something ... a nightmare she had put at the back of her mind, one that she tried to explain away as a figment of an overactive teenage imagination. After all, vampires weren't real. She had even tried to convince herself that the man at the center of those nightmares didn't exist either. But ten years later, she came back to Pleasant, accepted a job as detective with the Lane County Sheriff's Office after serving six years with the city PD in Eugene, and ran smack dab into the enigma. Kane hadn't aged, only appeared more menacing if truth be told. Cara kept her distance for personal and professional reasons. Lane County's Sheriff's Office knew the Sons of Sangue's clubhouse, of which Kane was the President, was located within city limits. Well before her time on the force, the Sheriff's Office had an unwritten agreement with them: keep any and all violence out of town and the S.O. would look the other way. After all, no one with half a brain would go up against an OMC without knowing there would be backlash. This kept the town of Pleasant, for the most part, violence free.

Until now.

Cara slapped the file closed, stood and grasped her light jacket from the coat tree. "Whereabouts?"

"North Fork Road. Just before you get to Bender Landing County Park."

"You trace the call?"

"GPS on the cell says Main Street near Tom's Deli."

"Send two deputies out there. See if they can find a witness to anyone making a call from that area. Tell them if they find the cell, not to touch it, but secure it until a tech comes. We need to print it. Damn it," she cursed, jamming her arms into her jacket sleeves. "Anyone else know about this yet?"

"Only you, Detective."

"Call the sheriff, let him know we have another possible homicide."

Cara headed for the door, Dispatcher Reeves backing out, his eyes beaming with excitement. She knew he couldn't wait until he could hit the streets as a deputy. Jeff Reeves had already finished the required courses, but with the current state of the economy, there had been no room on the force for new hires for deputies. Lane

County's Sheriff's Office operated on too few deputies as it was. The last round of layoffs had nearly crippled the office.

"You want me to call Hernandez?"

Cara nodded, not hiding her answering grimace. Joe wasn't going to be happy. "Looks like we're going to have to cut my partner's downtime short."

Joe had left the S.O. two hours prior, hoping to catch some alone time with his wife since the kids were at his mother's for the day. She'd no doubt catch shit for interrupting his sex life and remind Cara of her lack thereof. But she didn't have time for relationships. Besides, in her experience, sex was highly overrated anyway.

"Tell him to meet me out there. I'll grab the spotlights. It'll be black as sin by the time I make the drive. Have two deputies meet us. I'll need to get as much collected as possible. A storm is supposed to hit the area at any moment."

Reeves trotted off to do her bidding. He'd make a good deputy someday. For now, the kid had to bide his time until the economic crunch took an upswing. Cara walked to the back of the office, grabbed two of the large spotlights along with tripods, and exited through the rear of the building. As she pushed the remote, the lights on her car blinked twice and the trunk popped open. Cara quickly checked to see if the collection kits were well-stocked, then added the lights and tripods, slamming the lid down.

This time of the year, they lost daylight quickly. And with the promise of oncoming rain, they'd be under pressure to get as much collected as they could before the predicted heavy downpour washed away any evidence. Cara jogged back inside, grabbed a large tarp and some metal poles as an afterthought, then headed back for the Dodge Charger.

Fifteen minutes later, she spotted Hernandez' dark blue Toyota Camry pulled along the berm of the road. His hip leaning against the fender, Joe crossed his arms over his stocky chest and glared at her. Gravel crunched beneath her tires as Cara pulled up behind him. She exited her car and Joe pushed off the vehicle to meet her halfway. *Yep, he didn't look too happy.* She smiled, despite his mood.

"Just because you don't have a life, Brahnam, doesn't mean you have to look happy about interrupting mine."

Cara walked around the car and popped the trunk, handing him the spotlights and tripods. "Wow, look at that hair. Didn't have time to comb it? Looks to me like you just crawled out of bed, Hernandez."

He raked his free hand through the unruly dark curls, his dark brown eyes turning up in humor. "That's precisely what I did. Jealous?"

She laughed. As partners, they made a good fit. "Not in the least. I need a man who can last longer than two minutes in the sack."

"You're too damn picky, Brahnam. That's why you don't have a man to bed."

Placing a hand over her heart, she said, "You wound me, Hernandez. Now, let's get to work."

A black and white pulled up behind her Charger, the LED lights flashing brightly. They were losing daylight quickly. The two deputies she asked for exited the vehicle. With the pending storm working against them, they'd need to hurry. Cool humid air lifted the curls from her neck that had escaped her ponytail. She brushed the loose strands from her face as she told the uniforms to grab the kits and follow them to the posted hiker path through the forest.

The four of them slid down the deep ditch and climbed up the other side, mindful of where they stepped. A small path led deeper into the woods, exactly as the caller described it. Ducking beneath the cover of trees, Cara flipped on her light and followed the trail. She shined the light on the ground, catching several other footprints in the moist earth. They'd have to pour casts of every print, though it wouldn't likely help. The path was too well traveled to give them anything exclusive. The four of them carefully made their way just to the side of the trail, making sure not to add to the footprints already there.

About three-hundred-or-so-feet in, Cara came to a stop. Her heart sank. The caller hadn't been bluffing. A small mound of disturbed, fresh dirt lay before them. The head and upper torso were visible in the flashlight, appearing as though someone might have begun digging up the corpse. The victim had the same pale blonde hair as the last two victims, along with her neck being slit nearly from ear to ear. If Cara were of the betting sort, she'd wager that this one had been drained of most of her blood as well and they'd find squat for evidence.

"Another blonde," Joe said, looking at Cara. "You might want to consider dying your hair, Brahnam."

Cara didn't so much as crack a smile, although she knew it had been Joe's attempt at a joke. Lane County had a population of 330,000-plus people, but Pleasant only had a mere 3,600 residents, severely limiting the killer's targets if he continued to hunt in Pleasant for victims. The last two victims had been citizens of the small town. Cara bet this one wouldn't be different.

She tucked an errant curl behind her ear. "Hopefully this piece of shit moves on or he'll run out of women to choose from in Pleasant."

"Well, like I said—"

"Not funny, Joe."

He shook his head as he hunkered down to the shallow grave. The deputies went about setting up battery-powered lights to shine on the victim as a loud crack of lightning flashed across the darkened sky. "Maybe not, but I'd still consider the color change."

"How about we get off me as the subject. We need to hurry it along by the sound of the approaching storm." She looked at the younger deputy. "One of you call the ME?"

"Reeves already did," the smaller of the two deputies replied. "Said the doctor was coming himself. The ME also said to tell you not to disturb a thing until he got here."

"Of course he did." Cara looked above them at the small clearing in the trees, the sky growing darker by the minute. "Then he best hurry or we're not going to have a damn thing to find here."

Just as the words left Cara's lips, and to her own dumb luck, big fat drops fell upon her upturned face. "Son of a bitch," she muttered. "Get the tarp and quick."

Before they had the tarp fully in place, the sky let loose and rain poured into the valley. The deputies quickly finished setting up what little ground cover they could manage and then began to cordon off the scene with yellow crime scene tape. The tarp provided little shelter as water began running down the slopes and washing away some of the dirt and mud from their victim. Cara's hair plastered to her cheeks and water dripped from the tip of her nose.

She looked at Joe. "It couldn't be our luck that this would be just a quick shower, could it?"

"Watch the news, Brahnam? This is supposed to be an all-nighter."

"Shit," she grumbled just as she saw flashlights approaching from the road. The ME and his crew had arrived. "Looks like we're fucked."

CHAPTER TWO

KANE WASHED THE DIRT FROM HIS HANDS USING A BRUSH TO scrub beneath his nails. Mud swirled down the chipped, white ceramic sink to the drains. The last thing he needed was the law stopping by, and he had no doubt they would, and rapidly detect he had been recently digging. What the hell had he been thinking? Kane knew better than to mess with evidence. As much as he hated to admit it, Kaleb had been correct. They didn't need to borrow trouble from the law. And as president of the Sons, he should be looking out for them first and foremost, not worrying if the choice of victims again matched his preferred donor type. But his instincts had proved dead on. Someone wanted to make him sweat and was doing a damn good job at it.

That someone put a large target on his back.

This latest drainage had his name written all over it. Once the Sheriff's Office ID'd the vic, they'd be able to tie her to him. It's not like he'd kept their relationship a secret the last few years. Kane had never been one to lay low when it came to women. He hadn't been exclusive to Tab, not when it came to fucking. But she had been his only donor.

And she certainly didn't deserve to be bled dry because of her association to him.

17

He breathed out a heavy sigh as he held out his freshly cleaned hands before him. His flesh had begun to take on a translucent appearance and his body had a death chill to it. Damn it, losing Tab was going to present an immediate problem ... he'd need to find a new donor and soon. His kind couldn't go long periods of time without nourishment.

The door to the clubhouse restroom swung open, startling him. He had been so wrapped in his thoughts he hadn't detected one of his brothers had been within the same breadth. The fact that he had let his guard down, further aggravated him. Being in the MC, you needed to be aware of your surroundings and keep up your guard at all times. Anything else could get you killed. He threw the dirty nail brush into the sink with a clatter and faced his MC brother, Grayson Gabor.

"Don't you seem in a mood?" Grayson said with a smirk, his bright blue eyes twinkling with humor.

Kane unleashed on him, taking his anger out on someone who probably didn't deserve it. "You forgot how to fucking knock, Gypsy?"

Grayson grinned, not fazed in the least by Kane's outburst. But then again, very little rattled the man. "You afraid I'm going to see that small dick of yours, Viper? Try locking the door."

"Fuck you, Gypsy. I'm not in the mood."

"Talked to Hawk, said you guys found another drainage." He clapped Kane on the shoulder. "Sorry to hear it was Tab."

Kane shrugged. "Tab didn't deserve me, let alone drained. I think whoever is doing this, Gypsy, is looking to take me down."

Grayson's lips turned down. "That makes it club business. What do you want to do?"

"I say we find him and cut his head off."

"You won't get any argument from me," Kaleb said as he pushed his way past Grayson. "I say we fuck him up and ash the remains."

Kane grumbled as he shouldered past both of them. The bathroom was far too small to be holding a fucking meet-and-greet. "You guys ever think to give a man his privacy?"

Grayson followed him out, a deep chuckle bubbling up from his gut. "You just don't want—"

Kane whirled around on his heel, pointing a finger just inches shy from Grayson's nose. "My dick size is fine, Gypsy—I haven't had a complaint in that department. Not like you."

Grayson grabbed his crotch and gave it a quick tug. "The only complaint I get, Viper, is that it's too damn big."

Kaleb followed up the trio, slapping them both on the back of the head. "This ain't about the size of your dicks, boys. We need to find out who's trying to frame Viper and take them down. We need to call a church meeting. We have to get the word out on the streets—the Sons of Sangue are not happy with these recent bouts of dead bodies and we mean to retaliate. Put the fear of sangue in these fucks. We'll get answers. Someone out there knows something."

Kaleb thrived on this kind of action. So much so that he made stupid mistakes by not thinking things through. They needed a solid plan first, then action.

"I agree," Kane said. "But first I'll need to deal with the Sheriff's Office. No doubt they'll be heading our way yet tonight. They'll likely want to question us again. For some screwed up reason, they either think we know something or that we are somehow involved. They find out this latest drainage is Tab will only solidify that. We need to find this fuck like yesterday."

"We can thank mother nature for the rain, dude. It's coming down in buckets out there." Kaleb chuckled, shaking his shaggy dark curls. Water droplets sprayed the well-worn, pine flooring. "At least there won't be much evidence left to show you were digging around. The only thing they'll have on you is your tie to Tab. They won't have squat on the club."

"We don't have squat either, dipshit." Kane's reference hadn't fazed his twin a bit if Kaleb's smile was an indicator. "Don't you two have something better to do, like hanging somewhere that isn't in my vicinity? I can't even hear myself think with you two so fucking close."

Grayson flopped on the nearest leather chair, kicking his booted feet on the scarred wooden center table. Linking his fingers behind his head, he smiled. "I'm all yours, Viper."

"Lucky me." Kane headed for the cupboard behind the bar. He pulled out a clear shot glass and a bottle of Jack and poured himself a shot of the amber liquid, then downed it. The alcohol warmed him much like ingesting blood would, but without the nutritional factors. His stomach growled and his gums ached. The last thing Kane needed was the law stopping by. He needed to be out trolling for some new blood.

"I figure the pigs will want to speak to all of us eventually, why not get it over with? Right, Hawk?" Grayson looked at Kane's twin who seemed distracted, no longer listening to the two of them.

Kaleb's gaze fell on Grayson. "Come again?"

"What's got you preoccupied?"

"I was just thinking about that hot little blonde detective, the one that questioned us last time. Oh that's right, Viper—you got her partner. What was his name? Hernandez, I think. You never got a look at Detective Brahnam." He whistled. "Maybe she'll come by tonight. Think she might be single?"

Kane glared at his brother, knowing full well who Detective Brahnam was. Kaleb's assessment was dead nuts. Just the thought of her had his groin tightening. "Stay the hell away from her, Hawk. The last thing we need is you chasing the law's skirts."

Kaleb chuckled, holding his palms up. "Whoa, not interested, bro. Not my type. Now you on the other hand ... I was just thinking since Tab—"

"Don't even fucking finish it," Kane growled, clenching his jaw. Lord, he needed to feed. He had rarely gone three days without blood, and the fact he was nearing that timeline now, made his mood swing dark. Finding Tab dead meant he'd have to find communion the hard way. "I'm not your charity, Hawk. Besides, I'm not hard up enough to resort to fucking the law ... literally."

Kaleb winked as he sat on the sofa across from Grayson. "Whatever you say, Viper."

Kane poured himself another shot and knocked it back. "She's a fucking cop, Hawk. Don't allow your dick to overrule your head."

Grayson turned his nose up and sniffed the air, as though inhaling a fresh-cut vein. "Bet she has some sweet ass blood."

"You too, Gypsy. Keep your fangs to yourself. Besides, you both know the rules: no one feeds on outsiders. You get a donor from the Rave."

The Blood 'n' Rave was started several years back in Florence by a vampire lifestyler, a term used for a wannabe, giving young impressionable kids and misfits of society a place to hang where they wouldn't be judged by their peers. Psychedelics and Ecstasy ran rampant along with neon colors, glow sticks, and industrial dance music. It was a diverse crowd that drew in the curious. The Blood 'n' Rave soon became the "it" place in Florence. It was easy for real vampires to hide among the lifestylers when so many of the hang arounds dabbled in blood play. There were also those who knew the real thing existed among them. They began wearing tiny blood-filled vials on a leather cord or chain about their necks, signifying them as willing blood donors. A secret society of donors had been created, only the most trusted allowed in, giving vampires a safe anonymous way to feed.

"Yeah ... and that gets fucking old, Viper. We haven't seen anything new at the Blood 'n' Rave in months. What if I want new? I'm not like you. I get bored easily."

"Then go fuck to your heart's content, Gypsy, just don't feed off them. Rules are rules."

"Fuck the rules."

Kane clenched his teeth. His tolerance was definitely wearing thin. "The rules aren't negotiable, nor to be blatantly disrespected. You want them changed, then bring it up at the next church meeting. Put it to a vote. Otherwise, you follow them without question or pay the consequences."

"Fuck you," Grayson grumbled as his boots hit the ground and he stood.

Kane knew the man walked a thin line of control. Grayson never was one to be boxed in by a strict set of rules. He marched to the beat of his own drum. If he felt like acting out, he did and worried about the aftereffect later. Where Kaleb could be irresponsible at times, he still stayed within the boundaries of the MC's rules. Some days, Grayson could be downright reckless and left the club mopping up after him, though no one could ever fault his loyalty. Gypsy was always the first one to back you in a fight and the last one left swinging.

Grayson let out a harrumph and headed for the back of the clubhouse about the time a knock came to the door, stilling all sound within. Even though Kane's instinct was to ignore the call, he knew it was best to get the confrontation over with ... the sooner the better. He gave Grayson and Kaleb a look of warning, then headed for the door. He knew before opening it that the female detective stood on the other side. He could smell her and, hungry as he was, she smelled damn good. He had to fight to keep his canines from elongating.

The door swung soundlessly inward as he opened it to the caller. "Detective."

Kane saw the brief flash of anxiety in her eyes when her gaze collided with his before she quickly masked it. She squared her shoulders and tried to appear unfazed. It didn't work, his nostrils flared and he could smell fear on her.

"Kind of late for you to be out and about, isn't it?"

"Normally," she answered. "You going to invite me in?"

"That depends on what you want." Kane could think of all sorts of things he'd like her to reply, but he doubted they'd be of the same mind. "Dare I hope you came to party?"

Detective Brahnam rolled her eyes. "Come on, Mister Tepes. You and I both know we don't hang in the same circles, abide by the same rules."

His smile widened. "Touché. So what brings you to the skids, Detective?"

"Official business, I'm afraid." She held up a small note pad. "I have a few questions to ask you and your friends."

"Well, we wouldn't want to stand in the way of an investigation, now would we? Do come in." He stood back, holding the door for her. "Before you get any more soaked."

The detective stepped under the overhang and glanced back at her black Charger as her partner exited the passenger seat, flapping his phone shut as he jogged toward them. Of course she wouldn't have come on her own. Her, he could have easily tolerated; her partner would no doubt try his patience.

Detective Brahnam didn't wait for a second invitation once Detective Hernandez caught up. They both entered the clubhouse. Kane heard Grayson's growl, no doubt disapproving of her partner's presence as well. Kaleb never left his seat, nor did the smile leave his face. He certainly appeared to be the only one enjoying himself.

Kaleb sniffed the air. "Don't you just smell delicious."

Kane heard Detective Brahnam's slight intake of air, but she didn't allow Kaleb's comment to intimidate her. She walked over to him and nudged his crossed legs from the table until his booted feet thudded against the pine flooring. "Care to answer some questions?"

"I'm an open book." Kaleb chuckled, clearly amused. "Ask away."

"Where were you tonight?"

"I was here all night."

"Alone?"

Kaleb glanced at Kane. "No, the three of us haven't moved. We've been here all night, shooting pool and having a few beers." He turned his dark gaze back to her. "Why?"

"I have witnesses that say otherwise." She glanced at her notebook. "You and Kane were seen on your motorcycles out on North Fork Road earlier tonight. What were you two doing out that way?"

"We were enjoying the scenery."

Her facial expression told Kane she didn't believe Kaleb. Hell, he wouldn't have believed him either. "It's a pretty foggy night out there, and with the promise of rain I doubt your business had to do with sightseeing."

Kaleb laid his arms across the back of the sofa he sat on and crossed his booted feet back on the table. "Doesn't matter what you think, Detective. That's my statement." He used a finger to indicate what she should do. "Go ahead, write it down."

When she didn't do as told, he grabbed the pad and pen from her hand lightning quick. Detective Hernandez made a move, but Cara held out a hand to stop him. Kaleb wrote something on the pad, then handed it back.

As Brahnam read it, she nodded slowly, then looked at Hernandez. "Looks like we're done here. Kaleb Tepes can spell sightseeing. He even signed it. I'm impressed."

Detective Hernandez leaned down, his nose inches from Kaleb's and yet his twin never broke his smile. Kane knew better. He could feel Kaleb simmering beneath the surface with extreme dislike for Hernandez. Had Kaleb wanted to, he could easily kill the detective without breaking a sweat.

"What were you doing on North Fork?"

"Sightseeing," Kaleb reiterated, then winked at the man. "Ask me again, and I'll tell you the same thing. We can do this all night. The pretty lady has my statement. You don't believe that's what I was doing out there, then prove me wrong." The smirk left his face. "Now get the fuck out of my face."

Hernandez wisely backed off and looked to Grayson. "Where were you tonight?"

Grayson put his hands up. "Don't look at me. I just crawled out of bed, man. I'm sure one of the two ladies I woke up beside will corroborate that."

Detective Hernandez wrote down the names Grayson supplied him with and said, "I'll be sure to do that."

Kane finally stepped forward, stopping a good distance from both detectives. "Hawk and I were out for a ride, Detectives. You mind telling us what this is about?"

Detective Brahnam closed the gap between them. She looked up at him. Her clear blue eyes held his gaze. He had to admit Kaleb was correct. The pretty little detective was exactly his type. "We found another body off North Fork Road, near Bender Landing County Park. You boys out by the park tonight?"

"We passed the area."

"Notice anything different? See anyone?"

"As you said, it was foggy."

She narrowed her pretty blue gaze as though trying to assess him. As she tilted her face upwards, his focus landed on the pulse in her neck.

"So why go so far out of your way? There is nothing around for miles."

"Riding. It clears my head. You got anything else you need, Detective?" Kane leaned closer to her ear and whispered, "Because suddenly, I'm ravenous."

A shiver passed through her. He saw it in the slight tremor of her shoulders. "Then we're keeping you," she replied, barely audible.

Kane sniffed the crook of her neck, then said low enough Hernandez couldn't possibly hear, "Unless you're offering."

Detective Brahnam sucked in her breath, stepped back, putting space between them and looked at her partner. "No, we're done ... for now." She cleared her throat. "If we have any more questions, we'll be back. So don't leave town."

She started for the door with her partner, then stopped. She turned on a dime, then came back to Kane, her back ramrod straight. She grasped the collar of his tee and yanked him to her face level, causing him to smile. He liked her spunk.

She whispered, "You ever threaten to bite me again, I'll yank those canines out myself." Then she released him, turned back around and headed for the door, where she said, "We'll let ourselves out."

Kane smiled, watching the saucy sway of her ass in jeans that molded to her like a well-worn glove. His palms itched to take a handful.

The door slammed behind them, causing Kane to chuckle.

Hell, not only was he fucking hungry—now he could add horny as hell to his list of ailments.

So Detective Brahnam hadn't forgotten; she knew exactly what he was, no doubt remembering that night as much as he, for likely two very different reasons.

"Are you fucking crazy, Viper?" Kaleb asked as he jumped to his feet, only seconds after the door closed behind the detectives. Kane knew that Kaleb's and Grayson's acute hearing would have picked up their conversation. He hadn't cared. "What about the rules? If the law finds out about us, they'll definitely blame these drainages on us! If not have us killed on sight!"

Filling his glass again, Kane took the shot, then slammed it on the counter. "Relax, Hawk, she's known about my existence for ten years and hasn't breathed a word."

"How the hell does she know?"

"She came to the Blood 'n' Rave when she was all but a kid."

"So? A lot of people do."

"She caught me in the bathroom having sex with a donor."

Grayson approached the bar, grabbed the bottle of Jack and poured himself a shot, no doubt gloating at Kane's confession. "Oh, that's rich. You broke the rules, Viper? You weren't using good judgment and got caught with your fangs out and your pants down." A hearty chuckle followed his statement, deepening Kane's black mood.

"She hasn't said anything in ten years. She won't now."

Kaleb looked at Kane, obviously not trusting his brother's assessment. "And what if she does, Viper? She could expose us all."

"I'll take care of it."

"How, bro? How are you going to keep that pretty little detective's mouth shut?"

"I said, I'll take care of it."

No longer in the mood to be in the same company as his MC brothers, he grabbed his leather cut and headed for the door. He needed communion.

CHAPTER THREE

CARA PULLED HER SHIRT OVER HER HEAD, DISREGARDING THE buttons. Her fingers trembled fiercely; she doubted she'd have managed them anyway. Good thing for her she kept her panic at bay from Joe. The last thing she needed was her partner privy to the effect Kane Tepes had on her. She wasn't about to explain to him what had happened in the ladies' room at the Blood 'n' Rave ten years prior. Hell, *she* couldn't explain it.

Sometimes what the eyes observe cannot always be trusted— Cara knew that from her years on the force. It was the reason witnesses were sequestered and not allowed to talk with each other after a crime. One witness could influence another by their personal perception of the facts.

A few weeks after her hasty exit of the club, she had made the decision to leave behind the entire town, hoping to escape the nightmares that followed her night at the Blood 'n' Rave. But the dreams hadn't diminished. Large dark sulking figures with elongated teeth, and blood smeared mouths haunted her nights, along with snarls, growls and gnashing of teeth. She had always awakened in a pool of sweat, attempting to catch her breath as she convinced herself that vampires weren't real. Cara needed a straightjacket and a long time away, because everyone knew that vampires were a product of fiction. Lucky for her the Oregon State Mental Hospital, where One Flew Over the Cuckoo's Nest had been filmed ages ago, had been torn down in 2009 or she might surely be on the patient list.

Kane had wanted to frighten her with his growl and canines dripping of blood. And damn if he hadn't gotten the job done. Ten years and she had nearly convinced herself that Kane either didn't exist, of which he had already proven that theory incorrect, or he had purchased a good pair of very sharp molded dental fangs for which to better play the part at the Rave. That and he dabbled in blood-play like a lot of young kids there. Because the fact was: vampires weren't real.

A shiver ran down her spine.

Ten years and it was as fresh in her mind as if it had happened just yesterday. Cara had gone to the club out of curiosity and a bit of coercion by her best friend, Suzi. The name of the club alone had made her want to steer clear. Besides, Cara had never flirted with drugs and she knew the reputation that raves carried.

"Everyone that's anybody goes there, Cara," Suzi had said in her most convincing whine.

And Cara hated it when Suzi whined because she knew her best friend wouldn't stop until Cara relented. The last time she saw Suzi, just days before heading off to college, Cara noted her friend wearing a small vial of what looked like blood dangling from a black leather cord as a necklace. Lame? Maybe. But definitely strange. Cara hadn't bothered with a final goodbye the day she left. Suzi had immersed herself into a lifestyle Cara wanted no part of. So she had simply packed her bags and driven away.

There was no one to miss Cara except her aging grandfather, and she would stop back from time to time to visit him at the Pleasant Care Nursing Home. She hated placing her grandfather in assisted living care, but at eighty-two with a bad hip, he needed help with about everything and she couldn't trust him to be at home alone while she worked.

Her father, over-worked and mentally abused by the woman he married, died six-months after she had fled town and her alcoholic mother had moved on to abuse some other poor schmuck. Cara's upbringing could have been a case study for child neglect and abuse. Whenever her mother had gone on one of her drunken binges and meant to take her sucky-ass life out on her only child—one she frequently reminded Cara she hadn't wanted—her father had stepped in. Sometimes a bit too late. He'd been the one to take her to the hospital and lie about how Cara had broken her arm or finger or whatever part of her body that got in the way of her mother's tirades.

"Silly girl was on the swing set and jumped before I could get to her," was just one of the many excuses her father had manufactured.

Leaving had been easy. Coming home had not.

So why had she?

Because regardless of her past, Cara still thought of Pleasant as her home. She preferred life in a small town to that of the city, and she was much closer to her grandfather here. Better to keep an eye on him.

Besides, her mother no longer lived in Pleasant.

Thank the good Lord for small favors. She could be dead for all that Cara cared. And then there was the one unfortunate night in

Eugene, one she'd rather put to rest and forget ever happened. Best for all involved, at least that's what she had been told. It seemed she was always running from something.

Cara unzipped her pants and stepped from them, heading for the bathroom. A cool breeze wafted in through the opened window, the sheer curtains flapping in the breeze. She didn't worry about being seen. Not out here. Cara had chosen the old farm house because her nearest neighbor squatted a half mile down the road. Gooseflesh popped out along her skin, chilling her. A nice long hot shower was in order. Hopefully, it would help her relax her tired muscles and take away the stress of the day.

Kane came to mind, followed by a shudder.

Turning on the bathroom light, she looked in the mirror and pulled the rubber band from her still damp hair. The natural platinum blonde strands fell about her shoulders. Joe had been correct. Her hair color matched that of the recent victims. As well as matched the color of the blonde Kane screwed in the ladies' room at the Rave. Not that she kept tabs on Kane or gave a rat's ass the type of women he dated, but could Kane be responsible for these recent homicides? At this point she really had nothing to connect him to the murders other than his preference for blondes ... and his possible predilection for blood.

Cara's stomach soured. Even while on the force at the Eugene PD, she had seen nothing like these recent crimes. Something untoward had stepped inside Pleasant's limits, something foul and loathsome. Something preying on young blonde women, draining them of every last bit of their blood.

Shedding her under garments, she opened the glass shower door and stepped into the steaming water, allowing it to run down her skin. Vapor rose and gathered around her, fog rolling over the door and misting the room. She couldn't imagine a longer day. This time of the year, darkness came early, making the day seem much later than it actually was. Domestics actually rose this time of year due to depression and isolation that set in over the long gloomy months. With these recent homicides, Cara wasn't sure she was ready for the winter months to begin. She had enough on her plate trying to solve these cases, let alone add crazy spouses into the mix. Everyone knew domestics were some of the worst calls to answer. As a cop, you never knew what you were walking into.

Cara sighed, wishing the heated water would wash her worries down the drain, along with her thoughts of Kane Tepes. She didn't need the complications his presence in her life would most certainly cause. The perfect night would include making a batch of hot chocolate, grabbing a novel, and crawling into bed. But she knew nothing would stop her rolling thoughts. Once her head hit the pillow and the lights went out, her mind would replay the case, as well as its possible connection to Kane. Whether she wanted to admit it or not, the man was pretty pleasing to the eye. She chuckled. Pleasing to the eye didn't do him justice. The man was downright sinful.

Reaching for the shampoo, she lathered her hair, massaging her scalp, then rinsed the soap from the strands. Suds slid down her body and over her breasts. Her nipples tightened, teasing her, aching for a caress ... Kane's caress.

Her eyes flew open.

Where the hell had that thought come from?

Maybe Joe had been correct and she did need to get laid. Her imagination had started to take a turn for the dangerous. Since moving back to the small town, Cara hadn't bothered with a relationship. Didn't have time for one. In her experience a relationship took far too much time and energy for very little return. Even in her ten years in Eugene, at college and on the force, she hadn't dated a man for longer than a few months. None of them held her attention long enough to get serious, and most were more interested in getting drunk and going to bars. A piece of ass was just something they did after last call at the bar. No need to add complicated emotions into the equation.

Cara had little interest in sex when it didn't come in the form of a relationship. Call her old-fashioned. So after a few horrible tries at a relationship—one she refused to acknowledge because it had ended so badly—and a few bumbling mishaps in the sack, Cara swore off men and concentrated on her career. She figured she had a long life ahead of her to worry about family, babies and all that stuff she wasn't likely cut out for anyway.

Kane's image flitted before her. Not the one from her nightmares, but the man she encountered mere hours ago. He had been dark, brooding and angry. The angry she understood. The S.O. had targeted the Sons of Sangue since the very first dumped body. Each of them had been questioned at length and made to feel guilty ... maybe not of the crimes in question, but the Sheriff's Office knew the OMC were guilty of something. They always were. So they treated them like reprobates. Maybe the S.O. was looking to hang these crimes on someone ... anyone, and the Sons of Sangue seemed like a good target. At least that had been the view the Sons had taken. And she couldn't blame them. They didn't have squat for suspects. If Kane was indeed innocent of the homicides, then he no doubt had reason to be furious with her and the Sheriff's Office.

And an angry Kane was an intoxicating image.

With a lathered bath scrunchy, Cara ran the soap down her chest and over her sensitized breasts. Her breath caught, her nipples puckered, and a slow warm ache pooled between her thighs. Her heartbeat thudded heavy against her rib cage as she thought of Kane's large, muscular body. His chiseled frame looked like he lifted weights daily. She'd certainly like to run her hands down the solid ridges of his abs. Leaning back against the cool shower tiles, she allowed her hands to roam farther, heading south over her taut stomach. Lord, she hadn't felt a stirring of lust in years. She hadn't even allowed herself the pleasure of an orgasm. Cara had tried self-pleasure a handful of times, but it always left her unfulfilled and wanting. Her face heated at the thought of allowing herself the guilty pleasure now. Since when had she stopped thinking of Kane as anything but a nightmare?

His dark looks intrigued her, called to her as her hand drifted lower, wondering what it would feel like to have his hands skim her flesh and slide between her thighs. The ache grew. Her breath drew short.

The telephone jangled.

Shit!

Cara dropped the scrunchy, cursing herself for the notion of even thinking to pleasure herself. She quickly rinsed off, opened the door and grabbed a towel. Served her right. She had no business whatsoever daydreaming about Kane Tepes ... even if he was about the sexiest thing to ever land in Pleasant.

Grabbing the bedroom phone, she paced in front of the opened window. The chilled air cooled her heated skin. And, Lord, did she need cooling off.

"Hello," she answered on the fourth ring.

"Hey, Brahnam. What's up?"

Cara smiled. "What are you calling for at this hour, Hernandez?"

"This hour? Hell, Brahnam, it's barely eight-thirty. Some of us guys from the office are up to Murphy's for a beer. Why don't you join us?"

"I appreciate the offer, but I just got out of the shower. I was going to retire early and read."

"Christ, Brahnam, you're a candidate for sainthood! Now get your cute little fanny up here. I'll have a beer waiting."

Before she could decline the line went dead, causing her to chuckle.

Guess her plans for the night just got changed.

HIS BODY SHOOK WITH UNREQUITED desire. The vision in the window had his cock standing at full attention. Lust and hunger pumped through his veins, causing his fangs to lengthen and his eyes to sharpen in the darkened forest behind her house where he stood, hidden by the cover of night and surrounding trees. His animalistic nature demanded he act; his humanity kept his feet glued to the pine needle flooring.

Not a sound could be heard; not a cricket chirped. They sensed a predator among them, where she had not a clue of the danger that lurked just beyond her view. The air hung heavy with humidity and smelled of oncoming rain. Another scent drifted along the cool night breeze, one he couldn't quite catch, but nonetheless there. Probably nothing more than a rotting corpse of some critter of the forest.

His curiosity and desire to seek this woman out proved her to be his weakness, more than he cared to admit. His body demanded nourishment, yet feeding off the detective was completely out of the question. Not if he respected his brothers and his duty to the club as president.

So why the fuck was he standing here acting like a damned peeping Tom?

Hands in pocket, he stared up at her window. Because he hadn't wanted a woman with this ferocity in a long time. Getting a piece of ass had never been a problem. Being in the Sons of Sangue, not to mention wearing the president's patch, had women throwing themselves at him. Any given night, he had his pick of hardbodies. But biker bitches were a way of release to him, nothing more. Kane had no need for an ol' lady. He had tried that once in his hundred-plus-years existence and it hadn't ended well. He had yet to forgive her. Hell, Kane hadn't forgotten or forgiven himself for not arriving in time. She had been banished to Italy, back to her stepfather, and he hadn't heard from her since.

Nor did he want to.

Now here he stood, his libido going into overdrive like some randy teenage boy. Kane knew it had to do with desiring what you couldn't have. Mixing the MC with the law would be like placing a square peg in a round hole, no chance of the two ever fitting. But like it or not, he definitely wanted the pretty little detective hot, wet and naked, squirming beneath him calling his name during multiple orgasms. Just the mere thought of fucking her turned up the heat of his hunger. His fangs had fully extended and ached with the need to feed.

Talk about thinking with the wrong head.

Kane shook off the growing need, turned his back on her as she pulled a light sweater over her head, and fled into the woods. Following her home had been foolhardy, pushing his self-discipline to its limit. Kane had acted on impulse, which was a short hop, skip and a jump from being just plain stupid. When he left the club-house, his intentions had been to head for the Blood 'n' Rave to find nourishment stat, which he was still in dire need of. He raced through the forest, the trees and passing brush, nothing but a blur moving at speeds impossible for normal humans. Kane was anything but normal. As he reached the road running south from hers, he came across his bike where he had left it, mounted it, and hit the electric start. The bike rumbled to life. Kane kicked up the center-stand and headed for Florence.

A half hour later, Kane parked his motorcycle, killed the engine and stepped over the seat. He took off his skull cap and placed it on the handlebar and headed for the entrance of the club. Hunger hummed through his veins. Tonight—just about anybody would do. Normally, when it came to feeding, Kane was quite particular. But with blood hunger pulsing through his veins, he wasn't about to turn away any willing candidate. He had a singular goal in mind: find a woman wearing a vial and commence communion.

—

FROM HIS VANTAGE POINT, HIDDEN by the trees near the side of the house, he watched the detective exit her house and point her key fob at the black Dodge Charger. The headlights illuminated and the yellow caution lamps flashed twice as the driver side door unlocked with a soft click. Moments earlier, Kane Tepes had stood within the woods across the large expanse of lawn toward the rear of the home, watching the young woman as she showered.

Kane hadn't been aware, that while he spied on the woman, someone watched him. A very dangerous someone. *Tsk, tsk, Kane,* he thought with a chuckle. Kane's keen senses should have picked up on the fact he wasn't alone and that another of his kind, not to mention a primordial, stood but mere yards away. Kane's weakness for women made him unaware. The biker had fucked up, handing him his Achilles Heel on a silver platter.

The female, he had to admit, was stunning even in her plainness. She didn't wear much makeup and her hair she wore unadorned. Her bright blue eyes were rimmed with just a hint of mascara, while a bit of blush accented her cheeks. He could easily understand what Kane saw in this one. The detective was not at all like the last one he drained. As she opened the car door, her cell rang, the light from the car's interior softly highlighting her face. But with his vision he didn't need the soft glow to see her clearly. Every freckle, every nuance was clearly visible, even from his distance. She rummaged through a small leather purse, pulling out a red BlackBerry.

Hitting the TALK, she placed it to her ear. Not giving the person on the other end of the phone a chance to utter a word, she said, "Yeah, yeah, I'm on my way."

A smile lit her cheeks and put a twinkle in her vivid eyes. She might be worth toying with before he drained her like the others.

"I'm leaving now. Give me fifteen minutes." She paused. "And, Joe? That beer had better still be cold."

Hitting the OFF, she lowered herself onto the front seat and started the car, pulling on her seatbelt. He watched as the car slowly crawled down the long driveway, then disappeared out of sight.

Walking from the cover of the trees, he approached the backdoor. Making a fist, he punched through the thin glass of the door as if it were made of rice paper and entered the house. *Old wives' tales,* he thought with a chuckle. Vampire or not, he didn't need an invitation to enter.

SWITCHBACK BY CELLDWELLER filtered through the speakers as bright blue, red, green, and yellow laser lighting pulsed through the room to the beat of the high energy music. Klayton, the lead singer of the band, was nothing less than a genius. Kane had met the man years ago when he was in a band called Circle of Dust. The band had toured the States, and when landing in Oregon for a tour, they had hired the Sons of Sangue as bodyguards. He and Klayton had become fast friends, keeping in touch over the years. Whenever Celldweller came to Oregon, Klayton hired the Sons to keep violence out of the venues. Tonight, however, the DJ spun the music. Most of the ravers here were considered Darkravers and Gravers, as this crowd was more into the darker side of music and tended toward Gothic styles.

The patrons stomped and jumped to the beat of the music while others practiced glowstick twirling, their arms fluidly moving to the rhythm in liquid motion. Women ... men, they all danced as one, regardless of sexual orientation. The entire scene looked very erotic. Ecstasy ran rampant in the Blood 'n' Rave. X or Disco Biscuits, as they were known here, were easy enough to come by if someone wanted to get charged up for the night. Kane stayed away from the drugs, as it wouldn't do much for his kind anyway. His blood regenerated rapidly and the pharmaceutical wouldn't stay in his body longer than a few minutes.

Finding a piece of ass in this crowd to slake the itch that started watching Cara shower, wouldn't be a problem. Finding one that interested him would. Her provocative image, running lathered hands down her smooth taut belly, heading for the V of her thighs, had burned itself in his mind. Creamy pale flesh called to him, beckoned him to take her against the smooth shower wall and fuck her like his hundred-plus years would end tomorrow. Hell, his dick stirred just at the thought. Maybe he should appease his raging hormones on the first willing woman who happened by, and the hell with where his true desire lay. Here at the Rave, he bet that wouldn't take more than thirty seconds.

Kane shook his head and ignored the young redhead eyeing him up ... not even thirty seconds, and headed for the bar. Not only did he need blood, he could use a stiff drink as well. He cut through the crowd with ease, people parting, giving him homage. His MC cut introduced him to the crowd, for those who didn't already know him. The Blood 'n' Rave allowed the Sons' colors within the establishment, showed them deference. This had been their hangout, their turf, since the nightclub had opened. The owner liked their presence. It kept out the dregs of society, the underbelly—even if there were those who considered the Sons one and the same. To the Rave, the Sons of Sangue were treated like royalty, and there was always an abundance of willing women to slake all their needs, be it sexual or nutritional.

Cutting a path around the dance floor, Kane headed for the ornate bar, spotting the owner instantly. He stepped to the side of a leather-padded stool, placed one hand on the bar and a booted foot on the foot rail, giving a quick nod to the man he had considered a friend over the past many years.

"Draven."

Draven stood just over six foot in bare feet, but tonight he wore a pair of black leather platforms that brought him eye to eye with Kane. He held out his black-fingernail-tipped hand and shook Kane's.

"Not used to seeing you alone, my dear friend. What's your poison?"

The Sons rarely traveled by themselves because it was always safer to arrive in numbers, should trouble start. Tonight, Kane didn't need wisecracks from his brothers. He wanted solitude, time to reason with this crazy notion of sliding between the detective's smooth lean thighs. "Jack, straight up."

Draven nodded at the bartender who brought them a freshly opened bottle of Jack Daniel's Single Barrel and two vintage lowball glasses, etched in fine gold. He poured them each a half glass. Draven picked them both up, holding one out to Kane.

Kane took the offering, clinked glasses with the man, then downed a good share of the amber liquid, feeling the burn as it slid down his esophagus.

"You come to party? I got some sweet shipments that just came in."

Kane shook his head and wiped his hand down his mouth. Draven knew Kane didn't dabble in drugs, free or otherwise, but it never stopped Draven from offering. Maybe Draven felt he wouldn't be the complete host if he didn't. Kane's answer never changed. "Just here for the women, my friend."

Draven's hand indicated the dance floor. "Take your pick."

He tipped his top hat back a notch as he peered over the blue rimless glasses he wore perched on the end of his nose. Kane wasn't sure if Draven wore them to read or because he thought it made him look more like Gary Oldman from Bram Stoker's *Dracula*. He wore red contacts to enhance the look and a soul patch beneath his lower lip. The only thing missing was the mustache.

Kane took another sip from his glass, then turned his back to the bar and leaned against it, his heel now resting on the foot rail. His gaze swept the room, looking for a good candidate, when a lean, dark-haired woman approached the bar. The first thing that caught Kane's attention was the red vial hanging from her neck, marking her as a donor. He had seen her many times before, but usually on the arm of one of his brothers. She wasn't his normal type, but tonight beggars certainly couldn't be choosers.

"Can I buy you a drink?" Kane asked.

Startled, her blue gaze stopped on his. "I'm sorry?"

Kane pointed at her glass and grinned. "What are you drinking, sweetness?"

"Tom Collins."

Kane nodded at the bartender, who quickly brought her a fresh glass. "I didn't mean to frighten you."

"You didn't," the brunette said, nervously running a hand down her black pleather pants. On her top half she wore a white fur-covered bikini bra, an A-cup at best. "I just didn't expect you to speak to me." She chuckled. "That was certainly rude of me. What I meant is that I've been coming here for years and you've never once spoken to me before."

"Maybe it's about time I did." Kane's fingers graced the hollow of her throat where a blood-filled glass vial and red jewel hung from a black, leather cord. "I'm suddenly famished if you're game."

Her red lips tipped into a wide smile. "Really?" she asked, followed by a nervous giggle. The sound cut straight to his spine, enough to make him want to about-face and find food elsewhere.

She had to be in her late twenties, making the giggle sound a bit immature. But what did he care? Food was food. "Really," he repeated. "What shall I call you?"

She looked at him, confusion clouding her eyes. "Call me?"

Kane resisted the urge to tell her to forget it and move on. "Your name, sweetness."

"Oh. I'm sorry ... my name is Suzi."

CHAPTER FOUR

CARA WALKED THROUGH THE DOOR AT MURPHY'S, THANKFUL the earlier rain had paused for her ride back to town. She had been soaked through before her shower, chilling her to the bone. Truth be told, she wouldn't have agreed to the beer had the weather not cleared.

An eighty's tune from the band Poison blared on the juke box, already lightening her dark mood. Maybe coming out for a beer was exactly what she needed. She'd never tire of the classic hair band, even if she really wasn't old enough to remember them the first time around. Bret Michaels and his Rock of Love had made sure her generation knew who the rock icon was.

The bar's owner motioned her over the minute he caught sight of her weaving through the crowd. Even on a weeknight, Murphy's packed them in. She side-stepped several people, careful not to bump their hands or catch them off guard. A bar full of standing patrons with full glasses in their hands usually meant she was wearing liquor by the end of the night. No one had ever accused her of being graceful.

"Hey, beautiful," he said, gathering her into a bear of a hug. "Where've you been hiding?"

She backed from his embrace and smiled up at the very tall man. He could have been a basketball player for his height, but Cara knew that Lyle lacked the ambition for sports in school, opting for party-ing with his buddies instead of dribbling balls. "I've been working, Lyle. Some of us are busy with our jobs."

"Shit, them boys" —he indicated her fellow deputies with the towel in his hand— "work, too. But they got time to come in and patronize my bar."

"If that's what you want to call what they do." She smiled and winked at the six-foot-eight man, then headed for the table of fel-low officers.

"You drinking?" Lyle hollered after her.

"Joe was supposed to have a beer waiting," she said, smiling as Hernandez pointed at the frosty mugged draft already sitting on the table in front of the empty chair.

"Sit your pretty little behind down, Brahnam," Joe said. "You're already about three beers behind."

"Good thing." Cara pulled out the chair and sat, taking a healthy swig of the icy cold brew. She had to admit, the beer tasted great after the day she'd had. "Or I'd be heading home for bed already."

"Everyone knows you're a lightweight, Detective," Jeff Reeves said with a chuckle. She could tell he was well into several beers, his glassy eyes proving as much.

"Not a lightweight, Jeff. Just smarter than the rest of you fools. I certainly hope you have a designated driver."

Joe slapped Reeves on the back and chuckled. "We'll make sure he gets home and tucked in all right."

"So, what was all important to get me out of the house on a chil-ly night? To think I could be curled up in bed with a good book right about now."

"See, that's exactly why we called." Joe grinned, saluting her with his draft. "We're saving you from yourself."

A round of laughter followed Joe's taunt, which she shared in. They weren't poking fun at her but rather joking with her. Working with mostly guys, she needed to be able to take a good ribbing as well as laugh at herself. Besides, Cara liked to give as good as she got.

"Shouldn't you be home, Joe? I thought the kids were away. That wife of yours isn't waiting for you?"

His smile reached his eyes. "She told me to get the hell out, said I needed to give her space. I guess I'm just too much man for her and twenty-four-seven sex is a bit of an overkill."

The guys laughed and fist bumped each other.

Cara rolled her eyes. "More like annoying the hell out of her twenty-four-seven."

"Coming from the woman who never gets any."

She snorted. "You act as if I care, Joe."

The last thing Cara wanted or needed was lack-luster sex. Her mind drifted back to the shower and her straying thoughts. Somehow she doubted sex with Kane would ever be deemed boring. Though, not a thought she intended to share with her co-workers.

"Did we find out anything more about the dead vic?" Cara asked, hoping desperately to change the subject and get the topic off her. Last thing she wanted was the entire office talking about her lack of a sex life. Jesting with her partner was one thing, letting the entire office in on the joke was another.

Jeff said, "Just before I left, the ME called. Thought he shouldn't have any trouble IDing her. Somebody's got to be missing her. If she's from Pleasant, he said he'd probably find out by tomorrow afternoon at the latest who she was."

"Maybe if we get an ID we'll be able to discover who she'd been hanging with before she died and give us a clue as to what the hell happened." Joe held up his empty draft mug and nodded at Lyle for a refill. "Our best bet is going to be witnesses. That fucking storm killed our chances for footprints."

Cara had a bad niggling in her gut. Something about this latest victim didn't sit right with her. "Too many prints out there to be of much use anyway. But you're right, the rain certainly didn't help. We can go back to the site tomorrow, but with slope of the land-scape, our evidence is probably long washed away."

"We collected what we could," one of the attending deputies offered.

"Unfortunately, that isn't going to be good enough," Cara grumbled and took another swig from her beer. The alcohol sat like a rock in her stomach. Suddenly, she felt as if coming here hadn't been the best idea. She had never been much of a social butterfly, preferring to stay home more than not. Spending the night drinking at the local tavern had never been her idea of fun, regardless of what her co-workers thought.

Or maybe spending time in someone else's company held more appeal.

Lord, if she kept to that line of thinking, she'd be on her own slippery slope. Not like Kane would be interested. His taunts earlier had been just that. He'd never engage himself with a cop, not with the life he led. Cops and bikers didn't mix. They came from oppos-ing sides of the law. Like mixing water with oil, the two elements never blended, no matter how hard you shook them.

But like it or not, it was his vision that stuck in her head. Cara took another swig of her draft, disgusted by her train of thought. Maybe she ought to go see that psychiatrist yet. Unlucky for her, her libido had finally shown up and, like Cupid with his damn little arrows, had aimed itself right at the figment of her nightmares from the past ten years. Coming back to Pleasant might not have been the wisest choice after all.

Joe chuckled. "Brahnam? Did you even hear a word I said?"

Cara scratched her nape, giving him the best apologetic look she could muster. "I told you I wasn't much in the mood for mixing company, Joe. You're the one who insisted I come hang out and have a beer."

He shrugged off her accusation. "I was just saying that these killings were on the verge of being freakish, like something out of the Twilight Zone. What the hell is the guy doing with the blood? With no rope burns around the ankle, it's not like he's hanging them to drain. It's like he's sucking the blood right out of them."

She toyed with the damp napkin beneath her mug. "I'm sure when we find this sick bastard he'll be able to elaborate what the hell he's doing with it."

"You think this fuck is drinking it?" Reeves asked, his brows knit together over the bridge of his nose, excitement lit his blue eyes.

Cara didn't want to chime in, but she feared that's exactly what was happening. And if that were the case, then she feared Kane knew more than he was letting on. Her thoughts returned to the night she ran from the bathroom while blood dripped from his fangs ... *fucking fangs!*

Who has those?

A shiver passed down her spine. "I'm sure that's possible. But humans can't ingest that amount of blood and keep it down. Our digestive system would reject it. So there is no way this freak is drinking it all. Which means we have a crime scene somewhere with a hell of a lot of blood, or he's dumping it somewhere."

A petite redhead approached the table. She wore a tiny little pen skirt, barely covering her front end, let alone her back end. The teeny scrap of a tank she adorned on top left little to the imagination as it plunged deep between her perky breasts. A cinnamon-painted smile complimented her tanned skin. The worst part, she didn't even appear legal. Although she had to be old enough to drink or Lyle wouldn't have allowed her into his establishment in the first place. He wasn't one to mess with underage.

Placing her hands on the battered table, she leaned forward, giving everyone a good hint of what lay beneath her teeny top. After she got every man's attention, she turned to Jeff Reeves. The young dispatch smiled drunkenly back at the woman who proceeded to ask him to dance. Following a bantering from the table, Jeff took the redhead's hand and was led away from the group.

"Looks like someone might get some action tonight," one of the deputies said before shaking his head and taking another swig from his bottle. "The ugliest one of the bunch."

"You might want to look in the mirror, you ugly son of a bitch," Joe said, patting him on the shoulder. "What do you say, Brahnam? Reeves better looking than Higgins here?"

Cara's gaze landed on Reeves who danced behind the redhead, rubbing up against her backside. He was definitely the cutest thing at the station, but also the youngest. He reminded her of the cute actor from Gossip Girls, Chase something-or-other.

"Better looking than any of your ugly mugs." She chuckled, then finished the remains of her beer. Before she had a chance to politely excuse herself and rush off, though, Lyle set a fresh frozen mug in front of her. Cara sighed. So much for sneaking out early.

KANE WALKED SILENTLY ACROSS the plush burgundy carpet of Draven's office. A warm, gold paint covered the walls, while draperies, matching the floor coloring, covered the windows so that even in the daytime, no light shone through. The small table lamps flanking the sofa lent to the room's ambiance. A perfect vampire's lair, Kane thought with a wry smile.

Using the owner's space became a necessity since being spied upon in the bathroom by young and impressionable Cara Brahnam years ago. Even at her tender age back then, she had all the makings of becoming a stunner. Hell, it had been damn risky of him to take his donor to the ladies' restroom in the first place but she had been a bit of an exhibitionist. The thought of getting caught had always been a turn on to her. Sex in public hadn't been the problem, though ... feeding from her was. Worse yet, it had been pure idiocy on his part not to follow Cara and use the hypnosis they had mastered over the years to convince her the scene she had witnessed hadn't actually happened. Changing their eyes to an obsidian glass-like appearance made hypnosis easy. Using hypnotic suggestion, they could convince anyone of anything. It's how they kept their secret. For some reason he had allowed Cara to remember that night. Kane had broken a club rule and allowed an outsider to be privy to their kind. Only donors were given that right.

Donors, a reticent society privy to the vampires' existence, allowed his kind to feed from them, much like donating pints to the Red Cross. They provided necessary food to those who had need. Unlike the vampires of folklore or fiction, they only required about a half pint of blood every few days to keep them fully nourished. They had no need to attack and drain anyone dry, which made him think of his last donor falling prey to the murdering scum who had been draining women of all their life's blood. The more a vampire fed, the stronger they became. If Kane needed to hone his skills and keep himself sharp, then he made sure he fed regularly. But never had he drunk a human dry. Besides, feeding daily required more than one donor, and Kane preferred to remain exclusive. Not only was it safer, it was also less dramatic. No need for any female to go all territorial. Kane didn't need the melodrama.

His gaze fell upon the short-bobbed brunette patiently lounging on the Italian leather sofa, watching his every move. Hell, if he didn't know better, he'd guess her the predator and he the prey with the look of hunger in her blue gaze. Her long lean pleather-clad legs stretched out in front of her, giving her that model thin appearance so many women strived for. Kane preferred his women with a bit more curves, not that he was in a position for turning away a meal. Sex was an entirely different matter. Her sultry eyes had been rimmed with soft black kohl. Suzi really could be quite bewitching and held her own with most of the women in the club, even if she wasn't normally his type. Kane certainly wouldn't bitch about feeding from her, but she had been already passed around by the Sons, not only as a donor but perhaps for sexual favors as well. He didn't plan on tapping into where his brothers had already been.

She patted the soft leather beside her. "Why don't you quit pacing and come over here and keep me company. You're making me nervous."

One of his brows inched up. He chuckled. "I make you anxious? Interesting. You're a norm with the Sons. So, why the hell would I make you nervous? It's not like you don't know what we are. You wear the vial of blood around your throat. You freely offer yourself."

Suzi shrugged, toyed with the tiny vial between her thumb and forefinger. "Because you're different ... you're the President."

"You've been with Hawk?"

She nodded. "Once."

"He's VP."

"Yeah, but he's not you."

"He's my twin. What makes me so different?"

"You aren't exactly approachable, Viper. And frankly, sometimes you scare the hell out of me and some of the other girls here at the club. It's no secret that you're standoffish and moody."

"And Hawk isn't?"

She tilted her chin to meet his gaze as he approached the sofa.

"I don't want to talk about Hawk. He's history and not worth my time."

Her admission had him wondering what exactly Hawk had done to piss off the petite brunette. But then again, what Hawk did with his personal life was none of his damn business.

The pulse at the base of her throat called to him. He could hear the soft patter of her heart from a couple of feet away. Hell, this hungry, he would have heard it from across the room. His fangs lengthened in anticipation. Her slight intake of air told him she had noted his change. His eyes warmed as they changed to their black glassy appearance. Kane could smell her sexual desire as her interest in him heightened.

He'd oblige his thirst. But he had no intention on partaking in any sexual favors she might offer as well. Not being able to help himself, he asked, "What did Hawk do to earn your scorn?"

Suzi rolled her eyes and sighed, crossing her arms across her chest, clearly not wanting to talk about his brother. Kane's interest peaked even more.

"He's not exactly a gentleman and we are clearly not suited for one another. Hawk is straight-forward, I'll give him that. He lets you know from the get-go what he's after, whether or not you want to hear it." She paused, studied him, then said, "You? I'm not so sure. Even now I don't know if you want to feed from me or fuck me. You hang at the Rave; you don't socialize. You talk to no one other than your MC members and Draven."

"I have no need to."

"See, that's exactly what I mean. Hawk and the boys come here to party. They like to have fun. I'm never quite sure why you're here."

It was his turn to shrug. "I need to feed. The Rave provides that. Besides, I like Draven."

"Do you?"

"Why would you ask?"

"Because you give off a vibe, Viper ... one that says you don't like anyone."

"Good."

She chuckled. "And that's exactly why you make me nervous."

"You have no need to fear I would harm you or take your life."

"You would if you had to."

He narrowed his gaze. "Yes. But there is only one reason to eliminate a donor and that's if we fear our secret is no longer safe with you. You knew when you became one that the punishment for revealing our secret is death."

"You wouldn't be the one to do it if I did."

"No, that's handled by your own kind. We don't need your deaths on our hands. So again, why fear me?"

"You're dangerous."

"So is Hawk ... or any one of my brothers."

"Not here. They let their guard down, relax. They make us feel at ease. You're different: always on guard, always serious. Even now, I think you would rather take what you came for and then get the hell out of here. Am I correct?"

"I'd rather not be having this conversation with you, if that's what you're getting at."

She smiled as if she knew exactly how he would answer.

"Make no mistake, Suzi, if I the need to take you out, I wouldn't hesitate. None of the Sons would. We aren't to be crossed or toyed with."

The smell of her desire increased. Apparently her fear was also a turn on. "You're not only dangerous, but truthful ... like Hawk," she added as if in afterthought. "It's always good to know where one stands. But not one of the Sons has ever said they wouldn't hesitate to kill me if the need arose."

"Any one of my brothers is as lethal."

"My point is I've never had one of them threaten me."

"That's because they're trying to get in your pants, Suzi. It's bad form to scare the hell out of something you want to fuck."

"And you aren't?"

"No."

Suzi rose from the sofa and sauntered toward him. Stopping just inches from him, he could feel the heat of her blood. She grabbed his flaccid cock. Her face registered her disappointment in not getting a rise out of him.

She slid her palm over his jean-clad dick. "I can't change your mind?"

He removed her hand. "No."

Her ruby lips turned down in a well-practiced pout. He couldn't help but wonder how many men fell for that look. "Even if it's what I want?"

"Your desires are of no concern of mine, Suzi. You can take them up with one of my more willing brothers."

"Then why bring me up here if not to get me out of my pants? I've heard the talk amongst the women in the club. They say you're insatiable."

"Because I'm hungry, Suzi, and I am tiring of this conversation. I don't want to fuck you. I think I've made myself pretty clear. If you don't want to nourish me, then get the fuck out so I can find someone more willing."

She came within mere inches and grabbed his crotch again. "Oh, I'm willing. I just want to feed all of your hungers. I know you aren't exclusive when it comes to sex. So why not take what I offer?"

Kane's reputation no doubt preceded him at the club. He wasn't one to turn down a willing female, not when it came to getting laid. He was only exclusive when it came to feeding. And Suzi wasn't his normal donor type either, but tonight he was too fucking hungry to care.

"Don't take it personal, Suzi. I'm not looking to fuck. I just need to feed."

And he needed to in a bad way. It was as if he could feel his veins drying up just standing here talking. Kane needed nourishment. Being hungry hadn't helped his demeanor either. He was in no mood to stand here bullshitting about why he didn't want to take the piece of ass she offered.

"Sex has always come hand in hand with feeding your kind. What makes you so different?"

Kane had had enough. "Why is it so fucking important that I don't want to have sex?"

"Because I've always wanted to know what sex with you would be like." Her voice cracked and Kane feared in the next moment she might just break into tears. "I think it's the least you could do if I offer my blood."

"I'm not going to fuck you, Suzi, so get over it." He gripped her shoulders, tipped her chin, giving him access to her neck. "Now shut the hell up before I find another donor."

He bit down on her carotid artery and began to feed. The slight sucking noise and her intake of breath became the only sounds in the room, other than the ticking of the mantle clock. Blood rushed to his cock as it always did when he fed. Vampires were very sexual creatures. Suzi had been correct, normally sex and feeding went hand in hand. But not tonight, not while he had Cara Brahnam on his mind, and it was her tight body he wanted to be sliding into. His desire burned brightly just at the thought of getting the detective horizontal. Or vertical, or bent over the table ... any fucking way he could get her.

Suzi moaned as he continued to draw the warm tangy blood from her neck. Her hands skimmed down his chest as the scent of her desire wafted to his heightened senses. She smelled like a bitch in heat. Being fed from not only affected the vampires sexually but donors as well. Suzi was doing nothing more than acting on the sexual tension derived from his feeding.

When she grasped his cock for the third time, Kane released her, licked her neck wounds to aid in their healing and set her away from him before he did something like slaking his own urge. Her small breasts heaved, drawing his heated gaze. Lord, he really did want to taste them, draw them between his teeth and bury his cock to the hilt.

Christ, his emotions ran taut.

Kane turned his back, looked to the ceiling and waited for his libido to subside. Her warm hand flattened against his back, causing him to jump. He was so damn close to shoving her against the far wall and pounding his hardened cock into her until she screamed his name in climax.

"I can take care of that for you, Viper." Then she added in a whisper, "And you wouldn't be obligated."

Kane growled menacingly. He wanted to scare her, get her to back off before he stupidly gave in to the ache gripping his balls. Luckily, she complied. When he turned around, she had turned to retrieve her handbag from the sofa.

"Come on"—he felt like such a shit when he spotted the lone tear running down her cheek—"I'll walk you to your car." He grasped her hand and pulled her closer to him. Brushing a stray hair from her face with his free hand, he said, "Don't take it personally, Suzi. I have a lot of demons I'm dealing with right now and sex isn't going to fix it."

"Maybe I could help you forget."

He chuckled. "I'm sure you could, but it would only be a temporary fix. To be fair, I don't want to be thinking about another woman while I'm having sex with you. Understand?"

She nodded as another tear slipped down her cheek. He leaned down and kissed her forehead. "Let's get you out of here. You don't need to drink alcohol while dizzy from the lack of blood. You going to be okay driving home?"

She sniffed, swiping a hand beneath her nose. "I feel stupid for throwing myself at you."

Kane brought her flush against his chest and smoothed a hand down her spine. Being a nice guy was foreign for him. "Don't apologize. Any other day, I might have taken you up on your offer. Come on, let's get you to your car."

CHAPTER FIVE

THE COOL NIGHT BREEZE CARESSED CARA'S FACE AS SHE LEFT Murphy's Tavern. Tipping her face upward, she breathed in, detecting the scent of the ocean and the recent rain in the fresh air. The full moon found a break in the storm clouds and lit the parking lot as well, as the soft glow from the street lamps. It appeared she might make it home before the clouds decided to let loose again.

In spite of hoping for a good night's sleep, she was glad Joe insisted on her coming out for a beer. Her raucous fellow officers could be downright fun, taking her mind off the job. They all needed the distraction. Being an officer had its drawbacks. Too many times red tape got in the way of the conviction. Frustration from watching the guilty walk free burrowed beneath her skin. There were times she had thought about leaving the job behind for something less stressful. But in the end, Cara couldn't imagine devoting her life to any other profession. She loved her job, despite the grievances.

Had it not been for Joe's invite, it might have been just another long, boring night at home with nothing to do but pore over what little they had on the open cases so far or read the novel sitting on her bedside table like she'd intended.

Spending time alone had begun to lose its appeal. Normally, she cherished her serenity but it came at a cost. She had no one to share

63

life's joys or sorrows with, except for her weekly trips to see her grandfather. Grandpa was always willing and eager to hear anything she had to say, no matter how mundane the topic. Thinking of her elder brought a smile to her face. He had been the rock in her life, the one that grounded her.

The door opened behind her, startling her from her thoughts. Loud music and the din of conversation spilled into the night as a patron she didn't know exited the bar. Her fellow officers hadn't seemed ready to follow her out the door. Most of them, though, didn't have to work the morning shift with her either. The two beers she had consumed would hopefully help lull her to sleep and keep her thoughts of Kane at bay. More likely, he'd be the center of her dreams. Which, of course, was the last thing she wanted ... or at least she tried to convince herself. Thinking of Kane in any other way than a prime suspect would only spell disaster for her.

The damp, brisk night air picked up and caused Cara to shiver since she had not bothered with a coat. She pulled her sweater a little snugger about her shoulders as she rounded the corner, not paying attention to where she was headed and ran smack dab into the middle of a very solid chest. Her forehead bounced off his pectorals and snapped her neck. Cara grasped her nape as she was about to apologize for not being more considerate. But when she glanced up, her eyes locked with the black gaze of Kane Tepes. She sucked in air, swearing for a brief second his eyes shined like black glass before she shook off the notion as nothing more than the glow of the bar's neon lights reflecting in them.

"I'm sorry. If you'll excuse me," she said, trying to quickly pass by, saving herself from further embarrassment. That's when she realized he wasn't alone. To her mortification, Cara's best friend from years past, Suzi, had her arm linked through Kane's, with a smug look on her face. Which, at the moment, Cara felt like slapping off.

But what did she care?

After all, Cara didn't want Kane ... or shouldn't for that matter. Not only was he her lead suspect, he was an outlaw biker. As a cop, she had no right being jealous of the man Suzi had wrapped herself around at the moment. So why, then, did she feel like beating her chest caveman style and staking her claim on the biker, vampire, nightmare, or whatever the hell he was?

"Cara Brahnam," Suzi said, her perky smile condescending. "I haven't seen you in years. Not since you drove out of town without so much as a good-bye. How's your family, sweetie?"

"My father passed away years ago. But then you already know that. My mother left town and I haven't heard from her in years. Not that I care," Cara mumbled, then she tried to sidestep the both of them.

Cara wasn't in the mood to entertain two of her least favorite people. They could humor each other, for all she cared. Suzi hadn't bothered to call Cara after she had left town. Although that wasn't exactly being fair, since Cara was the one who had her number changed and hadn't passed it along. When Cara left behind Pleasant, she left behind everyone in it as well. She could hardly blame Suzi for her own actions. And Kane ... well, who the hell knew what the biker was up to? Although her job as lead detective was to find out and nail his well-formed ass to the wall.

Kane grasped her shoulders, stopping her from fleeing as she intended. The heat from his touch seared through her sweater and into her flesh as if he had caressed her bare skin. The man couldn't be accused of being stone cold, which meant he was indeed flesh and blood, ruling out the ridiculous vampire notion. She stiffened her spine and looked back up at him, hoping her gaze told him to leave her the hell alone. But apparently he wasn't getting the message.

"Where's the fire, Detective?" Kane asked, a smirk turning up a very sensual set of lips. Lord, she could imagine how soft they would feel against her own. Her heart picked up a beat and her breath stuck in her throat.

Cara willed her libido back into its dormant stage. "It's my bedtime," she said, filling her tone with sarcasm.

His smile widened as though humored, before it dawned on Cara where his thoughts likely had led him. *Great, Brahnam, why not just invite him into that bed of yours?*

Cara gritted her teeth and shook off his hold. "It's late."

"I beg to differ," Kane said as he allowed her to step back. "The night is young. Care to join us, Detective?"

"No. You and Suzi can have fun entertaining one another." She tried a second time to brush past him, only to have her efforts stymied again. Settling one hand on her hip, she glared up at him. "Is there something you want, Mister Tepes?"

His smile deepened. "It depends on what you're offering, Detective."

Suzi grunted, obviously annoyed by his taunts of Cara. Not that Cara cared one iota what Suzi thought, but she'd be damned if she allowed Kane any farther under her skin. "Go to hell."

This time, Cara managed to stomp by him and headed for her car in the parking lot. She had forgotten that Murphy's Tavern and Blood 'n' Rave shared the same mall parking lot. Unlucky for her, she had quit Murphy's the exact time Kane and his date had left the seedier bar. Kane had some nerve hitting on her while in the company of Suzi. She might have felt sorry for the girl had Suzi not been glaring at her.

Cara reached her car, clicked her remote to unlock the Charger, then crawled behind her seat, taking one final look back to see Kane had thankfully let her go without following. Good. Maybe he had finally gotten the message she wasn't interested.

Now, Cara needed to convince herself.

CARA GRABBED HER PURSE FROM the passenger seat and stepped out of the car, locking the doors. The night was heavy with humidity, curling the escaping tendrils of her hair. She blew a couple from her face as she dug for the house keys from the bottom of her purse, making her way through the dim security lighting to the back of the house. Glass crunched beneath the soft soles of her shoes as she stepped onto the stoop. Her gaze followed the sound. Clear shards scattered the cement, twinkling from the porch light. Her heart raced and her mouth dropped as she spotted the large hole in the window of the door. Reaching for her purse again, Cara withdrew her Glock and held it at the ready.

Her blood pounded in her ears.

Slowly, she pushed open the back door, holding her breath as the small creak echoed through the still house. More glass crunched beneath her feet as she stepped over the threshold, indicating the window had been broken from the outside inward. Cara stopped, trying to detect any sound over the pounding of her heart. Hearing nothing but the blood rushing through her ears, she stepped over the remaining glass strewn across her hardwood-floored laundry. Thankful for the soft soles of her shoes, Cara made her way quietly through the back room, past the washer and dryer to the kitchen. She flattened against the wall next to the door before slowly peering around the frame.

Her house yawned silently before her.

Whoever had broken in seemed to be long gone. Not yet ready to sheathe her gun, she crept into the next room, glad for the open floor plan. The only two rooms she couldn't see from her standpoint was her master bedroom and bathroom up the stairs to the left.

Her office door stood open. Beams of moonlight slid across the rich cherry flooring. No one would be able to hide in that room without being seen from her viewpoint, and the closets were far too stuffed to be able to hide inside. Cara was positive she stood alone on the main floor. Whoever took the time to break in, she hoped they'd taken what they were after and fled. Using her forefinger, she flipped up the light switch, illuminating the kitchen and living area. Cara blinked a few times, allowing her eyes to adjust to the sudden glare and willed her heartbeat to slow and her anxiety to subside.

She needed to call the station, report the break in and have her house checked for prints, but first she'd need to see if anything was missing. Cara laid her phone on the small rounded kitchen table as she tucked her Glock into the back waistband of her jeans. Running a shaken hand across her nape, she let out an unsteady breath.

Who the hell would want to break into her house?

Flipping on lights as she went, Cara headed for the stairway on unsteady knees, holding the railing as she ascended. At the top her breath caught in her throat again. Clothes were strewn about, drawers upended, and her closet emptied. Makeup smeared the mirror of her bathroom, lipstick drawn in awkward patterns. Approaching the smaller room, she realized the waxy pink color actually formed a message.

"Open your eyes ... and believe. Your turn to die."

Cara covered her open mouth. What the hell? She needed to call Joe. Surely he'd leave the bar and come—

Just as she pivoted on her heel to return to the kitchen and grab the cell, she bounced off the wall of a very hard chest for the second time in one night. Cara screamed, but before she had time to reach for her Glock, the man easily immobilized her and pulled her flush against him. Cara couldn't have moved if she'd wanted. The sense of being trapped washed over her and panic set in as she envisioned the sightless eyes of the last three victims. But instead of hurting her, one large hand smoothed down her back, attempting to soothe, not frighten her. When the man spoke softly, quietly hushing her, she knew the voice to belong to Kane. His hold loosened and she glanced up to see his gaze traveling her ransacked room.

Jesus! Was he responsible?

"What the hell happened?" his deep voice reverberated from his gut, telling of his fury. Kane had to feel her heart beating heavy against her ribs.

Trying not to further embarrass herself, Cara pushed from his embrace. And thankfully he allowed it as she didn't think she had the energy left to fight him on the issue.

But what the hell was Kane doing here?

"The better question is, what the hell are you doing here?" Her eyes widened as the possibility of him being the intruder dawned on her. "Did you do this?"

His dark gaze immediately dropped to hers and his brows came together. "Why the hell would I break into your house?"

"You tell me?"

A lazy grin curved his lip. "Frightening you is not what I have in mind to do to you, Mia Bella. Trust me."

"And just what the hell is that supposed to mean?"

He ignored the question and instead canvassed the room. "Anything missing?"

"How the hell would I know? I just got here and found it like this!"

Kane's nostrils flared as though detecting a scent. Cara followed suit and sniffed the air but didn't detect anything out of the ordinary. His gaze narrowed and he emitted a low growl.

"What?" she asked as she bent to retrieve some of the strewn clothing.

"Son of a bitch." Kane grumbled. "This isn't good."

Cara stood, shirts, undergarments, and shorts clutched to her chest, and looked at Kane. "What is it?"

He shook his head, and tried to mask his expression. But he wasn't fooling her. Something bothered Kane. "It's nothing."

"You can't just open a can of worms then clam up about it. What is it that has you so bugged?"

His gaze studied her for a long moment and Cara was sure he wasn't about to open up to her when he said, "One on my kind has been here."

Kane was talking complete nonsense. "One of your kind? What the hell are you talking about? Who was here?"

His eyes darkened to deep fathomless slits. Lord, she needed to get her vision checked. Certainly, it was due to the low lighting in the room. "I'm different than you, Cara ... and you know it. That message on the mirror is telling you that something exists beyond what you deem as humanity. You need to believe, because this intruder, he will kill you. You need to take this threat seriously."

She scoffed at the idea something else might exist, but the word vampire began to surface in her thoughts again. "You're talking nonsense."

Kane turned on his heel and grasped her shoulders, giving her a light shake. "Cara, we aren't playing games. What you saw ten years ago does exist."

Cara slowly shook her head, refusing to believe what her eyes had seen that night. She had spent too many years running from her nightmares and refused to buy into it now.

"There have been three dead bodies in this county and you're nowhere close to solving any of the cases. You won't either."

She shook off his grip and backed from him. "You underestimate my skills as a detective, Mister Tepes. I'll catch this perp. And if you have anything to do with these deaths, I won't hesitate to take you down."

KANE JAMMED BOTH HANDS through his hair and blew out a steady stream of air. Damn infuriating woman! Pacing the small confines of her ransacked room, he weighed the option of laying it all out for her. He knew the rules and the consequences. Making her see the truth was foolhardy, if not downright idiotic. She could expose his kind, unwittingly putting targets on their back, risking capture, experimentation, and possibly elimination. For their own survival, they kept their true nature hidden from the masses.

It's not like she didn't already have an inkling that something else existed, following her exit of the restroom some ten years back. But should his brothers get word that he solidified, instead of suppressed, her fears, they could not only strip him of his president patch but of his Sons of Sangue rocker as well.

He lived for the MC.

Kane had no family outside of it. But rules were rules and no one could know of their existence outside of the club. To all appearances, they were an outlaw motorcycle group, not a coven of vampires.

But what choice did he have now?

This unknown son of a bitch had put a target on Cara Brahnam's back and she wasn't even aware of what she was dealing with. Cara and her entire office of deputies could not match the power this primordial vampire had. He knew this vampire was an original by his scent, centuries older than he and Kaleb. The question was, what the fuck was this primordial doing in the States? All the primordials he knew lived in Italy, where the Sons of Sangue formed many years ago, long before the existence of the motorcycle club.

Stopping his pace, he stole a glance at Cara. She stood ramrod straight, arms crossed beneath her breasts. Her cleavage spilled over the V of her tee beneath her sweater, making his mouth water for a taste. She presented a very tempting picture, one his gaze was irresistibly drawn to. His canines ached within his gums, wanting to sink into her pale flesh and draw her life's blood into his mouth, to suckle from them like a newborn babe. Damn, she looked hot enough to fuck—but then again, when didn't she? He shook off the notion and tore his gaze from her. Maybe he should have taken what Suzi had offered in Draven's office, appease the need he tried damn hard to ignore in Cara's presence. Because now, one look at Cara and his dick was as rigid as her spine.

He needed to focus.

"You want to tell me what's really going on? Otherwise, I'm tempted to run your ass into the S.O. for B and E and threatening a police officer."

Kane chuckled, running his palm down his slightly whiskered jaw. "You think I did this?" His tone rose in disbelief. "You think I came in here, dumped your clothes and threatened you on your bathroom mirror? If I were to threaten you, Detective, it wouldn't be to forewarn you that I intended to kill you. If I wanted to kill you, you wouldn't know it until a moment before you sucked your last breath. My threats toward you would be much more of a sexual nature."

She sucked in air; her gaze widened. Her mouth dropped, but no words came out. Kane had finally rendered her speechless. Though he wasn't sure if it was because of his threat to take her life or whether it was the sexual innuendo that followed. He was betting on the latter.

Her pulse beat a heavy cadence at the base of her throat. And even though he had recently fed from Suzi, the temptation to draw from Cara was pretty fucking heady. Coupled with the desire of sex, it became an intoxicating combination, one Kane was reluctant to resist. Had he not been positive she would have fought him within an inch of her life, he might have taken exactly what his animalistic nature demanded.

Instead, he held his position and smiled devilishly. "I assure you, Detective, you're safe from me. I wouldn't take anything not freely offered."

"Well then," she said, raising one brow, "that means I'm perfectly safe within your company because I'll never freely offer you anything."

"A challenge." Kane smiled. "Never say never, Mia Bella."

Cara made an unflattering noise from her pursed lips, then began picking up dresser drawers and clothes, as if easily dismissing him. He closed the gap between them, close enough that the scent of her blood humming through her veins wafted to his nostrils, close enough he could also detect the increase of her pulse with his acute sense of hearing. His presence affected Cara; he'd bet his President patch on it. She could deny with her words all she wanted, but her body told a different story.

Cara Brahnam was hot for him.

Her hands trembled slightly as she folded a faded classic rock tee and replaced it in one of the drawers, smoothing it more than necessary. Kane contained his chuckle as he gathered a few articles of clothing, resisting the urge to take them to his nose. Damn if her scent didn't affect him the way the smell of a raw steak might a ravenous dog. And right now, he was insatiable. Kane's nostrils flared. What he wouldn't do to give into his urge, to taste her lips, nip her tender flesh and allow her silky blood to slide over his tongue. Kane couldn't help wondering what her blood might taste like. Gritting his teeth, he bit back the urge. If he didn't get a handle on his rising lust, hard telling where this little conversation of theirs would lead. No doubt with her kicking him out of her house and refusing to come within a thousand yards of him. But she needed his protection, whether she was too stubborn to admit it or not.

Kane roughly shoved several shirts in Cara's direction. His fingers brushed hers. Cara quickly withdrew as if she had just brushed against the skin of a snake.

Biting back an expletive, he turned to her and instead said, "Cara, you need to take this threat serious."

"What? That silly thing written in lipstick?" she asked, not bothering to stop her task and look at him. The tremble in her response gave away that it actually bothered her. But she wouldn't allow her tough exterior to slip; Cara was far too proud for that.

"It's not silly, Cara. Whoever came here means to kill you. You shouldn't brush that off as nothing."

"Well, it really isn't your problem now is it, Mister Tepes?"

"Jesus! Call me Kane already!"

She hardened her jaw and squared her shoulders. "I don't need your rescue, Kane. I'm sure Suzi would be—"

He grabbed her arm, perturbed that she would not take this warning seriously, and even more angry that she assumed there might be anything between him and the little brunette. Suzi wasn't his type and he had made that much clear to the young woman back at the Blood 'n' Rave earlier.

"What the hell is it between Suzi and you anyway?" he asked.

Cara's startled gaze looked up at him, his hand still gripping her biceps.

"I don't know whether to shake you because of your ridiculous, unfounded jealousy, or because you won't take this threat serious."

"Jealous? Ha!" She laughed, shaking off his hold on her arm. Fists jammed on her hips, she glared at him. "You give yourself far too much credit, Kane. What the hell would I ever see in—"

He hadn't meant to, but shutting her up became imperative. He seized her shoulders, getting the exact response he had hoped for as her eyes widened and her mouth gaped. Kane pulled her flush against him, her chest flattening against his ribcage. Cara's heart beat heavily, her blood rushed through her veins. Kane ignored his first primal instinct: to sink his elongating fangs into the artery beating at the side of her neck and instead kissed her.

CHAPTER SIX

THE MINUTE KANE'S LIPS TOUCHED CARA'S, HIS BLOOD HEATED. His temperature shot up quicker than mercury in a thermometer tossed into a pot of boiling water. His heart pounded in his chest and his fangs fully extended. His eyes heated in their transformation to obsidian-like glass. He couldn't hide what he was from Cara now if he wanted to. If she didn't feel the points of his fangs, then she wouldn't miss his more prominent brow and black gaze should she open her eyes to look at him.

His erection nestled against her abdomen. No way she couldn't feel the effect she had on him. Kane wanted Cara in a bad way. And kissing her wasn't helping that predicament as he closed his own eyes and slid his tongue into the soft cavern of her mouth. She tasted of hot, cinnamon candy, no doubt trying to mask the alcohol consumed earlier at Murphy's.

Kane expected her to fight him tooth and nail, to push him away and curse him for daring to take such liberties. Instead, her hands lay flat against his breasts, trapped between them. Not exactly a caress, but she wasn't shoving him away either. When their tongues touched, Cara responded in kind, a slight moan escaping her lips. That small, barely audible sound unleashed his desire. He growled in return. One hand anchored her as it rested on the small of her back. He had to fight to keep himself in check. Her response had turned up the heat, and he couldn't think straight for the want of fucking her.

He had craved to slide deep inside her from that first day ten years back when she stood innocently behind him, watching him have carnal relations with a woman he hadn't given two shits about. Kane had followed her from the club, but she had quickly disappeared. Not that he couldn't have caught up to her, but doing so would have frightened her irrevocably, if what she had witnessed hadn't already. Kissing her now, he had a small taste of what he had yearned for, and Lord help him, he wanted more.

Sliding his free hand down from the soft curve of her back, Kane cupped one cheek of her ass, pulling her abdomen tightly against his erection. He didn't think he had ever been so close to embarrassing himself.

What the hell was it with this woman that had him acting so out of character?

Females were nothing more than nourishment and to scratch an itch. Yet this one seemed to crawl inside his head, cause him to feel things he didn't wanted to feel. Kane, wrapped in his thoughts, didn't realize Cara no longer participated until the heal of her hand, placed squarely on his sternum, shoved hard in an attempt to push him away. Kane could have easily taken what he wanted, Cara was no match for the strength he held in check, but her withdrawal was like being doused with a bucket of ice water. He stepped back and shook his head, turning away from Cara and willing his fangs to retreat. He hoped like hell she hadn't noticed the changes.

Her breathing hitched as she stood precariously close behind him. Close enough that if he chose the animal side of his nature, he could easily catch her and toss her atop the messed bed and take what he so hungered for. He could still feel her heat, hear her blood rushing through her veins. But Kane had never taken what wasn't given. And he wasn't about to start now.

He took several deep breaths before facing her, his eyes and teeth returning to their more human state. Cara clutched a tee to her chest, fingers on one hand resting against her kiss-swollen lips, eyes wide and glassy as she stared at him. Christ, he didn't want to be the reason for her tears.

Had she felt the points of his fangs?

"You're staring at me as though I'm some sort of monster, Cara."

She shook her head. "I just hadn't expected—"

"You hadn't expected what? A kiss?"

Kane knew if she mentioned his fangs, it would be his responsibility to hypnotize her, use mind control to get her to forget what had occurred between them, but damn him if he didn't want her to remember. Just as he had wanted her to remember him ten years ago. He already walked a fine line with the MC. How much would they be willing to overlook? "You kissed me back … and quite well, I might add."

Cara stepped forward, raising a hand to strike him. Kane clasped her tiny wrist, lightning quick. "I wouldn't do that, Mia Bella. I might be tempted to think you liked it."

Cara yanked her wrist from his slackened grip. "You arrogant ass!"

A chuckle bubbled up from his gut. He had every right to be arrogant. Cara's body responded in kind whether she was ready to admit as much or not. His senses were far too keen for her to deny it.

"I may be an arrogant ass, but at least I'm not a liar." The smile left his face. He needed to get back to the real issue at hand: the warning from the primordial. "The threat against your life—"

"Is my problem," Cara said as she returned to gathering her clothing. Damn her stubborn hide for not seeing the seriousness of this. If this primordial vampire wanted her dead, then no matter what she did to try to prevent that from happening, the end result would be the same. Dead.

"Cara," he whispered as he approached her. Gripping her biceps gently, he turned her to face him again. He had to take the chance she wouldn't breathe a word. Her refusal to see the seriousness of the situation had pushed his hand. "What you saw ten years ago…"

The shirts in her hands dropped to the bed as she lifted her gaze. He could see the fear residing there, regardless of what her words said to the contrary.

"We're real."

Her brows knit together. "Of course, you are. You're standing right before me."

"No, Cara, not as a human. At least not fully."

He allowed his face to transform, his brow becoming more pronounced, his eyes turning blacker than coal, and his teeth elongating. "Vampire," he told her.

Cara sucked in a breath, but to her credit, didn't scream, though she struggled in his unyielding hold.

"Let me go," she hissed between clenched teeth.

Kane couldn't allow her to escape, lest she do something stupid like tell someone what she had just witnessed.

"You need not fear me, Mia Bella," he whispered, still holding her firmly in his grip. "I won't hurt you."

"Vampires don't exist," she said as she continued her fruitless struggles.

"Then how do you explain what you see?"

A stray tear rolled down her face as she stilled. "That I'm certifiably insane."

Releasing her, he used the pad of his thumb to wipe the wetness from her cheek. "Mia Bella, you're not insane. We exist. We have for years, but we do so in anonymity. No one can know, or surely we'd be hunted like animals. And though our strength surpasses humans, we are far outnumbered. It wouldn't be long before we would cease to exist."

"You can't have fangs." She raised her hand and ran her fingers across his more prominent brow. "Your face doesn't change shape," she said, her fingers traveling his hollowed cheeks.

"Cara, damn it, focus!" he growled. "This isn't about me or your sanity. This is about that threat on your bathroom mirror. It's real. And the person making the threat will carry it out unless I can stop him."

"But if you say you are a … a … vampire." Her breath hitched. "Then surely you can just bite him or something."

Kane released her and began pacing, his features returning to their human state. It hadn't missed his attention that Cara's gaze stayed glued to his face.

"The person who threatened you is not to be taken lightly. I wouldn't have shown you my nature if I thought there was another way."

He stopped, nailing her with his stare. "Mia Bella, you have to take this seriously. The vampire who threatened you is a primordial. That means he's an original. He is older than I am and much stronger. If he wants you dead, then I can't stop him. At least not by myself."

"So you're saying that there is nothing I can do. This primordial vampire will kill me."

"Not unless I've drawn my last breath. I have my brothers to back me. Chance are, he's here in the States alone. The primordials rarely leave Italy."

"Then how are you so sure that a primordial wrote the message? Did you see him?"

"No. I smelled him."

Her brows came together over the bridge of her nose as her nostrils flared. "I don't smell anything."

"You wouldn't, Cara. But I can and I know he's been here."

Cara tilted her head to the floor, shook her head then started laughing. "I can't believe I'm buying into this bullshit!" She glanced back at him, steeling her jaw, her lips a harsh thin line. "I don't know what kind of parlor trick you just pulled, but get the hell out of my house, Kane. I don't need your help. For all I know, this is your way of trying to scare the living hell out of me. Vampires! What-the-fuck-ever! I am not some teeny bop groupie you can lead around like Suzi."

"Cara," Kane said, his tone meant to warn her.

She advanced on him this time, stopping inches from his chest. She looked up as she pointed her finger into his chest. "I'll say this one more time, Kane: get the hell out of my house! If I find out you had anything to do with this and the dead girls we've been finding, I'm going to be the one taking your ass down! You don't scare me.

"Now. Get. The. Fuck. Out!"

CARA SAT AT HER DESK, STARING into space when the phone on her desk jangled, startling her. The pencil she had been toying with dropped to the wooden surface with a clatter as she grasped the receiver. Ever since Kane had exited her house via the broken windowed-door, she was nervous as a long-tailed cat in a room full of rocking chairs. Not to mention her concentration had been off. She needed to focus on the open case, and not on who the hell had ransacked her house.

"Detective Brahnam," she said.

"Good morning, Cara. We have some good news. We've ID'd your vic," the ME told her, his voice deep and raspy due to the excessive weight he carried. "Turns out she died like the other two vics: bled out. Never seen anything like this in the thirty-two years I've been doctoring."

"Who was she?"

"Tabitha Perkins. Twenty-two. Last known address was 252 Crestview Drive, Florence. She lived alone."

"Richey part of Florence to be that young and living alone. What did she do for a living?"

"She didn't. Spoon fed. Her father is the CEO of National One Bank. Her mother passed away ten years ago and her father never remarried. Tabitha was an only child. You can imagine he's not taking this well."

Cara rubbed her forehead with her fingers. Lord, this was about to get ugly real quick. No doubt CEO Perkins was going to demand answers and fast, answers she didn't have. Not that she didn't want help from the Forensic Services Division which would surely come in now and want to see all their evidence, but she didn't want the Oregon State Police breathing down her neck and telling her how to do her job, especially since she had past history with one of their troupers.

"TOD?" Cara asked.

"Best I can do is approximately a day, day and a half. Find out who last saw her alive and it will pin that time down better. It was cool so it preserved the body better than if it had been blazing hot out there."

"Thanks, Doc."

"If you need anything else, Cara ... you let me know," the ME said.

Her life was about to get a lot more complicated. Immediately, her thoughts turned to Kane. How much more muddled could they get?

"When are you releasing the body?" she asked the ME, still hanging on the other end of the line.

He cleared his throat. "Not until the Forensic Service Division says they're done with it."

Cara groaned. "You called them?"

"Sorry, Cara. I didn't have to. Mister Perkins did and they called me. Seems he's been reading about these cases and watching the news. Now that his daughter was just added to the growing list of numbers, he's fighting mad. He called the State and demanded they come to the Lane County's Sheriff Office and take this case over."

Cara let out a long sigh. *Great.* "Thanks for the heads up," she said and disconnected the call. Just as she ran both hands down her face and sighed again, Joe entered the office.

"What's up, Brahnam? Looks like you're having a day from hell."

"Something like that," Cara responded as she motioned for her partner to take a seat. "That was the ME on the phone. They've ID'd the vic."

The corners of Joe's eyes turned up with his smile. "I don't see how that could be deemed bad news. Let's see who we can tie her to."

Cara nodded slowly. "Let's find her known friends, who she'd been hanging with, acquaintances ... anyone she had been seen with in the last few months. Now that we have a name, we can match her friends and acquaintances with those of our past vics. We do have a problem, though."

Joe's grin faded as he leaned forward. "What's that?"

"Our vic ... Tabitha Perkins. Ring a bell?" When he shook his head, she continued, "Her daddy is the CEO of National One. Seems he's already called the State for us. Forensic Service Divisions is no doubt on the way here to take a look at our evidence, and we look like we've been chasing our tails. They'll think we're a bunch of buffoons and inadequate at our jobs."

"Have we done everything we possibly can to find this suspect?"

"You know I have."

Cara wasn't about to mention her personal business and how she knew one the troupers. Hopefully, he wouldn't be assigned anywhere near the case.

"Then stop worrying, Brahnam. We could very well use their help at this point. I don't know about you, but other than retracing our footsteps, looking at friends, family, and acquaintances, I'm just about out of ideas. We could certainly use a fresh pair of eyes on this case. Not to mention someone broke into your house last night. That could very well be related to the case."

Her gaze shot up to his. "Why would you think that?"

"Because, face it, you fit the perp's MO. And there was a threat made on your life on your bathroom mirror, Brahnam. We have to consider the possibility. We didn't get a latent, no blood from the broken glass. The perp likely wore gloves. At this point we don't know he's the same perp, but we have to consider the possibility. We need to make sure you're protected from this fuck."

Cara slumped in her chair. "It could have been just a random break in."

"Anything missing from your home?"

"No."

Joe tipped his head and leveled his gaze. "You're a better detective than that. A thief that doesn't take anything?"

"Maybe it was someone I arrested in the past. You think of that? There are a lot of possibilities that don't point to these unsolved murder cases."

"Of course, I thought of that, Brahnam. I have Deputy Higgins going through your past arrests and checking to see if anyone has been released recently. But I still think it's going to be a dead end. Call it a hunch. I think we need to get you some protection."

"Now you sound like Kane."

Joe stood and crossed his arms across his chest. "What does Kane Tepes have to do with any of this?"

Cara hadn't meant to bring him up. But now that she had... "He was at my house last night."

"When?"

"Before I called you."

"Was he there when you arrived home? Do you think he had anything to do with this?"

"No," Cara said so quickly it must have looked as if she were defending the man when clearly she wasn't sure if she should be. "What I mean is, I doubt he was the one who broke in. He was worried about my safety, too."

"How did he know where you lived?"

Cara rubbed her forehead. "I don't know. We ran into each other after I left the bar. Maybe he followed me home. He had been with Suzi at Blood 'n' Rave."

"Suzi?"

"Stevens. An old friend of mine. Back in our school days. I'm sure she'd more than willingly be his alibi."

"That still doesn't explain why he followed you."

CHAPTER SEVEN

"WE GOT PROBLEMS," KANE SAID AS HE WALKED INTO THE motorcycle shop he owned with Kaleb.

His twin was the first to look up as he laid his wrench on the cement flooring and stood, wiping the grease from his hands on his red work rag. "What's up?"

"Primordial vampires."

"What about them?" Kaleb narrowed his gaze, the word primordial no doubt piquing his interest as well as that of any other vampires within hearing distance.

"You hear from any of them?"

Kaleb chuckled. "Why the hell would I hear from them?"

"Because I think there's one here in Pleasant."

Grayson hung up the phone and headed in their direction, his sunglasses perched on top of his head. Some of their kind frequently wore them during sunlight hours, their eyes being sensitive to UV light. Grayson's seemed a natural part of the top of his head. "Why would you think a primordial would come here? I'm not aware that one's left Italy in more than a decade."

Hearing the conversation and the word primordial got most of the other brothers' attention as well, those that worked in the shop next to Kane and Kaleb. Nicolas, Alexander, Anton and Joseph quickly dropped what they were doing and filed around to hear what Kane had to say about the originals. That one simple word had a way of instilling fear in any vampire.

Nicolas "Wheezer" Bazil crossed his beefy arms over his massive chest, a small wheeze leaving his lungs, hence his nickname. Even though the big man topped the scales at easily three-sixty, the breathing sound had always been a part of him. Kane couldn't remember him without the tell-tale wheeze.

"So what makes you think a primordial is here?" he asked, his voice deep and just above a whisper.

"I smelled him last night, Wheezer," Kane said, propping one black-booted foot on the round of a stool. The vinyl seat was emblazoned with their motorcycle shop logo: K & K, which stood for Kane and Kaleb since the two brothers were the ones to open the shop some twenty years back when the Sons of Sangue first landed in Pleasant.

"You're sure?" Nicolas asked. Not that he doubted the President of the Sons. No one did. Nicolas more than likely fished for details.

"We all know the Sheriff's Office has been on our back about these peculiar deaths. We suspected that a vampire was behind them." Kane paced. He wasn't sure how the brothers would take the news he had been keeping an eye on the detective ... well, maybe not so much an eye on her as much as a keen interest. For now he'd downplay the last part. "I saw Detective Brahnam outside of the Blood 'n' Rave last night and followed her home."

"What was that detective bitch doing at the Rave?" Alexander "Xander" Dumitru asked. "She's a hot little number, but she don't watch out, she's going to get her own throat sliced."

The hairs on the back of Kane's nape stood on end. "What the hell is that supposed to mean, Xander? You know something about these murders?"

The man didn't even look affronted. "Fuck, no. I was just meaning she's got that look. You know, the same kind you seem to be hot after and the same one that's getting these bitches killed."

Alexander wasn't far from the mark and Kane was sure the rest of his brothers thought along the same lines. He ignored the comparison.

"She wasn't at the Rave. She was coming out of Murphy's Bar. I quickly got rid of my donor and followed the detective. Best to know where our enemies live," he added as an afterthought. "When I got to her place, it had been broken into. I decided to check it out.

"That's when I caught the scent, the primordial's. No mistaking it. He had been there, ransacked the place, and wrote a threat on the mirror to take her out next."

Kaleb slowly nodded. "Makes sense. She's the one trying to put him away and she matches his MO. Sucks to be her."

"Exactly what I was thinking, Hawk," Kane agreed, then his gaze scanned the rest of the brothers present. "And that's why the Sons are going to keep an eye on her."

"Are you fucking crazy?" Xander growled. "She's trying to pin these murders on one of us and you want to save her hide? I say let this primordial have her. Good riddance!"

"Sorry, Xander. That's not going to happen. If I say we keep an eye out for the detective, then that's what we do." Kane then added, "Without question. Until these murders, the Sheriff's Office has always stayed out of our business. Let us live in peace. We need to show them our allegiance as well."

Anton "Blondy" Balan rubbed the back of his neck, looking nervous. Kane figured whatever he had to say, he probably didn't want to hear it. Anton spoke up anyway. "Maybe we ought to take it to a vote, Viper. Most of us, we don't like that bitch anyway. She's always coming here, treating us like dog shit. All high and mighty. Blaming us for shit we didn't do. I say we call a meeting to church. Put it to a vote."

Anton, Secretary of the Sons, had always been the one to push for church meetings and putting decisions to a vote. Personally, Kane didn't feel this needed a vote, nor did he think he'd get the majority of those present behind him on this one. The three missing Sons weren't likely to side with him either, as they had their own reasons for hating the law.

"Unless everyone here vetoes me on this, Blondy, I'm calling this one as club Pres. There isn't going to be a vote. Keeping a close eye on the detective means we have a better chance at finding the primordial. Then maybe we can find out why this fuck is trying to pin these murders on the club … more specifically me."

Kaleb nodded. "I agree with Viper. Our first order of business needs to be finding this primordial, see what the hell he's doing in Pleasant and why the fuck he seems bent on the Sons being blamed for his shit."

Joseph "Kinky" Sala, usually the quiet one of the bunch, spoke up. He ran his hand through his large curled 'fro, hence his nickname. "I agree with Viper and Hawk. We just might have a chance at finding the original if we keep a close eye on the detective. Really ain't no reason to vote. If this primordial doesn't want to be found … we ain't finding him. I say this bitch detective is our best bet. We need to find out what the fuck this vampire wants in Pleasant, and what he wants with the Sons."

"CARA, YOU AREN'T GOING TO believe this," Joe said as he entered their shared office, a child-like grin reaching his deep brown eyes.

His khakis rode low on slim hips with a blue dress shirt tucked into them, left unbuttoned at the collar. His shirt sleeves were rolled up to the elbows, revealing lightly hair-dusted forearms, while his tie had been left abandoned over the back of his office chair. Cara knew he hated the constraint of a tie, being a bit claustrophobic, but the sheriff had insisted he wear them. So, Joe followed the rules … any time he had to leave the office while on duty. But at the S.O., he left them hanging on the chair, the desk, the coat rack, or whatever he happened to be near the moment he walked through the office door and unhooked the clip-on.

Cara sighed, closing the files in front of her, feeling the frustration of not being anywhere closer to solving this thing and knowing the State would arrive sooner than later. She hoped Joe came bearing something that might help break the case.

"What do you have, Joe? Good news, I hope."

"Our vic?" he asked, his white teeth standing out in contrast against his dark skin. Cara nearly chuckled as Joe was clearly unable to contain his excitement. He tapped his forefinger on the solid desk surface. "Tabitha Perkins dated Kane Tepes. Seems that they were an item for a few years."

What? Cara sat up straighter, pushing the files to the corner of her desk. She stood and met Joe's gaze. "Kane and our vic were an item? Incredible."

"Seems Kane's choice of women runs along the same line as the appearance of our dead victims." Joe rubbed his hands together, oblivious to her unease. "I think we may have our first viable suspect."

"You think Kane is responsible?" Cara gave Joe her back and glanced out the window. The gray clouds hung heavy with the threat of more rain in the forecast. The same guy she allowed to kiss her the night before, could he be responsible for three dead women? *Vampire,* flitted through her thoughts. She hadn't been imagining things and she certainly wasn't certifiable. Kane had shown her what he could become, even if she wanted to deny it with the deepest part of her being.

"Could he possibly be responsible?" she asked as she turned on her heel and faced her partner again, arms now crossed over her chest to ward off the sudden chill of the room.

Joe's face went from pleased to perplexed. "For real? His last known girlfriend winds up dead. His previous known girlfriends even match the perp's MO for victims. Not to mention Kane was the first person at your house following the break in."

"Oh, for goodness sake, Joe. I told you he had an alibi. He was at the Rave with Suzi while my house was being tossed."

"Not good enough. I want someone else besides his date to corroborate how long he was there. If he showed up at the night club later than you did at Murphy's, he could have easily ransacked your house."

"Even if you're correct, no one will give him up. It's the Sons' regular haunt."

"Then we'll subpoena the Rave's security videos. He's bound to be on them. We'll be able to see what time he walked through the door."

She slowly nodded, hands on hips. Cara couldn't very well continue to defend Kane without implicating herself and her mixed emotions where he was concerned. "I'll call the Florence PD and see if we can get them to subpoena the video feed. Keep a lid on this, Joe, I don't want those videos erased before I get a chance to look at them."

Seeing those videos might just put her own mind at ease and prove to herself that Kane hadn't been the one to write that threat on her mirror. Affirm that it was nothing more than a coincidence that he had arrived at her house shortly after finding the damage.

"While you're contacting the Florence PD, I'm going to pay K & K a visit and see what the Sons have been up to."

Cara didn't want Joe to confront Kane on his own. Truth be told, she wanted to see Kane's reaction first hand. How would he respond to the fact his girlfriend had been the one lying in a shallow grave, not far from where he had been out joyriding? Not to mention, she wanted to see if those damned butterflies still existed in the light of the day.

"I'm going with you," Joe said.

"What about the phone call to Florence?"

"I'll put Higgins on it. I want to see the look on Kane's face when we tell him the vic was his fuck buddy."

———

"HERE COMES THAT DETECTIVE bitch," Anton said as he returned from the front of the motorcycle shop and stopped at the opened door of Kane's office. "What the fuck you think she wants this time?"

Kane looked up from the paperwork. He knew Anton referred to Cara Brahnam. Just the mention of the detective started his blood humming through his veins. Hell, he didn't have to be a psychic to know that he'd be fucking her someday. No doubt about it. Kane was used to getting what he wanted. And right now he wanted the detective in the worst way. The memory of their kiss had him standing and heading for the front counter of the shop. He definitely wanted to see her no matter what brought her to K & K, which he was pretty sure was official business. Cara wouldn't likely seek him out on her own, at least not yet.

The front glass doors swung open, sounding the bell in the backroom, announcing someone's arrival. Kane stepped through the swinging doors separating the backroom from the showroom, bringing him face to face with the object of his obsession, and there was no doubt she had become one. Lord, she was hotter today than she'd been the night before, if that were even possible.

"What can I get for you, Detective?" Kane asked as the outside door swung open a second time and her partner graced them with his presence as well. Her gaze stayed fixated on his as Kane approached them both, stopping just short of running into her. She no doubt prayed he wouldn't mention *everything* that occurred the previous evening. The thought of making her squirm put a smile on his face. Kaleb entered the showroom behind him. Kane didn't need to turn around to know he was there.

Cara produced her shiny deputy badge in a small leather wallet. As if he needed to see it. "Official business, Kane. I have a few questions I'd like to ask you," she said, then hooked the leather wallet on the waistband of her tan trousers.

"What sort of questions, Detective? I don't believe I have any more information for you than when you stopped by the clubhouse last night."

Kane leaned his backside against the counter. His gaze traveled to her tasty lips, her pulse picking up its beat in the base of her throat as a result. Kane had no doubt she detected where his thoughts centered.

Cara cleared her throat, flipping his gaze back to hers. "Do you know Tabitha Perkins?" she asked.

Shit. He knew sooner or later the Sheriff's Office would figure out the connection. Kane shrugged. "What about her?"

"Miss Perkins is dead." She paused. Her gaze narrowed, no doubt trying to gage his reaction. He wouldn't give her the satisfaction. "She's the vic we questioned you about last night. Seen her around lately?"

"A few days ago."

"Where?"

"The Blood 'n' Rave. We met there a few times a week."

"Your girlfriend?"

"I don't have girlfriends, Detective. They're more trouble than they're worth ... that is unless you're offering." He winked at her. "Maybe then I'd have a change of heart."

Her gaze widened. "Seriously? You've been seeing this girl for a good period of time, you just find out she's been murdered, and you're now, what? Auditioning for a replacement?"

He kept his expression guarded. "I told you, she wasn't my girl-friend."

Detective Hernandez stepped forward, a smug look on his face that Kane wouldn't mind wiping off. "Not what I hear, Tepes. I heard you've been fucking her for a few years."

Kane glanced at Joe briefly. "Three to be exact." Returning his gaze to Cara's, he said, "But fucking does not equate being my girl-friend or a relationship."

Cara's expression darkened and she glowered at him. "You're a piece of work, Kane."

"How so?"

"You think Tabitha Perkins thought she might be your girl-friend, had she been asked?"

Kane chuckled as did Kaleb, who stepped beyond Kane and leaned his forearms on the glass showcase that separated them. "Ta-bitha knew exactly what she was getting with Viper. Everyone knows Kane hasn't had a girlfriend in a very long time. It's not Kane's fault if she came back for more. Besides, Detective, I bet if you two do your homework, you'll find others that my brother's been fucking over the past few years as well."

Cara turned back to Kane, ignoring Kaleb as though he hadn't spoken. "Care to tell me where you were last night?"

"Back to this again, are we? I'm assuming you mean before you saw me leaving the Rave. As I told you, Kaleb and I were out riding our bikes."

"On North Fork Road—joyriding," Joe recited from their last statement, sarcasm dripping from his words. "Just happened to be in the area we found your dead girlfriend."

Kane clenched his jaw, having had about all he wanted to take from her partner. Although he never minded indulging in a little word play with Cara, Detective Hernandez got beneath his skin and he was in no mind to humor him. "I told you, Detective, she wasn't my girlfriend."

Hernandez straightened, coming to his full five-foot-ten height. "Sorry. Your fuck buddy."

Kane towered over him at six-foot-four. He placed his hands on his hips and looked down his nose at the shorter man. "Call it what you want, but she and I did not have a relationship outside of the physical."

He wasn't about to add his feeding as part of that relationship. Dismissing Hernandez, he turned back to Cara. "I wasn't with Tabitha yesterday. I hadn't seen her in a few days. That's the truth of it."

"When did you last see her, Kane. And be specific about day and time because you know we'll want to verify your statement."

"I wouldn't expect any less, Detective. Four days ago at the Blood 'n' Rave. You can verify that with anyone who was there. I arrived at dusk, stood at the bar with Draven for about an hour when Tabitha joined me. We went to Draven's office. That was around ten o'clock."

"You do that often?"

"Do what?"

"Go to the owner's office? What do you do in there?"

Kane's grin widened. He'd definitely enjoy watching her expression. "We fucked, Detective. And yes, I use the office often."

Her cheeks flamed and Kane had to suppress a chuckle. "Do all the Sons use Draven's office for the purpose of intimate relations?"

"No. Only I use Draven's office for that purpose. Call it perks of being the president." He leaned in, sniffed the air, and smelled the rich scent of her blood rushing headily through her veins. What he wouldn't do to take Cara Brahnam into his own office and fuck her on his desk, his sofa, bent over the chair, and all the while suckling her rich blood. "I could show you the inner sanctum at the Rave if you so wish."

Kane didn't miss the tiny sound of her quick intake of air. He knew she would never admit as much, but the idea of being alone in Draven's office excited her. He could smell it on her. "I may want to do that, Kane, but I'll ask the club owner for the tour."

"As you wish," he said, his humor still visible. "But I assure you, it would be much more enjoyable if I gave you the tour personally."

"You're exasperating." Cara shook her head and gritted her teeth. Kane loved rattling her cage. She glanced at her notepad and ignored his open invitation. "Four nights ago, ten o'clock is the last time you saw Tabitha?"

Kane nodded.

"Anything else you want to tell me about that night?"

Kane leaned back against the counter again, crossing one booted foot over the other. "She left an hour later. I haven't heard from her since. You can ask any of my brothers. I've been here and at the club, other than last night's ride. That's it."

"I may want to question you further." Cara looked up and boldly held his gaze, squaring her shoulders. "Don't leave town."

This time Kane didn't suppress his humor. "Straight out of the movies."

"Excuse me?"

"I assure you, Detective, if I need to leave town, I will ... with or without your permission. But you're welcome to accompany me if you think it's necessary."

Cara glared at Kane, no doubt pissed at his mocking her authority. "I'm finished here. Joe?"

Hernandez glared at the twins, before placing a hand in the small of her back and guiding her toward the door without another word. Fucking pussy. Kane wanted to rip the detective's throat out for the familiarity with which he handled Cara.

As soon as the door closed behind the two, Kaleb growled, turning his censure on Kane. "And just what the fuck was that about?"

Kane pivoted on his heel, heading for his office, ignoring his brother's inquisition into his goddamned business and passing an eavesdropping Anton on the way. He was not in the mood to entertain his twin or any of his brothers. Kaleb dismissed Kane's foul mood and followed him to the office anyway, slamming the door behind them. The wood rattled the frame and shook the photo frames on the wall from the force.

"Are you fucking crazy?" Kaleb asked.

Kane turned and faced him, his thunderous mood skyrocketing. "About what?"

"Don't give me that shit, Viper. I'm your twin and I can smell you're hot after that little bitch. I didn't need to hear your little word games with her to get that."

"So what?"

"She's a cop."

Kane shrugged. "She's also a sweet little piece of ass. Besides, since when did you take an interest in who I want to fuck?"

"Since you got a hard-on for a pig."

A chuckle bubbled up from his gut. "It's no secret she's my exact type. It shouldn't come as a surprise."

"She's trying to pin these murders on us. That doesn't mean anything to you?"

"Of course it does." Kane ran a hand through his overlong black hair, pushing the strays from his face. "All the better reason to keep her close."

"I can't argue with keeping an eye on her. But I hardly think you need to fuck her to do that. What if she sees what you are? You know what happens when desire or hunger takes hold."

He wasn't about to reveal to Kaleb that the little detective had already seen his transformation. Kaleb would go apeshit if he knew.

"You don't have to worry. Cara Brahnam isn't coming within a football field of me unless she has to."

Kaleb narrowed his gaze, meeting Kane's dark eyes. "No, brother, what I smelled was a bitch in heat."

CHAPTER EIGHT

FOLLOWING A DISAPPOINTING TRIP TO THE BLOOD 'N' RAVE with her partner, Cara decided she needed to return ... this time without Joe. She wanted to experience the Rave and its clientele after the sun went down, when nightmares go bump in the night. A black lycra halter and dark blue denims with bleached thighs had been the best outfit she could throw together so she wouldn't stand out like a sore thumb, let alone as a cop. This crowd wouldn't know her or her profession, so she hoped to go unnoticed.

Cara toyed with the large golden hoop in one of her ears as she stared at the darkened entrance. The owner certainly went out of his way to make the club uninviting. A certain type of person frequented the Rave and she wasn't it. Tonight, she hoped it wasn't so obvious. Her heart stuck in her throat as she leaned against her car, reminding herself she was much older, no longer that young naive girl who fled the establishment years ago, thinking never to return. Hard to believe ten years had passed.

Yet, here she stood.

Her thoughts flitted back to that night and seeing Kane for the first time. He had been elusive, intriguing, and, well ... hot. Even as a young girl she could easily see his appeal, the ultimate bad boy. He rode motorcycles, wore a leather cut marking him as a member of the Sons of Sangue, and women seemed to take notice when he

103

walked by. He had a commanding appearance then, just as he did now. That appeal had her following him to the restrooms, too damned naive at the time to understand why he would go into the ladies' room in the first place. After long moments of looking for courage she didn't have, she had passed through the same door, only to find he wasn't alone.

Kane copulated with a blonde as Cara stood unable to exit the room as propriety called for. No, instead she had stared wide-eyed, rooted to the floor, a bit turned on, if she were being honest, by the erotic scene before her. That was until Kane turned and spotted her, his fangs scaring the bejesus out of her. Then she had run like the hounds of hell had been nipping at her heels, causing her to fear the man that had since become the cause of her night terrors, the same man who now made her insides hum with liquid desire. Just looking into his dark, hungry eyes left her one touch away from a screaming orgasm.

The club's owner, Draven, hadn't given away any of Kane's secrets when Cara and Joe had been there earlier. He hadn't told them anything more than they had already deduced. Kane had indeed been there with Tabitha four nights prior just as he confessed. No one had seen him since, not until the night Cara spotted him outside the club with Suzi. They were more than welcome to view the video feed if they didn't want to take his word for it, Draven had assured them. Joe, not wanting to wait for the subpoena from the Florence PD, took him up on the offer and asked for a copy, which he planned to take back to the S.O. for viewing.

Cara's thoughts returned to the tour and, more specifically, the office Kane used frequently. Was Kane using that very room to have sex with Suzi as well? She couldn't help thinking of him with her ex-friend, entangled together, giving her what Cara could only fantasize about, making her heart ache for the unattainable. Disgusted with herself, she shook her head.

What the hell was wrong with her?

Her gaze had held the Italian leather sofa for far too long, wondering what secrets it held and how many girls Kane had lain with on its supple surface. Cara wasn't sure she really wanted the answer.

Ignoring the jealousy snaking its way through her, Cara pushed away from the car and headed for the club. She had a job to do and standing by the car entertaining thoughts of Kane wasn't accomplishing a thing. In a self-conscious gesture, she tugged at the hem of the tank, it resting an inch above the waistband of her jeans. Maybe she should have dressed a bit more conservatively. Too late to turn back now. Taking a deep breath, she pulled open the door and entered the building before she could talk herself into heading for the safety of her home. Truth be told, the only thing she really feared was running into Kane.

Cara nodded at the doorman as she slipped past and paid the cashier the five dollar entrance fee. Once inside, she quickly cased the place for the least obvious place to sit. Neon lights glowed from every corner, as strobes and spotlights of bright yellow, red, green and blues flashed about the fog-generated room. The music blared and the bass beat heavily against her chest. Cara skirted the crowd gyrating on the dance floor, opting for a table at the back of the room. Even if she didn't run into Kane, she didn't want someone telling him that she'd been snooping around his regular haunt. Sure, he expected Joe and her to interview Draven, to verify his claims.

But coming here at night wasn't part of that investigation, at least not the way he would view it.

She had barely taken a seat when a scantily clad barmaid approached, asking what her poison was. Cara ordered the house Merlot, thinking the preferred draft more suited for Murphy's. The little barmaid returned quickly, placing a small, half-filled wine glass on the round scarred table. Cara handed her a ten, telling her to keep the change. The young girl smiled and tucked it quickly away, leaving Cara free to observe the room. Dancers raved to the music, glow sticks waved to the beat like extensions from dancers' hands. She hadn't recognized the song, but these days she didn't keep up with the trends or listen to the radio.

Halfway through her glass, the alcohol began to sooth her anxieties. No one from this crowd would even recognize her. Kane didn't seem to fit in with this young crowd either. Most seemed barely legal. Hell, she probably appeared ancient compared to a big share of the partiers. Coming here had been a mistake. Not like she'd discover any of Kane's secrets.

Movement by the entrance caught her attention, stopping her from making a speedy exit. Kaleb Tepes strode up to the doorman, shaking his hand and butting shoulders with him. His grin widened by whatever the man said, he winked at the cashier, though no money exchanged hands, and headed for the bar at the back of the club. Apparently, the Sons' money wasn't good here. Her best bet would be to finish her drink and wait for Kaleb's attention to become preoccupied. Once he ordered a drink and engaged in conversation, she'd slip out the nearest exit.

As she took another sip of Merlot, she heard "Looking for me?" just above the din of music.

Warm breath whispered across the shell of her ear, causing a shiver to pass along her spine before large hands cupped her bare shoulders, rooting her to the chair and preventing her from rising. Her window of opportunity just slammed shut. *Shit.* Cara glanced to the left. Kane's lips were scant inches from her cheek, a disarming smile on them.

"Surprised to see me?" Kane asked before grabbing the chair beside her and sliding into it without waiting for the invite she wasn't about to give.

He certainly hadn't lost his appeal after all these years. Kane Tepes was still hot as sin, with no more wrinkles than he had sported ten years ago. The black, form-fitting wife-beater that he wore beneath his motorcycle cut, left his arms bare. His shoulders and biceps flexed as he crossed his forearms on the Formica table and leaned toward her. The black tribal tattoo covering his left shoulder snaked down his arm and reached his elbow. She couldn't help wondering what he might look like without the tank and how many more tattoos he sported. Her mouth watered at the idea of his six-pack of abs, her fingers gently running over the contours.

"Something tells me you were hoping to run into me."

"Mighty sure of yourself," she scoffed, fearing her thoughts were plainly written on her face as heat rose in her cheeks. "Just because I came here, doesn't mean I was looking for you, Kane. Or should I be calling you Viper here?"

One of his eyebrows rose. Obviously, she wasn't a good liar. But rather than calling her on it, he said, "You may call me anything you want, Mia Bella, but I do prefer Viper over worse things I've been called."

Damn, if he didn't look good enough to ... what? Sleep with? She needed to get a handle on her libido, for crying out loud. No matter how sexy and mouth-watering Kane was, she couldn't allow herself to go there. Ever. Bad enough he rode on the opposite side of the law. Add vampire into the mix and the fact he was a strong possible suspect in her murder cases, she had reason enough to not allow him between her sheets.

Cara shrugged. "I told you I'd check out your story," she said, hoping he'd buy her excuse.

"You did that this afternoon."

No such luck. She might have guessed Draven had called Kane the moment she and Joe walked out the door.

"So why come back if not to see me?"

"I like the atmosphere."

His smile widened. "Try again, Detective. How about the truth this time? You came here to check up on me."

"Maybe."

"You wanted to see me again?"

"Kane—"

He leaned in and whispered, "You can deny it, Cara, but I won't believe it."

Cara held Kane's gaze, judging whether to try to dispute his claim. The words died against her lips. She couldn't even form the lie; he'd see right through it anyway. So instead she looked toward the bar where Kaleb stood, engaged with some pixy-haired brunette.

Kane's gaze followed. "Yeah, he wouldn't be too pleased if he found us talking. Hawk thinks you mean to put me away. Throw the book at me for these murders."

"He's not far from the truth."

Kane returned his gaze to her, looking serious. "You think I could be responsible for killing three women?"

"I don't know, Viper. You tell me."

"I might not have been in love with Tab, but I wouldn't have taken her life. I did care. I wasn't a total ass."

"Could've fooled me with your flippant attitude earlier."

Kane grasped her glass and took a sip of the Merlot. "Good choice."

"Are you always that cold with your girlfriends?"

"I told you, she wasn't my girlfriend. Besides, if I was such an ass to her, you think she'd stick around for three years?"

"I don't know. Seems like you have a way with the ladies," Cara said, earning her another chuckle.

"There's only one lady's attention I want right now."

Cara wasn't sure if he was being straight with her or playing games. Either way, his admission had her blood humming through her veins. Like it or not, her body responded to the man and she wanted him in the worst way. Best that he never find out, because if he ever turned on the seduction, she'd be a lost cause.

"You want to go up to Draven's office?"

This time Cara chuckled. He was shameless. "You don't miss a beat, do you?"

"As much as I'd like to wrap those long legs of yours around my waist, I'm only thinking right now it's in both our best interests if Kaleb or any of the other Sons don't spot us together."

Cara supposed she wasn't exactly high on their list of hang-arounds, so she quickly agreed. Grabbing her glass of Merlot in one hand and his fingers in the other, she followed him through the back of the club and up the curtained stairway. Once the curtains closed, darkness enveloped them. Cara couldn't see an inch in front of her face without the benefit of the tiny lights that illuminated the staircase. Kane took them as though he didn't needed a visual. Cara tried hard not to stumble in his wake. Reaching the office, Kane closed the door behind them, sliding the lock into place, and flipped the switch, filling the room with a warm glow.

Cara's stomach somersaulted. She certainly hadn't thought her actions through. If she had been wrong about Kane and he had indeed killed the three women, then she had just put herself into a precarious situation. Even as a black belt, Cara was pretty sure she wasn't a match for Kane's strength.

Kane must have guessed her apprehension. Pulling her to him with the fingers he still held tenderly in his clasp, he brushed her cheek with the back of his free hand, before tucking one side of her hair behind her ear.

"You're safe with me, Mia Bella. As I said to you before I would never take from you what is not offered."

"I haven't changed my mind, Kane. I'll never offer you anything."

Kane's eyes lit with humor. "I'll remind you of that when I'm fucking you."

Cara sucked in breath. She might have slapped him for his vulgar declaration had his statement not been like a shot of pure desire. Lord, she couldn't let him know the power of his words.

"Not only egotistical, but crude. You attract a lot of ladies with a mouth like that?"

"Confident, Mia Bella." He framed her face with his palms. "There's a difference. As for being crude, do I remind you of a gentleman so much that you think I should act like one?"

That earned Kane a smile as she quickly stepped back from his touch. "No, I don't suppose. So why are we here?"

"Because I wanted to talk to you—off the record. I want to be straight."

"Why?"

"I don't know. For some asinine reason I trust you. It could be because for ten years you've known that I was a vampire and yet you haven't told a soul."

"Who would believe me?"

"You didn't tell anyone, Mia Bella, because somewhere deep inside, you know I'm not a monster."

And she did, but she had to ask anyway. "Have you ever killed anyone?"

"Yes, a man. Never a woman." He paused, waiting for a reaction that didn't come. Then he said, "And not because I'm a vampire. One of the Sons' old ladies had wandered away at a biker rally. Not the smartest thing to do, but she didn't fear being hurt as no one with a lick of sense would touch someone belonging to us, but she was attacked. The man beat the shit out of her after he fucked her in every way possible. He left her for dead, thought the Sons would never find out. She lived for a short while, long enough to tell us who did it. It's not pretty what I did to the man. So don't ask. Just know he no longer draws a breath. If I've killed, Mia Bella, and I have, it's always justly deserved. Does that shock you?"

"No."

"Does it frighten you?"

"You scare the living hell out of me, Viper."

"Why?"

"Not because you've taken a life. Not because of what you are. But because I fear one day you'll be correct and I won't be able to resist you."

Kane stepped closer, his hand palming her cheek. "Lord, I hope not," he whispered and lowered his head, his lips claiming hers.

It wasn't a sweet, chaste kiss, but a total possession of her mouth. His kiss told her what his body desired, leaving no doubt where they were headed if she allowed him to continue. Just thinking about Kane doing to her what she had only dared to dream, numbed her limbs. Her grip slipped on her Merlot she had brought with her from the club and the glass fell to the tiled end table, shattering. Cara gasped, stepped back from Kane and reached for the broken shards, the pieces cutting into the flesh of her palm in her clumsiness. Red blood oozed from the wound and ran down her palm and between her fingers. Kane seized the injured hand before she could snatch it back and took it to his lips. His tongue wrapped each finger, licking the red fluid before moving to the deep cut on her palm.

Cara's heart beat heavy in her chest, not from fright but from a craving so strong it scared the hell out of her. The act of Kane suckling her blood was ecstasy in its purest form. The sweet sting of the wound as his tongue touched it caused her to suck in more air as her legs threatened to give out. She had to get as far away from Kane as possible before she did something incredibly stupid like draping herself around a vampire and telling him to take what he hungered for.

Problem was, she wasn't certain if he'd fuck her or bite her.

That last thought had her snatching her hand from his clasp, cradling it to her chest, and running from the room, not stopping or looking back until she reached the safety of her car. Cara sat heavily into the driver seat, willing her breath to return to normal before considering the depth of the wound. Surely, she'd need to get stitches. But when she opened her palm, holding it near the interior lamps of her car for a better view, only a thin red line remained. The wound had miraculously closed.

"ALEC, YOU STUPID IDIOT! YOU fucking imbecile!" came the irate screech through his cell as he pulled the phone from his ear. How dare she resort to name-calling after all he had done. And for what? Love? *Hardly,* he snorted! Maybe a few good pieces of ass.

"Careful, darling. I might be tempted to come back to Italy tonight and allow you to clean up your own fucking mess."

"How stupid of you to threaten the woman detective! I want to destroy everything Kane Tepes has worked for. I don't want him knowing a moment's peace. The goal here is to take him down, get his brothers to start questioning him as the Sheriff's Office closes in on their number one suspect. I want them to turn on him, remove his Pres patch, toss him as a member. They need to be convinced he's guilty, going off the deep end and draining these women. The Sons will never believe he threatened that lady detective when he trails her like a dog looking for a bitch in heat!"

He could hear her intake of breath, could easily imagine her standing there, hands on hips, glaring at the ceiling, wanting to wring his regal neck.

"Look, what I did will make the cops think the President of the Sons wants this all to go away, which would mean that Kane would want Brahnam dead. And hopefully, his brothers will draw the same conclusion. The end result will be the same: Kane will be exiled, and you'll be once again happy. If that is indeed possible."

He knew she paced the large expansive bedroom they shared, fuming that he hadn't followed her every directive, daring to set out on a plan of his own devising. She fascinated yet frustrated him to no end. He had committed to memory her every nuance, the way she ate, the way she moved, the little temper tantrums she threw. No love was shared between them, only the shared desire for power.

Together they were a force to be reckoned with. Any vampire would fear them, and rightly so. They were both primordials, origi-nals, but Rosalee came from the very loins of Vlad Tepes' brother's last wife, making her the much stronger of the two. Vlad's offspring hadn't been so lucky, their blood watered down over the years, leav-ing Kane and Kaleb the closest living relatives, many years removed. Alec had been turned by one of Vlad Tepes' now dead spawns, which gave him the title original, though he was not an actual rela-tive on the Tepes' family tree.

So for the time being, he humored Rosalee. After all, the perks were well worth it. No one fucked with, or like, Rosalee. The woman was an animal in the sack and out of it. He usually bore the claw marks to prove it. And when Rosalee wanted something, she could become downright insatiable. He grew hard just thinking about fucking her from behind, his fangs buried deep into the flesh of her shoulder.

Rosalee wanted Kane Tepes ruined, so much so it bordered on the obsessive. He could care less the reasoning behind it, just knowing Kane and Rosalee were once an item, was enough for him. Alec could have easily come to the states and ended the bastard's life upon his first sighting, But Rosalee had expressed her desire that he live. The younger vampire was no match for a primordial. His powers well-surpassed that of Kane's, but Rosalee had been adamant about making the bastard squirm. Who was he to deny her the pleasure? Besides, killing Kane was too easy. He'd rather watch him suffer.

"Alec? Are you listening to me?" came the shrill accusation, bringing his focus back to the phone call. "You know how I can't stand it when you aren't paying attention."

He rolled his eyes and released his breath. She could be exasperating at times. "My dear Rosalee. Of course I am listening. You want Kane Tepes disrespected and ruined. What more do I need to know?"

She harrumphed.

"Look, how about you don't worry about what methods I use and I won't question your reasoning? I'll see that Kane Tepes loses everything he holds dear in life and you can finally feel vindicated."

CHAPTER NINE

LORD, WHAT THE HELL HAD HE DONE?

Drinking from a non-donor was strictly forbidden and against club rules. Technically speaking, it was just a taste, nothing of real substance. At least that's what Kane tried to convince himself. If the rest of his brothers found out, there would be certain consequences. Rules had been put in place to protect his kind. And since first laying eyes on Cara some ten years back, he had been breaking those rules. Starting with allowing her to remember what she had witnessed in the bathroom at the Rave. He should have hypnotized her, taken her memory of him away ... but after following her into the night, he couldn't bring himself to do it. Kane wanted her to remember. The Sons had recently found out about that slight and allowed it to pass without penance, likely since Cara had kept their secret thus far. That and his promise to make sure she continued to keep it.

If they found out he had tasted her blood, suckled the wound, they'd be forced to call a meeting. President or not, his actions should have disciplinary actions. Kane had been reckless and he should be held accountable, as any other member would be. For now, he'd stay quiet about his latest discrepancy, keep his fangs to himself, and stay the hell away from Detective Brahnam. Because one small sample of her exotic blood had him craving another sip like wine to a wino.

"We got issues, Viper," Alexander said as he entered the clubhouse meeting room where Kane sat by himself at the large table that sat fourteen, staring out the double-paned window overlooking the Siuslaw River.

He shook off his musings and looked up, the hair at his nape bristling. Something told him whatever Alexander had to say wasn't going to be good. "What's the problem, Xander?"

Raking a hand through his long black hair, Alexander stopped before the long wooden, hand-carved table, leaning forward and bracing his hands on the worn wood. "Knights are in town."

Kane's brows knit together as he stood. His nape continued to tingle, a trait he and his brother shared when trouble lurked around the corner. The Knights were a rival club and had not asked for permission to enter the Sons territory. No doubt the Knights were up to no good.

"What the hell are they doing in Pleasant? And why am I just now hearing about this?" he roared. Kane overreacted due to his earlier musings. But at the moment he didn't give two shits who was on the receiving end of his morose mood.

Alexander stood, crossing his arms over his massive chest. "What do you mean? I'm telling you now."

"We should have known well before the Knights hit town. Who was on watch? What the fuck are we getting? Lax? I want to know when they cross the fucking state border."

The six-foot tall biker ran a hand through his black hair again, looking as though he wanted to tell Kane to go fuck himself, but thought better of it. "I'll grab Blondy, Wheezer, and Kinky. We'll ride out and see what they're up to."

"Where the hell is my brother?"

Alexander cleared his throat, clearly agitated by Kane's tirade. "I'm not sure. Last I knew, I wasn't his keeper."

Kane walked around the desk and pushed the curtains further aside, peering out at the cloudless night. A sliver of the moon stared back at him and reflected off the rolling river. Damn it, he knew exactly where Hawk was, likely ramming into some willing bitch. "I saw him earlier at the Rave."

Kane allowed the curtain to fall back into place as he turned and looked at his comrade. "I'll go."

"We need to retrieve Hawk ... the Sons' business is top priority. He'll want to be there."

"We aren't sure what the hell the Knights are up to yet. The five of us will ride out. Go get Blondy, Kinky and Wheezer. Tell them to meet me out front."

"Hawk would want to be there. He's VP."

"He's twenty minutes out at best. I'm not waiting for him. Are you questioning my judgment?"

"Absolutely not."

"Then get the other three and meet out front in five."

Alexander nodded, then trotted out of the office. Kane saw the excitement in the younger vampire's eyes. The Sons were always ready for a good fight, especially if it meant spilled blood. Kane's eyes warmed at the thought, but it wasn't the Knights' blood he desired. Damn the little detective to hell for making him desire something taboo.

"Shit," Kane cursed as he grabbed his cut off the back of the chair and shoved his arms into his vest. Tonight he'd have answers or bloodshed. One or the other. And given his present mood, he'd much rather have the latter.

THE WIND RUSTLED KANE'S HAIR beneath his skull cap as he leaned into the curves of Highway 126 at a high rate of speed, heading past Cox Creek to the outskirts of town. His motorcycle cut flapped behind him, the unseasonable warm weather dampening his tank, molding it to his sweat-slicked back. Anger simmered beneath his skin … furious that the Knights would dare to disrespect the club's domain, annoyed that Kaleb wasn't at his right side and indubitably getting a piece of ass, and mostly pissed at himself for even allowing his desire for Cara to become a cock block to him in the first place.

Christ, he was spoiling for a good fight.

He hoped to hell the Knights didn't have a good reason for crossing into Sons' territory, giving him the excuse to throw the first punch. The rival MC had been spotted gassing up at Riley's Gas Station and Dairy Mart on the edge of town. An adjacent picnic area had been set up for patrons, complete with shelter house, awnings and tables. Those tables were where they found the Knights lounging. As he drove into the parking area, gravel crunching beneath his tires, Kane wondered what the hell brought them to Pleasant. His brothers' Harleys followed him into the lot.

Kane brought his bike to a stop, kicked his centerstand down, and easily stepped over the seat of his bike. He took his skull cap off and let it dangle from the handle bars as the president of the

Knights rose to greet him. The rest of the Knights stayed their positions. There were ten in all, leaving the Sons out-numbered at the moment. Kane wouldn't think twice about picking a quarrel with two to one odds. He knew their strength outmatched the Knights and they didn't stand a chance should a fight break out. Kane narrowed his gaze, stopped before the six-foot-two president and crossed his arms over his chest. The pres sported weathered, tanned skin, no doubt from spending hours on the road and leading a hard life of alcohol abuse. His mouth made a grim slit across his face, barely noticeable through the heavy dark-red beard that reached the center of his chest. The Knights were a long way from their home turf of Seattle, Washington, about three-hundred-and-fifty miles south of it.

"Mind telling me your business in Pleasant?" Kane asked, not really caring about the reason. Truth was Pleasant was Sons' territory and to come here without permission meant you were looking to scrap. Kane would be all too happy to oblige.

"I don't want trouble," the president said, one hand toying with the tail of his long beard, which looked pretty grimed from the road. Kane wondered about the last time the man had graced a shower.

"If you're just passing through, then I suggest you get back on your motorcycles and keep moving. Next time you're in the area, I advise circling Pleasant or I might not be so courteous."

A smile split the muscular man's beard. Kane knew by his size he'd be a worthy opponent, though the man wouldn't stand a fighting chance with Kane's enhanced strength.

"I need a favor."

"A favor?" One of Kane's brows arched north. Being a rival gang, Kane had serious doubts he'd want to grant it. "What could you possibly want from the Sons?"

"We have some guns coming in via Florence. We need your permission to cross through Pleasant on a monthly basis. You're a straight shot for us from Interstate 5 to Florence. It's the easiest and quickest route."

"So you want our permission to run guns through our town?" Kane chuckled, then looked at his men still seated on their motorcycles behind him. None of them so much as smiled. He sobered his expression and returned his attention to the Knight. "You are either incredibly stupid or extremely vain to think we would allow you to bring that kind of trouble across our doorsteps."

"Hear me out."

"I'm listening."

"We need to run through your town. Allow it and run a distraction, and I'll see you profit."

Kane didn't need the added attention of the Knights driving through Pleasant monthly, not to mention the law taking notice and come down on the Sons for not holding up their end of the bargain of keeping all illegal activity and violence outside city limits. The Knights no doubted counted on the Sons' relationship with the locals to get them to turn the other cheek.

"So what's in it for us?"

"Ten percent."

Kane chuckled again, rubbing his temple with the tip of his middle finger. "Not even worth my time. Besides, you're potentially bringing violence within our city's limits, which we promised to keep out of Pleasant. That directly breaks our agreement with the Sheriff's Office."

The man was low-balling him and Kane knew it.

"Fifteen percent and we'll stay off the main streets."

The added income would be beneficial to the Sons as well as give them an alliance with the Knights, should they need one.

"Forty percent and you don't ride through Pleasant, but around it. You keep to the outskirts and don't ride before midnight."

The cover of night would be more beneficial to the Sons. Daylight posed too many problems and would draw unwanted attention.

"Forty-percent is bullshit and you know it."

"You came here asking for my help."

The president rubbed his beard as he stared at the gravel beneath his boots for long moments. Kane wasn't about to back down. His was a take-it-or-leave-it kind of offer. The income would be a bonus and a lucrative deal without much effort on their part, but he wasn't about to borrow trouble for little benefit.

Kane closed the gap, forcing the shorter man to gaze up, his expression grim. The rest of the Knights stood, ready to hit the dirt should the red-bearded man give the order. Behind Kane, the gravel crunched as his brothers left their Harleys and stood at his back.

"Don't insult me by offering less than forty percent. You want to run guns near Pleasant, then you'll give me what I ask. And," he paused, knowing the next request wouldn't be as easily won, "you give your allegiance to the Sons."

"Hell no." The man spat at Kane's feet, then wiped the remaining spittle off his beard with the back of his hand. "The Knights will not align themselves with any other MC."

Kane shrugged, turned his back and headed for his Fat Bob. "Suit yourself."

"The Knights aren't a puppet club."

Turning on his heel, Kane retraced his steps, leaving mere inches between their noses. "I'm not giving you a choice. You run guns through my territory, then you agree to an allegiance. Nothing happens with the Knights that doesn't go through the Sons first. In return, the Sons will have your back as well. If you don't agree, then you best not be seen in Pleasant or Oregon for that matter. Oregon is our state. No MC rides through it without our consent or an allegiance to us. If that makes you a puppet club, then consider yourselves lucky. Otherwise, no deal and you won't be running your guns through Oregon."

"At a mighty high price."

"It's a high risk. We may have the Sheriff's Office keeping out of our business, but the state dicks don't look the other way where we're concerned. So if you don't like it, then take your business elsewhere and stay the hell out of Oregon or we will go to war over this."

The president glared at Kane for a moment, then said, "Other than forty percent, what's in this for you? Why the fuck do you want our allegiance to you?"

"We have an issue that may become a problem down the road." Kane wasn't about to tell him about the primordial, but they might need an extra hand keeping an eye on things ... or better yet an eye on Cara. Like it or not, her life had been threatened and Kane couldn't keep her in his sights twenty-four-seven. "Should we need your help, you'll be there, no questions asked."

After a long pause, Kane thought the man might reject him outright when he stuck out his hand. "The name is Red. You have my word that the Knights will be in allegiance with the Sons. You need us, you call."

"The name's Viper." Kane shook his hand. "You run your guns at night and skirt the city. We'll make sure the Sheriff's Office turns a blind eye. After every run, I'll expect the forty percent in cash. Should you run into trouble," he withdrew a card from his motorcycle cut breast pocket and handed it to Red, "you call this number. You double cross me and you die. Don't make the mistake of playing me or the Sons for a fool."

"You have my word," Red said, tucking the card in his vest pocket, handing Kane one of his own.

With that, Red turned and headed for his Harley, motioning for the Knights to follow suit. Kane and his brothers watched the MC ride back down Highway 126, their rockers, the circular patches on their cuts that told other bikers their MC affiliation and what chapter they belonged to, and taillights fading into the distance. Kane turned, headed for his Fat Bob, swung a leg over the seat and looked at Anton.

"You think that's a wise move, Viper? Maybe we should have taken this to church and voted on it. I'm not so sure we would have all agreed to an alliance with the Knights."

Kane steeled his jaw and glared at the Sons' secretary. "You want to take it to a vote, Blondy? Then call the meeting when we get back. End result will be the same because it's a good business deal. We get money for doing nothing other than looking the other way. And, when I'm ready to bring them in, it couldn't hurt having a few extra eyes looking for this son of a bitch trying to take us down."

Without waiting for a response, he pushed the start on his bike. The sound deftly ended any argument his men might have. Kicking the centerstand up, he made a wide arc in the parking lot, then headed for town, hoping none of his brothers followed. First thing tomorrow, he'd make a trip to the Sheriff's Office to talk to the sheriff about their new business venture. But for now, he needed to see for himself that Cara was safe before heading for the clubhouse, calling it a night.

Kane glanced up, noting the cresting sun. He'd best hurry if he hoped to catch Cara.

CHAPTER TEN

CARA AWOKE WITH A START, HER HEART POUNDING LIKE A jackhammer. Her stomach lodged in her throat, cutting off a steady breath. Blinking, she focused on her surroundings. What the hell had she been dreaming to cause such hysteria? Her mouth tasted dry as dirt and her sheets wrapped her legs tighter than a mummy. Kicking her legs free, she swung them over the side of the bed and peered out the window as the sun slipped over the horizon, lending an eerie glow to her room.

Just a dream.

Tears stung the back of her eyes. Hell, she couldn't even remember the nightmare other than the complete sense of loss and panic as she awoke in a tangled mess of bedding. Cara scrubbed both hands down her face, grateful that something had roused her.

The remnants of sleep hung heavy, making her sluggish. Cara rubbed her eyes, hoping to dislodge the fogginess clouding her brain. Standing, she crossed the carpeted floor to the window, curtains billowing in the breeze. Cara brushed them aside and looked across the dew-misted lawn. Footprints disturbed the wet blades, heading in a direct path to and from her opened window. Large footprints at that. A sense of unease washed over her. Since her bedroom was located on the second story, surely no one could have gained access to her room. The rest of the house had been locked up tight.

Kane's words haunted her. *Whoever came here means to kill you.*

Cara didn't want to admit as much, but Kane had scared the bejesus out of her. What if someone really did want her dead? Someone like Kane. Black eyes and elongated white teeth ... a shiver passed over her spine. She wrapped her arms about her middle, suddenly feeling more vulnerable than she ever had. Cara couldn't help thinking that the three dead women, as Joe pointed out, looked very much like herself. If what Kane had warned her about was true, then there wasn't anyone strong enough to stop this psycho from following through with his threat. Cara's fear shook her to the core. Although for years she had mocked the very existence of what stood before her, less than twenty-four hours ago Kane had proven the reality of it.

Vampires.

The epithet alone made her tremble. Maybe she didn't fear Kane. But what about the others? The threat on her mirror proved they weren't all like him. Some were blood-thirsty killers. Some would stop at nothing to get the one thing they desired: human blood. And it appeared one of them had put a big red target on her back.

Suzi came to mind as she left the Rave two nights prior, hanging on Kane's arm and none to glad to see Cara. She couldn't help thinking her friend was somehow a part of all this nonsense as a tiny vial of blood hung from her throat that she never seemed to be without. Cara wondered at its significance. Did Suzi know of vampires' existence? Was she part of some underground culture, a den of real-life vampires?

Maybe Cara needed to put the past to rest and pay Suzi a visit, see what she knew about Kane and his brothers. Cara planned to find out the truth, whether she wanted it or not.

Her life might just depend on it.

As she looked back out the window, a brown smudge on the frame caught her attention. Fresh dirt marred the painted sill. Cara ran a finger over the brown soil, noting the freshness of the mark. How the hell was that possible? She didn't even have a trellis leading up to her window on the second floor. Yet the someone who had trekked from the woods behind her house, leaving a trail in the dewy grass, had been at her window. Cara went to pop out the screen so she could get a better look, when she noticed that some-one had already popped it out and hadn't fully reseated it in the track.

Jesus, Mary and Joseph.

Cara knelt in front of the window, brushing the slightly damp carpeting before it. Wet blades of cut grass stuck to her fingers. Not only had he peered into her window, he had climbed in, stood over her while she slept.

How naive and stupid of her to leave her window unsecured, especially following the ransack. Kane had warned her and she had all but ignored his concern. And for what, fresh air? She could have easily been added to the list of growing victims.

Cara stumbled back to the bed and sat heavily onto her rumpled sheets. Who the hell could she even call? The S.O. certainly would never believe that an age-old vampire meant to slice her throat. Get out the straightjackets now. Joe would be concerned, sure, but he'd never understand what she dealt with. Hell, she didn't even understand it.

Kane.

Like it or not, he might be her only hope in getting out of this alive. Cara hadn't ruled him out as a suspect in the murder cases, nor had she completely ruled him out as the one who had ransacked her room. And now she thought him her last hope? Cara took a deep breath and released it. What a mess. She didn't even trust herself to be in the same room with him for far more reasons than the open murder cases. Cara thought about the hot possessive, toe-curling kiss. The one that came right before she panicked, broke the glass and ended with him sucking her blood. Her heart quickened and her blood raced through her veins. The man was one hell of a turn-on. She had no doubt that if she were ever to cave and actually take him up on that piece of ass, it would be the best sex she'd ever had in her lifetime.

Not that she had a lot to draw on.

Cara looked at her palm. The palest of scars remained. She ran her forefinger across the thin, pink line. His actions should have had her praying to her lucky stars that he hadn't decided to drain her. The three women left in shallow graves came to mind. Surely, he wasn't capable of anything so heinous. But instead of swearing off of ever being in the same room alone with the man again, she thought him her savior from this whole debacle. Not only that, but she actually fantasized about him sinking his fangs into her neck and taking his fill. Just the thought had her panties wet.

What the hell was it about the man?

Kane had tasted her blood, his tongue following the red path down her fingers and encircling the digits. The sharp points of his canines had scraped her flesh as he suckled the cut. She should have been running for the hills, not dreaming about getting him out of his pants and into hers. A dull ache centered between her thighs. She had done gone and lost it.

Walking to her closet, Cara pulled her thin nightgown over her head and tossed it into her laundry basket, then stepped out of her panties. She needed a shower. A very cold shower, she thought with a chuckle. She had no business entertaining thoughts of Kane and how she'd like to lick every hard, contoured inch of him. The man was a walking wet dream if she had ever seen one.

A knock sounded on her back door, startling her. Cara glanced at the clock: six-fifteen. Who would be calling at this hour? Grabbing her silk bathrobe from her closest, Cara shoved her arms into the sleeves and headed for the door. Whoever it was, the person better have a good reason for disturbing her fantasies of one very hot vampire.

Cara peeked through the venetian blinds that hung over the door window, one of the four panes now covered by plywood. Kane Tepes stood on her stoop, as though the very thought of him had conjured him up. Cara hesitated, hand on the knob. Her heart stuttered to a screeching halt. Hadn't she just convinced herself that being alone with him wasn't a good idea? And here she stood, nearly naked, and ready to invite him in. Cara slapped her palm against her forehead. She needed a reality check. Besides, if Kane had been the one to stand over her bed last night, then she wanted to know why.

Opening the door a crack, not wanting to give him the impression he was welcome, she asked, "What do you want, Kane?"

His smile warmed her and tickled her libido. Damn, she hoped she wasn't about to hand herself over to a psychotic killer.

"That's one hell of a greeting."

"I'll save the pleasantries for those that are invited."

Kane laughed. "I'm wounded."

Great, her jibe hadn't fazed him. She opened the door and allowed him in. "Aren't you supposed to be sleeping, going underground, getting in your coffin or something about now?" she asked as she shielded her gaze from the morning sun.

He rolled his eyes as he stepped into her laundry room. "Maybe if I were dead."

Gripping her hand, he placed it over his heart, which beat heavy beneath her palm. His flesh was hot … very hot against her hand.

"Does that feel dead to you?"

"Vampires are supposed to be cold."

"We aren't fictional. We don't need to be invited in, crosses don't scare us, holy water won't harm us, and our eyes are only sensitive to the sun. We won't go up in flames if that's what you're worrying about."

"More like hoping."

Kane pulled her so close her breasts grazed his chest, hardening her nipples. No hiding them beneath her silky robe. Damn her Benedict Arnold body, but she wouldn't give him the satisfaction of pulling away and allowing him to see her reaction. So instead, she stood her ground and tilted her chin up, glaring at him.

"That isn't true, Mia Bella, and you know it. Your heart beats fast." He winked at her. "One of the benefits of being a vampire, our senses are more acute."

"Then maybe you can tell how annoyed I am right now."

"Annoyed that you desire me?"

"Annoyed that we're standing here having this conversation. I have to get to work, Kane. So unless you're here to tell me you caught the son of a bitch who threatened me, I don't have time for your bullshit."

"It's a Saturday, Detective."

She steeled her jaw, debating how much to tell him. "I still have a murderer to catch."

Kane's expression turned serious, obviously detecting her unease. "What's wrong?"

Cara looked away, not wanting him to see the lie. "Nothing. I really should get to work."

Using the pad of his thumb on her chin, he brought her gaze back to his. "Mia Bella, I smell your fear. What is it?"

Cara gritted her teeth, cursing his over-ripened senses. "Where were you last night?"

"Why?"

She took an unsteady breath, hoping her leap of faith wasn't right into the arms of a killer. Cara didn't want to believe Kane had crawled through her window, so she had to ask, had to hear it from his lips that he had been nowhere near the vicinity. And maybe because she needed to trust in someone other than herself. Cara had to admit she was out of her league on this one. Kane, like it or not, might be all she had.

"Someone climbed through my window while I slept." Moisture gathered in her eyes, but she didn't want to show her weakness. Blinking away the tears, she stepped back from Kane's touch. "The evidence is upstairs. I'm not going crazy. God, at least I hope not."

When Kane said nothing, she feared misplacing her trust. She continued, "My sill had dirt on it as proof."

When Kane still had not reacted to the fact someone had been at her window, her mouth formed an O. Her heart clawed up her chest, and goose flesh popped out along her forearms.

She glared at him. "Why the hell would you stand over me while I slept?"

He took a step in her direction but stopped just short of touching her when her expression rooted him to the floor. "I had to know you were okay."

Cara's ire peaked. "You could have called."

"I wanted to see for myself."

"Well then, looking in the window should have sufficed." Cara steeled her jaw, the ache traveling to her ears. "How the hell did you manage to look in a second story window without a ladder?"

"Jumping that high is not a problem for my kind."

"So why climb through it?"

"Cara." He took another step and gripped her shoulders. "What the hell are you talking about? I held onto the ledge and only looked in. That's it. I didn't climb through your window. Are you telling me someone was in your room last night?"

Kane didn't wait for her answer. He dropped his hold on her and stormed around her. Cara followed him through the kitchen and the living room, as he crossed the carpeted floor and took the stairs two at a time. Cara tried to keep up, and nearly ran into him as he stopped abruptly just outside the bedroom door, and sniffed the air.

"Fuck." He turned, his eyes turning black in his anger. "You can't stay here. Pack your shit."

SON OF A BITCH.

The primordial's scent drenched Cara's room. Kane wanted to destroy something ... better yet, Kane wanted to kill a primordial. This fucker wasn't getting bold, he was downright cocky. He shook his head, hands on hips as he looked to the floor and mentally kicked himself. Did he expect anything less? Primordials weren't known for doing things quietly among the vampire community. When they did something, it was usually to prove a point or teach a lesson, and it was done so in grand fashion. So what the fuck was the point and what did it have to do with Cara?

He hadn't heard of a primordial leaving Italy in better than a decade. Last time...

Christ, he refused to think about it, let alone voice her name. Things had not ended well between them. As a matter of fact, their parting had left someone dear to him dead. Kane wasn't the forgiving type. She was the reason Kane no longer believed in relationships. How did the saying go? *Screw me once, shame on you. Screw me twice* ... he had no intention of being screwed a second time. Women were good for two things: sex and nutrition.

It was that simple.

Women couldn't be trusted.

He'd do well to remember that as he stood before his latest interest, dressed in nothing more than a silky robe and lord only knew what lay beneath. Kane hated to admit as much, but Cara Brahnam had woven her way beneath his skin all those years ago. Then she was nothing more than a stunning teen ... today, she stood before him as one hell of a gorgeous woman. One who tripped his libido, left him hot and wanting. His semi-erection was proof of that. She really needed to get dressed.

"Pack your shit, Cara."

She crossed her arms over her chest, shoving a great deal of her cleavage above the neckline of her robe. Kane swallowed. Maybe he could throw her ass on the bed, fuck her first, then get her the hell out of there.

Nope, bad idea.

"What makes you think you can protect me any more than the S.O.?"

Kane did chuckle this time. "Are you fucking serious? I'm one of them. The Sheriff's Office doesn't stand a chance against me, let alone a primordial."

"You've said this vampire is older than you, more powerful. So basically, you're saying I'm screwed. He wants me dead and he's stronger than you. How the hell are you going to protect me?"

Shit, she had just voiced his own fears. "I don't know, Cara. But I promise you I will protect you with my own life."

"Why risk your life for me? I've done nothing but try to pin these murders on you."

Kane wasn't ready to face his feelings. Hell, beyond wanting her horizontal, he didn't even know what they were. "Because you're a pawn in his game. The primordial likely killed Tab. And the other women? They all looked very similar to you, Cara. That's not by accident."

"I don't understand. Why target my looks?"

The last thing he wanted to do was freak Cara out, but she had a right to know. And even though she was his preferred type, she was far different from the rest. Truth be told, it was because of her that he preferred his women blonde and blue-eyed. "Because it's my preferred type."

"Preferred type?"

"Women I like." He glanced back at the floor, not wanting to see the reaction in her beautiful gaze. Christ, she was likely to think he stalked her. "Women I like to fuck."

Kane heard her slight intake of air. He brought his gaze up, and before he could offer her any sort of explanation, she stayed his words with a raise of her hand.

"What you're saying is that I've been targeted by this psycho vampire because you want to fuck me?"

He nodded, feeling like a heel. "If he's after you, then his real target is me."

"Oh, that's just rich!"

"I can't help how I feel. You have to know I would never willingly get you involved in anything that would see you harmed."

Her throat bobbed as she swallowed, her eyes glassed over with unshed tears. "How do you know he's been here?"

"Because I can smell him, Cara. His scent is all over your room. He didn't merely stand over your bed. He paced the fucking room. And you know what I think?"

"What?" she asked, her voice catching.

"He did it on purpose. The motherfucker wanted me to smell him all over this room. He was sending a message to me, Cara. Otherwise, he would have just killed you when he had the chance."

The scent of her fear seeped from her pores. Good, he needed to frighten her. And the fact she now probably hated him would work in his favor as well. She wouldn't let him come within ten feet of her, let alone toss her onto the bed like he so desired. Kane needed to keep his head on his shoulders and stop breaking MC rules. He needed to get back to business and catch this motherfucker. Getting involved with the detective would only complicate matters and turn his brothers against him. And right now he needed their help.

"He wants me to know that he's targeted you."

She wet her lips, the tip of her pink tongue nearly having him forgetting his latest resolve.

"I don't understand any of this."

"I know what he's capable of, Mia Bella."

"But why would they use me to get to you?"

"Damn it!" Kane shoved his hand through his hair and pushed it from his face. "Just pack your bags, Cara. I'm moving you to the MC clubhouse where I can better keep an eye on you."

"I'm not moving, Kane, not until you tell me how I got involved in the middle of a pissing match between you and some ancient vampire."

He ground his teeth. Damned stubborn woman. "Why can't you just do as I say? I can't protect you here, Cara."

"Well, apparently"—she stepped so close he could smell her blood rushing through her veins— "had I not ever met you, I wouldn't need protecting. So I think you owe me the truth, Kane."

"I don't know the answer, Cara ... other than he wants you dead. Why? Because it would hurt me."

She spread her arms out, the gesture causing her robe to slip, revealing more of her cleavage ... answering the question of what lay beneath her robe. Nothing. His breath left his chest in a hiss. How much could one vampire take? They were sexual beings, for crying out loud, not used to practicing restraint. His cock hardened. He wanted to bury himself to the hilt, feel her walls surround him like a silk glove and forget this primordial even existed.

"How could my death possibly hurt you?"

"Because I want you, Cara, I have for ten years." When she didn't comment, only gaped at him, he continued, "Is that what you wanted to hear, Mia Bella? You have one vampire who wants to fuck you senseless, who can barely contain himself in your presence, and one who wants to take your life because of it."

Kane's eyes blackened as his fangs elongated in his rising desire. He could see his crazed reflection in her gaze. *Damn,* but he wanted to throw her on the messed bed she had just crawled out of, push aside her robe and run his hands along her silken flesh, take what he'd fantasized about as he watched her sleep. He didn't think his actions through, just knew the need sluicing through him was more powerful than anything he had experienced before. Grasping her biceps, he pulled her flush and slanted his mouth over hers, his tongue sliding between her parted lips. God help him, but he was a hair's breadth away from losing all control.

CHAPTER ELEVEN

KANE FELT HER HESITATION BUT A MOMENT BEFORE HER ARMS slipped about his neck. He took her compliance as an invitation and deepened the kiss. Her answering moan drove him forward as he backed her toward the bed. Her kiss wasn't tentative by any means. It was begging for what he was more than willing to give.

Hot, sweaty sex.

That's the thought that crossed his mind. Not his need to feed. Not his need to protect. Not the primordial. And certainly not Rosalee. No, his only thought was burying himself to the hilt in a woman who didn't think she needed protection. Hell, she needed protection all right. Cara not only needed it from the ancient vampire, but she needed it from him as well for his intentions were of the X-rated sort.

Kane had passed the point of trusting himself.

He grabbed a cheek of her ass in each of his palms and lifted her. Cara wrapped her slender thighs about his waist, bringing her center flush with his cock. Her robe parted, leaving nothing between them but the rough material of his jeans. Her breath drew short and her wide-eyed gaze told him Cara was a scant inch from bolting, and damn him if he shouldn't be the gentleman and give her the opportunity.

The Sons would doubtlessly strip his P patch if they caught an inkling of how frequently his thoughts turned to the woman who meant to incarcerate him for crimes he hadn't committed. He had lived and breathed the MC for as long as he could remember. Not that they would strip him of the presidency for his idiotic choice of whom he chose to fuck, but for the likelihood that he would feed from her in the process. If he followed through with his intentions, he prayed for the willpower to keep his fangs to himself. His one taste of her had his mouth watering for another. His brothers had looked the other way when he hadn't hypnotized Cara into forgetting. No way could they allow him to break another rule without repercussions.

Needing far less clothes between them, Kane laid her upon the rumpled sheets. Taking his off was near to impossible the way she had wrapped herself about him. He desired her that way, but with nothing on. He wanted to feel her flesh sliding across his in a sweat-slicked dance that went back to Adam and Eve. Cara had scooted up the sheets to the pillows, hugging her knees, staring at him with a heavy-lidded gaze of desire mixed with that of fright. Her complexion had paled. He knew she waged her own battles. On one hand, Kane had been her every nightmare. On the other, a huge temptation, evident in her desire now scenting the room.

Stripping off his shirt and tossing it to the side, Kane closed the gap between them. He needed to make sure the right side of the equation won and planned to make himself hard to resist. Cara's decision to walk away wouldn't be an easy one. Grasping an ankle, Kane pulled her slender foot toward him. He brought the gentle arch of her foot to his nose, sniffing the rich blood that flowed through it, then licked a path along the soft slope. Cara gently tugged at her foot in his grip, her tiny gasp filling the quiet air.

His fangs ached at the warm scent of her blood. Biting her and slaking his urge to feed would be so damn easy. But he also knew she'd flee from him faster than she had the first time he tasted her. He'd be left with a whole lot of regret and a raging hard-on. Kane fought back his animalistic nature, hoping to hold it at bay. This close to Cara's flesh made it damn near impossible.

His blackened gaze reflected in her eyes and yet she hadn't run screaming from the room. He took that as a small victory in his favor. He spread her smooth thighs, running his palms up the satiny flesh. His cock throbbed. Kane slid up the bed, his tongue following her hip bone to her stomach, circling her navel, hearing the catch in her breath and smelling the heat of her desire. Cara couldn't deny she longed for the same release.

Kane challenged her, needing to hear her say she wanted the same thing. "What is it you want, Mia Bella? You need to tell me. Do you want me here?" he asked as he ran a finger along her swollen flesh, feeling how damn wet she already was.

Her breath hitched and her legs quivered.

"Or do you want to stop now and forget what we started? This is your last chance to turn back. Because if I go any further, I'm going to fuck you ... let that be understood. And if that's what you want as well, you best take the opportunity. Because once we hit the clubhouse, you will not only be protected from the primordial but from me as well."

She rose up on her elbows and locked gazes with him. "Why would I be protected from you if I were to move into the clubhouse?"

"Because my brothers won't allow me within a mile of you."

CARA DIDN'T UNDERSTAND. WHY would the OMC care who Kane chose to sleep with? She was under the impression that every one of them slept with multiple women. Not like Kane hadn't had numerous lovers, so why was she so different? An unsteady breath left her as she wondered just why they were having this conversation in the first place. Shouldn't they be getting to the part where Kane … ah, hell. She needed her head examined.

Kane's obsidian gaze studied her. The change in his eye color should have been her first sign to run, but for some reason it was a huge turn-on, right along with those ridiculous fangs and his more prominent brow and hollowed out cheeks. She might have regrets, should she decide to take Kane as a lover, but one look at that chest and abs and she was a goner. It certainly wasn't the body of a … how old was he anyway? Did she even care?

"I may want you in every position possible, Mia Bella, but you and I are against club rules."

"Why would we be any of the club's business?" she asked as she slid back up the bed to a sitting position, putting distance between her and his hand.

She couldn't think straight, let alone talk, with his hand so close to stroking her. She detected his dislike of her pulling away. Her body screamed at the distance. She didn't want to be having this conversation. No, she wanted the promise of the best sex ever.

"Please don't tell me they have a list of fuckable women and I didn't make the cut."

A genuine chuckle bubbled up from his gut. "My brothers couldn't care less who my flavor of the—"

"Don't say it!"

His smile widened. "What I should have said is my brothers don't dictate who I sleep with. Nor do I care who they have sex with, providing it's not breaking any club rules."

"So what are we doing that breaks the rules? Is a cop off limits?"

He shook his head. "Not exactly. Though keeping us high on the suspect list doesn't exactly put you in their good graces."

"Then why would we be breaking your stupid rules?"

His face sobered. "The rules are not stupid, Cara. They're put into place to protect us."

"From whom?"

"From outsiders knowing about us ... vampires. No one can know that we exist."

"And yet I do. The MC knows that I know what you are?"

He nodded.

"So what are you supposed to do about it? Kill me?"

"I could hypnotize you."

Whatever she expected him to say, it wasn't that. "Have you ever—"

"No. If I would have, it would've been ten years ago when you fled the Rave. My job was to follow you and make sure you remembered nothing."

"But you didn't."

"I followed you."

She sucked in a breath.

"But I couldn't bring myself to take away your memory."

"Why?"

"Because I wanted you to remember."

His admission hung heavy between them. Neither said a word as their gazes locked. Slowly, Kane's eyes returned to their normal deep brown. She supposed that meant he'd reined in his desire, thanks to their conversation. Looks like she'd be left speculating how good Kane was in the sack. Lord, she couldn't help being jealous of Tab ... a dead woman. Cara pulled her robe back over her shoulders and tied the sash, hiding her body from his view.

"I'm sorry, Mia Bella. I desired you then, just as I want you now."

"And what does that have to do with your brothers?"

"I told them that you knew about us and had for some time. They were willing to look the other way because you kept our secret."

"So sleeping with me would anger them how?"

"I broke one club rule by allowing you to remember. Should I feed from you—"

"Whoa, fang boy. Back up! You're insane if you think I would allow you to sink your teeth into me!" she nearly shrieked. How the hell had they come to this? Five minutes ago she was ready to have sex with the man ... scratch that ... a vampire who wanted to bite her? Okay, well maybe at the time she might have even allowed it. But yep, she would have definitely regretted her actions later. "Can't you have sex without biting?"

Kane laughed again. "Had I been normal and I bit you, you might have thought it part of the foreplay. Or maybe you'd even have been into the idea."

Cara couldn't help but share in his humor. "Nipping is normal sexual play, Kane, drinking one's blood isn't."

Though she'd be lying to herself if she denied she'd been a little turned on by the idea of Kane's teeth sinking into her arteries. Cara rubbed the side of her neck, as Kane stood and left the bed. He gave her his back and retrieved his tee, pulling it over his head. His muscles moved with the exertion, making her wish she had just kept her damn mouth shut. His departure was like a cold bucket of water, dousing any remnants of desire. Cara covered her eyes, leaned back against the headboard and groaned. Certifiably insane. What the hell had she been thinking?

Kane turned back around just as she scooted to the edge of the bed. "Get some clothes on, Cara. You aren't safe here. Pack a bag. I'm taking you to the clubhouse where you'll be safe."

"Wow," Cara said as she stood, yanking the lapels of her robe tightly about her, not that he hadn't already seen it all.

His gaze told Cara her reaction confounded him. Stupid boy. And here she'd been ready to throw caution to the wind. Moment over. Time for reality to sink back in. Kane had been correct. She definitely needed the club's protection. *From him.*

"I'll see you at the clubhouse, Viper. I need to get a shower," she snapped, leaving out the word cold. "If you want me to stay at the MC clubhouse, fine, but only at night. I don't need a babysitter during the day."

Kane didn't say a word. Probably confused by her quick turn-about in moods. How was she supposed to act? One moment they were on the bed, headed for the best orgasm of her life, and the next he was standing over her, demanding she pack her bags and follow him like one of his groupies. Cara wasn't anyone's flavor of the month and she certainly wasn't anyone's puppet. She'd allow him to keep an eye out for her while she slept, but she'd be damned if she'd allow him to dictate her days. And no way in hell would she ever allow her guard to be down around him again. Kane Tepes was off limits and she would do well to remember that.

"Why are you still here?" she asked as she grabbed a shirt and a pair of slacks from her closet. "I expect to find you gone when I get out of the shower."

Without waiting for a response, she slammed the bathroom door behind her and locked it. Not that the bolt would stop him should he want to get in, but she had a feeling Kane wouldn't go anywhere near that door knob.

CHAPTER TWELVE

C ARA KNOCKED ON THE DOOR OF AN APARTMENT IN A COMPLEX that had seen better days. The hot water radiator hissed at the end of the hall, as if proving her point. This dive had come up on her office computer when she looked for Suzi's last known address. Suzi came from a well-off family, old money. Surely, her father wouldn't have allowed his only daughter to live in such a crappy dwelling. What the hell had happened? Maybe she should have kept in touch with her old friend over the years instead of running away from everyone.

Glancing down the hall, Cara noted the dim bulbs and the ratty, filthy carpet, trash littering the corners. Suzi wouldn't want her pity, but Cara couldn't help sympathizing with her current living conditions and worrying about Suzi's safety. Not that Pleasant had been riddled with crime over the years, but if Pleasant had a bad side of town, this was it.

In high school the two friends had been inseparable, meeting in grade school. They had spent nearly every weekend together at each other's house on sleepovers. So why, when Cara left Pleasant behind, had she not bothered to stay in contact with her oldest and dearest friend? Because, she feared Suzi had become part of the scene at the Blood 'n' Rave, her entire reason for turning tail.

She raised her hand to knock again just as the door creaked open. Suzi's expression changed from one of surprise to displeasure in a heartbeat. Cara couldn't blame her.

"Slumming, Detective?"

Even though Suzi hadn't invited her in, she hadn't slammed the door in her face either. Instead, Suzi walked away, leaving it open, putting the ball in Cara's court. She stepped onto the small square patch of linoleum, closing the door quietly behind her. Beyond the entryway proved to be a pleasant surprise. Cara had been incorrect with her earlier assessment. Though not lavish, Suzi kept a clean, nicely decorated apartment. Who knew that such a nice place resided behind the horrible exterior?

"Can I offer you coffee?" Suzi asked from the kitchen. She leaned one hip against the counter, waiting for Cara, looking no more pleased with her visitor than when she first opened the door.

"Sure," Cara said. She took a bar stool next to the breakfast nook and folded her hands atop the clean Formica countertop.

Suzi grabbed a white ceramic cup from the cupboard, placed it in front of Cara, then poured a generous cup of java from a glass carafe. Steam rose from the hot liquid.

"Cream or sugar?"

Cara shook her head. "Black is fine. Thank you."

"So why are you here, Cara?"

She smiled uneasily. "Right past the pleasantries."

"You haven't called or stopped by in over ten years. I'm not going to assume you suddenly wondered about me."

"Vampires," Cara said truthfully, hoping to catch Suzi off guard and have her admitting to something she might later want to retract.

The momentary shock on Suzi's face told Cara everything she suspected. Suzi knew Kane's true nature.

Recovering quickly, probably hoping Cara hadn't caught the slight, Suzi asked, "You wanting to go to the movies or did you just finish reading *Twilight?*"

"Let's not pretend I'm stupid. You know they exist and that they're living here in Pleasant. You were with one of them last night."

"And just who do you think is a vampire?"

"Kane."

Suzi studied her, then likely thinking better of confessing secrets, opted for the obvious. "We're friends."

"And lovers?" Cara couldn't help throwing in, allowing the little green-eyed monster to take up residence.

"What's it to you, Cara? I haven't seen you in years and you coming knocking on my door for what? Jealousy?"

Cara's face heated. Suzi wasn't far off the mark, but Cara would be damned if she admitted as much. "What you and Kane do is normally none of my business."

"Then why ask?"

"He's a suspect in a murder case. Maybe you ought to be more aware of who you're sleeping with."

Suzi jerked her own ceramic mug from the cupboard, her actions speaking highly of irritation, and poured herself a cup of coffee.

"I can see you're going to be here awhile," she said, then took a sip from her mug. Suzi returned her gaze to Cara's. "Kane didn't kill anyone."

Cara noted Suzi avoided the lover connotation. "How could you possibly know that?"

"Although you've been AWOL for the past ten years, I haven't. I know Kane and his brothers. They've been protecting this town. If they were to kill someone, trust me, it wouldn't be within miles of Pleasant."

"You say that as if you have first-hand knowledge."

"Look, Cara, what're you really here for? I'm sure it's not to talk about my love life. Are you here as a detective to question me about Kane's whereabouts?"

"If I honestly believed Kane was guilty of the murders, I would have called you to the office and interviewed you on the record."

"So instead you're here as a concerned friend for who? Kane or me?"

"I deserve your scorn—"

Suzi laughed cynically. "You ran away from Pleasant and never looked back. You didn't call—"

"You never called me!"

"Really? You wouldn't know because your phone number had been changed and someone forgot to give me the new one."

"I—"

"You what? You're sorry? You could have stopped by any number of times when you came back to visit your grandfather. And you didn't."

Cara hung her head. When she had left Pleasant and the nightmare of Kane Tepes, she had known that Suzi had a connection. But rather than questioning her, she avoided her, pretending the incident at the Rave hadn't been real. Shunning Suzi had been a necessity to keep her head firmly planted in the sand.

"What happened, Suzi? Why are you living here?"

"Had you been around or called, you would know." Suzi took another sip of her coffee. She tried to act nonchalant, but Cara knew better. "My dad passed away a few years after you skipped town."

Cara had been self-centered. She had no idea Suzi's father had passed. And anytime her grandfather brought Suzi into their conversation, she had informed him that Suzi was past news, that she didn't want to hear anything revolving around her ex-friend. Her grandfather looked thoroughly chastised, and maybe even angered, but he had abided by her wishes and never talked about Suzi again.

"I'm so sorry."

"Spare me your pity, Cara. I've come to terms with it. My stepmother left town ... with all his money, I might add. I didn't get a dime and I haven't seen or heard from her since. She's always hated me, never understood me. And Dad? He was too busy working when he was alive to see what was going on. Surely you remember I was a bit on the rebellious side. So?" —her arms stretched out from her sides— "Welcome to my life."

"I can't make up for the past, Suzi. I had my reasons for wanting to leave town and forget Pleasant."

"And me?"

"You're a part of it."

"A-plus for honesty. Care to elaborate?"

Cara knew she owed Suzi an explanation. "My father died and I was in a dark place."

"I could have helped you through that."

She hung her head, knowing she hadn't given Suzi the opportunity. Glancing back up, Cara said, "Things were getting weird for me. You hanging at the Blood 'n' Rave all the time. The people that hung there, they knew you better than I did. I mean, what's with the vial of blood you wear around your neck? It's blood, correct?"

Suzi's hand encompassed the vial. "Just jewelry."

"Jewelry you never seem to be without. Besides, you weren't the only one I saw wearing them. What the hell is it? A secret club or something?"

"I really don't think what I wear or do is any of your business, Cara."

"It's part of the reason I left. I was weirded out by what you were becoming."

"What was the other part?"

Time to let it all out, spare no details. Suzi could either think Cara was ready for the psych ward, or Suzi had been keeping secrets herself and already knew Kane was a vampire as she predicted.

"Ten years ago, the last time I went to the Blood 'n' Rave with you, I'm sure you remember, I ducked out without saying goodbye."

"You left me wondering what happened. At first, I was worried. Then when you didn't answer my calls and I heard you left town, I began resenting how you left me behind. When I tried to contact you again, your cell number had changed."

"I knew you wouldn't understand. I couldn't even fully believe what I saw. You started wearing that vial of blood around your neck like a token. It was too much to process."

"Exactly what was so hard to process? It's just jewelry, Cara."

"Again, jewelry you never seem to be without. For ten years? You don't find that strange?"

Suzi shrugged. "I'm sure my taste in jewelry wasn't the real reason you left town."

"No, it was Kane."

"Go on."

"That last night at the Rave, I went into the ladies' room. Kane was in there."

Suzi's brows creased at the bridge of her nose. "What was Kane doing in the ladies' room?"

"Fucking some blonde."

Suzi choked on her freshly sipped coffee. Once she regained her composure, she asked, "Seriously?"

"Yeah." Cara averted her eyes, embarrassed to be confessing what she had tried so hard to forget Or that it had been a huge turn on, something she'd never admit ... not even to Kane.

Suzi chuckled. "I realize it may have been a bit unorthodox to fuck in a public place, but enough to make you want to leave town? I find that hard to believe. You might have been a virgin, but you weren't that naive."

Cara smiled, her cheeks heating. "No, I would have been embarrassed and fled the restroom, but not town."

"Then what was it?"

"He was biting her neck." Cara could tell her admission hadn't fazed Suzi. "I don't mean just biting it. I mean sinking full-fledged fangs into her neck."

"It was probably dental moldings. Nothing to get excited over."

Cara didn't believe that lie for a minute, nor could Suzi look her in the eye as she uttered the words. Her hands fidgeted with the dish towel lying on the counter.

"You don't think I haven't tried to convince myself of that and about a million other possibilities? The truth is, Suzi, he was biting her neck and drinking her blood. Christ... Kane is a vampire!"

Suzi didn't say a word. Just glanced up and stared at Cara.

Get a clue, Brahnam, Suzi already knows what Kane and his brothers are.

"Kane told me," Cara finally said, though she should have kept her big mouth shut, just on the off case that her intuitions were incorrect. But why stop now? She had already said far too much.

"He told me the truth, Suzi. You don't have to say anything, because I already know more than I'm comfortable with. But don't worry, I haven't told a soul. No one would believe me anyway. My question is what do you have to do with the whole grand scheme of things? Are you one of them?"

Suzi grabbed a bar stool and pulled it to the other side of the bar, sitting across from her. She folded her hands on the countertop and looked at Cara, her expression serious.

"I could lose my life for what I'm about to tell you. There are rules, Cara. And consequences. Should anyone find out that I spoke with you about it, I could be killed."

"Kane and his brothers—"

She shook her head. "Not them, the society of donors I belong to. If I talk about what we are or what we provide, then the society can and will have me eliminated. Keeping their secret is first and foremost, the number one rule. If people find out about their existence, they would be hunted and killed."

"This is crazy talk." Cara ran both hands down her face. "And you wonder why I left Pleasant. Better yet, why the hell did you stay?"

Suzi shrugged. "I don't know. I wasn't much more than a kid. I was turned on by the whole idea of vampires and seduced into the lifestyle. But unfortunately, once you're in, you don't leave. Not that I'd want to anyway."

"You want this lifestyle?"

She offered a weak smile. "I guess I do."

"You offer your blood to them. What do you—" Cara stopped in mid-sentence.

She knew without asking. Suzi was, in a way, food for them. This society that she talked about nourished the vampires.

"And the necklace?"

"Signifies that I'm a donor. At any time, I'm willing to offer myself for their … needs."

Cara shivered. Maybe tomorrow she would wake up and this would all be one bad nightmare. Surely this couldn't be real. But mere hours ago, Kane stood in her bedroom … correction, slinked between her spread legs and she was ready to give her all to him. Sex, blood, the whole nine yards. That is, until they both came to their senses. And he insisted she stay at the clubhouse because one of their kind had marked her for death. Someone more powerful than Kane or his brothers. Some ancient vampire or crazy shit. What the hell had she gotten herself into?

KANE PACED THE OFFICE OF Sheriff Ducat. The balding man sat back in his wooden desk chair, his portly belly hidden by the polished wood, hands clasped behind his head, looking more smug than he had a right to. He bet the only run the sheriff had ever made was running for election. Kane could easily rip out his throat and end the man's life, should he outlive his usefulness.

"So you want us to look the other way? Guns being run through—"

"Not through Pleasant. Around," Kane corrected. He'd play this game with the sheriff for the time being to get what he wanted. Kane didn't need the extra attention brought to the Sons by being disagreeable, not with the ongoing murder investigations. "And yes, I want you to look the other way. The Sons of Sangue stand to make a good deal of cash off this."

Sheriff Ducat sat forward. "And what does the S.O. stand to get out of this lucrative deal?"

"Our continued protection. We've kept Pleasant a peaceful little town."

The sheriff laughed. "Somehow, I think we're getting the short end of the stick, Viper. You see, Pleasant would be a quieter town without you in it."

"The Sons aren't going anywhere."

Sheriff Ducat sat forward and clasped his hands on his neatly kept desk. "I want ten percent of your take."

"Seriously? You think I'd give you a share of our take? That's laughable."

"What's laughable, Viper, is I have murder investigations going on. And from what my detectives are telling me, the Sons are prime suspects."

Heat rose up Kane's neck as his ire rose. They needed to catch this son of a bitch and fast. He was tired of being in the law's spotlight. "The Sons aren't involved in those murders and you know it."

"You wouldn't be honest with me if you were. Ten percent, Viper, and I'll make sure my deputies are very busy when the Knights come to ... or around town."

Kane leaned against an old wooden bookshelf, crossed his arms over his chest, and shook his head, not about to give into the sheriff's demands. "No deal."

"If I agree to allowing the Knights to skirt the town, running guns under the cover of night, then you have to give me something."

Kane gritted his teeth. He had a feeling he wasn't going to like any deal the sheriff had in mind. "What else do you want, Ducat? Because you aren't getting a payoff from the Sons."

Ducat leaned back and smiled broadly, as though he had just caught his meal ticket in his web of corruption. Kane had a feeling he should have agreed to the ten percent.

"My detectives are having a hell of a time solving these latest murders, as you well know. I want this son of a bitch caught and dealt with before the feds come down on us."

"Word on the street is they're already interested, due to Tab's murder."

The sheriff nodded. "Then you're aware of who her father is?"

Kane nodded.

"Which means I'm pressed for time. You find this son of a bitch and bring him to me. I don't care how you do it. I need to close this case and fast. The State Police and FSD coming here isn't good for me or the Sons, if you catch my meaning. Not to mention you wanting to let the Knights cross through with illegal arms. That could bring a lot of unwanted attention to my county."

"I couldn't agree with you more."

"You do that for me and the Knights can run their damned guns. I'll make sure my deputies are too busy to take notice. That and if I ever need a favor called in, you'll owe me. Are we in agreement?"

"Favor?"

"There may be a time or two I need to see someone disappear. No one upstanding, I assure you. But when the law fails and the pieces of shit hit the street again, I may call in your favor to see justice done."

"Justice how?"

"Run out of town, maybe even out of state. If that doesn't work, then I might even want them eliminated, if the punishment does not suit the crime."

"Depending on the case, agreed."

"And about this bastard killing women?"

"We agree on taking this piece of shit out, but not on me bringing him to you."

"I'll need cold-hard evidence that he's been dealt with, Viper. No one is just going to take your word for it. I need something to give to the feds that this case has been closed and the murderer has been found."

"I'll give your detective the heads-up once he's been dealt with. But you'll get nothing more than ashed remains of the prick. That, I promise. I'll make sure you have physical evidence to show you got the right man."

"And how do you intend to keep my detectives in the loop?"

"I'll keep a personal eye out on Cara."

"She's chasing her damn tail in this case. She and her partner don't have a clue what's going on. Following their lead will gain you nothing. I was hoping for better."

Kane chuckled this time. "I'm not following anyone's lead, Ducat. I'll find this shitbag without your detectives' help. I'm keeping Cara under my care for other reasons."

"How's that?"

"I have reason to believe she's in danger, and that's all you need to know."

"My detective is in danger and you don't think that's something you should share?"

"I said I'd catch this guy, and you'll get your evidence. Cara, however, is my business."

"How so?" Cara asked as she strode into the office, her gaze boring into Kane. "I'm a big girl, Kane. I don't think I need your help or protection."

Kane growled beneath his breath, knowing her bravado was a facade. "I'll see you at the clubhouse by nightfall, Cara. If you aren't there, I'll come looking for you and carry you there myself. That's non-negotiable," he said, then left the office, slamming the door behind him.

Damn, stubborn woman was going to get herself, and likely him, killed before this damned nightmare was over.

CHAPTER THIRTEEN

"SO WHAT THE HELL WAS THAT ALL ABOUT?" CARA ASKED Sheriff Ducat, pointing her thumb in the direction of Kane's exit. "You want to tell me why you two were discussing me and how I became Kane's business?"

The sheriff's gaze spoke of his annoyance. He hated being caught with his pants around his ankles. Cara knew that Sheriff Ducat and the Sons had an unspoken agreement and were in bed together. But that didn't make Ducat happy for anyone to be privy to the fact.

"Don't get all worked up over nothing, Brahnam. Kane wants to see you're protected is all."

"Since when did he drop off the suspect list?" Cara's tone rose, angry that the sheriff was now in on the fact she needed the biker's protection. "I'm now being protected by a murder suspect? Doesn't that cross you as a bit odd? Come on, Sheriff, you can't seriously think I would be better off under the OMC's care."

She was tired of being thought of as helpless, even though in this instance she might very well be. So then why was she fighting Kane's offer of protection so whole-heartedly? Because she feared being alone with him, and not because he was high on the suspect list. She just hoped Kane was correct and his brothers would do a damn good job of keeping them apart. The last thing she needed was to be caught in a moment of weakness again.

"We aren't even sure he's innocent of murdering these three women in cold blood. And yet you hand me over, someone who matches the look of the dead victims, to the man who very well may have drained them of their blood. Hell, Sheriff, why not just take out your gun and shoot me yourself?"

The sheriff leaned back in his chair, his face tired and deflated. These cases seemed to have aged him, the worry lines in his forehead were much more pronounced, as were the frown lines between the bridge of his nose. She knew the pressure to solve these cases was much harder on him, not to mention the promise of the State Police and Forensic Services Division coming to Lane County. Cara and her partner could look like boobs in the investigation with little fallout, but these unsolved cases could cost Sheriff Ducat his next election.

Maybe her outburst had been unwarranted.

Cara braced her hands on the top of Ducat's desk, not a paper covering the fine oak surface. Ducat was OCD when it came to his office. On hers, however, you couldn't find the desk surface.

"Look, I'm sorry and you didn't deserve my tirade. But where Kane is concerned these days, you can't blame me if I'm a bit defensive."

"You really think he might be involved in these murders?" The sheriff cleared his throat. "You should know I would never willingly put you in danger, Cara."

She took a seat opposite the sheriff and sighed heavily. "I know you wouldn't. And I don't know what to think where the president of the Sons is concerned. We have the State wanting to come here and look over our shoulders, thanks to Tab's murder and her father thinking we aren't doing our jobs."

"Are you doing everything you can to solve this thing?"

"Of course, Hernandez and I are, sir. I want this son of a bitch caught more than anyone."

"So what Kane is saying is true then."

The last thing she wanted was Ducat privy to her believing in vampires. Surely, he didn't know. Or did he?

"What's true?"

"That you're in danger."

She shrugged, not being able to form the lie. Besides, had the sheriff bothered to read the reports on her recent break-in, he'd know about the threat on her bathroom mirror. Had he been so preoccupied he hadn't heard about it? Or had he brushed it off as a nothing more than a pissed-off convict wanting to put a little scare into her? Either way—he should have known.

"My house was broken into Thursday."

He nodded slowly. "I'm sorry, Cara, I've been so busy, but I should have asked you about that. I haven't read the report yet. Any clues?"

"Not yet. I don't think anything was taken. There was a threat aimed at me written on my mirror. I believe that was in the report as well."

The sheriff's complexion reddened. "I didn't read the full report and Hernandez hadn't elaborated. The threat was aimed at you specifically?"

"The message said, 'Open your eyes … and believe. Your turn to die.'"

Sheriff Ducat pursed his lips as he rubbed his chin, clearly perplexed. "Believe what?"

Maybe he didn't know Kane and his brothers were bloodsucking vampires after all.

"I don't know." Cara thought it best not to expound her knowledge to the sheriff. She could see a straightjacket in her future. "But the 'shall die' part is pretty clear. And not only that—"

"There's more? Why wasn't there a second report?"

"I didn't report it. It just happened. I woke up this morning and discovered someone had been in my room while I was asleep."

The sheriff's complexion deepened in color. "What the hell? Who?"

"I don't know. At first I thought it was Kane when he showed up at my house early this morning. But he swears it wasn't."

"What do you think?"

Cara took in a deep breath. "Call me crazy, but I don't think it was Kane either. I believe him."

"Which is the entire reason Kane wants you moved out of your house and under someone's protection."

She smiled sadly. "Not someone's ... his. And he's not taking no for an answer. For some reason, he thinks he's the only one who can protect me."

"You want to stay at my house for a while? I can talk to Alice about it. We have an extra room now that the kids are all off to college. It wouldn't be a burden and you wouldn't have a biker hovering over you."

"Thanks, but no." Cara couldn't involve two more innocent people in this twisted nightmare she found herself a part of. Like it or not, Kane was her only sole choice. If this primordial vampire was real, then Kane and the Sons were her only hope at staying alive. "I'm going to take Kane up on his offer. If this threat on my life is real, I don't want Alice, or you for that matter, to get hurt."

Cara knew the sheriff would agree. He adored his wife and wouldn't want to put her in jeopardy.

He cleared his throat. "If that's your decision."

"It is."

"I hate like hell to put you in an uncomfortable position, Cara, but I'm confident the Sons will keep you safe ... that is, if this threat is real and not a prank by some young punk or thug you might have brought in." Ducat tapped his desk. "I'll have some of the deputies go through your past cases. See if anyone you arrested was recently released, someone who might have a beef with you. We'll catch this guy. You won't have to stay under the protection of the Sons for long."

"Check with Higgins. Hernandez had him looking into my past cases last I knew. I do hope something turns up and soon. Staying at the Sons' clubhouse and under Kane's protection isn't going to set well with all the Sons."

Lord, how the hell did she get herself into such a mess? Stay with the Sons of Sangue? She had to be battier than the nut who wrote on her mirror to even consider such a proposal from Kane Tepes.

Living under the same roof with the sexiest man alive was downright dangerous in itself, not to mention a whole coven of vampires. Maybe instead of heading for the clubhouse at nightfall, she should just head for the state mental hospital and check herself in.

"IT'S A SATURDAY, BRAHNAM. DON'T you want to take some time off?" Hernandez asked, glancing up as Cara entered their small office.

It looked like Joe had already been hard at work with papers and manila files littering the desk surface, quite the contrast to Sheriff Ducat's. Pictures of the dead women were push-pinned to the cork-board adjacent to their work surface, with not a single suspect tacked up. Cara approached the folders on Joe's desk and withdrew a photo of Kane.

She had meant to get an earlier start, but due to Kane's unexpected visit and her chat with the sheriff, she had gotten to the office much later than intended. As for giving up her day off, it wasn't like Cara had anything more pressing than the cases they worked. After all, who did she have at home waiting? She glanced down at the picture in her hand, but quickly shook off the notion that he might actually be waiting for her. Arriving at the clubhouse at dark would be soon enough to deal with her conflicting emotions. She needed to keep her mind on her job and not her rising libido. Spending too much time in Kane's company had a very dangerous effect on her. Cara felt as if she were on a slippery slope with nothing much to grab onto to stop her descent.

Nightfall would come soon enough, but first Cara planned to stop by the nursing home and take her grandfather a piece of peanut butter pie, following her day at the office. It had been a week since she last seen him and she could use the added distraction. He'd undoubtedly give her hell the minute she walked into the room. Cara smiled. She loved her grandfather's spunk. That's what kept him alive and kicking at ninety-two.

"I could ask you the same thing, Hernandez. You got a wife and kids at home waiting for you. Why the hell are you here?"

"Let's see, spend the day with the kids fighting and my wife pulling her hair out or working the case. Yeah, tough decision."

Cara chuckled. "You know I don't believe that for a New York minute. You adore your wife and kids."

Glancing back at the photo of Kane, Cara walked over to the corkboard, pulled out a silver pushpin and pinned his photo, front and center.

"Wow." Joe sat back in his seat and stared at the board, a smile of satisfaction rose on his lips. "Are you really ready to call him a suspect, Brahnam?"

Cara stepped back and viewed her handiwork. "We have anyone else?"

"Nope."

"Then at this point, Kane is our only suspect," she said, not voicing the fact she was handing herself over to him later this evening. For now, she'd keep that between her, Kane and the sheriff. Besides, what better way to keep an eye on him? "I'm still not sold on the fact he did it. But at this point we have little else. I just want to keep a close eye on him and his band of outlaws."

"I can't argue. I've been saying that all along."

"I know, Joe." Though, she wasn't ready to fully commit to the idea either. "You find anything else that might stand out in these files?"

He shook his head. "Nothing really. But I think we should visit Tom's Deli about suppertime."

Cara narrowed her gaze, a frown creasing the bridge of her nose. "You needing a supper companion?"

Joe laughed heartily. "Appealing, Brahnam. At least it would be a quiet meal for once. But, no, I was thinking of interviewing some of the customers. See if maybe anyone saw someone making a call from their cell near the restaurant. Our uniforms didn't turn up anyone, but by the time they arrived, the supper crowd had departed.

"The cell phone they retrieved was reported stolen several days ago and wiped free of prints. The only call made after the call had been reported stolen was to the S.O."

"Visiting at suppertime, we might catch the same crowd," Cara said, likely voicing what Joe had been thinking. "You sure you don't want to head home and catch up with me later?"

"Nope. I'm yours for the day. Char and the kids are going shopping. I really didn't want to spend the day at the mall." His gaze turned serious. "You have any other problems at your house since the break-in?" he asked, changing the subject.

Cara shook her head, not ready to reveal last night's intruder. Besides, that brought up her conversation with Kane, and she wasn't about to let Joe in on the fact he had shown up at her house at the break of dawn. Or the fact that she could have easily fallen into bed with him. What the hell was wrong with her? She needed to get a handle on her libido and come to the realization that Kane might very well have killed these three innocent women. She would do well to keep her guard up and her enemy close.

As though knowing where her thoughts were, Joe said, "How about we pay Kane another visit today?"

Her gaze snapped to his. "For what purpose?"

He shrugged. "I don't know. Maybe lean on him some more. I think the bastard knows more than he's telling us. There's no way he and his brother, Kaleb, were out for a joyride two nights ago. You and I both know that. And yet we take their word for it?"

"We took their statement, Joe," Cara said, annoyed he would think she'd take their word verbatim. "That doesn't mean we believe them. There's a big difference."

"Then I say we visit the clubhouse and question Kane again." A smile grew on Joe's face. "Besides, I kind of like annoying the hell out of him."

Twenty minutes later, they pulled into the clubhouse parking lot. Three motorcycles sat to the left of the building. Kane, Kaleb, and Grayson looked to be inside. Cara bet at least two of the three were still asleep. She already knew Kane was up ... unless he had gone to bed following his visit to the S.O. If Joe enjoyed harassing him, waking him up ought to accomplish that in spades. Cara wasn't sure whether to bask in Kane's misery or her own, should he take it out on her when she returned for the evening.

Joe opened the passenger side door to her Dodge and climbed out before she had a chance to turn the key off and cut the engine. He headed for the scarred front door with one purpose in mind: pissing off the biker. Cara unfastened her seat belt, climbed out of the car and jogged up the beaten path behind him, dread sitting in her stomach like a rock. Kane swung the door inward after Joe's incessant pounding, the look on his face none too friendly, even when he turned it on Cara.

"Let me guess, social call?" Kane grumbled, his glare centered on Cara and ignoring her partner altogether.

By the look of his sexy bed-rumpled hair, she'd bet Kane had been sleeping upon their arrival. No wonder he seemed to have a continuous stream of women. One look at him and she was mighty tempted to join him in that bed herself.

Whoa, Brahnam ... Mind on case.

As though knowing the path of her thoughts, Kane ran a hand through his mussed hair. His scowl turned to a smirk as he winked at her. Damn him for the insight. Arrogant bastard. Her face heated, no doubt reddening her cheeks.

"Look, Mister Tepes—"

"Don't you two have something better to do ... like catch a murderer?"

"That's exactly what we're trying to do," Joe said with a cocksure smile. "And you need to let us do our job."

"Are you here to arrest me?"

"No, not yet anyway." Joe pulled out his small tablet and pen from his jacket pocket. "We're here to ask you a few more questions. Like why you were really out on North Fork Road the night we got the tip about the dumped body in Bender Landing County Park."

"Joyriding. Last time I checked, it wasn't a crime."

"Cut the bullshit," Cara said, stepping past Joe and jamming her forefinger into his sternum. "You and I both know that's not the reason you and Kaleb were out there. Visibility that night wouldn't have been great for sightseeing."

"I assure you, Detective, I had no problems with my vision that night."

"Did you stop near Bender Landing County Park?"

"No."

Cara narrowed her gaze. "I think you're lying."

Kane stepped closer, leaning forward so their noses nearly touched. "Prove it."

"You see, Mister Tepes—"

Kane chuckled when she placed her palm on his chest and shoved. Though her effort wouldn't have made him budge, he backed up anyway and gave her some much needed breathing room.

"So formal, Cara? You can call me Kane, or Viper if you choose … but we're way past the formalities."

Hell, she'd much prefer picking up her tail and running as far away from him as possible. Being this close to the man, or vampire, or whatever the hell he was, played havoc on her senses. *Mind on case, Brahnam.* Could she help it if the man was a walking, wet dream?

Cara sighed, then said, "We have footprints leading back to the area where the body was found."

"You have casts? Then match it to my boot and prove I was there. But considering the amount of rain we had that night, I'm betting your evidence washed down the hill. How far off am I?"

If Joe hadn't been standing mere feet behind her, she might have pummeled his smug chest. Kane knew she bluffed and that they had no evidence at all to point to him or Kaleb having been at that site before they arrived to cordon off the area. But someone had been digging up that body and messing with the crime scene, and she would bet her grandfather's life that it was either Kane or Kaleb. The brothers, no doubt, covered for one another. Call it intuition, but she knew.

At Kane's obvious lake of respect, Joe started to step around her. But Cara held out her arm, staying her partner. She wouldn't allow Kane to think he could best her or that she needed her partner to go to battle for her. Besides, where would Joe be tonight when she showed back up at the clubhouse under Kane's protection?

"You know, Mister Tepes," —she stuck with formality since he said he preferred her not to— "you aren't helping your case if you are in fact innocent by not cooperating."

His gaze darkened, and Cara swore she could see just hint of the obsidian-like glass his eyes turned to in his vampire state. "Just so you know, Detective, I *am* cooperating. If I weren't, you'd still be pounding on the fucking door."

"Then why lie about being at the scene."

"You haven't proven I was, therefore you can't make the assumption I'm lying."

"Someone was out there. That much we know. Someone disturbed the make-shift gravesite ... maybe someone who had a stake in this."

"And what stake would I have?"

"She was your girlfriend."

"I thought we already established that I didn't have a girlfriend. Don't embellish the facts or put your own spin on the truth. She was someone I fucked on occasion. And that's all she was to me."

"So did you get rid of the annoyance?"

Kane's brow furrowed. "Now what direction has your inquisitive little mind taken you? Why the hell would I want to rid myself of a good piece of ass?"

"Was she?"

He laughed, humor twinkling in his gaze. "Why would you or your case care whether my last fuck was any good?"

"Because if she were, then maybe you wouldn't have killed her."

"Or maybe you have a personal interest."

Cara looked briefly at Joe to see his reaction. She couldn't tell if her partner was angry at her for the line of questioning going south or mad at the biker for insinuating she might be jealous. She certainly hoped for the latter or she'd have a lot of explaining to do.

"You live in a dream world, Mister Tepes, one where every blonde haired, blue-eyed woman cannot resist you."

He raised one brow. "I haven't found one yet who could."

"Then your ego is inflated, because this blonde is resistant to your charms."

His smile widened. He didn't believe her. And why should he? She hadn't given him any reason to. No, just mere hours ago she damn near gave him everything he desired from her.

"Let's get back to the questions, Viper," Joe growled, his temper showing.

"That's Mister Tepes to you, asshole." Kane's humor quickly retreated. "Ask your questions, then get the fuck off my property. But if you even start with whether I was at Bender Landing County Park the night in question, you should know, my answer hasn't changed."

"And my belief that you were there hasn't either," Joe retorted.

"Then we're at a standstill. It's your job to prove I was, Detective. Why not go do your job?" Kane glanced back at Cara. "And unless you can prove I had anything to do with Tab's murder, or that I even had a motive, I suggest you find someone else to harass. I'm done here."

With that, he shut the door in their faces. A complete waste of time, Cara thought. Not to mention they had probably put Kane in one hell of a mood, for which she would likely pay later. Cara let out a steady stream of air, turned on the step and headed for her vehicle, hoping that Joe would let the innuendoes go without question.

"WHERE THE HELL HAVE YOU BEEN?" Cara's grandfather griped, his voice raspy from years of smoking, even before she passed through the open doorway, a slice of his favorite peanut butter pie in hand.

The late afternoon sun poured through the opened, west-facing window as a cool, fall breeze caused the tan sheers to float softly across the tiled floor. She had been running late, due to the busy supper crowd at Tom's Deli. Joe and Cara put their time to good use. After a filling supper, they interviewed the crowd. Finding someone who might have seen a person dropping the cell phone used to call the S.O. across the street two days prior, though, didn't happen. Had it not been for the great food, Cara would have called it a complete bust. She purchased a slice of pie to go and parted ways with Joe.

"You know some of us have to work for a living, Grandpa," she said with a smile as she bussed his cheek and laid the pie on the din-ner tray, still sitting on the bedside table next to him. A roast beef open-faced sandwich, dripping with brown gravy, and a perfectly rounded scoop of potatoes appeared all but untouched. "Doesn't look like you ate much for supper."

"'Cause I was waiting for that pie. I had to save room, you know." He patted his slightly rounded belly. "Watching my figure for the ladies."

Cara chuckled. "They don't stand a chance with you around, Grandpa. And if you don't learn to eat better, you won't have the energy to chase them."

She took a seat on the edge of the bed, grasping her grandfather's weathered hand. The veins stood out in contrast from his brittle bones; the skin-covering seemed to get more loose and transparent every day. She knew her grandfather's years were numbered and she wanted to cherish each and every one of them. After all, to her, he was the last of her family. Cara turned his hand over. A dark bruise marred his right wrist. At his age, it didn't take much to purple his delicate skin. She rubbed the injured area.

"Where did you get this one from?"

"Getting out of bed." He glanced at the wrist she held. Cara knew he loved the close bond they shared. "They put those bed rails up every night like I'm some damn child."

"They don't want you falling out of bed, Grandpa." Cara smiled. "If a bump caused this bruise, imagine what a fall would do. Don't you be giving these ladies a hard time here. They take good care of you. I can't be looking for a new home for you, one that would be willing to put up with your old cranky ass. I have a job to do."

"Bah! Cranky! You go right ahead and find me a new place, missy. These gals don't give me no slices of peanut butter pie! That's for sure."

Cara laughed again. "Then you best be nice to me or I won't bring them either."

"Ain't it a Saturday?"

"You know it is, Grandpa. I come every Saturday evening to see you."

"You should pick another day."

Cara smiled. She knew what was coming. He never stopped chiding her about not having a man in her life.

"Saturday is for courting. You should be out on a date."

"Don't worry, Grandpa. You aren't taking some man's time. I'm still not seeing anyone."

His weathered brow creased. "You best stop playing so hard to get. You ain't getting any younger and I ain't dying until I get me a great-grandbaby. How about that nice detective you work with?"

"Joe?" Cara laughed. On occasion, Joe would stop in to see her grandfather, said he liked the old fart … made him laugh. "He's already married. Don't you be pushing me off on someone else's man. I can get my own."

"Well, you sure ain't doing a very good job of it."

Her grandfather picked up the remote, turned on the television set and changed the channel to the news. Settled, he reached for the pie and began taking large bites.

"You best not fill yourself with dessert. You need to eat some roast beef, too, old man."

"Who you calling old?" he said around a mouthful. "I can still outrun you on a bad day."

"I'd like to see that. You can barely get out of that chair."

Finished with the pie, he set down the empty plate and turned to look at Cara, his gaze serious. "You need a man in your life, girlie. You can't spend the rest of your life alone. I only have so many good years left. Then who's going to take care of you?"

"I can take care of myself. I've been doing it for over ten years."

He sighed, moisture misting his eyes. "Don't I know it and it's a damned shame. Your mother was a good-for-nothing whore. Worked your father to death and took every damn dime he had. Made too many excuses for that one, he did."

"You don't have tell me...," She patted his weathered hand. "I lived it, remember?"

"Exactly why you need to find yourself a good man. You've had enough unhappiness in one lifetime. You deserve to have a nice family."

Cara smiled, hugged his hand to her chest. She knew he meant well and only wanted the best for her. But finding a man hadn't been a priority, let alone had she ever thought about the word family. She lived for her career, which didn't provide her a lot of time for dating. Besides, the men she came across on a daily basis weren't worth having. No, she was better off alone.

Kane came to mind.

Her nights were about to get a lot less lonely. She didn't plan on telling her grandfather that, though. He'd likely want to meet him, Cara thought with a chuckle. But Grandpa wasn't ready for the vampire.

"I have to go, Grandpa. There's someplace I need to be tonight. I hope you don't mind me cutting it short."

"You going to see a man?"

"In fact, I am ... but we're just friends. Don't you go getting no ideas."

"Bah!" He waved his hand in the air. "No such thing as a man friend. You go. Don't keep him waiting on my account."

Cara kissed his cheek again. "I'll be back next Saturday."

"You come see me another night." His nearly toothless grin always brightened her day. "You save Saturday for that new friend of yours."

"Fine! No sense arguing with a bullhead."

"Not when you know I'm right. Now get on, get out of here."

Cara waved at him as she left the room, dread settling in her stomach as the sun began setting, casting an eerie glow down the long hallway to the entrance. Time had just about run out, and she had an angry vampire waiting for her.

CHAPTER FOURTEEN

THE DOOR OPENED AND KANE STEPPED BACK, HIS HAND GES-
turing for Cara to enter. Her stomach fluttered. Hell, forget
the butterflies, it felt more like a nest of angry bees. The entire ride
from the nursing home here had her more nervous than a long-
tailed cat in a room full of rocking chairs. She had packed an overnight bag before leaving the house that morning, knowing if she
hadn't shown up at the clubhouse, Kane would have in all probabil-
ity retrieved her. She'd rather save herself the embarrassment and
show up unescorted. No sense making him go all caveman on her.

Cara squared her shoulders and stepped beyond Kane without a
word, her soft soles nearly soundless as they struck the wooden
floor. A quick glance about, to her good fortune, told her they were
completely alone. Thank goodness for small favors. Better to get
settled before any of the other members descended on the club and
discovered her presence.

"Dare I hope you're the only one here?"

"For now," Kane said, shutting the door quietly behind her.

She hadn't heard his footfalls but knew he stood very close, felt
the heat of him through her clothes as his breath whispered across
her nape. "Did you intend on pissing me off earlier?"

Cara turned and looked up at him, his expression absolutely murderous. She steeled her resolve and wouldn't give him the satisfaction of seeing her cower.

"It's my job, Kane. You need to let me do it."

"If you're so fucking sure I killed Tab, then why the hell are you here without your shadow?"

"Because, honestly, I have no one else to trust. You're it. Is that what you want to hear? That my life may very well depend on you? Besides, you said you would retrieve me if I didn't show up. I thought I'd save you the effort."

Kane appeared too damned pleased with himself that he was her only option for protection. At least he no longer looked at her as though he wanted to add her to the growing number of victims.

"Does anyone know that I'm staying here?"

He shook his head, then ran a large tanned hand through his unruly black hair. "Looks like you'll be tonight's surprise."

"Who all lives here at the clubhouse?"

"Just me, Kaleb and Grayson. With any luck you'll only have to contend with the three of us tonight. There's been no meeting called, so hopefully the rest of the Sons will be otherwise occupied."

"And how many bedrooms are there?"

"Three."

That was probably something she should have inquired about before her arrival. Certainly, he didn't think— "I'm not sharing your bed, Kane."

Kane rolled his eyes, then reached for the bag she had slung over one shoulder. "Get over yourself, Detective. I'll be sleeping on the couch. Even if I had intended to fuck you, this afternoon's visit squashed any desire I might have had."

Cara wasn't sure if Kane jested. But either way, she was glad to have dodged that bullet for the time being.

"Remind me, then, to piss you off the next time you think to change the status of our relationship."

Living under the same roof, she planned to steer clear of him, arriving at dusk and gone by dawn. The less time she spent in the man's exasperating company, the more she'd not have to worry about exposing her vulnerability. She almost laughed at the irony. The clubhouse was to be her safe haven from this unknown killer, this primordial Kane had referred to. But who was going to keep her heart safe from Kane?

She certainly hoped Kane was correct that his OMC brothers would be an impassable barrier, making sure the two stayed polar opposites. Because just being alone with him threatened to break down her walls, not to mention what it did to her libido. Cara had a bad feeling that if she were ever stupid enough to sleep with Kane, he'd crush her far worse than the man who was instrumental in forcing to leave her job and home in Eugene. After all, Kane had said from the beginning women were only good for feeding his needs. She'd do best to remember that.

Cara wasn't about to be a one-night stand or another notch on Kane's bedpost. If she had wanted a relationship without emotions, she could have stayed on the PD in Eugene and put up with Robbie Melchor. Just the thought of the overbearing, obnoxious, lousy excuse for a man sent her blood to boiling. Robbie had not only ripped out her heart, he had pissed all over it. She'd never forgive him for their last meeting. Cara shuddered at the remembrance. The word "no" had never entered his thick skull. He took what he wanted.

Cara had kept the incident to herself, shutting herself off emotionally, knowing no one would ever believe the decorated officer had raped her. It would've been his word against hers. She had heard he moved up the ladder to the Oregon State Police and hoped he wouldn't be part of task force sent to Pleasant to take over their investigation. Cara doubted she'd be able to be in the same room with him and not go for his balls. No, she'd doubtlessly give Kane permission to rip out his throat and drain the son of a bitch dry.

"Cara?"

She blinked, focusing back on the present: her current problem and temptation standing only a few feet away.

"You look as if you've seen a ghost."

Not about to share her memories and past history with Kane, she said, "I have a job to do, Kane. If my partner wants to question you again, or any of your MC brothers for that matter, then that's what we'll do. I may not have a choice in the matter of where I'm staying at the moment because for some fucked up reason an ancient vampire wants to make me food, but that doesn't mean you're off the hook. How about we skip the pleasantries and you kindly show me to my room."

She yanked her overnight bag back from his grip. "I'm tired and morning will come way too early as it is."

"It's a Saturday, Detective. You feeling the need to go into the office on a Sunday?" He raised one brow. "You must have one hell of a social life."

"My social life is none of your business. My room?"

Kane's hand indicated the back of the club. "Down the hall, second door to the left. Make yourself comfortable."

"Don't worry about me. I'll make myself scarce. Maybe you won't even have to tell your brothers of your decision to offer me protective custody. I'll be long gone before they even crawl out of bed tomorrow."

Cara gave him her back and headed for his quarters, but his answering laugh caused her to stop and glance back.

"Mia Bella, I won't have to tell them you're here. They'll smell you the minute they hit the door."

"Smell me?" Cara resisted the urge to put her nose to her armpit. "I showered this morning."

"Trust me, Cara, your scent isn't unappealing. But that wasn't what I meant. I was talking about the scent of your blood."

"Oh," she mumbled. Jesus, they could smell the blood running through her veins? "Then you deal with them. Goodnight, Viper."

Cara entered the second door to the left, closed it and leaned against the cool wood. She was way out of her league. No way in hell would she leave Kane's quarters before the rise of the sun. Becoming someone's midnight snack was not on her bucket list of things to do. Besides the less time she spent in the sexy vampire's company, the better off she'd be.

A king-sized bed sat flush against the far wall, its sheets rumpled and unmade. Cara's gaze traveled to the indention in the center of the mattress, causing her to think of Kane lying there. Did he sleep naked, a sheet tossed over his center? Just the thought had Cara fanning her face as her heart picked up its beat. Thinking of the man in his natural state was doing nothing to help her craving of

186 | PATRICIA A. RASEY

the unattainable. Okay, so maybe it was attainable, but definitely off limits.

Three large pillows reclined against the oak-paneled wall, making up for the lack of a headboard. A couple of other pillows tossed on the mattress bore his head print. Kane appeared to be a restless sleeper, if the tossed sheets and bed pillows were any indication. Cara really didn't want to hazard a guess at how many women had shared his bed. Best not to even speculate or she'd be looking for a new place to sleep. Kane had said he used Draven's office for his sexual liaisons. Did that mean she was the first female to step foot within his room? It certainly didn't appear as though he did a lot of entertaining from here. Maybe he hadn't tidied up because he hadn't believed she'd actually show.

Truth of it? She was too damned scared not to.

One set of dresser drawers sat to the left of the bed against the side wall, nothing decorating the top. No pictures, nothing personal. To the right was a small bedside table, a silver lamp with a red shade and a black book the only items to adorn the surface.

Cara tossed her overnight bag onto the mattress and approached the end table. *Tales of Edgar Allen Poe* was stamped in gold on the hardbound black leather. Cara picked it up and thumbed through the gold-edged pages, before cradling the book in her hands and glancing behind her. A large bookshelf lined the wall next to the opened door to the bathroom. Books crammed its surface in no particular order. The fact that he read at all surprised her and had her wondering what else she didn't know about the man.

Unzipping her bag, she pulled out her white button down nightshirt and plaid sleep shorts, laying them next to her bag. Very conservative and not the least bit sexy. She didn't need to be prancing around a vampire den wearing anything less. She might have chosen her flannels, had the weather been any cooler, an outfit that wrapped her neck better than a wool scarf. Cara was thrilled Kane's room had an adjoining bathroom, giving her no reason to leave his room at all when she decided to freshen up before crawling into bed and calling it a very long day.

The knee length pencil skirt and dress shirt she had chosen for tomorrow's trip to the office needed to be hung. Cara looked for a chair or anything to drape them across, coming up empty. The man apparently didn't believe in extravagances. Cara opened the small closet door where a variety of tees and vests nearly filled the steel rod. She spied a few extra hangers and helped herself. The soft material of one of Kane's black tees brushed her knuckles, causing her to want to take it to her nose and see if the material smelled of outdoors and man.

Instead, with a groan, she closed the door and leaned her forehead against it. *Yep, she had just hit pathetic.* Cara turned to the bed and flopped down. Even though exhaustion nipped at her heels, she wasn't about to get much sleep, not knowing that Kane lay just beyond the door on a couch entirely too small for his long, muscular body. *Not my problem.* After all, he had been the one to insist she stay beneath his roof, even if it was for her own good.

The outside door banged off the wall, causing her to jump, followed by booted feet entering the living area. Some of Kane's brothers had no doubt returned, causing her stomach to somersault. Curious on how exactly Kane would handle the situation, Cara crept to the door and opened it a crack.

"Now what the hell have you done, brother?" Kaleb demanded.

"Since when is it your business what I do?"

"When it involves this club. Don't pretend to be stupid. I smell her all over this room. I'm betting she's still here."

"That detective bitch?" The words came from a second voice, probably Grayson. "You save seconds for me, Viper?"

Furniture screeched across the floor and knocked about, then something slammed hard against the bathroom wall. From the strength of the thud, Cara was betting Grayson had just been pinned to the wall separating the bathroom from the living area.

"Jesus, Viper, get a grip. I was only joking. You may want a piece of that, but I sure in the hell don't. She's a pig … figuratively speaking, before you decide to actually push me through the fucking wall."

"Don't even joke where she's concerned, Gypsy," she heard Kane hiss.

"You want to tell us what the deal is, Pres?" Kaleb asked, his tone accusatory.

More rustling could be heard, doubtlessly Kane letting loose of Grayson. "I told you we needed to keep an eye out for her. That's what I'm doing."

"Yeah, an eye out. Not invite her into our fucking home. The rest of the Sons aren't going to like this one bit, bro. You know we need to vote on this kind of shit. You've been taking advantage of that P patch a lot lately."

Footsteps sounded off the wooden flooring. Cara could imagine Kane pacing. "I went to her place this morning to check up on her."

The footfalls stilled. "The primordial's scent was all over her damn room. We don't keep an eye out for her and she's dead."

"And we should care, why?" Grayson asked.

"Because we aren't fucking animals, Gypsy. She'll stay in my room. I'll take the couch."

"Be sure that you do, brother," came from Kaleb.

"As I said, Hawk, my business is none of yours. If I decide to fuck her then I don't intend to ask your permission."

"It's club business when it involves that bitch. She's trying to pin these murders on you … us! And you think we need to make sure she's safe and cozy? Quit thinking with your dick." Grayson's voice rose. "Why not get it the hell over with then toss her out. I don't give a rat's ass what that primordial does with her."

"Watch yourself, Gypsy," Kane threatened. "Anyone touches the detective and they answer to me."

"Is that a threat?" Grayson asked.

"I don't make threats."

Booted footsteps came her way, causing her to back farther into her room when she heard a door slam.

"Be sure that fucking her is all you do," Kaleb said, his tone hushed.

"What the hell is that supposed to mean, Hawk?"

"The canines better stay to yourself. You know the rules. You step over that line and I'll cut the P patch from your chest myself."

Several seconds later another door slammed, followed by silence. Cara hedged past her doorway and back to the living area where Kane stood in the middle of the room, hands on hips, head hung so his hair hid his expression. She must have stood there a few seconds before he growled, "Wanting something, Miss Brahnam? If not, I suggest you make yourself fucking scarce."

Cara turned, ran back to his quarters and slammed her own door.

Well, that certainly went well.

"ARE YOU FUCKING SERIOUS?" Rosalee squealed through the cell's ear piece.

Alec held the phone away and grimaced. He knew she wasn't going to take the news of Cara Brahnam moving into the Sons' clubhouse well.

"I'll still have access to her. She can't be with Kane or the Sons twenty-four-seven. Stop going all dramatic."

"I swear to the god you believe in, Alec, that I will be in the States before you can formulate a plan to stop me if, you don't do something soon."

Alec rolled his eyes, not that she'd see. Sometimes Rosalee could be a royal pain in his ass. How the hell had Kane put up with her as long as he had? Because then she wasn't a bitter vampire bent on revenge. Just a few short years with her and Alec was ready to throw his hands up and say fuck it. Let her fight her own battles. He wasn't some imbecile she could order around so easily. After all, he, too, was an original.

"Stop threatening me, Rosalee. You and I both know you don't want to be anywhere near the States when I take down Kane. He'd suspect you the minute he laid eyes on you, if not figure a way to kill you on the spot." He bit back an expletive, and instead added, "and stop ordering me about like a fucking child."

Alec took a deep breath. What he really felt like doing was a disappearing act and letting Rosalee mop up after her own mess, which Alec already knew she wouldn't. No, she'd find someone else to screw, and get them to do her dirty work. Besides, he wasn't quite done with Rosalee yet. His goal was her stepfather's respect, and damn if he wasn't going to get it ... one way or the other.

"Alec? Are you still there?"

"I'm here, Rosalee ... where the hell did you think I went off to?"

She made an unbecoming sound into the phone, but left his question hang unanswered.

"Look, this is nothing more than a snag in our plan. Kane will still pay."

"You best hope so, Alec—or you better not step one foot back into Italy."

"Idle threats, my dear. You can't stop me. You may be older than I, but we still stand on the same ground. Your stepfather actually likes me; he wouldn't allow you to turn your revenge on me."

"My stepfather allows me anything I desire."

And that's why you're such a spoiled brat.

No one would dare cross her stepfather, except her step-uncle, if indeed Vlad Tepes were still alive and the rumor of the empty tomb to be believed.

"Come now, Rosalee, you know you wouldn't harm a hair on my head. Who else would put up with your tirades? I said I would take care of Kane and I will. In my own time. I do have a plan. I'm not the complete idiot you think me to be. But first, I'll toy with him. Have a little fun."

"Toy with him how?"

"You do want him to suffer, no?"

"Of course I do. That's what this is all about. Kane humiliated me, stomped on my heart. Sent me back to Italy and my stepfather as if I was a nuisance. I was forced to suffer alone. I lost my son—we lost a son and he didn't even have the decency to help me grieve."

Alec was about to ask her if she even had a heart but thought better of it. If she had one when she met Kane, the arrogant vampire had most certainly ripped it to shreds.

"Rest assured, when I'm finished Kane will wish he were dead."

CHAPTER FIFTEEN

SILENCE CLOAKED THE CLUBHOUSE. HIS BROTHERS HAD NOT shown their faces, nor had Cara left the sanctity of his room following his tirade. Jesus, since when had he taken to treating women with so little regard? Not to mention, she had followed his order without question. Kane paced the floor in his bare feet, wearing nothing more than his unbuttoned jeans, low on his hips, and a pair of boxer briefs beneath. He had wanted to strip, being accustomed to sleeping nude, but having a woman in the house had not allowed him the luxury.

Instead, he lay on the couch, watching the ceiling fan slowly circle, hunger gnawing at his gut. He had fed two nights prior, but having Cara in such close proximity made him ravenous, and not just for communion either. Never had a woman led him around by his dick. Oh, he enjoyed sex, quite regularly in fact. But this woman had him turning away perfectly willing candidates. He wanted the detective in the worst way. And since she had gotten beneath his skin, no other woman would do. His desire for her bordered on obsession.

Kane ran his hand through his hair, frustration clawing its way through him. Glancing at the clock on the wall, he decided a quick trip to the Rave was in order—maybe he could appease at least one of his aches. With Cara occupying his room, though, a change of clothes was out of the question. He wasn't about to knock on her door. Not because he didn't want to disturb her, but because he didn't trust himself to keep his hands off her. His animalistic nature lay too close to the surface, while his hunger spun dangerously out of control. And although he desperately needed to get laid, for now he'd look for a donor only, not a willing sexual partner.

That meant avoiding his last donor like the plague.

Suzi had made it quite obvious she had designs on him, but he wasn't about to selfishly slake his desire while thinking of another. Christ, when had taking any willing party become so distasteful? A few months earlier and he would have gladly taken her offer. Kane had known of the cute, petite brunette donor before. But never once had she approached him, making Kane wonder why the sudden fascination. Besides, she seemed more to Kaleb's liking. When Kane had brought Kaleb into the conversation, though, she hadn't wanted to talk about his twin. Kane couldn't help being curious about their history.

He'd best steer clear of that one, if for no other reason than her mysterious past with Kaleb.

Decision made to partake in communion, he'd make a quick trip to the Rave, feed, and be home within the hour. He supposed it was his only chance at finding rest. Kane headed for the bathroom, wanting to take a quick shower and wash away the day's grime from the road.

Kane paused by his closed bedroom door and listened to the silence coming from his room. Cara was likely fast asleep, alone, in his bed. A bed large enough for them to share. He groaned. A cold shower seemed in order. He turned back down the hall and opened the door to the bathroom.

Light spilling into the hallway was his first clue that the room had an occupant. The second was Cara's shriek. Kane's heart leapt to his throat and his gut clenched like a vice. She sat, perched on the edge of the tub with razor poised in hand. Sans clothes.

Jesus, Mary, and Joseph.

His gaze dropped to her now crossed legs. A small trickle of blood ran down where her feminine hair had been freshly removed, disappearing between the V of her thighs. Shit, the scent called to him as she stared at him wide-eyed. Blood rushed instantly from his head to his dick. His unbuttoned jeans did little to hide his exact reaction to the vision in front of him. And what a vision it was. Cara's gaze caressed his bare chest and slowly trailed to the front of his unbuttoned jeans, barely containing the heavy bulge. She couldn't miss his reaction to her.

He slowly closed the bathroom door behind him, as his canines elongated and his eyes heated in their darkening. His face took on the shape of the hungry animal barely contained within. His refection in the mirror told him as much. Why his appearance hadn't caused Cara to flee from his presence he didn't know.

"You have about thirty seconds to gather your things and get the hell back to my room."

"Or what?" she whispered.

The scent of her answering desire traveled to his flaring nostrils. Lord help him.

"Or, make no mistake, I will follow through with my promise to fuck you."

Her mouth rounded in an O, but she didn't move. Kane wasn't sure if it was fright or desire that held her in place. And frankly, he didn't care. If she didn't move soon, he'd make good on that threat.

Cara laid the razor carefully on the side of the large tub. She took in a shaky breath. Her gaze held fast to his. By the scent of her arousal, he knew she waged the war to run as suggested, or take him up on his promise. She couldn't lie, couldn't tell him she didn't want this as badly as he. Perched on the tub, completely exposed, her thighs quivered and her nipples pebbled. His mouth watered with the desire to draw one between his teeth, to nip it and taste her sweet-ass blood, then soothe it with his tongue. Hell, he wanted to dive between her thighs and take his fucking fill.

"Your time is nearly up, Mia Bella," he said as he slowly advanced. "I'm not a patient man. When I make a promise to take what I want … I follow through."

He stopped, mere inches from reaching out and touching her, breathing in her blood's rich scent before releasing a growl.

"Fuck it," he said and dropped to his knees.

A palm on the inside of each of her thighs easily uncrossed them. His gaze trailed the blood as it disappeared between her swollen folds. His mouth went dry. Never had his eyes feasted on anything so erotic. The time for her to flee now past, his eyes held hers briefly before descending on her. His lips closed over the small cut on her bare mons, suckling it just before his canines pierced the soft flesh.

Cara gasped, one hand steadying her on the tub's edge as the other fisted his hair. But instead of pulling him away as he thought she might, she held him tight to her center. A moan escaped her throat. Her thighs trembled on either side of his head.

Kane's blood roared through his veins, drowning out all sound as he drew her life-giving fluid into his mouth, loving every blessed drop. Hell, he was dizzy with want. Never had he thirsted so deeply, never had he desired so strongly. He had known that it would be like this, all the more reason he should have abstained.

Another moan left her body, her fist tightened in his hair. The scent of her desire increased. He used his hands to further spread her thighs, gliding his fingers down her moist slit, into her slick folds. His dick ached, wanting appeasement.

The time for turning back had vanished.

Kane spread her wetness across her clit, mixing her juices with her blood. Slipping two fingers inside, he felt the tremors of her approaching climax.

Kane quickened his rhythm, his fingers shoving in and out of her as he wanted to do with his cock. Her breath hitched, drawing his gaze, and she glanced at him, heavy lidded. Her thighs tightened about him, her face tipped heavenward, and she whispered his name. Kane felt the answering pulses of her orgasm against his fingers.

Slowly he withdrew his fangs and his hand, sitting back on the tiled floor of the bathroom, wiping the remaining blood from his mouth with the back of his hand. His own breath labored as he looked up at her.

He wasn't done by a long shot, but he'd put the ball in her court. If she wanted more, then she'd have to ask for it. He watched as her breathing leveled. Her eyes stayed focused on his. He couldn't tell if she were ready to take flight or wanted a round two.

"What's it going to be, Cara?"

Long seconds passed as she said nothing. A final shiver passed over her shoulders and she took a deep, steadying breath.

"I had no idea."

His brows knit together. "Of what, Mia Bella?"

"That sinking those teeth of yours into me could be so … so orgasmic."

Kane chuckled. Whatever he expected her to say, that wasn't it. "You really have no idea then how talented my dick can be."

"I suggest you shut the hell up and show me."

ANOTHER SHIVER PASSED THROUGH her as Kane moved from his sitting position and crawled in her direction. The man oozed sex. Of course, she'd never doubted that for a second. But the last few moments he spent touching her had laid proof to it in spades. She hadn't had an orgasm in … scratch that, had never had an orgasm that epic!

Who would have thought the act of drinking her blood could incite such rapture? No wonder Suzi and all her donor friends had signed up to the Suck-My-Blood-Club so willingly. She had been the one missing out all these years. Lord, she needed an industrial size fan just to cool her heated skin.

Now to see him advancing on her like a cat to prey, her body hummed in anticipation. She had no doubt his lower anatomy was quite talented. After all, his past experience with women meant he had plenty of time to hone his skills.

He braced himself on the tub, his arms hemming her in, then bent to capture a kiss. And kiss her he did. His mouth slanted over hers, his tongue snaking out, touching hers, the coppery taste of her blood still evident. Cara drew his tongue into her mouth and deepened the kiss as her hands slid up his chest and to his nape, anchoring him. Damn, if he was half as good in the sack as he was at kissing, she'd want to chain him to the mattress. Stephen King's *Misery* came to mind. She doubted *bored* would ever enter the equation.

And exactly when had she stopped thinking of him as a cold-blooded murderer? As a blood-sucking vampire who drained people of their blood? About five minutes ago when he sank his fangs into her.

Oh lord, she had to stop thinking about the case, vampires and psychotics, or she'd embarrass herself right into running for Kane's quarters and locking him from the room. Not to mention missing out on the best sex she'd probably ever have. She needed to think of him as a fantasy, the perfect lover, pretend the darker side didn't exist, at least until she discovered how talented his cock really was. Just the thought made her heart slam against her chest. The man was a walking wet-dream.

His finger and forefinger tweaked her nipple, stealing her breath and stopping her from all sane thought. Well, the parts of her musings that weren't living in a fantasy land, that is. As he twirled the tight bud between his fingers, Cara moaned against his mouth, wanting very much his mouth where his fingers were at the moment. She was going to enjoy ever inch ... er, minute of him while she could. The morning would be early enough for regrets.

And no doubt she would have them.

Kane stood suddenly, lifting her, his large hands now cupping her backside. Her legs slipped about his waist, bringing his erection flush with her center. Were all vampires this well-endowed? She suddenly wondered how he'd possibly fit.

"You have far too many clothes on, vampire," she grumbled against his lips, earning her a chuckle.

As he shoved at the waistband of his jeans and briefs with one hand, Cara used her heels on his rock-hard ass to help divest him of the barrier. The less between them, the quicker she could get to the best-sex-ever part. After the orgasm he had given her, she had no doubt he'd deliver.

His erection sprang free. The soft steely skin rubbed against her wet clit. She wanted him inside her, to feel him completely fill her.

"I don't suppose you have a condom?"

Cara could feel his answering humor rumble up from his gut since she was thoroughly wrapped around him like a cat clinging to a tree. She loved that his spirits were high, but at the moment, his laughter was not what she needed. She just might die from extreme longing. Was that even possible?

"I don't need one, Mia Bella."

"That's all fine and dandy, but I'm not on birth control since having sex in the last couple of years wasn't a priority."

His humor died as he looked at her point blank. Damn it, but Cara hadn't meant to confess how long it had actually been since she had slept with a man.

But rather than comment on her admission, he said, "I can't get you pregnant."

Vampires couldn't spawn babies? "Sterile?"

"Not that I'm aware."

"Then why so certain?"

"Because you aren't a vampire."

"Oh." She made a mental note to ask him about that later. "Diseases? It's not like you've been celibate."

"As a vampire, I can't get those either, Mia Bella. My blood regenerates at too high of a rate. You're safe. I can't get you pregnant and I won't give you any STDs. Are we done with the questions?"

His smile was so cute; she could hardly fault him for his lack of patience at her sudden inquisition. Instead of answering him, she brought her lips back to his and kissed him again, taking control of his mouth and receiving an answering growl.

Kane turned and backed her against the wood paneling of the bathroom and entered her swiftly. Her gasp at his size lasted mere seconds as he started to move within her. Her back slid up the wall with each of his powerful thrusts, as he seat himself to the hilt, stretching her completely, before withdrawing and doing it all again.

Words failed her. She couldn't form a phrase if she wanted to. Her heart beat at the base of her skull as another climax rapidly approached. This wasn't making love, nothing slow and gentle about the way Kane took her. No, he had been correct when he said he had wanted to fuck her.

And he was doing a damn fine job of it.

Their sweat-slicked bodies slid together as he continued to pump into her. Her mouth left his to nip his shoulder, giving him access to her throat. But instead of biting her like she desired, he ran his fangs over the flesh, teasing her with the points and causing a series of shivers to pulse through her, right before another orgasm slammed into her, rocking her to the core.

Not that the first one hadn't sent her to the moon and back, but this ... this she couldn't even describe. Kane shoved into her one last time before his ass muscles tightened and he reached his own peak. She could feel his cock pulsing inside her as the last of her own tremors subsided.

No foreplay, no tender kisses, though she wouldn't have had it any other way. After all, they were just two beings enjoying the moment, copulating due to the stress of being thrust together by some psychotic primordial vampire bent on sucking every last drop of blood from her.

Kane slowly released his grip on her backside and allowed her to slide down the length of him. Cara wasn't so sure she was going to be able to stand, but her wobbly knees held up. She was just about to ask him, "Now what?" when he patted her rear and told her to head for his room.

"Lock the door this time, Mia Bella," he said as she turned back in the doorway. She so wanted to invite him to join her but wasn't sure she'd last another round. Besides, if the rest of the club members found out, Kane would suffer the fallout.

Kane winked at her. "You better do as I say, Mia Bella, or you won't be getting any sleep this night."

Cara smiled in return, then shut the door and turned the dead bolt. She leaned against the door for support. Had she really just given herself to her worst nightmare? Nope, she thought with a smile. She had just taken hold of a very sexy vampire and screwed his brains out.

"WHAT HAVE YOU GONE AND done now, dear brother?" Kaleb asked, his lips turned down as he entered the living area of the clubhouse.

His hands made tight fists at his side, telling Kane what came next wasn't going to be pretty. So much for waking up in a great mood. Kane didn't care one iota what Kaleb or Grayson might have to say about his late night activities and wasn't about to make this easy for his twin. What he and Cara shared last night, well, that was their business. End of story.

"I have no idea what you're talking about," Kane said, pulling last night's tee over his head.

He walked to the kitchen area, fetched a mug and poured himself a cup of coffee. He blew the steam across the surface before taking a healthy sip, feeling the answering warmth. The morning chill filled the air. This time of year, the nights cooled to the mid-thirties. Since he had yet to turn on the furnace or throw logs into the fireplace, the clubhouse was brisk. If Cara was going to spend her nights here, he'd need to change that. Kane took another sip from his coffee, and even though regular food didn't do anything for him, he still enjoyed a good cup of coffee the way he did a shot of whisky.

"You fucked her. Don't even try to deny it. I could smell her desire the minute you entered the bathroom."

One of Kane's brows quirked upward. "Listening against the door, were you? I believe that's even beneath you."

"Like I had to. You could have been in the next building over and I still would have heard the two of you. Maybe you ought to learn the word discreet."

"With our close quarters and acute hearing, no way to avoid it. I've heard you and Grayson many a night, and you haven't had to hear my opinion once on the matter. What you two do behind your own closed doors is no business of mine. Just as who I choose to fuck in none of yours."

Kane took another sip and hoped Kaleb would take the hint and leave him the hell alone. He was in no mood to discuss what had happened between him and the detective last night. He held no regrets when it came to the great sex they shared. Hell, no—he planned a repeat performance. Had that been all there was to it, there wouldn't be a problem. But he had drunk from her, taken communion.

Shit.

If Kaleb or Grayson even suspected as much, there would be consequences. There *should* be consequences. But as long as there was a primordial running loose, threatening to drain Cara of her blood, he needed her close. And he needed the club's cooperation to take him down. He couldn't do it alone, and the club turning their back on him now could only prove deadly to Cara. So for now he'd keep that particular activity to himself, just as he would his fangs. He couldn't allow himself another slip, no matter how tempting.

Kaleb walked around the island, grabbed his own mug and poured himself a cup of coffee as well. Kane could feel him stewing beneath the surface. He knew his brother didn't approve of his actions. Kaleb had never held his tongue before, and he doubted he'd start now.

After glaring at Kane over his coffee cup, he finally slammed it on the island, brown liquid spilling over his hand and onto the counter. Most men would flinch at the scalding liquid splashing onto their flesh. But then they weren't most men.

"Just say it and get it over with, Hawk. My patience is wearing thin."

"Did you bite her?"

"I'd like to know the answer to that question myself," Grayson said as he exited his room, buttoning the front of his jeans, though opting to go shirtless.

"Jesus, what the hell is it with you two?"

"You knew when you brought her here this wasn't a good idea," Grayson said. "Why not pick up someone from the Rave like the rest of us?"

"Oh, that's rich coming from you, Gypsy. You who gets tired of the same ol' too often to count. If I recall, it was you who pitched a fit a few days ago."

"I never said I only fuck girls from the Rave. I screw who I want and color their memories before I leave so that my appearance while fucking them doesn't leave a lasting impression. Can't very well conceal that. But communion? That's another story. I may not like the rules, but I abide by them because I understand the need to keep our nature secret. Did you alter the detective's memory from what she spied, Viper?"

"You both already know she's aware of what we are. I didn't have to change her memory."

"And what happens should she decide she's bored with you? Or better yet, threatens to tell others because you decide she's not worth your time any longer? Bet you hadn't thought of that."

"I'll take care of it if and when the time arises."

"See that you do, Viper. I don't care what you do, but we can't risk her exposing us. Now stop dodging the real question," Hawk said. "Did you bite her?"

"No," Kane lied, taking a quick sip of coffee so that his brothers wouldn't detect it. Besides, from where he had left the twin holes, they'd never spy them.

"Pray you don't, brother."

"Or what? Are you threatening me, Hawk?"

"You know the rules. You break them, I'll see the entire club knows about your indiscretions. There won't be a single Son who comes to your defense. She's a cop, Viper. You best keep that in mind. She has the power to take us down. Can you imagine what would happen if she decided to take this shit to the media?"

"I'm well aware of what she does for a living and her power in this community. If she proves to be a threat, then I'll take care of her myself."

"What will you do to me, Kane? Kill me?"

Damn it, he couldn't catch a break. "Cara—"

"No, Kane." Cara glared at him, her gaze as hot as pokers. "I heard enough to know I'm not wanted here."

"You can't defend yourself against this threat."

She laughed without humor, slinging her overnight bag over her shoulder. "It appears I cannot defend myself here either, nor can

I trust you to defend me. I think I'll take my chances with the primordial. At least with him, I know where I stand."

Cara walked to the front of the clubhouse, where she turned on the trio. "Don't worry, boys ... your secret is safe with me. Hell, I don't even believe this supernatural shit." With that, she turned and stalked out, the door closing behind her.

"Great! That went well," Kane grumbled.

Thankfully, Grayson and Kaleb remained remarkably silent.

CHAPTER SIXTEEN

K ANE HAD TOO MUCH TO DO TODAY TO CONCERN HIMSELF with what the hell the detective was up to or what she had been thinking following her untimely entry into the club's main room this morning. He had received a call from Red and knew that the Knights planned to run guns around Pleasant's borders once the sun set. And since Cara had stupidly refused to be in his company for protection, he didn't have a spare man to track her down and babysit her either. The Knights needed to be given clearance. Kane had to make sure the Sons were onboard, so a church meeting was called.

This could be a very lucrative deal for them, income with little or no effort on their part. Plus, on the flip-side, he had to make sure he upheld his promise to the Sheriff's Office and kept any violence out of Lane County. Knowing the Knights would likely try to run their guns under the radar, with or without the Sons' approval, Kane wanted to spare the county the war that would surely ensue had he not agreed to the arrangement. By giving the Knights his backing, he ensured they wouldn't go to battle over the needed route on the Knights' end. Kane had chosen the path of least resistance.

Besides, an alliance with the Knights could be to their benefit. Having a puppet club in their back pocket meant they always had backup when needed. Should anyone have issues with the Sons, then the Knights would have their back.

Sitting at the head of the long table, Kane watched as each member filed in, Kaleb and Grayson sitting at his left and right respectively. He hoped to hell they kept their mouths shut about his late night activities, as Kane didn't want to have to answer for his actions, at least not yet. Eventually the truth would come out and if need be, he'd step down as president. He had broken rules. Plain and simple. Being the president didn't exempt him.

But for now he needed time to figure this thing out with Cara and where it was heading. Having the primordial in town and targeting her meant he needed to keep her safe. Resigning as club pres would take away any control he might have over finding this son of a bitch and could put her at further risk without the Sons' protection. Kane was only one vampire. Against a primordial, like it or not, he need the power of the MC.

The door to the meeting room closed behind the last member. The large table seated fourteen with only one empty seat remaining, bringing Rosalee to the forefront of his thoughts. She had been responsible for the loss of Ion, his son, the empty seat he now stared at. Kane's jaw ached from tension. No meeting ever went by without him feeling the loss burning a hole like acid in his gut. He should have taken her head and dealt with the repercussions of killing an original. Instead, he had turned his back and dismissed Rosalee from his life, leaving her no choice but to return to Italy and the rest of the primordials, as her stepfather demanded.

In her own way, he knew Rosalee had loved him deeply, and he supposed he had felt much the same way at the time. But Rosalee had been a selfish bitch, not considering the possible ramifications of her cavalier actions. Actions Kane had forbid. With one single act of defiance, she had managed to destroy everything he had ever felt for her. In the end, Ion had lost his head because she hadn't used hers. She had thought herself far superior to even Kane, that she was somehow untouchable. The cartel funding the rival MC had wanted restitution for the loss of one of their own.

Yes, Rosalee was a powerful, ancient vampire.

But taking on the drug cartel was pure idiocy on her part. The cartel wasn't of the forgiving kind, and Ion had been the one to pay the price for Rosalee's arrogance. Kane had warned her that the Devils of East L.A. were backed by a Mexican cartel and were not to be toyed with. Regardless of his charge, she had set out to teach the MC and the cartel a lesson for daring to cross state lines with their drugs, for trying to take over the entire West Coast, therefore disrespecting the Sons.

Setting out with Ion in tow, she took matters into her own hand. She had killed one of the heads of the cartel, sending a message loud and clear to his troops. His brother, not cowering from her actions, had given the order to take a Sons' life.

A life for a life.

Kane would've rather given his own life.

Rosalee had tried to get Kane to see reason that she, too, had suffered. But an agreement had been made with the cartel, Kane banished Rosalee not only from the Sons but from the States as well, sending her back home to Italy, leaving her no choice but to return to her stepfather. In the end, her stepfather had agreed that Rosalee had acted recklessly and forbade her to leave Italy ever again as punishment. When Mircea II of Wallachia spoke, all of the vampire community listened ... including his wayward stepdaughter. Over ten years had passed, but he still felt the betrayal like it was yesterday.

Kane raised the wooden gavel, tired of reminiscing, and slammed it against the sound block. Conversation ceased as one by one all eyes trained on him.

"I called this meeting to inform everyone that the Knights intend to run guns tonight through Lane County. I'm sure you've heard by now of our deal with the MC from Washington."

The room remained quiet, no one pointing out that aligning themselves with the rival group had never been taken to a vote. Kane was sure there were those who opposed. Grigore cleared his throat, toying with the black rubber bands circling his left wrist.

After all the members looked in the muscular man's direction, he raised his chin a notch and leveled his gaze on Kane's. "I don't believe we ever voted on this alliance, Viper. Can I ask who took the liberty to make the deal without the full club's approval? There are those of us who don't feel an alliance is in our best interest."

Kane's face heated in his rising ire. As president, no one should ever question his decision once made, even if the issue at hand had never been voted on. And Grigore knew damn well who made that decision. By asking the question, he forced Kane to bring it to the table.

"I made that decision and I didn't ask, Wolf, because it was a good one. We stand to make a good deal of money off these runs."

"Allowing another club to run guns through our state makes us look weak," he pointed out. Several members nodded their heads in agreement.

"We can use the Knights as a puppet club. They will answer to us. Sometimes it's best to take the road of least resistance. We give them a lending hand from time to time, and when we need help, they'll be there for us. We already know that going up against an opposing club can cause us more trouble than we're willing to take on at the moment."

No one had to voice Ion's name, but everyone in the room knew Kane spoke of him. Not to mention the drainages in their county now causing them unwanted attention from the law.

"So what do we get out of this deal with the Knights—other than them being our puppet club?" Grigore asked.

"We get forty percent of their cut, Wolf. Pretty lucrative deal for doing nothing more than allowing them to skirt Pleasant on their way to Florence and back. Not to mention we have their backs should they get any grief from the law in Oregon. They'll run under the cover of night. If the state catches on or tries to stop them for any reason, we'll create a diversion."

"Are we just watching out for them as they pass through Lane County? Or are we following them through the entire state?"

"Two of us will follow them to the Washington border. Make sure they don't run into trouble, as well as keep a close eye on their activities while in our state. The rest of us will just make sure they get clearance through the county. Any questions?"

Nicolas rubbed a hand down his banded beard that nearly reached his chest. "What kind of diversion are you talking about?"

"Anything that will cause us the least amount of trouble, Wheezer. I'm not willing for you guys to do jail time over something that isn't our gig. The Knights know that. So you do whatever you have to, within reason, to draw the heat from the Knights." Kane shrugged. "Cut off the cop car. Get them to chase you. Worst we get is a traffic violation. Am I clear?"

All heads nodded in unison and thankfully no one argued. Kane wasn't in the mood for opposition.

"Good. I want Kaleb and Grayson to follow the Knights back to their home state on this run. Everyone else, just be on guard and make sure this goes smoothly as they pass through our county. I've already cleared it with the Sheriff. He'll see to it we have no trouble from him or his deputies on duty. Any objections?" When no one spoke, Kane slammed the gavel back on the sound block again. "Then we're done here. I'll see everyone back at the clubhouse at dusk. No exceptions."

Everyone began filing out of the meeting room one by one. Kane grabbed Kaleb's wrist and indicated that he shut the door behind the last of their brothers. Kaleb did as instructed and returned to his seat. The club meeting room had been soundproofed for confidential meetings. Kaleb's expression told Kane he still wasn't too happy with his twin's late night activities.

"Thanks for keeping this morning quiet. I appreciate you and Gypsy not saying a word."

Kaleb leaned back in his chair and crossed his arms behind his head. His booted feet stretched out in front of him. "Telling our brothers about your indiscretions wouldn't do any of us any good at the moment. We have bigger issues to deal with."

"Agreed."

His brother leaned forward, the legs of the chair scraped the wooden floor. "Make no mistake, Viper. I'm not agreeing with what you're up to. I think you ought to throw that bitch out and make her fend for herself. We shouldn't care one way or the other whether she gets her throat sliced and drained from this primordial."

Kane's jaw ached from tension. He wanted to rip his brother's heart from his chest for speaking so callously. But putting the boot on the other foot—he might have felt much the same. He'd known getting involved with the detective would not sit well with any of his brothers. Besides, after this morning, she wasn't about to return to the clubhouse willingly any time soon, no matter what he had to say about the matter. Kane didn't plan on giving her a choice once his job here tonight was finished.

"Look," Kaleb continued, "I know she's your type, but so are a lot other women out there. Can't you—"

Kane interrupted, "I know getting involved with the detective isn't good for the club. No one, especially you, has to point that out to me. But I can't change what happened. I fucked her last night."

"We heard," Kaleb grumbled.

"And all I want to do is fuck her again. Damn, Hawk, she's got me by the balls." He ran a hand down his face and sighed heavily. "Maybe, you're right. I should stay the hell away from her. But I can't honestly sit here and tell you that's going to happen."

Kaleb stared at his brother for long moments before he whistled low, leaning back in his seat.

"Jesus, Viper! You didn't just fuck her, did you? You drank from her."

It wasn't a question, but an accusation. Kane couldn't hide the truth if he wanted. His brother would spot the lie. "I hadn't meant to."

"No one feeds from an outsider. That rule is in place for a damn good reason, Viper. If she tells anyone—"

"She won't."

Kaleb leaned forward, anger evident in his darkening black as coal eyes. "How do you know?"

Kane massaged his forehead between his fingers. Damn, if he hadn't gotten himself into deep shit this time. "Look, Hawk, give me your word this is between us."

Kaleb shook his head and slammed both palms on the wooden table. "You have my word, brother ... for now. But you hear me, you best make sure she keeps her big mouth shut. For if I even think she'll tell anyone about this—I'll take her life myself. You won't have to worry about the damned primordial."

THE DOOR CRACKED OPEN AND Cara offered a feeble smile. No doubt Suzi wondered what she wanted this time. The suspicion on her face said as much. Cara had left the clubhouse and headed for the S.O., but after spending a few hours poring over the files in the nearly empty station, she decided to call it a day. Being Sunday, the deputies on duty were out in the field, leaving her alone with the dispatch. She hadn't been able to keep her mind on business, not after last night's festivities and Kane's telling admission this morning.

Cara sighed. She had been nothing more to him than a piece of ass. But what did she expect? By Kane's own admission, he didn't have girlfriends. Although some sort of compassion would have been preferable to threatening her life should she get chatty. She needed someone to talk to, a friend. Something she suddenly found missing in her life. That's where Suzi came into the equation. She was likely the only person who would understand what Cara had gotten herself involved in. Besides, not only would she be thought of as a quack, she wasn't willing to put Kane and his club in jeopardy. Kane and his brothers had a right to be paranoid. If word got out about the vampires, the public wouldn't understand and they would be hunted to extinction.

Cara wasn't callous enough to allow that to happen.

Regardless of what his twin, Kaleb, or Grayson thought of her, she wasn't heartless. She might not understand what they were or how vampires existed, but they were still ... what? Human?

"What do you want, Cara?" Suzi asked, jerking her from her reverie.

"Can I come in?" Cara shifted her stance uneasily. It never occurred to her Suzi might not want to be her confidant. "I really need someone to talk to, and you're the only one who might understand."

Suzi shook her head, her mouth twisted in indecision, then stepped back. "Come in. I'll make us a couple of ice coffees."

Shutting the door, Cara followed Suzi to the kitchen. Suzi grabbed the half-filled carafe of cooled coffee from the coffee maker. After pulling two tall glasses from the cupboard and adding ice, she poured about a half cup of strong black coffee into each. Cream and a shot of caramel syrup followed the coffee. Sticking a straw into each, Suzi handed a tumbler to Cara.

She held up her glass, clicked it with Cara's and said, "Cheers."

Taking a sip, Cara savored the creamy goodness.

"This is delicious. I should stop by more often," she said, earning her a chuckle.

Cara had hoped to break the ice as she wasn't sure how Suzi would feel about her rendezvous with Kane last night since Suzi had all but dodged her questions about her relationship with Kane last time Cara had asked.

"So why did you stop by? Miss me?"

Cara suddenly felt the loss of the last ten years. "I do miss having you in my corner, having someone to talk to. I miss our friendship."

Suzi propped her forearms on the countertop and leaned forward. "Yeah, I kind of miss that, too. So what's eating you? I know that look too well not to know something is bothering you."

"Am I that transparent?"

"Like rice paper. Spill it."

"It's Kane."

Suzi scratched behind her ear, clearly uncomfortable talking about the man. "What about him?"

Cara hoped her intuition was correct and Kane hadn't slept with Suzi. Nor did she think Suzi appeared head-over-heels with the man … scratch that … vampire. What the hell was he, anyway?

"Are they still human?"

Suzi laughed again. "Yeah, they're still human. Don't believe Hollywood's version of vampires, Cara. They breathe, eat, and sleep just like we do. Their hearts beat, which means they can be killed. Granted they're harder to kill than we are."

"How so?"

"Their blood regenerates at a very high rate of speed. Any injury they receive will heal ... except one straight through the heart or a head wound that stops their heart from beating. Any other injury they'll survive."

Cara thought about the wound on her hand. "Can they heal others?"

She shrugged. "To a point. If you get cut, they can lick the wound and their saliva will speed up the healing process. Anything more life threatening is a bit more complicated. That, you'll have to ask Kane about as I've probably already said too much."

"I won't tell anyone, Suzi. Surely, you know that."

Suzi harrumphed. "Don't push the shaky bridge we're building here, Cara. I'm not real sure about anything where you're concerned these days."

"I've already apologized. What more can I do to make up for my running away?"

"Coming here again is a start."

Cara smiled, tears welling in her eyes. "I was hoping you would say that."

Suzi reached across the counter and gripped Cara's fingers and squeezed. "You want to tell me about it?"

Her simple question opened the dam as tears made watery treks down Cara's cheeks. Suzi let go of her hand, walked around the counter and pulled Cara into her embrace. Sobs shook her. Kane's admission this morning had cut her straight to the heart. She had no doubt, that if need be, he'd make sure she kept his secret, even if it meant shutting her mouth permanently. The idea she meant so little to him, even though he had made her no promises, still stung.

Cara stepped back, wiping her cheeks. "I'm sorry, Suzi. I have no right involving you in the mess I've made of my life."

Suzi pulled out a bar stool and sat, indicating Cara should do the same. "I don't have anywhere to be. You want to tell me about it?"

"Maybe I should go."

"Nonsense. We're friends, right?"

A hiccough escaped her lips. "I'd like to think so."

"Then tell me what's plaguing you."

"Are you and Kane ... I mean, are the two of you...?"

"No." Suzi sighed, then grabbed her drink and took a sip. "I may have wished otherwise, but Kane turned me down flat. He wants nothing more from me than the nourishment I offer. Are you two...?"

Cara tucked one side of her hair behind her ear. "It wasn't supposed to happen. I hadn't meant to allow Kane within ten feet of me. Are you mad?"

"For screwing Kane? Why would I be? Although I'm curious how he relates to his brother," she said with a chuckle.

"You slept with Kaleb?"

"Once. A long time ago. Before you left town."

"Wow, I certainly was blind to what was going on."

Suzi shrugged. "I wasn't exactly forthcoming."

"If you slept with Kaleb, then why go after his twin?"

"Because I hate Kaleb. I'd do anything to get under his skin and piss him off."

"What did he do to you?"

Suzi grimaced. "Long story. But the short of it: I was young and dumb. Kaleb started using me frequently as a donor about six months before you left town. I fancied myself in love with him. I wanted to give him everything, including my heart. In fact, I did. But once we slept together, he walked away without a backward glance. He didn't speak to me, never fed from me, acted as though we were complete strangers. I was crushed. So I started hanging with another of the Sons, Ion. We were friends, but Kaleb thought there was more to it. Anyway, when everything went south, I no longer had Ion either. Shortly thereafter, you were gone. I had no one to talk to. I was devastated. I would have left the donor society then and there if I could have."

This time Cara gripped Suzi's fingers. "I'm sorry. I was so self-ish."

"It's okay." Suzi offered a weak smile. "That was ten years ago. I don't even know why I tried to sleep with Kane, other than to make Kaleb jealous. He lost his latest donor, so I knew he'd be in the market. I thought maybe if I could get Kane to pay attention to me, I'd be able to get back at Kaleb. There was a problem with my theory, though."

"What's that?"

"Kane didn't want me either. But enough about me, tell me about you. What happened between you and Kane?"

"You've heard about these murders in Pleasant?"

Suzi nodded.

"The three dead girls, all pale blonde hair and blue eyes."

"And because you have the same look, Kane feels the need to protect you?"

"Not exactly. We have no suspects, well, other than Kane."

"Kane didn't kill those women."

"He's our only suspect because we don't have any others. I really don't think he's responsible either. I feel like we're chasing our tails. Now that Tab's been murdered, her big-shot father is coming down on us to find a suspect. It won't be long before the State Police come in and take over our case. We aren't any closer to finding this perp than when the first victim was found. Then there's the break-in."

"What break-in?"

"Someone ransacked my house, didn't take anything, just messed up the place and threatened my life. The night before last, someone stood over my bed while I slept. My carpet had dirt on it and the window sill had smudges."

"You think Kane?"

"No." Cara quickly cut her off with a shake of her head. "The night of the break-in, he was with you. You were his alibi and I had witnessed as much."

"What does Kane say about all of this?"

"He thinks it's an ancient vampire. Said he could smell him on my property, in my room. That's why I stayed at the clubhouse last night. For some reason, Kane feels the need to protect me."

"Ancient vampire?"

"Kane called him a primordial."

Suzi nodded. "I've heard the term, know they're from Italy. But I wasn't aware any of them ever came to the US."

"Apparently one has and he wants me dead."

Her breath hitched. "You can't be serious. What are you going to do?"

Cara shrugged. "I don't know. Since Kane's appointed himself guardian, he's demanded I stay at the clubhouse at night where he can keep an eye on me. That's why I spent last night there."

"In his bed."

"I spent the night alone in his bed."

"I thought you and Kane—"

"We did. But it was in the connecting bathroom. I was getting around for bed. I had just showered and was finishing up shaving when he walked in. I thought the door was locked. Besides, they'd all gone to bed. I didn't even think about the second door until Kane walked through it.

"There I sat, without a stitch of clothes. He startled me and I nicked myself shaving. The next thing I know, Kane was drinking from the small wound. I can't tell you what a turn-on that was."

One of Suzi's eyebrows rose. "Kane fed from you?"

"I guess that's what you call it. I could feel my heart beat right where Kane suckled. It was so erotic. I don't think I've ever wanted a man as much as I wanted him at that moment."

"You know it's against their rules for Kane to feed from you. Right?"

"They have rules about who they can feed from? The donor thing."

"I know it sounds crazy, but it's the only way for them to protect themselves. They are to feed from donors only. Do the others know?"

Cara thought about the conversation she had walked in on earlier this morning. She had overheard Kaleb asking Kane if he had bitten her and he had denied doing so. At the time she had wondered about his denial. Now it made sense.

"No. I think the argument I walked in on this morning had to do with them overhearing us having sex. I thought we were being quiet. Apparently not."

Suzi smiled. "They have very acute hearing."

Cara's face heated as she groaned. "Nice to know. That's certainly embarrassing."

"Living under the same roof as those three do, I doubt it's nothing they haven't heard before."

The Blood 'n' Rave came to mind. No wonder Kane preferred to use Draven's inner office.

"That may be true, but they were certainly unhappy about the fact it was me. When I walked out of the bedroom, they were arguing with Kane, telling him he'd have to take care of me, ensuring I kept my mouth shut, or they would. Which of course, he agreed to.

"That's another reason I'm here, Suzi. I can't go home with this primordial wanting to kill me and I can't go back to the clubhouse either. I didn't know where else to go."

CHAPTER SEVENTEEN

KANE PULLED INTO THE DARKENED DRIVEWAY, ONE LONE SECU-rity lamp lighting the way. He wouldn't have needed it but was thankful Cara's house had the small security. This far from town on a cloudy night, her surrounding yard and woods would be pitch black without it. He glanced at his watch. Three-fifteen. Turning the key, he cut the rumble of his bike short. Silence greeted him, other than the sound of crickets and critters scurrying close by through the dense woods. Kane didn't detect any other sounds, no heartbeat, no breaking twigs, nothing to indicate he wasn't alone. The air hung heavy with early morning dew, not to mention the promise of oncoming rain.

Thankfully, the Knights' gun run had gone off without a hitch and the rain held off, allowing him to check on Cara. Kane pulled off his skull cap and dangled it from the handlebar before stepping over the seat of his motorcycle, glancing at the dark house before him. If Cara was here, then she had parked the car in the garage and lowered the door, since her Charger was nowhere in sight. Maybe she hoped to fool the primordial into thinking she wasn't in residence.

The ancient vampire wouldn't need to see her car, though. He'd be able to detect the beating of her heart from anywhere near the house, whereas Kane would have to be within. The dark windows yawned before him. Either she was fast asleep or not home. Kane needed to find out, to see for himself that she was safe. The entire evening he hadn't been able to get his mind off her well-being and hoped like hell the primordial hadn't found her. Jesus, he didn't even want to think about the alternative.

Bile soured his stomach.

If anything happened to her, he'd never forgive himself for making her walk out, rightfully pissed, the previous morning. His temper had ruled his mouth. And once voiced, he couldn't take it back. Cara probably thought him the worst of bastards and he couldn't blame her. Kane and taken communion from her, fucked her, then threatened to take her life, as if she had meant nothing at all to him. He'd screwed up. Plain and simple. His only hope lay in Cara not believing the condemning words leaving his lips.

Fat chance.

Kane had never given her any reason to trust him. He rubbed a hand down his days' stubble of beard. Dwelling on her opinion of him wasn't finding Cara. Pushing off the bike, he headed for the back of the house and stopped just short of the door, trying to detect any movement. The house seemed deathly still.

A hollow ache gripped his chest. Dread washed over him. Reaching for the knob, Kane found the lock held fast. He could have easily twisted the knob, and snapped off the cylinder. But instead of further damaging her door, he used the palm of his hand to break away the plywood nailed over the broken pane, sending the wood skittering across the floor inside. Kane reached through the missing window and turned the lock.

The door creaked inward. Kane stepped into the back room, the soft soles of his boots striking the wooden flooring. By now he should have been staring down the barrel of Cara's gun. Any good cop would have heard the intrusion the minute he struck the wood covering the broken window. He'd bet his life she wasn't within.

Why the hell hadn't he insisted the Sons do the run without him, hunted down Cara and insisted she take his offered protection? Instead, he had allowed her to walk out of the clubhouse and take her chances with the ancient vampire. An encounter she had no hope in surviving. Only his loyalty to the Sons had kept him from chasing her down and shaking her senseless until she saw reason.

"Cara?" he called out.

Eerie silence greeted him. Kane quickly moved through the kitchen to the living area, then took the stairs to her bedroom three at a time. On the landing, his gaze did a quick sweep of the area, her made bed, the opening to the bathroom. He was completely alone.

Where the hell had she gone?

Detective Hernandez came to mind, though he had no idea how to get in touch with him. Pulling his cell from his jeans' pocket, he scanned his contact list for the only person who might know how to get a hold of Cara. He touched the number next to Sheriff Ducat's name. Several rings later came a groggy, "Hello?"

"Tell me Cara's with you."

"Who the hell? Kane?" Rustling of bedcovers traveled through the cell's speaker. "I thought she was staying with you?"

"If she were, I wouldn't be calling, now would I?"

"Damn it, Kane. You check her house?"

"I'm standing in the middle of it. Trust me, she's not here. You have any other ideas? Her partner?"

"She wouldn't go there."

"Why?"

"Because he has little ones. Whatever danger she's gotten herself into, she wouldn't want to place Joe's family at risk."

"You sure about that?"

"Positive. She wouldn't even take my offered help."

"Friends? Family?"

"She has no family other than her grandfather. He's in a nursing home here in Pleasant. She wouldn't be able to stay there. And other than her fellow deputies, I'm not aware of any other friends. At least none that she speaks of."

"Any other ideas of where she might go?"

"You call her?"

Kane ran a hand through his messed hair and blew out an unsteady stream of air, quickly losing any patience he'd had. "If I had her number, would I be calling you?"

He'd sure as hell change that fact once he found her.

"I'll call her," the sheriff said. "Give me a few minutes, then I'll call you back."

"Thanks," Kane said ending the call.

Kane paced to the window and looked out, his thoughts turning to the primordial who had stood over Cara while she slept two nights prior. Anger welled in his gut. The son of a bitch stood within a hair's breadth of taking her out and easily could have, which told Kane she wasn't his true target. He was using Cara to flush him out and doing a damn good job of it. He took in a deep breath, hoping to tamp down his rising ire. Getting pissed now would help no one.

Cara's scent stamped the room, bringing to mind their assignation the night before. If anything happened and this primordial was responsible for hurting her, Kane wouldn't stop until he hunted the vampire down and severed his head from his shoulders. He'd face the originals for his actions later and not make excuses. This fuck better pray he didn't touch one hair on Cara's head.

Her closet doors stood open. Kane peered inside, flipping through several of the garments. Several hangers hung empty at the center of the rod, tempting Kane to believe maybe she had hastily packed a few things hours earlier, although it could have been for her stay at the clubhouse. He slammed the closet doors closed, frustration clawing at him.

He needed to find Cara like yesterday.

Kane walked back to the window and brushed aside the sheer curtains, staring into the night. The primordial was out there somewhere. Kane could feel it in his bones. If he could figure out what the hell he wanted and what his weakness was, he might stand a better chance at catching this vamp.

Kaleb or Gypsy had yet to check in, but he'd lay odds the ride to the Washington border had been without incident. The Knights had shown up on schedule with a commercial van filled with wooden crates carrying illegal firearms. Kane opened the rear doors, peered at the crates, then waved them on. He wanted nothing to do with the deal the Knights had made or who they dealt with. The Sons were in it for the profit and to keep their town free of violence ... period. After following the Knights through town, Kane allowed his men to finish the job so he could track Cara before anything untoward happened to her.

The Knights' timing had sucked.

When Kane slammed his palm against the frame of the window in frustration, the wood split beneath the force. His jaw ached and his ears rang. He hoped to hell his promise to the Knights hadn't cost him Cara.

The phone vibrated in his hand. Kane turned it over, slid the lock on the face of the smart phone and said, "Where is she?"

"She's fine, Kane. Mad as a hornet for being tracked down, though."

"That's too damn bad."

"She told me to tell you to go fuck yourself."

Kane chuckled. "I'm sure she did. Where is she?"

"She spent the night with a friend."

"Who?" Kane's ire rose. He didn't have time to play twenty questions with Ducat.

"Do you know Suzi Stevens?"

"Fuck."

"I take it that's a yes."

"Goodnight, Sheriff."

Kane stabbed END on the screen, then pocketed his phone. This was about to get ugly.

"OPEN THE DAMN DOOR, SUZI."

Cara bolted upright, startled from a deep sleep. Following the sheriff's call, she must have been tired enough to fall right back to sleep. After all, given Kane's history with Suzi, she hadn't thought that the arrogant jerk would show up here. She should have known better.

"Open the damn door, or I swear to whoever you pray to, you'll be calling a carpenter to replace your fucking door."

Nope. Not a nightmare. Crap!

More clamorous pounding came from down the short hall to the foyer. Cara struggled with the knitted quilt wrapping her feet as she tried like hell to wrestle herself free and make herself scarce before Kane came busting through the door. The last thing she wanted to encounter at four in the morning was a pissed-off vampire.

And, boy, did he sound pissed.

Just as she managed to flop from the couch with a thump, banging her knee in the process on the steel and granite coffee table, the sound of splintering wood followed her into the half bath.

"Jesus, Kane," came from a shocked-sounding Suzi making her way to whatever was left of the door.

Cara had just gotten the restroom door closed before the imposing force made it fully into the apartment with a resounding growl.

"Look what you did to my door!"

"I'll buy you a new one. Where is she?"

"Who?" Suzi feigned ignorance. "Do you even know what time it is?"

"You know damn well who. The sheriff told me I'd find Cara here. Now go retrieve her before I start breaking down more doors."

"I highly doubt she's going to want to see you. Have you completely lost it? Just look at the damage you've already done! Damn it, Kane, even I don't want to see you right now."

"I'll fix the door. Now, I'm not leaving here without Cara, so you might as well go get her. She's not safe with you." He paused and Cara bet his facial expression was murderous. "I think I've just proven that point."

"Of course, it's not now, you big oaf! You just made firewood out of my door. Don't even think to start on the bathroom door!"

Cara leaned her ear against the bathroom door, trying to better hear their conversation. Something bounced off the wood, jarring her head. She quickly backed up, fearing Kane might just make good with his promise and start with the door separating them next.

"If you two think that door was any kind of a barrier between you and a vampire hell bent on getting in, then you're both seriously delusional."

"Obviously."

Cara couldn't allow Suzi to take any more of Kane's ill temper, not when it should've been focused on her. She had been the coward, the one to run.

Opening the half bath's door, Cara stalked into the room, shoulders squared. She'd take the bull by both horns and not give him the satisfaction of seeing her cower. Cara gripped the afghan tightly about her breasts, although Kane had already seen all there was to see beneath the thin tee she wore as a nightshirt.

"What do you want, Kane?"

"Get your things, Detective." His anger rose from him like waves off hot asphalt in July. No doubt he was plenty angry he had to come looking for her. "You aren't staying here."

"I was perfectly safe until you came traipsing in, making kindling of Suzi's door."

Kane raised one brow. "Exactly the reason I needed to come retrieve you. You two need your heads examined if you think that Suzi is a better match for this primordial than I."

"I'm safe, or at least I was, because no one knew I was here."

"I found you easy enough."

"Because you talked the sheriff into helping you."

Kane shrugged, not feeling guilty in the least for his caveman antics.

"Really, Kane. What were you thinking? If this ancient vampire didn't know where I was before, he probably does now. You led him straight to Suzi's door."

"He's not after Suzi."

"No, but now my association with Suzi puts her in danger as well."

His brows met over the bridge of his nose, clearly perplexed at Cara implying this was his fault. "Don't blame me for involving her. That was your decision. You chose to come here over my protection."

Kane glanced from Cara to Suzi, grumbling beneath his breath, something sounding darn close to boneheads.

How dare he?

Before she had a chance to admonish him, he said, "Get your things ... both of you. You're going to get into Suzi's car and follow me to the clubhouse. You're no longer safe here."

"What about my car?"

"It stays. This fuck surely knows your car, but he doesn't know Suzi's. I'd like to keep it that way."

"He does if he followed you."

"I don't think he did. I would have smelled his presence. Now get your things and meet me out front in five minutes. You think you two stubborn clowns can manage that?"

"Gee, when you demean me that way, Kane, it makes me go all gooey inside."

"Your sarcasm is lost on me, Cara."

Kane didn't wait to see if they'd follow his orders. His arrogance spoke volumes. He knew damn well they would do as he demanded. After all, they didn't have much of a choice.

Cara looked at Suzi and grimaced. "I'm sorry. I didn't mean to get you involved in my mess."

Suzi gave her half a smile. "What are friends for?"

"This certainly goes beyond." Cara unwrapped herself from the afghan, folded it and draped it over the back of the sofa. "I guess we best get our stuff before we rue the day we tested Kane's patience."

"I'll get my things."

Several moments later, Cara sat in the passenger side of Suzi's car as they closely followed Kane on his motorcycle. The sidewalks stood uninhabited this early in the morning as the red Neon traveled down Main Street and past Tom's Deli. Street lights illuminated their way through the hazy layer of fog descending on the valley. By morning the fog would likely be dense, hampering visibility, a common occurrence in the cool fall temperatures.

Cara glanced out the side window, seeing the red glowing brake lights of a patrol car as it stopped at the corner of Washington and Monroe, then slowly rolled through the intersection. She suddenly missed her uncomplicated life in Eugene where she started out as a uniform. She had thought by moving back to Pleasant that life would be slower paced, even if she had taken on the job of detective. After all, what cases had Lane County seen in the past eighty years? A few drug trafficking cases, one bank robbery, and a couple of open and shut suicides. But not one murder case in the last twenty years.

That is, until now.

After letting out a long sigh, Cara returned her gaze to the back of Kane's motorcycle and that of his backside. His jeans stretched nicely over his muscular rear, Cara remembered all too well the cords of muscles beneath his taut skin as her heels dug into his ass. Her mind couldn't help traveling back to the previous evening when he walked in on her shaving. Truth be told, she hadn't thought of much else in the last twenty-four hours. The question was would she want a repeat?

Desire pooled in her lower abdomen, numbing the inside of her thighs, causing her to cross them. Cara had never experienced anything so erotic in all her years. Hell, with the way her love life had been going, she'd be a fool to turn down round two. With a shake of her head, she stifled a chuckle. Last thing she wanted to do was admit was how much she really had been thinking about Kane, let alone wanting to revisit last night's activities.

Cara glanced at Suzi. She wasn't sure who all would be at the clubhouse this time of night. But for once she hoped Kane's club members were out feeding or whatever it was they did when the sun went down. Noting Suzi's death grip on the steering wheel, Cara figured she undoubtedly worried about Kaleb being at the house when they arrived. After what she had confided in Cara, she didn't think Suzi would be in too much of a hurry to see him.

"What?" Suzi asked as she glanced briefly at Cara, having caught her staring.

"I feel horrible, Suzi."

"You already apologized. Don't sweat it."

"But you hate Kaleb."

Suzi didn't respond right away. Instead, she returned her gaze to Kane and the road. Finally, she said, "Does Kaleb still live at the clubhouse?"

Cara nodded.

"Then, I guess I'll just have to deal with him when I see him. I doubt pretending he doesn't exist will work."

That caused Cara to snicker, and Suzi joined in on the humor. "That will be as easy as trying to ignore Kane."

Moments later, Cara's prayers were answered as they pulled into the clubhouse's empty parking lot, gravel crunching beneath the tires. At least now they could get settled before the other members discovered who the little red Neon belonged to.

One look at Suzi told Cara she wasn't as brave as she let on. Truthfully, she looked ready to bolt as she stared at the wood-sided cabin. Kane didn't wait to see if Suzi and Cara followed, nor did he bother to see if they had bags they might need help with. She supposed his pissed state of being had a lot to do with his lack of manners at the moment. He clearly wasn't too pleased he had to chase her down in the middle of the night. She supposed he had better things to do, like feed.

How often did a vampire need to drink blood anyway?

That question brought back their late-night rendezvous in living color. Desire shot through her at the thought of Kane's fangs sinking into her flesh. She knew damn well that if the opportunity arose, angry at Kane or not, she'd cave. No one had ever given her an orgasm of that magnitude. There was no question about it. Kane not only knew how to make a woman peak, but being food for a hungry vampire had its tremendous draw as well.

Exiting the small Chevy Neon, Cara grabbed her overnight bag and headed up the walk behind Suzi. She had to hand it to her old friend. Since exiting the car, Suzi hadn't faltered her steps. Cara would bet her insides were tied into knots and no doubt hoped Kaleb wasn't inside.

CHAPTER EIGHTEEN

KANE SLAMMED THE DOOR UPON ENTERING THE CLUBHOUSE, not waiting on the women. Jesus! Bringing Cara back to his home, his bed, was the most insane, idiotic thing he could have possibly done. He had little or no willpower when it came to her, no matter that he really didn't have another option. Not only did she need safeguarding from this psychotic vampire bent on taking her life, she needed to shield herself from him. Cara hadn't asked to be in the middle of some pissing match between two vampires. But there she was. One wanted revenge for some yet-to-be-known reason, while the other just wanted her out of her pants and in his bed. Stupidly, he had allowed his interest in the detective to cloud his good judgment and place her in harm's way.

Kaleb and Grayson had every right to be angry with the way he had handled this situation. Not only had he brought one female into their home, he now had two under foot. No doubt they'd want to stake him once they found out. He hung his head and stared at the wooden planks beneath his feet. This had disaster written all over it. Kane hadn't forgotten how Suzi had nearly begged him for sex when he had fed from her a few nights back. Throw Cara into the mix and their late night activities ... well, let's just say Kane had no idea how the two would react if one found out about the secrets of the other. Add Kaleb to the equation...

Kane shook his head.

He still had no clue about their history, and normally he couldn't have cared less. But now that they might all be residing beneath the same roof, he second guessed his earlier rationale of tracking down Cara at Suzi's house. The wiser choice would have been to retrieve her at the Sheriff's Office the following day. He certainly hadn't been using good reasoning as of late. He sighed heavily. Cara had him acting irrationally and not thinking with his head.

The door opened, drawing his attention, and the two women causing him so much distress entered the living area. One look told him neither was too happy with her present situation. No more than he anyway. His eyes zeroed in on Cara, his dick also taking notice. Kane clenched his teeth so hard he feared breaking a molar. Cara definitely had him thinking with his head ... just not the right one.

"Welcome home, ladies," Kane grumbled.

Cara tossed her bag on the sofa, where it landed with a thud. "Really, Kane? It was one thing to involve me in all of this, but now Suzi?"

His ire rose. Balancing his fists on his hips, he glared at them both. "You don't think I know that? Don't get all self-righteous on me here, Cara. You're not the only one being inconvenienced. You think I'm enjoying playing babysitter? Now I have two of you to worry about when I should be out there looking for this son of a bitch turning my life upside down."

Cara's cheeks reddened as her gaze narrowed, pinning him where he stood. Apparently, he needed a lesson on how to handle a hard-headed woman, because he was doing nothing more than pissing this one off.

"I didn't ask for this!"

"Look, Cara," he said, taking a deep, calming breath. "I know this hasn't been easy for you, but it would go a whole hell of a lot smoother if you'd just start doing as I say."

"I'm not your doormat. I have a job to do, which may include arresting you, I might add."

Kane's gaze widened. "Are you fucking serious? You still think I could've had something to do with these murders?"

"You drink blood!"

"It's called survival, sweetheart. But when have I ever made you feel threatened because of it?" He looked at Suzi, who wisely kept her mouth shut as she watched Kane and Cara's exchange with amused interest. "Suzi ... you allow my brothers to feed from you. You fed me a few nights ago. Have any one of us ever made you feel your life was in danger because of it?"

She put her hands up, palms out. "Oh, no ... don't get me involved in this."

"Throw me a bone here."

Suzi glanced at Cara, her smile crooked. "You just have to know the signal to get them to stop or they might just suck you dry."

Cara's face paled and Kane wanted to throttle the petite brunette. She must have detected Kane's reaction to her little joke, for she quickly followed up with, "Relax, Cara. Kane or his brothers have extreme self-control. They never take more than they need, and no more than your body can replenish easily. It's like going to the Red Cross and donating blood."

Cara's gaze narrowed. "Oh, no you didn't. You didn't just compare what they do to giving blood at Red Cross."

Suzi smiled and shrugged.

"Okay, fine." Cara turned back to Kane. "I really don't believe you murdered these women, or I certainly wouldn't be following you into the night and right into the lions' den. Let's just say I don't extend the same courtesy to your brothers."

Kane thought about the men who followed him, the rest of the Sons. Could one of them be the miscreant they hunted? That made zero sense since the primordial had targeted Cara, had said that it was her turn to die, and Kane had smelled his presence all over her room. Could it be possible the ancient vampire wasn't guilty of the other murders? Kane had only assumed...

"You think one of my men could be responsible for killing these women? On what basis?"

Cara's shoulders slumped ever so slightly, but Kane caught the defeated gesture. She was grasping at straws. The fact he and his brethren drank blood made them her probable suspect. Kane knew without a doubt that one of his kind was indeed responsible. The complete draining told him as much. But one of the Sons? Ludicrous.

"You're grasping at straws, Detective."

"Maybe. But at the moment, I don't have anyone else to look at. Give me a reason to look outside this club."

"It's a primordial who wants you dead."

"So you say, Kane. I don't have anything but your word that this phantom exists. You're asking an awful lot from me to buy into this supernatural shit. Hell, I can hardly believe that you exist. And now

I'm supposed to suspend disbelief even more and believe this ancient, powerful vampire wants me dead." Tears welled in her eyes as her bravado slipped. "And if that's true, I don't even know what I did to piss him off."

Kane's heart ached. Damn, a hard-headed woman was tough enough to deal with. But a vulnerable one? Kane was completely out of his element. He wanted to go to Cara, wrap her in his arms and never let go. He knew, though, she would welcome his comfort about as much as she did his protection. Especially after the stupid remarks that came out of his mouth the previous morning, words he never intended her to hear. Words meant to placate his brothers.

Just how the hell he'd managed to get himself into this mess, he wasn't sure.

"Look, it's late. Why don't you two get settled. We can discuss this tomorrow. You both look like you could use some sleep."

"Suzi can sleep in your room with me. No reason to put out Kaleb or Grayson when we can both fit in your massive bed."

Kane's gaze jerked to Cara's. Oh, hell no. He'd rather put Kaleb out of his bed than allow Suzi to share Cara's, scratch that, *his* bed. Not that there would be a repeat of last night, mind you. Or at least he made half an effort of convincing himself.

Who the hell was he trying to kid?

One taste of Cara and he wanted more ... though this time, he needed to keep his fangs to himself. And if he planned on getting Cara horizontal, he didn't need Suzi blocking his efforts. Nothing short of a beheading would keep him from having sex with Cara again.

Suzi sharing Kane's bed was unacceptable, so Kaleb be damned if he didn't like the new living arrangements. Kane nearly laughed. Kaleb would no doubt be mad as a hornet. But there were two sofas, both large enough to support Kaleb and Grayson. Besides, Kaleb usually didn't come crawling in until daybreak anyway. If he wanted his bed, he could just wait until Suzi crawled out of it.

"You'll be taking my bed and Suzi can have Kaleb's."

Suzi and Cara both gaped at him, clearly neither happy about his decision. Too damn bad.

"I won't sleep in Kaleb's bed," Suzi declared.

"You will."

"Kaleb won't like it."

"I'm sure he won't, but then he'll probably stay out all night as he usually does. I'll not have you both sharing my room."

Cara's shock turned into suspicion. "Why would you care if we decided to room together? Seems like that would be the best solution for everyone."

Kane held his ground. "It's not."

"If you're using the sofa, then why should you care if Suzi and I share your bed? It's large enough for both—"

"It's large enough should I choose to join you."

Cara's gaped mouth snapped shut. By the look of her reaction, it was going to take a whole lot of persuasion before he charmed his way back between those sweet thighs. Fine. He could be just as hard-headed.

He didn't care if Suzi hadn't been aware of their relationship status, or what she thought. Kane wanted a repeat performance and he'd be damned if he didn't get his way. Vampires were sexual beings and went after what they wanted, and right now he wanted Cara.

"I can see this conversation would be better suited for another time, like next time we're alone."

"Dream on, fang boy. What happened between us isn't going to happen again."

Kane smiled. "If you say so."

"It's not." She crossed her arms across her breasts. "It shouldn't have happened in the first place."

"Maybe."

"Maybe? Are you serious?"

"As a snake intent on biting you. Mark my words, Cara, I'll have my way and you'll be begging me to. I already proved that once."

Her cheeks reddened but she didn't have a retort.

"Suzi, Kaleb's room is last door on the right down the hall. Make yourself comfortable. I'll intercede should my brother return before you wake."

Suzi glanced at Cara, probably to see if Cara needed her presence.

"I'll be fine," Cara assured her. "He doesn't scare me."

"Are you certain?"

"I can handle Kane."

Suzi looked at Kane briefly. "You"—she pointed at him—"better be nice. If you need me, Cara, just holler."

Suzi hugged Cara, then headed down the hallway. Kane waited until the door latch clicked behind her. But before he could say a word, Cara glared at him.

"Don't even think about entering your room." Her gaze narrowed, brooking no argument. "Or the bathroom, should I be using it. You and me aren't happening, vampire."

With that, she grabbed her bag from the sofa and headed for Kane's room. The soft click of the bolt sliding into place told him going to her tonight might not be such a good idea. Kane pulled off his tee, draped it over the back of the sofa, kicked off his boots and lay down. Crossing his arms behind his head, he stared at the ceiling.

Cara might be angry and not allowing him to share his bed at the moment, but at least she was safe. Besides, judging by her response last night, it was only a matter of time before she caved, and he could be patient man if need be. He closed his eyes and smiled, knowing full well Cara's thoughts were on last night's festivities. After all, he could smell the rise in her desire the second he mentioned it.

"WHAT THE HELL WERE YOU THINKING?" Kaleb slammed his fist on the wooden bar separating him and his twin. His hair lay in wild disarray, his cheeks ruddy from his recent ride to the border and back. "Jesus, Viper! It's bad enough to bring one woman into this house. Now two? Wasn't this the whole reason we decided women were not to reside here? Fuck 'em and send them home. That's always been understood."

"It's temporary, Hawk."

"Good, then they can both find another place to stay tonight. Who else did you bring home?"

Kane ran a hand down his jaw, not yet ready to reveal the name of their second guest. Instead, he side-stepped the question. "You know we have to protect Cara until this primordial is found. She's being targeted because of me. Get busy finding him and we can all move on. That is, if these murders are his doing."

"What do you mean?"

"Cara brought up a point. She's thinks maybe one of the Sons could have an ax to grind with me. It's a feasible explanation. Maybe someone wants my seat at the head of the table."

"Yeah, me, asshole." Kaleb sat on the closest bar stool and folded his hands on the bar top, looking up at Kane. "You seriously think one of us murdered your exes?"

"One girlfriend. I didn't know the other two. At least I don't re-call them."

He chuckled. "I stand corrected. I think. If you can't recall them, I sure in hell can't be expected to keep track of your women. You know it's possible you might have met them briefly, maybe even slept with them. After all, the victims were all your type, Viper. But why would Cara think one of us would kill women you may or may not have dated or slept with?"

"You tell me. I didn't say I believed her theory, only that it's a valid one. But what makes this anymore improbable than a primor-dial coming to the States and killing women fitting my dating pref-erence? The first two, I'm not aware of, but Tab was my donor. Now this shit has targeted Cara."

Kane walked around the bar, the heels of his boots striking the wooden flooring. He leaned his back against the bar next to Kaleb, shoving his hands deep into his pockets. They needed to hunt this shit down and find out what the hell he wanted and why he was bent on destroying Kane. He'd bet the primordial camped out in the area, close enough to keep tabs on the club.

Kane looked down on Kaleb. "How did the rest of the run go last night?"

"Fine. Grayson and I watched their backs until they hit the state line. No problems came up. We U-turned at the border, no longer on our watch. Grayson met up with a couple of biker bitches and went back to their place to party. I wasn't interested, so I came here. Why?"

"You didn't see anyone or anything unusual on the road?"

Kaleb shook his head. "Not much traffic that time of night."

"Didn't detect this primordial?"

"Nope. But we never stopped. Why?"

"I can't help thinking that maybe this asshole is keeping tabs on all of our activity. If he's trying to undermine my authority, it might also benefit him to make our deal with the Knights go sour."

"What makes you think he would even care what we do?"

Kane pushed off the bar and walked to the front windows of the clubhouse. Clouds hung low over the horizon, painting the sky blood red. The forecast called for impending storms, doing nothing to improve his blackened mood, which brought his thoughts back to the woman lying in his bed. Kane hadn't slept a wink after she locked that door. Not that a lock would hinder his entrance had he wanted to get in, but he'd respect her wishes for now.

An ache started low in his groin. *Stop thinking with your dick, Tepes.*

He had thought, or at least hoped, that having sex with Cara would diminish his desire as it had with most women. But instead it had intensified it. And Kane wasn't used to curbing the sexual hunger now burning deep in his gut.

He ran a hand through his hair.

Damn, if she didn't have him by the balls. No woman had ever captivated him the way she had. And the hell of it? He scared the hell out of her. Sure, she had responded to his advances and he had given her one hell of an orgasm. But when desire didn't enter into the equation, she feared the monster in him. He could see it in the way she looked at him. Once this case was over, she'd undoubtedly run as far from him as possible. He'd have no other option but to let her go.

Kaleb cleared his throat, bringing Kane back to the unanswered question. He turned from the window, squared his shoulders and looked at his brother.

"That's the hell of it, Kaleb. I don't have a fucking clue what I've done to piss off one of the ancients."

One name weaved its way into his musings: Rosalee. His gaze narrowed as the thought took purchase. If he was correct, she'd have every reason to hate him and want to see his liaisons taken out.

"You don't think Rosalee?" Kaleb asked, thinking along the same lines.

"Mircea would never allow her to leave," Kane responded, yet he wondered at the validity of his statement even as it left his lips. "Rosalee broke his heart, and he's not likely to forget or forgive her sins any more than I."

"Don't be so sure, Viper. Rosalee is used to getting her way. At one time his stepdaughter could do no wrong. Ten years is a long time to heal wounds."

"A decade is but a blink of an eye in our time, not nearly long enough for me. A century could have gone by, and I'd still not welcome her sorry ass back into my life."

"You know your anger won't bring Ion back."

Heat rose from his gut and burned in his ears. How dare Kaleb brush off his son's death so easily? "She's the reason Ion is dead. What the hell are you defending her for?"

Kaleb looked at him queerly. "Have you lost your fucking mind? Did I say I forgave anything that bitch did? I was playing devil's advocate, for crying out loud. Speculating on why Mircea might have pardoned her. As far as I'm concerned, she can rot in hell for all eternity. If she steps back in the States, I'd be happy to be the one who ends her immortality."

"You'll have to get in line behind me, Bro."

"What's going on?" came from a groggy Cara as she shuffled her bare feet down the hallway, running her hands through her sleep mussed hair.

Kane wanted to replace her hands with his. Damn but he wanted to pick her up, throw her over his shoulder, and return her to his bed. She looked cute and sexy as hell in a loose pair of pink sweats, hanging low on her hips with white tank clinging to her breasts on top. He could just make out the outline of the dark pink bra beneath. Cara might not realize it, but she made quite the tempting package. His groin semi-hardened just at her appearance. He had it bad.

"We were discussing how you, and whoever the hell else is here, will be finding other digs tonight," Kaleb told her.

Cara glanced at Kane, all sleep quickly gone from her gaze. "You found someplace else for us to stay?"

"Hawk is jesting, Cara. You're welcomed to stay here until we figure out who this primordial is and we take him down."

"Or her," Kaleb added.

Kane could have kicked Kaleb's biker ass for that slip. And by the look on Cara's face, she wasn't going to let it pass.

"Once we—" Kane began, hoping he could quickly move past his twin's slight.

No such luck.

"Wait, Kane. *Her?* You mind telling me what that's about?"

"It's only a theory."

"Fine," Cara said as she crossed her arms beneath her breasts, causing the soft flesh to spill over the neckline.

Kaleb's gaze went right to the swell of her breasts, causing Kane to want to cold-cock him.

"Eyes up here, brother," Kane warned.

Kaleb's brows pinched. "Seriously?"

Cara moved right past the brothers' pettiness. "I appreciate that it's only a theory, Kane, but I want the details anyway. Stop glossing things over and give me the straight facts. I'm a detective. I deal better with facts."

Kane grasped her beneath the armpits and sat her on a stool beside his brother. "Then sit and listen. I'll tell you the everything if you promise not to interrupt."

She nodded.

Cara deserved the unvarnished truth of who might be after her and what she was capable of.

"Her name is Rosalee. I'm not saying she's the primordial after you, but it is a very good possibility. What Kaleb and I were talking about is we can't figure out how she's even left Italy, if it is her."

"Why?"

"Rosalee did something that upset her stepfather. He's the eldest primordial in their clan. Mircea II. He banned her for eternity from leaving his side. She's not allowed outside of the country. To do so could mean certain death for her."

"What did she do?"

"She's a fucking cold-hearted bitch," Kaleb added.

Kane nodded, then continued, "She caused her son's death, Mircea's beloved grandson."

Cara's breath caught, her shock evident in her rounded eyes. "Surely, the death of her own son was certain punishment. What happened?"

"Rosalee lived here, in the States. Her son was born here. He was a good kid, always trying to please his mother. He would have done anything she asked. She used that to her advantage.

"About ten years ago, the Sons had a rival club in Oregon. They made their way north from California. Their hope was to take over the coast. The Knights and Sons were to band together against this club. But they had powerful men backing them. The cartel had special interest in taking control of the coast. Running their drugs was the main focus, and the Devils would do their grunt work."

"So what did Rosalee and her son have to do with all of this?"

Kane didn't want to relive the ugliness, but Cara needed to hear it. Those final days with Rosalee were some of the darkest days of his life.

"Rosalee is a beautiful, seductive vampire. Most men could not resist her charm, even if they wanted to. But these men were ruthless killers. They didn't do anything without having something to gain. And if you got in their way, they wouldn't simply kill you, they'd send you a fucking message."

Kane paused and took a deep, steadying breath. Ten years had done nothing to dull his pain. He felt the knife to his heart as if it were just yesterday. Cara watched him, hanging on his every word. He wondered how she would react to the fact he had created a life with not just any woman but a mate. When vampires mated, they mated for life. Rosalee would no doubt try as she might to remind him of that. Kane, however, would never honor it.

"Against club decree she took Ion with her. She met with one of the drug lords. She seduced him, stupidly believing herself far superior in all ways. In the end, when she demanded he pull the Devils from Oregon, he laughed in her face. Rosalee took that as a direct insult. She bled him dry and tossed his carcass aside, knowing his brother would find him. She hadn't counted on the retaliation, thinking the way she had murdered the brother would send the superstitious men fleeing south."

Tears filled Kane's eyes but they didn't fall. Cara laid a hand on his forearm.

"What happened?"

"His brother tracked her. She hadn't even gone twenty miles before they caught up. Rosalee hadn't bank on them finding her. She thought that finding the drug lord had been killed by a vampire would make the brother and other members of the cartel so scared of the unknown that they'd pull their puppet club, the Devils, from Oregon. Instead—"

Kane cleared his throat. "Instead, they caught up with Rosalee and Ion. They staked Rosalee and Ion to trees facing one another. They beat them both mercilessly. Rosalee lost enough blood to make her weak. All she could do was stare in horror as they lit the other tree on fire and burned Ion to death, then separated his charred skull from his shoulders."

"My god. She must have been horrified. How did she get loose?"

"She grieved for two days before we found her and released her from the tree. She wanted to die there. I wanted her to die on that damned tree, but I knew I'd suffer the wrath of her stepfather."

"So the cartel killed her son and Mircea's grandson? Why didn't he retaliate?"

"Because the cartel agreed to pull their MC from Oregon and Washington, to never enter our states again. They get to continue running their drugs in California, and we agreed not to go to war against the Devils. A life for a life."

"And Mircea ordered his daughter back to Italy as punishment?"

"And away from the love of her life who now hated her."

"Who is Ion's dad? The love of her life?"

Kane stared at Cara for a long moment before her mouth rounded. Tears filled her eyes and slipped down her cheek before she stated the obvious. "Ion was your son."

CHAPTER NINETEEN

KANE'S STORY RENDERED CARA SPEECHLESS. SHE HAD NO IDEA what to even say to someone who had lost a child. Surely, he didn't want her sympathy. That wasn't what his confession was about. But her heart went out to him anyway. Parents weren't supposed to outlive their children. Cara couldn't begin to imagine the pain and loss he had endured.

Tears slipped down her cheeks as Kane watched her. Cara took a deep breath, feeling the biggest kind of sappy fool as she tried to get her emotions under control. His glassy eyes were the only sign at all that the remembrance affected him. No wonder he hated Rosalee. She might have meant well, wanting what was best for the club, but her arrogance had cost them their son's life.

Kaleb drummed a nervous tempo with his fingers against the bar top, watching them both, the only sound in the clubhouse as silence continued and tension mounted. If Kaleb hadn't been there, she might have gone to Kane and attempted to comfort him in some small way. But Kaleb's dislike of her kept her from doing as she desired.

Finally, for lack of anything better to say, she commented on his relationship with Rosalee instead. "So you were married?"

Kane grimaced as he rubbed his temple. Obviously, his relationship with Rosalee was something he'd rather not talk about. "As far as I'm concerned, she's free to mate with whom she pleases."

"But you were together?"

"We were mated. Yes."

"Is that the vampire form of married?"

Kane winced. It seemed Cara put more weight on the fact he had been mated than he did. Rosalee was obviously no longer a part of his life. Fifty percent of marriages ended in divorce, so it really wasn't something that should bother Cara.

"There's no need for a union to be docketed on paper. No vampire would touch another's mate. It's a sacred bond."

"So what happens then? I assume there is no such thing as a divorce since there is no marriage. You just, what? Go your separate ways?"

"No, Cara." Kane scratched his nape. The sorrow in his gaze vanished as he suddenly looked as if he rather be anywhere but standing here having this conversation.

Kaleb smiled. "This should be good."

Kane glared his twin into silence before answering her. "When vampires mate, Mia Bella, it's for life."

"Oh, well ... what about the other night? Is that considered an affair? Am I now a mistress?" Her voice cracked in her distress. She couldn't help it. Cara would never consider an affair. And the thought of being a mistress to a vampire was unthinkable.

"Rich," Kaleb said with a chuckle. "Yes, dear brother. Care to respond?"

"Butt out, Kaleb. Don't you have something better to do?"

"Nope. Don't believe I do."

Kane shook his head, tilting his gaze to the floor. Cara's heart lodged in her throat, making her want to gather her things and leave. Suddenly, she felt like a complete outsider, one who had no business at all standing here having this conversation. When she screwed up, she did so royally. What the hell had she been thinking when she opened herself to Kane and let him in? Jesus, she had had the best orgasm of her life with another vampire's mate. The last thing she needed or wanted was a psycho vampire after her because she had the audacity to sleep with another vampire's mate. Her gaze snapped up.

"You think Rosalee is the one after me? Of course,"—she snapped her fingers—"it all makes sense."

"Cara, you slept with me after that message appeared on your mirror."

"True, but maybe she didn't know that. She could be killing off your lovers one by one."

"You forget I didn't know the first two victims."

"At least you don't think so, dear brother," Kaleb added, earning him another warning glare from Kane.

"Something you need to tell me, Kane? If you knew these women—"

"I didn't. At least I don't think I did. I can't be expected to remember every woman I have slept with."

"How many?"

"You really don't want that answer."

"No, I don't suppose I do."

"This isn't about my sex life."

Cara rolled her eyes. "Of course not, Kane. Are you serious? It looks as if it has everything to do with your love life."

"Sex life," he corrected.

"Whatever."

"If she's here, trust me, she already knows everything about me … us."

"Great. And if she's not the one who wrote on my mirror, then I'll have two psychotic vampires wanting to drain me. Just shoot me now!"

Kane gripped her shoulders and looked down upon her, his dark gazing blackening in his intensity. "Cara, no one is going to hurt you. I won't allow it."

"You might want to talk to your wife about that."

Kaleb started laughing again. At least someone was having a good chuckle at her expense. Cara wanted to knock his sarcastic ass from the stool. Instead, she ignored him and turned to Kane.

"Get this straight, Cara. Rosalee is not my wife or my mate."

"Well then, color me confused. You just said you mate for life."

"Normally, yes. But there is nothing normal about this. I would never take Rosalee back into my life. My life is my own and I will see whom I choose. Rosalee no longer has any say in how I live my life. When she went against my wishes and cost me the life of my son, she broke that bond."

"What do you think Rosalee would say about that?"

Kane jammed his hand through his hair and blew out a stream of air. "I don't care what she'd say. It doesn't matter. And trust me, she knows that. Rosalee is anything but stupid."

"So you're free to mate with another?"

There was no mistaking the truth in his eyes. Kane had no desire to travel down that path again.

"As I said, my life is my own. I see whom I choose. Rosalee proved to me that finding a mate is not something I ever desire again. Not in my lifetime."

His confession shouldn't have hurt. But damned if it didn't. It cut her straight to the heart. Not that she wanted to be strapped to a blood sucking vampire for life, even if he had been the best sex she'd ever had.

Cara needed to distance herself the only way she knew how. "I need to get to work."

"So that's it? We're finished with this conversation?"

"What more is there to say? I have a job I need to do, and that's to find this person who's taking innocent lives. Even if this person is a blood sucker."

Kaleb laughed again, clearly amused at their expense. She might have shared the humor at the ridiculous situation, had she not been so damned miserable because of it.

"Look, I'm going to go get dressed and head for the office." The look on Kane's face had her quickly adding, "I promise I'll be back by dark."

"You're leaving me here alone with them?" Suzi asked as she made an appearance, her eyes wide and weary.

Kaleb's gaze snapped to the petite brunette before glaring at Kane. "This is the other woman you brought here? Un-fucking-believable!" He stormed from the room.

Cara gaped at Kane then Suzi, who didn't seemed surprised by Kaleb's outburst.

"Well, that was certainly rude," Suzi said as she flopped down on one of the sofas and propped up her feet. "What's for breakfast?"

KALEB SUCKED IN A DEEP BREATH, the icy-cool morning air feeling good to his lungs. His heart drummed against his sternum and his pulse beat a tempo in his ears. He hadn't been this angry since Rosalee had caused his nephew's death. Out of all the women Kane could have brought to his home, why this one?

His thoughts returned to some ten years back when he had first laid eyes on her: petite, brunette and a svelte body that made his mouth water and his dick hard. He had always preferred his women diminutive, loved wrapping himself around them. But he also preferred them spunky, and Suzi fit both bills to a tee.

She had walked into the Blood 'n' Rave, wearing a very short black leather skirt barely covering her small but muscular backside. He remembered his first thought was to mold his palms perfectly to those taut glutes, to pull her flush against the massive erection she had caused. He never could resist a great ass, and damn if hers wasn't first rate. Upon meeting her, he did exactly that and filled both hands, resulting in a dressing down like none he'd ever received. Suzi had promptly told him that her ass was off limits, and she would damn good and well tell him when or if he could ever touch it. Just the thought of this tiny five-foot-two stitch of a woman scolding a man who easily stood a foot taller, brought a smile to his face.

She had spunk all right.

Probably the reason she was the one woman who had grabbed him by the dick and never let go. And damned if he hadn't tried to forget their one orgasmic night. Kaleb had fucked immense amount of women since, but none had managed to scrub her from his thoughts. Reason enough to run like hell. Which he had and never looked back.

Kaleb liked variety, a different woman every week if he could help it. The idea of one woman having so much control over him pushed every one of his panic buttons. Mating wasn't something he could ever commit to. Better to take what he desired and send them on their way.

Mutual gratification. No questions asked.

Suzi Stevens had been the first and only woman to jeopardize that way of thinking. One taste of her and he had turned tail and run like hell as far and fast as he could. For weeks following their one sexual encounter, he had managed to avoid her, find other donors to meet his needs. That was, until Suzi had become Ion Tepes' main focus. Not that Kaleb could blame him. Suzi was a vampire's wet dream. Ion had not been one to confide in his father, and certainly not his mother, leaving his Uncle Kaleb his main confidant. He had made it known that he planned to win Suzi over, take her as his mate. And though Kaleb had no idea what her true feelings were where his nephew was concerned, she seemed pretty interested in Ion whenever Kaleb was within the vicinity, causing the green-eyed monster to simmer deep within his gut.

The night Ion had been burned at the stake, Kaleb had gone to the Rave to tell Suzi the news. The cold-hearted bitch hadn't even shed a tear. She had squared her shoulders and looked him straight in the eye, thanked him for the news, and walked out of the club.

Kaleb had only seen her in passing since ... until now. And he had his brother to thank for that.

Kaleb wanted to crawl on the back of his Ironhead chopper and head for the hills. If Kane hadn't needed his help catching this son of a bitch trying to frame him and destroy the Sons, he might just do exactly that. Instead, his duty to his brother kept his feet deeply rooted. That didn't mean he needed to share a roof with the one woman who made his gut burn with twin fires of hatred and desire.

One look at her moments ago made him want to throw her over his shoulder, take her back to his bed that she had just crawled out of and fuck her from his thoughts.

Damn her for showing back up in his life.

Damn her for making him desire her like no other.

Damn himself for allowing her to be his weakness.

And damn Ion for loving her.

Placing fists on his hips, he tilted his face skyward and roared loud enough to wake the dead. The door to the clubhouse opened and shut as footfalls sounded across the gravel. At first he thought maybe Kane had followed him into the parking lot to see just what the hell Kaleb's problem was. But the sound of the crunching gravel was far too light for someone of Kane's size.

Suzi's appealing scent wafted to his nostrils, just before she stopped short of touching him. He could have easily picked her pheromones from a crowd of donors. No one made him lose control the way she did, one minute wanting to strangle her, the next wanting to bury himself to the balls. Kaleb wasn't sure which side would win out.

"What the hell do you want, Suzi?"

"I thought I'd see if you were okay."

He turned on his heel so quickly she jumped back with a yelp. Good, she needed to keep up her guard around him.

"You don't have a caring bone in your body. You proved that when my nephew died, the one who loved you. Why the hell would you care about someone who loathes you?"

Suzi shrugged, unaffected by his harsh set-down, proving his belief that ice ran through her veins.

"You don't know anything about my relationship with Ion."

Kaleb laughed, though he felt no humor. "You're right. All I know is that your heart is made of stone. I lost my nephew and you lost a lover. I would have thought you would've shown an ounce of compassion."

Her jaw tightened, a muscle ticking in her cheek. "Regardless of what you think, I don't want to be here anymore than you want me to be. I thought we might be able to co-exist under the same roof and not see one another."

Jesus! There was no way they could both live under the same roof. "You seriously think that could work?"

"I'll show up at night when you're at the Rave. You spend the night in whatever bed you choose and I'll be gone before daybreak."

"And sleep in my bed? Why not sleep with Cara?"

Suzi sighed and crossed her arms over her breasts, drawing his gaze downward. "Because Kane forbid it."

The admission shouldn't have surprised him, but it did nonetheless. Kane played with fire. If he kept on the same path, he'd expose them all. His brother was a fool. Kaleb knew he had fucked the detective and had drunk from her as well. Kaleb would lay odds Gypsy hadn't been fooled by Kane's pretense either.

Cara wasn't a donor and never would be, due to her profession. She'd be deemed untrustworthy. Even if Kane decided to mate with Cara, should he be given the right to take a second mate, he'd never get a unanimous vote from the MC required to turn her. Kaleb would be the first 'nay'.

His twin needed his head examined.

Kaleb gritted his teeth and returned his thoughts to the tiny brunette before him. "So naturally you chose my bed over Gypsy's."

Her brow furrowed. "Get over yourself, Hawk. I was told to sleep in your bed."

"Since when do you do what you're told?"

"You really are impossible. I came out here to see if you were all right. Now? I'm sorry I even bothered. Go fuck yourself, Hawk."

"I'd rather be fucking you."

Suzi sucked in air. Good. His admission had shocked her.

"*That* will never happen again."

Without thought of repercussions, Kaleb grasped the hair at her nape and growled, "I am always up for the challenge, sweetheart." And then he kissed her.

CHAPTER TWENTY

"Y OU'VE GOT TO BE FUCKING KIDDING ME?" CARA SAID AS
she entered her office.

Talk about an instant migraine. Christ, she wanted to run back
to the clubhouse. Suddenly spending time with Kane seemed like a
day at Disney World. Had she known her day was about to get a lot
worse, she would have called in sick and taken her chances with the
biker vamp. Much more appealing than spending an hour with
someone who never learned the word *no*.

Cara tossed her handbag to the desktop with a thud. Her partner's gaze swung to her in surprise, no doubt wondering about her
off-color greeting. Of course, he had no idea of the history she
shared with the State Police Officer now standing by her desk, a
smug smile inching up one corner of his lips. Her life had just gone
from bad to worse. Cara wanted to turn tail and run like hell, but
she wasn't about to give the bastard the satisfaction.

Upon leaving the clubhouse, Cara had discovered Suzi had taken
her Neon and left Cara without a ride. She couldn't help wonder
what had happened. Both Suzi and Kaleb had disappeared without a
word. Swallowing what pride she had left, she about-faced and
asked Kane for a lift to her vehicle. A ride across town on the back
of his Harley and about an hour later, she finally made it to the office thirty minutes late. Thankfully, Sheriff Ducat wasn't a stickler

about time clocks, not when she had been putting in so much over-time.

Robbie Melchor.

Wonderful.

The last person on earth she wanted to encounter. Couldn't she call the Criminal Investigations Captain and request he put some-one else in charge of her case? Cara grumbled beneath her breath, having a very bad feeling that her day was about to get a lot worse, and no phone call from her to the State Police would make a differ-ence. At least not without some kind of explanation ... not one she would willingly give. Suddenly, the idea of spending the day in Kane's company didn't seem like a bad idea after all. Maybe feigning being sick could still work, except that tomorrow¬ Robbie would still be here.

"Nice to see you could join us, Brahnam," Joe greeted, eyeing her wearily.

Cara ignored her partner's jibe and inquisitive stare, and focused on the sorry excuse for a man gracing her office. One, she might add, she had hoped never to see again.

"Robbie."

His smile widened. "Nice to see you as well, Detective Brahnam."

"I don't believe I said anything about it being nice to see you. What the hell are you doing here?"

Cara walked past the man and his outstretched hand to grab her coffee mug from the shelf. Stopping by the Mr. Coffee, she poured herself a steaming mug of the black liquid. She couldn't stomach the thought of touching him, even if three years had passed since she last laid eyes on him. A lifetime wouldn't have been enough time.

"Captain Melchor came—"

"What?" Cara gasped, coffee sloshing over the side of the cup in her surprise.

She shook the scalding liquid from her hand, not really feeling the pain. She supposed a phone call to the very guy who stood before her would have done her little good to have him removed. Just her fucking luck. Robbie had been promoted since the last time they had seen one another.

"You made captain?"

"Why should that surprise you?" Robbie asked. "And careful how you answer that," he added with a wink, but she knew it for the warning it was and not the jest he tried to brush it off as.

Cara had no intention of sharing their past with her partner. Gritting her teeth, she turned, set the coffee cup on the desk for fear of spilling it again, due her now trembling fingers. The lech made her skin crawl. She took her seat, putting the desk between them, hoping to ward off any close encounter. Hernandez looked queerly between them, no doubt curious at her strange reaction to the Criminal Investigations Captain.

Sheriff Ducat took that moment to enter her small office. The room seemed to close in on her. Much more, and she'd be running outside, gulping air and praying to ward off an oncoming panic attack, something she hadn't had since returning to Pleasant.

"I heard you'd arrived," he said, shaking the captain's hand.

"Sheriff," Robbie acknowledged. "I've been sent to go over the files of your last three murders. It seems CEO Perkins has some concerns about how the investigation is progressing. He contacted

Superintendent Wilkes, asked that the State take a look into the case."

He aimed his condescending smile in her direction. "I can't say as I blame him. So, until this case is solved, I'm at your service. I will be personally overseeing these open cases."

"Whatever you need, Captain Melchor, Detective Brahnam and Detective Hernandez will be happy to assist you. We want nothing more than to catch the son of a bitch and rid ourselves of this monster."

Cara wouldn't be happy to do anything where Robbie was concerned but kept from saying as much aloud. The last thing she wanted was her fellow officers privy to her past in Eugene. Robbie made her want to go home and shower ... just by the way he looked at her. He made her feel dirty. The captain was worse than a criminal; he was a criminal who wore a badge. But she'd be damned before she ever allowed anyone to see her fear of him, nor would she give Robbie the satisfaction of seeing it.

Instead, for the good of the case, she'd square her shoulders and try hard to act as if his presence didn't bother her. The sooner the case got solved, the sooner he'd leave Pleasant.

"Very well, Captain Melchor. I do have some paperwork I need to finish. If you need anything, please let me know. I'm sure my detectives will be of help to you and the Criminal Investigations Division."

"Thank you, Sheriff. I'll be sure to let you know," Robbie said, shoving his hands into his pants pockets and rocking back on his heels as the sheriff turned and quit the room.

"So, how's Eugene?"

Robbie glanced back at Cara and smiled. She shivered.

"I no longer reside in Eugene, Cara. Surely, you know the CID is in Salem. Feel free to move back to Eugene any time you wish."

"I'll remain here. I have some very bad memories of my time there. Surely, you remember."

He pursed his lips. "Mmmm, no. Don't believe I do."

Cara glared at him, no longer caring if Joe saw the animosity in her gaze. "I'm here to help you solve these murders, Captain. I'm not about to reminisce with you."

Robbie cocked one brow. "Have it your way. I'm sure there will be time for that as we'll be spending a lot of time together."

"Not if I can help it," she mumbled.

"I'm sorry?"

"You will be if you ever bring up the past again. Now, can we please get to work." Cara turned to Joe. "Mind filling me in on what you've shared with Captain Melchor so far?"

"Uh…" His gaze went from Cara to Robbie's, then back. "Sure. I was just showing the captain Kane's photo and the file we have on him."

"Which isn't much," Robbie interrupted. "I think I'd like to question him myself. Can you see to it he comes in later this afternoon for a little Q & A?"

"WHAT THE FUCK IS THIS?" KANE all but growled, his boots thudding against the tiled flooring as he entered the interrogation room that the young punk of a dispatch had escorted him to upon arrival.

He had been formally invited in for a Q & A. But the question was why Cara hadn't had the balls to call him personally. Undoubtedly because she knew damn well he hadn't committed these crimes and knew he'd be good and pissed. No doubt she was getting pressure from somewhere or someone to solve them. Tab's father wasn't likely sitting tight while the Sheriff's Office chased their tails. But Sheriff Ducat wouldn't dare jeopardize their agreement where his club was concerned, especially if there was no evidence at all to point in their direction.

Kane's gaze landed on an unknown man gracing the back of the room, the only person in attendance he didn't know. The smug look on his face told Kane exactly who was responsible for his presence. He wore an expensive cut of black pants that sat arrogantly low on his hips, a grey, button-down shirt tucked into them, and a pair of black, Steve Madden shoes on his feet. Kane got the impression the man was full of himself. He bet if he had the notion to grab his striped silk tie and pull the man within an inch of his nose, he'd have the pencil pusher pissing himself. His kind rarely had any balls.

"Mister Tepes," Cara greeted.

The sound of his proper name rolling off her lips grated his last nerve. Though he knew she strived for formality in front of this unknown fuck, he'd make her pay for it later. Preferably her calling his name in the throes of ecstasy. The mere thought of her pretty lips wrapped around his cock brought a smile to his lips and an ache to his groin. Her cheeks glowed pleasantly pink. Good, at least she had the decency to be embarrassed for treating him as though they had no knowledge of each other. Kane wondered what this man would think if he knew the detective assigned to the case had wrapped her legs around him while he rode her up the wall of his bathroom just two nights back.

Next time, he'd fuck her in his bed.

"What can I do for you, Detective?" Kane asked, his eyes boring into her.

Cara knew damn well what she could do for him. He planned on collecting later at the clubhouse. He'd make sure Kaleb, Grayson and Suzi all had better plans.

"Have a seat, Mister Tepes," the pencil-pusher directed.

Kane resisted the urge to wrap his large hand around the man's thin throat and squeeze until his eyes bulged. He might have done just that if he knew Cara would walk away unscathed. Instead, he pulled out a chair, turned it backwards and straddled it, resting his arms across the back.

"You got something you want to ask me, Detective?"

"Captain Melchor," he corrected and stepped forward. "You mind telling me what you were doing last Thursday night?"

"I've already been questioned about that evening. My answer hasn't changed." Kane's forefinger indicated a manila file lying on the table. "It's probably all in there. That is, unless you can't read."

The smug shit pointed at a one way mirror. "For the purpose of the video. You don't mind that we're recording this interview, do you?"

Kane shrugged. "I have nothing to hide."

"Good." Melchor's grin inched up on one side. "Let's start with your name then."

"Kane Tepes."

"And your affiliation with the outlaw motorcycle club, Sons of San … you mind pronouncing that for me?"

"Sangue. San has a short A sound like ah and gue sounds like way but with a g added before it."

"San-gue," the captain pushed sounded out slowly. "You mind telling me what that means? I don't believe that's an English word."

"Blood. It's Italian for blood."

"Sons of Blood. Doesn't really give one a nice impression."

"It's not meant to."

He nodded, though letting the subject of his motorcycle affiliation drop. "Back to my original question again. Where were you last Thursday? For the video of course."

"I was out for a ride … sightseeing. There is no crime in that last I checked."

"Mind telling me where you were?"

"North Fork Road. Great night for a ride."

"As I recall, from your statement of course, it was foggy that night."

Kane looked briefly at Cara. "I believe that was Detective Brahnam's description. Not mine."

"So you're saying it wasn't foggy?"

Kane grinned. "I didn't say that either. You never asked."

Captain Melchor braced his hands on the table and leaned forward. "Was it foggy that evening, Mister Tepes."

"I do believe it was."

"You think it's wise to be sightseeing, on a windy road, in thick fog? Surely visibility in these woods would have been slim at best."

"I didn't have any problem with my vision that night, Captain. Any other questions?"

Kane could tell the captain didn't believe he could see a foot in front of his face that night, let alone navigate the turns. He didn't give a damn what the pencil-pusher thought.

"You anywhere near Bender Landing County Park?"

"I was out that way."

"You stop? Get off your motorcycle?"

"No. Next question?"

"You alone?"

"No. I was with my brother Kaleb. We frequently ride together."

"And neither of you stopped near the hiking trail leading into the woods there."

"No. And unless you have proof otherwise, I suggest you move on to the next question. I already answered that one."

"You know Tabitha Perkins?"

"I knew her."

"So then you know she was murdered."

"Detective Brahnam and Hernandez informed me. Too bad. Nice girl."

Melchor stood and began pacing the floor, hands locked behind his back. As if he could put the fear of god into Kane. Laughable is what he was. He stopped and turned his attention back to Kane, narrowing his gaze.

"Word is she was your girlfriend."

"Then the word you heard would be incorrect." Kane tapped the table next to the folder. "Read the file, Captain, I'm sure it says I've already denied that. I didn't have a girlfriend."

"Then what was Tabitha to you?"

Kane sat up straighter and glared at the smug man. "A fuck buddy."

"What do you think CEO Perkins would say to that?"

"I don't give two shits what the old man says. I call it for what it was. We met occasionally and we fucked. We didn't go to the movies; we didn't go for ice cream. We met at the Blood 'n' Rave and we had sex from time to time. What would you call it?"

The captain leaned back on the table again. "I don't believe you realize how serious this is, Mister Tepes. You're a suspect, our only suspect, in the murder of three women who match your dating, scratch that, fucking habits. What do you have to say about that?"

"I didn't do it."

"Prove it."

Kane tipped his head back and genuinely laughed. Shaking his head in his mirth, he leveled his smile and gaze on the man. "You prove I did. Now, am I free to go or are you going to charge me with something? And if that's the case, talk to my lawyer."

One of Melchor's brows angled toward the ceiling. "You saying you need one?"

"I'm saying I didn't do it. If you want to question me further about this then get in touch with my lawyer. I'll leave his name and phone number with that young man out there minding the desk. Now, unless you have reason to hold me, I'm heading the fuck out of here."

"No one said I was through questioning you, Mister Tepes."

"I did."

With that, Kane stood, turned the seat around and slammed it against the table and walked out of the room. He could hear the son of a bitch issuing threats against Cara and her sidekick. The captain ought to be glad that Kane didn't want to cause Cara further distress.

Stopping by the young blond, he said, "You know Charles McCreary?"

The boy nodded. "He practices law down on Main Street."

"You might want to make note of his name and number. Because if that fuck back there wants to question anyone from the Sons again, you tell him to call McCreary."

The boy said nothing, only nodded, showing he had heard.

"Then I'm done here," Kane said as he walked out the security door, through the small lounge and out into the blinding light.

Damn, he hated daylight. He grasped his glasses from his vest pocket and centered them on his face. Stepping over his Fat Bob, he turned the key and the bike roared to life. Without glancing back, he headed off down the road with a smile on his face.

No doubt, Cara would be at the clubhouse this evening wanting to apologize for Captain Pencil-pusher. He knew exactly how she could make amends.

CHAPTER TWENTY-ONE

CARA GRABBED HER HANDBAG AND HEADED FOR THE BACK OF the Sheriff's Office. Before she even got to her car, she heard footsteps rapidly pounding the pavement, coming from behind her. Heart in her throat, she turned to find Robbie closing the distance. Not that she was any more pleased to see it was him, but at least it wasn't the psycho vampire who wanted her dead.

She'd rather take her chances with the date rapist. At least now she knew his true colors. No more poor, trusting Cara.

"What do you want, Robbie?"

"I thought maybe we could go somewhere ... get a drink."

He certainly had nerve, she'd give him that much. "What makes you think I would go anywhere with you?"

He held his hands out, palms up. "Old times?"

Tears filled her eyes, but she refused to let them fall, or allow him to see he could still affect her.

"How dare you?"

He looked at her queerly, as though she were truly clueless. "Dare I what? It's just a drink, Cara. Nothing to get all up in arms over. A drink between two old friends."

"Friends? You raped me, Robbie."

He did a quick glance about to make sure no one had heard. "It's not like we hadn't had sex. And you were more than willing."

"Last I checked, no still means no. Go fuck yourself," she said, giving him her back and heading for her Charger.

Robbie grabbed her shoulder and turned her before she could get a hold of the door handle. "Look, Cara, I said I was sorry."

"Get your hand off me."

Thankfully, he listened, shoving his hands deep into his pants pockets and rocking back on his heels. "I just think maybe we could talk over the case."

"I'm tired. Go call on Hernandez."

His gaze turned hard and he clenched his jaw. "You really don't need to be such a bitch."

Cara's hand itched to strike him, but instead she made a fist at her side. The last thing she wanted was to provoke him further.

"Go back to the hotel, Robbie ... or better yet, why not head back to Salem. You're not wanted here."

A grin rose on his smug lips. "You may not want me here, but if you'd been doing your job—"

"Stop right there." Her voice shook in anger. "I'm doing my job. This piece of crap isn't leaving us anything to go on. But if you think you can do better, you go right ahead."

"I plan to."

"Just so you know, pissing off the one man who can possibly help us isn't the smartest thing you've done since you've been here."

"Kane Tepes? You can't be serious? Why the hell would I care if I pissed that piece of shit off? Have you forgotten he's an outlaw? I would say, I'm surprised...but frankly, Cara, you've always been a bit of a disappointment."

He leaned in and lowered his voice. "That includes in bed, dear."

Cara gasped as if he had openly slapped her. She stepped back and glared at him. "Get out of my face, Robbie. If you so much as touch me, I'll tell the world what you did."

His lips turned up again. "Go ahead, dear. No one will believe you. Why don't you run along. I'm going to go back inside and do your work."

Without another word, the smarmy bastard turned and walked back to the station. He knocked on the door, waited for someone to let him in, then looked back and winked, just before the door closed behind him.

How dare he?

Cara fought back tears as she turned toward her car. But instead of getting in, she turned and leaned against the door, staring into the distance. She hadn't even been aware of Robbie's promotion until this morning when she found him pouring over her case. Where was the justice in the world that a slime like him could be put into a position to convict others?

A tear slipped down her cheek and she batted it away. For however long it took to get this investigation over with, she was stuck with him. Like it or not. This time, it wouldn't be as simple as packing her bags and moving away.

The rumble of a Harley caught her attention just as she was about to get into her car. Cara caught sight of Kane sitting astride the Fat Bob, and her heart picked up a beat as butterflies took over her stomach. Just like that, Kane chased away all the haunting memories of Captain Robbie Melchor.

He brought his motorcycle to a stop at the rear bumper of her car. "You got a minute?" he asked over the rumble of the powerful bike.

She smiled. "For you, yes."

For once, she was actually glad to see Kane. "What do you need?"

"There's someplace I want to take you."

"You want me to follow?"

He turned, unstrapped a skull cap from the rear seat of the back and handed it to her.

Cara glanced behind Kane. "Last time I looked, your Harley was a one-seater."

"The benefits of owning a motorcycle shop. I added the bitch, uh … sorry, fender pad this afternoon. After I left here."

"I got the idea you preferred to ride alone."

"I do, don't get used to it." He laughed. "Now get on."

Kane helped her strap the helmet beneath her chin. Skull cap secured, she stepped on the foot peg and, with his help, lifted her free leg over the back fender of the bike. Cara sat, tucked her small hand bag between them, then wrapped her arms around his waist.

He glanced back at her. "Ready?"

She answered with a nod. Pushing off slowly with his feet and gently pulling back on the gas, Kane did a wide arc in the parking lot, then headed for the exit. Looking both ways, he headed down the road and out of town. Once they hit the coast and turned south on Oregon Coast Highway, Cara's curiosity got the best of her.

She leaned forward and spoke loud enough for Kane to hear her over the wind and the rumble of the motor. "Where are we going?"

He turned briefly. "Bookings."

Bookings? "You asked if I had a minute. That's a three and a half hour trip down the coast."

"We'll be there in three."

She caught his smile as he hit the gas and leaned into a curve. Wrapping her arms securely about him, she settled into the ride, knowing whatever he had in mind, it must've been important enough to add an extra seat to his bike.

THE SUN'S DESCENT CAST THE horizon reddish-orange as they reached their journey's end. Thankfully, the daylight hadn't completely dissipated as Kane wanted the benefit of light, though more for Cara than himself. Flipping on the turn signal, he leaned into the turn and pulled the motorcycle into a gravel parking lot, the tires crunching over the fine stone next to a picnic area. He felt Cara lean forward and peer over his shoulder as they approached a grassy knoll where he brought the bike to a stop and cut the engine. Cara lifted her leg and stepped over the back of the bike, stretching her arms and legs. Obviously, she wasn't used to riding on the back of motorcycles for long periods of time. He hoped to change that. Guess he'd need to keep the bitch seat on his back fender.

Kane had put off making this trip, not wanting to relive the pain of losing his only son. Thankfully, Cara had agreed to come along without question so he wouldn't need to face the grief alone. She had surprised him by remaining silent for most of the long ride down the coast, her gaze taking in the scenery whenever he'd peered at her through the rearview mirror. Maybe the quietude had helped her shed stress over the case and the threat coming from one of his kind.

Cara unsnapped the helmet from beneath her neck and waited for Kane to dismount the bike before handing it to him. He hung both skull caps from the handle, then took her hand and led her to a path leading into a small copse of Oregon Ash just beyond the picnic area. The farther into the forest they traveled, the heavier his heart beat. His chest felt as though an elephant had sat on it. Kane hadn't been back since the fateful night that had changed his life forever.

Cara trotted to keep up with his long gait, ducking beneath a few low hanging branches and stepping over fallen limbs and debris. "Where are we?"

Kane gave her fingers a slight squeeze. It had been easier to stay away, than to face the cold ugly truth. Returning to the site made it real, a bitter pill to swallow. Kane had hoped by coming back he would finally be able to come to terms with the loss. Cara made the heartache bearable.

"I've wanted to come back here for years now but haven't had the courage. I think somehow I convinced myself if I didn't see it, I wouldn't have to let go of my anger."

"Where's here?" She tugged his hand, causing him to stop and look back at her. "Where are we, Kane?"

He didn't reply, just turned and pulled her further into the thicket until they stood before the wide base of a dead tree reaching toward the heavens about twenty-five yards from the picnic area. Dim light filtered through the trees, illuminating the small area where they stood. After all these years, the tree stood like a shrine, hollowed out. No bark or vegetation ... just bare and dead like his soul.

Although many years had passed, it pained him as if it had only happened yesterday.

How did one come to terms with losing your only son?

"Kane?" Cara tipped her face to his. "You brought me to see a tree?"

"I brought you to the place Ion died," he said.

Cara gasped.

Kane stared at the gnarled dead wood that had held his son upright before the assholes had taken his head. Once it, too, had been a living and breathing thing.

Anger directed at Rosalee burned like fire deep in his gut as he recalled her tears, her repeated apologies when he broke the chains that bound her. She could have easily snapped the thick iron links herself had the cartel not beat her and Ion repeatedly, had she not lost a great deal of blood. Kane supposed Rosalee had been slumped, chained to the tree for at least a week after witnessing the beheading. She probably hadn't even tried to free herself, maybe even wished to follow her son's fate.

Her skin had the translucent, dead chill, telling Kane it had been a long while since she had ingested human blood, but he hadn't given a rat's ass. Had it been his choice, he would have left her there to die. Only repercussions from her stepfather kept him from doing so.

"I haven't been back since the night I found them, which was a few months shy of when I first laid eyes on you at the Rave." He turned, cupping her chin with his palm. Kane tilted her face upward and said, "Both nights altered my life forever."

Her brow creased. "Why would you not return after all this time?"

"I didn't want to face the pain. By staying away, I was able to bury the hurt, act as though Ion made his choice when he followed his mother. But every time I walked into the meeting room at the clubhouse, I saw Ion's empty chair and the truth stared me in the face. Ion followed his mother because of blind devotion, because he trusted his mother more than he did me, and the weight of that nearly crushed me."

Cara reached out, smoothing a palm down his whiskered jaw. He leaned into warmth. Kane suddenly understood his desire to bring Cara here. She had begun to fill the hole in his heart left by Ion. Christ, his feelings only put Cara in further danger. He couldn't risk losing her, too. If Rosalee had anything to do with this threat on her life, he'd make sure she paid with her own...her father be damned.

"I knew I had to come back, to bury Ion for good, and let go of the guilt that I felt somehow responsible."

"How could you blame yourself for Rosalee's actions?"

"Because I chose her. I mated with her."

"Without Rosalee, there would've been no Ion. How could you wish those years away?"

"He wouldn't have had to suffer and die because of me."

"You can't focus on the end of his life, Kane. Think of the years you had with him. No one can take away your memories. Focus on the good. Let Rosalee go. She's not worth your time."

"And I no longer want that part of my life to define me. I hate the man I've become."

Cara ran a hand down his chest, stopping just over his heart. His flesh heated from her mere touch and his blood raced through his veins. She made him feel things he never thought to experience again. That maybe he could trust someone other than himself.

"So what does this have to do with me? Why bring me instead of coming here with Kaleb?"

"Because with you I am no longer dead inside." Kane picked up a tendril of her hair that had escaped her braid. "I can't allow this son of a bitch to take you from me, Cara. I can't lose you as I did Ion. You need to start taking this threat on your life seriously. Let me protect you."

"What are you saying?"

"That I want you in my life. I think I always have from the moment I saw you." He paused, now running a finger along her jaw. He needed to touch her. Hell, he wanted her naked and beneath him.

"I'm not sure it's possible. The rules state I can sleep with anyone I want as long as I hypnotize them into believing I'm as normal as the next guy, that my facial features are no different than any man's. You weren't supposed to know what I become."

No more secrets. It was time to tell Cara everything, screw the repercussions. If she didn't run for the hills, then he'd do everything in his power to keep her at his side. That is, if this shit bent on destroying his life didn't get to her first. Kane shivered at the thought.

"Rules?"

"Vampire law. MC rules. They're one and the same."

"If you could've hypnotized me into not remembering ten years ago, why didn't you follow me? Why didn't you take away my memory then?"

"Because I didn't want you to forget, Cara. I never did."

Her large blue eyes rounded. He could easily drown in their depths.

"I can have sex with you, be with you, as long as you don't know what I or my brothers are. Feeding from you is strictly forbidden."

"But you already have."

"Yes, and I don't apologize for it. I can't feel bad for something so damn sweet." His fingers touched the pulse point at the base of her neck, felt her answering shiver. "You know that we can never mate either."

Cara intertwined her fingers with his again. "Because you're already mated or because vampires can only mate with each other?"

"Not because of Rosalee. She is dead to me. But, yes, vampires can only mate with their own kind."

"Would you even want to mate with me if you could?"

Kane released her hand and took a deep breath, hoping to calm the frustration and insecurities clawing at his gut. He couldn't stop thinking about this woman, couldn't stop wanting her ... hell, he had broken rules that he would have never thought to because of her. And yet, he didn't have an answer to that question. Mating wasn't something he ever thought to do again.

Not waiting for his answer, she asked, "How does one become a vampire?"

Kane wasn't sure what he expected her to say, but that sure the hell wasn't it. He glanced at her dumbstruck.

"I mean," she stammered, "should someone want to become a vampire."

"You would want to be like me?"

"I was just curious, is all," she quickly amended, her gaze darting from his, unable to look him in the eye.

She might desire him, that much he knew for certain, and maybe even care for him on some level. But he couldn't allow her to give up her humanity. Ever.

Kane gripped her chin again and forced her to look at him. "No one should ever desire to be like me. It's a curse, Cara. One you can't just take back because you've changed your mind."

"How so?"

"You never stop thirsting for human blood. Some days, it's all you can think of. Over the years you learn to curb your thirst. But it's hell getting there. You've seen what I look like when I get excited, hungry ... or angered. I become the animal inside. A thing of nightmares."

"It's not so bad."

He had to give her credit for the lie. It wasn't that long ago that he scared the living hell out of her.

Kane smiled. "Then you humor me, Mia Bella. I'm a monster. And although I'm not guilty of draining those women, someone of my kind did, and I can guarantee he doesn't feel bad about it. He'd take your blood without a care that your life is fragile and precious. And when he drains you, he'll toss you aside like yesterday's garbage. Who would want that life for themselves?"

"Someone who wants to be with you."

He raised a brow. Heaven help him. "It's not that simple, Cara."

"Then tell me why it's not."

Kane looked back at the tree as he spoke, the setting sun now casting heavy shadows upon it. He didn't want to think of the pain

Ion had suffered before they took his head. He would have gladly given his life for his son, taken his place. There was a dark time in his life he contemplated going to the cartel and asking for the same fate. Instead, here he stood with a woman who offered him a chance to be happy again, and he wasn't sure he even deserved it.

He glanced back at Cara, her eyes moist with unshed tears. "Kaleb and I are descendants of Vlad."

"The Romanian ruler? The Impaler?"

"One and the same. He's a distant grandfather, guilty of many dastardly deeds, but he is my flesh and blood. Vlad believed that there was life-giving energy in blood, and he was correct. His blood line continued the practice for many years following his disappearance. The tomb he was buried in was later found to be empty. But he has never been seen since. Metamorphosis began and through the drinking of blood over the centuries, our bodies began adapting to the practice. We grew fangs to better feed, our night vision sharpened to better hunt at night, we became stronger to subdue our victims.

"And as long as we continue to drink blood, we stay forever young and do not die. It's our fountain of youth. Our DNA has changed. Because of it, our blood regenerates at such a rapid rate that we can't be killed because we are able to heal ourselves. The only way to take out one of our kind is to instantly stop the heart from beating."

"Does that mean you're all descendants of Vlad?"

Kane grinned, realizing where her thoughts had taken her. "No, we aren't all related. We're not dating distant cousins or anything like that. If I were to give you my DNA, you would become like me."

"How?"

"You drink my blood. And before you say something you might regret, Cara, that's against the rules, too."

"I'm not saying that I—," she started, her cheeks reddening. Instead of finishing her thought, and further embarrassing herself, she said, "Then how do you get new vampires if it's always against the rules?"

"Should I, or any of my brothers, decide to take a mate with someone not of our blood, or if a prospect wants to join the club, it's taken to a vote. If all members agree, then our brother is given the okay to mate or the prospect becomes a member. Then he can give her his blood. Or in the case of a prospect, his sponsor turns him."

"And is that how you and Rosalee—"

"No, Rosalee was already one of us. She's the stepdaughter of Vlad's older brother, Mircea II. She's years older than I. Vlad's brother made her after he mated with Rosalee's mother, which means she's no relation to me. But that makes her a primordial, much older and stronger than I."

"Like the primordial after me?"

Kane nodded.

"Is Rosalee the one who wants me dead?"

"I honestly don't know, Cara. She's not supposed to leave Italy. Her stepfather forbid it after she recklessly caused his grandson's death. But I can't say for sure. I haven't heard from Rosalee in ten years, not since she went back to her stepfather."

Cara took a shaky breath as her gaze took in the burned-out tree. Kane wished he knew what was going through her mind, what she thought of the life he just expounded.

Long moments later, she looked up at him. "Even if you were allowed to turn me, you and I could never mate because of Rosalee."

"No, Mia Bella," Kane said. "I told you, I'm a free man. I'm no longer bound to Rosalee because of her actions. No vampire would hold me to that vow, except for maybe her stepfather."

"Not that I'd want to be your mate," she quickly added. "I was just speculating."

"No." He smiled. "Of course not."

He could see she had more questions, knew she pondered all she had been exposed to. Kane wanted to be open to her, allow her to get any answer she sought. No more secrets between them.

"Why, if not because of Rosalee, would I be against your club rules? You said yourself, I only need to drink your blood. You already drank from me."

"You're the detective who's trying to pin some very public murders on us." Kane ran a knuckle down her smooth cheek. "Some of my brothers detest you for that. Not to mention you're a civil servant in a pretty high-profile job. I would never get the unanimous vote required by the Sons to allow it. One nay vote and it becomes end of discussion. And once it's voted upon, it can never be brought up for a vote again."

"Oh."

He framed her face with his palms again. "Thank you, Cara."

And he meant it. She had touched his cold heart by her very desire to be with him, even if she hadn't actually come right out and admitted it. It seemed possible she might be willing to give up everything she knew as normal in order to drink blood and commune with him. Her desire to do so made his heart open up even more.

"For what?"

"For even considering to become a vampire to be with me."

And with that he drew her against him, touching his lips to hers, reveling in how well her body fit against his. Cara smoothed her hands up his chest and about his nape, anchoring him to her. He could feel the desperation in her kiss, smell the rise of her desire. Gently pulling on her bottom lip with his teeth, he heard her gasp but a second before he slipped his tongue past her lips. His groin instantly hardened as she responded in kind.

Lord, he wanted this brave woman.

Sex with Cara hadn't been just about fucking. For the first time in years it had been so much more, not just a brief joining of bodies but a connection of two souls. It felt like freediving without scuba gear, having the faith to take the dive without the benefit of any security and feeling more free because of it.

After Rosalee, he thought it impossible to love again. She had shredded his trust in the opposite sex. Kane had never wanted to go down that road again, to count on another for his happiness. But somehow this little slip of a detective, had managed to slip through the cracks in his armor and change his perspective.

He wanted more.

And damned if he didn't wish to be able to take her as a mate. Warmth spread over him, wrapping around him like an angel's pair of wings. It was almost as if Ion reached down from the heavens, wrapped them in his embrace and gave them his blessing. He broke the kiss, his breathing labored, as he rested his forehead against hers.

"I need to be inside you."

"It's a long ride—"

He shook his head. "I can't wait, Cara. I want you now."

Cara cleared her throat and whispered, her voice husky with desire. "What do you suggest then?"

Kane glanced back at his bike.

"Oh, hell no," she laughed. "That little fender seat you added was hard enough to take the whole ride here. No way in hell are we going to try and balance on that thing."

"Going anywhere in my present condition will no doubt give any desk clerk nightmares."

Cara reached up, ran her fingers over his more prominent brow, down his cheeks, and to his lips, where she felt the sharp points of his fangs.

"I can see where that might be a problem," she chuckled. "But I'm not about to go all commando out here, digging sticks and pine needles into the cheeks of my ass. That might just ruin the mood for me."

"Speaking of dampening the mood."

"That's the point, fang boy. Calm down, don't let your emotions rule your head. Then, maybe we can take this up in a room down the road where we can both enjoy the ride."

She took a few steps back, putting herself just out of his reach.

"You need to get the hell away from me, Detective, before I rip those khaki pants from you and take you against a tree. I have no problem fucking you right here."

"Those are the exact kind of thoughts that caused your issue in the first place." She waggled a finger at him before turning her back and heading for the break in the woods. Her sexy, swaying ass did little to help the situation.

Just as she reached the picnic area, Cara called back, "There's a motel right around the corner. I'll meet you there. You best hurry before I'm forced to take matters into my own hands. But don't worry, if you're a good boy, I'll let you watch."

His growl followed her as she slipped from his view. Damn, her confession of starting without him had his balls tightening. Cara certainly wasn't helping him get rid of his raging hard-on or his damn fangs.

CHAPTER TWENTY-TWO

ALEC HAD THE PERFECT PLAN. KANE WOULDN'T BE ABLE TO hide his little bitch away forever. She'd make a mistake sooner or later … and that's when he'd nab her. It was time to go for Kane's jugular.

Flush out his weakness.

This started out as Rosalee's desire to get revenge. But now Alec took it personally. The last thing he needed was Rosalee running her mouth all over Italy at how a lowly vampire got the best of him, a primordial. His position in Italy wouldn't be worth squat.

He glanced at himself in the mirror and adjusted the collar to his pristine white shirt, which accentuated the paleness, the dead chill his flesh had begun to take on. He needed to feed. Five days was far too long for him go without. Truth of it, he could go much longer but what was the point of abstaining?

Tonight, he'd drain another. Drink his fill. He'd make sure that little bitch had no choice but to arrest Kane, put him behind bars. They'd never hold him, not without causing himself a lot of attention by easily bending the bars or pulling them from brackets. Kane would have no choice but to comply with the law or risk exposing his brothers.

Step one: get Kane behind bars.

Step two: drain his little bitch.

By the time Alec was finished, Rosalee would be bragging about him all over Italy. She'd be proud to hang on his arm, to take him as a mate. He'd certainly get Mircea's attention. They'd create the most powerful family in all of the world. No one would dare defy them.

Kane had become a liability by shunning Rosalee, and Alec was about to teach him some manners. After all, the primordials couldn't have lowly vampires making them look bad without repercussions. Alec might allow Kane to walk away with his life, but his little bitch wouldn't be so lucky.

Alec's cell chirped. He picked it up from the tall dresser next to the mirror where he stood. Sliding the lock screen on his phone, he tapped the message icon that told him he had one unread message.

What's the status?

Lord, that woman was impatient. Damn good thing more than five thousand miles separated them, or he'd wrap his fingers around her pretty little throat. Two days had passed since her last phone call. What the hell did she expect? Impatient bitch.

Curbing his anger, he figured it best to placate her. The last thing he need was her running to Step-Daddy. Besides, Mircea might not be happy to hear they schemed against Kane Tepes. After all, her defiance of Kane the last time had caused Rosalee her present predicament. He didn't want her stepfather aiming his exasperation in his direction.

Kane will be set up on the morrow to take his fall.

And as soon as he finished up here, he'd put his plan into motion. His target ended his shift promptly at eleven. He'd follow him, and when the opportunity afforded him no witnesses, he'd drain him, stage the scene, then sit back and watch the show.

His phone chirped again. Alec gritted his teeth.

Don't fuck this up, mocked him from the screen.

Oh for fuck's sake, he thought, give him patience.

CARA'S HEART BEAT SO HEAVILY in her chest, sending blood pounding through her ears, she thought maybe she ought to worry about going into cardiac arrest. Staring at the back of the heavy steel door, Cara waited for Kane to enter. Time seemed at a standstill. What was taking him so long anyway? If he didn't hurry it along, she might just follow through with her threat to get started without him. The ache between her legs was damn near unbearable.

She had walked from the clearing in the woods and headed for the hotel just down the road. It had taken her all of fifteen minutes to arrive, another ten to secure a room, and five to strip naked and crawl beneath the white, cotton sheets. She had left a key card for him with the concierge. By her estimation he should have been following her through the door.

He hadn't changed his mind, had he? Please, please don't let the answer to that question be yes. Her libido had hit a high note and nothing short of Kane crawling between her thighs and burying himself to the hilt would assuage that ache he had started moments ago. The man was like a walking, talking sex toy. One she couldn't wait to unwrap and play with. Cara licked her lips, and ran her hands down the white sheet, pebbling her nipples that begged to be touched. Instead, she fisted the sheet at her sides and groaned her frustration. Hell, he knew exactly what he was doing, the rogue.

A half hour passed and the infuriating vampire had yet to make an appearance. If he wanted her hot enough to beg, then he had accomplished that in spades. Cara wasn't above pleading for what she wanted ... scratch that ... needed. And damn if she didn't need him right this second. Where the hell was that vampire, anyway? She had left him hard and wanting back in the woods. That part she wasn't mistaken about. His erection lay proof, trapped between them as he leaned down and kissed her. And oh what a kiss it had been. One hot enough to melt hell.

Maybe he had decided to feed first. After all, Kane had made it clear that drinking from her again was out of the question. Quenching his thirst might help him keep those fangs to himself. Damn the donor society for taking away all her fun. Cara had a strong feeling that if Kane ever decided to latch onto her neck, she'd never allow him to use the society again, not if it felt anything like what she had experienced two nights back. From zero to orgasm in two-point-one seconds.

A shiver passed through her.

Cara shifted beneath the sheets. The ache between her thighs had become damn near intolerable. If fang boy stayed away much longer, she'd wrap the sheet around her and go find him, to hell with who saw. She had needs, damn it.

Cara groaned. She had it bad. Somewhere along the way she stopped caring what Kane was or what he became when they got all hot and heavy. Truth of it, his vamp boy look was kind of a turn-on, especially knowing she could be the reason for the change in him. Come to think about it, his morphing into vampire certainly had its benefits. She'd always know if he were angry, hungry or horny. A heavy sigh escaped her. Cara just wished he'd hurry it along because she was more than anxious to get to the hot and heavy part.

As if on cue, the key card sounded on the door handle and she found herself pulling the sheet to her chin. Where the hell had her bravado just gone off to? Now was not the time to second-guess jumping into the sack completely nude, regardless whether he favored his women a little less forward. No time to worry about who he preferred to be the aggressor, she thought as the door swung inward. He could beat his chest caveman style for all she cared. At least she wasn't going to have to go it alone. Cara never had been a fan of one-sided orgasms. No, she wanted a repeat performance of the kind Kane had given her two nights back.

The door closed and the most gorgeous man she had ever laid eyes on leaned against it. His thick black hair lay in wild disarray, one that begged her to run her fingers through. His brow remained pronounced, accentuating his high cheek bones and hollow cheeks. His eyes shined like twin obsidians. Cara knew without a doubt his full upper lip hid two razor sharp fangs ... two fangs she wouldn't mind sinking into her flesh again, even if it was against his nature to break his stupid rules. Shouldn't that be her decision if she wanted to share her blood or not?

Maybe when they got back to Pleasant she'd have a talk with Suzi about joining the Please-Suck-my-Blood club. Although, the only one to be doing any sucking from her veins would be the magnificent vamp before her.

"You look as though you're ready devour something." Kane grinned wickedly. "Should I be scared?"

Cara ran her forefinger across her lower lip, then stuck the digit into her mouth and suckled it before slowly withdrawing it, earning her a groan from Kane as his smile left his face.

"You should be very scared, biker."

"Jesus!" he blasphemed.

His deep voice smoothed over her like an aphrodisiac, causing the ache to grow between her thighs. She swore if he just stood there, whispering the naughty things he wanted to do to her, he wouldn't even have to lay a single finger on her and she'd likely orgasm. Dear Lord, the man oozed sex.

Cara allowed the sheet covering her to slip just a bit, one of her nipples appearing just above the stitched hem. Kane drew in a sharp breath before stepping away from the door. His black gaze focused on her chest, then moved down the length of the sheet.

"Why don't you toss that sheet aside, Mia Bella. You won't be needing it."

"I don't know. I was a bit chilled."

"And now?"

"Why don't you come over here and find out?"

The animalistic growl that came from deep in his gut, sounded much the same as the one she had heard in the ladies' room what seemed like eons ago and had frightened her into fleeing. This time, that growl called to her in a more carnal way, rooting her to the bed where she wished he'd hurry up and join her. He certainly seemed to enjoy torturing her.

Kane shrugged out of his motorcycle cut and easily tossed it atop the bedside chair in the corner, narrowly missing the floor lamp beside it. Next came the black, long-sleeved tee he wore beneath the vest. Cara's gaze fell upon his chest and abs. Her fingers itched to walk up the contours and run her palms across the planes. The man didn't have an ounce of fat on him. No, he had a body like one of those Greek statues except with a slight dusting of dark hair, making the silver chain around his neck stand out in contrast against his dark skin.

Her eyes followed his muscular abs to his oblique, resting just above the waistband of his low slung jeans, arrowing straight for his groin. But it was the bulge that rested beneath the rough material that had her mouth watering. Cara wanted to please him as he did her two nights ago.

Just as he released the button and reached for the zipper, Cara dropped her hold on the sheet, and crawled toward him on all fours atop the mattress. His actions stilled as he watched her advance. Stopping at the edge of the bed, she sat back on her calves. His fathomless black eyes locked with hers. Cara tucked her tongue at the corner of her lips as she reached for his fly and moved his hand.

She ran her palm over the jean material, feeling the hard length of him beneath, earning her another growl. Cara's tongue ran the length of her lower lip again as she gripped the tiny zipper and carefully lowered it over his erection. He wore white boxer briefs beneath. Hooking her thumbs in the band of his jeans, she pushed them from his hips, allowing them to fall and pool at his knees. The boxer briefs barely contained his large erection.

"Cara," he whispered, his voice husky with desire.

Cara pulled the wide band down on his boxers, the steel length of him springing free. Cara wrapped a hand around his width, marveling at his size. Had she not already had carnal knowledge of him, she might wonder how he could possibly fit. But he did ... perfectly. As she began moving her hand slowly up and down his length, Kane watched her with avid interest. He looked about a half second from tossing her onto her back. She'd be damned if she'd allow him to deny her the pleasure.

Kane had tasted her. Now it was her turn. Leaning forward, her tongue darted out and captured the drop of pre-cum that had gathered on the tip, hearing his answering hiss just before she wrapped her lips around the head and took him as fully into her mouth as possible, gently sucking him. Withdrawing, she used her tongue to lick a path up the thick vein on the underside from balls to the tip, before taking him back into her mouth again.

Kane's thighs tightened as he mumbled something sounding like blasphemy. His ass muscles tightened against her palms. Gripping the hair at her nape, he pulled her away.

"Jesus, Mia Bella. You'll end this before we've even begun."

"Oh, I am far from being done."

Cara grinned. Grabbing the band of his boxer briefs that still stretched beneath his ass, she slid them the rest of the way off to gather with his jeans at his ankles. "Now why don't you get naked and join me in this bed like a good vampire?"

His black eyes gleamed and he winked at her. "Mia Bella, you have me all wrong. There is nothing good about the thoughts running through my mind or what I plan to do with you."

She raised one brow as she slid back up the bed. "I certainly hope not."

CHAPTER TWENTY-THREE

KANE'S BREATH LEFT HIS BODY, WATCHING CARA DO A BACK-ward crawl up the bed. Her pale white skin called to him as his hands itched to trail over every silky smooth inch. And he would. They had all night. He planned to take his time appealing to every one of her erogenous zones, so that she'd never think of another man. He'd be the only one playing out in her fantasies.

He shucked his boots, followed by his jeans and briefs before crawling onto the bed. The mattress dipped by his added weight as he made his way to join her. Her wide blue gaze darkened, the pupils nearly swallowing the irises. The scent of her heightened desire wafted to his nose, like a beacon of light beckoning in the dark. His fangs grazed his lower lip, reminding him that drinking from her again was not an option, no matter how heady the fragrance of her blood.

Grabbing her behind the knees, he slid her down the sheets toward his waiting mouth. If he couldn't taste her blood, he'd damn well for sure taste her another way. Cara gasped from the swift alteration that brought his mouth just scant centimeters from his intended destination. Kane dragged the sharp points of his canines over the tender flesh of the inside of her thighs. Never had the urge to feed been so strong. Had he been smart, he would've taken care of that temptation before following her to the hotel.

303

Instead of giving purchase to his strong desire to take communion, he followed the path of his canines with his tongue. Using his forefinger, he slid it between her wet folds and dipped within her moist center.

"God, you're so wet."

Cara squirmed above him, as she fought to catch her breath. Her thighs quivered beneath his touch. Kane added a second finger, dragging them slowly in and out of her, feeling the walls of her vagina clamp around them in response. The tip of his tongue circled her clitoris as his fingers continued to slide in and out of her like his cock ached to do. Cara's hips came off the bed, her hands fisting the sheets. He savored the sweetness of her, almost as delicious as that of her blood. His balls tightened and he wasn't sure how long he'd be able to hold out.

Sweet agony.

He wanted her wringing his cock as tightly as she did his fingers, knowing they already fit like perfect pieces of a puzzle. Drawing the sensitive bud between his lips and teeth, he gently suckled it. Cara's breath quickened, her chest quivered.

"Kane, I—" she said, seconds before the spasms seized his fingers and her head tilted heavenward, calling out his name again.

Hearing his name cross her lips in the throes of an orgasm was nearly his undoing. If he didn't sheath himself inside her soon, he'd most definitely embarrass himself. Kane removed his fingers, gripped one of her legs and wrapped it about his waist as he crawled the rest of the way up the bed. His lips hovered over hers as his black gaze fastened on the tip of her pink tongue, darting out and smoothing over her lower lip. His cock rested intimately between them, throbbing against her slick folds. Kane gritted his teeth to keep from selfishly driving home and ending this all too quickly.

Cara, her gaze heavy-lidded, flattened her palms against his ribs. Kane felt the heat of her touch like the flame from a candle. His breath drew in sharply as she leaned forward, pressing tiny kisses against his throat, before licking a path from his Adam's apple to his ear. She caught the lobe between her teeth, gently nipping it.

Bracing himself on one arm, he turned her head and captured her mouth in a deep, possessive kiss. There was nothing chaste about it. No, it was meant to be one of possession as his body longed to do, and he would soon, as he was quickly reaching his breaking point. As if Cara had sensed his desperation, she raised her hips, riding the length of his hard-on, giving him permission to take her.

She threatened his self-control like no woman before her. No longer willing to deny himself, Kane gripped her other leg and hooked it over his shoulder, opening her to him as he swiftly entered her. Cara's breath hitched and her gaze widened. His cock filled her completely as his hips rose and fell with each thrust.

His free hand palmed one of her breasts, dragging it slowly over the hardened bud before tweaking it between thumb and forefinger as he balanced on one arm. Kane watched her nipple harden and pucker. His mouth watered for a taste, but he didn't trust his fangs anywhere near her delicate flesh, not when his hunger rode at an all-time high.

God, she had great nipples.

Kane knew the moment she teetered on the edge of yet another orgasm as her lids lowered, hiding her sky blue eyes from him. Her head tilted into the pillow and she arched her back from the mattress, taking him more deeply into her, if that were even possible.

"Cara," he requested, willing her gaze back to his.

She blinked, her breath hitched as she focused on his vampiric features.

"Know that I claim you."

She nodded once in acknowledgement, the only clue that she had heard. But he meant every word, every syllable. Pity the man who tried to take what now belonged to him. She might not realize yet what his confession meant, but to him it held the same level of authority as being mated, without her having to become one of them. A tear leaked from the corner of one of her eyes. Kane leaned down and licked away the salty wetness, before licking a path to her ear.

"Come for me, Mia Bella," he whispered.

Cara's breath stuttered and her lids closed as her convulsions began, this time squeezing his cock as thoroughly as she had his fingers. Kane grunted, tipped his head back and uttered the word, "Fuck," as he let go and tumbled over the cliff with her, his release spilling hotly inside her.

His thigh muscles and ass cheeks tightened as white lights exploded behind his eyelids before collapsing his weight on top of her. He quickly rolled to his side and tucked her against him. Cara laid her head against his breast, feeling the gentle wisps of air she breathed, tickling the fine hairs on his chest. She used her free hand to smooth her blonde hair from her brow.

"Wow," she said. He could feel her lips curl in a smile against his chest. "And I thought it couldn't possibly get any better."

Kane chuckled. "I'm only getting started, Mia Bella."

A shiver passed through her. Tightening his grip, Kane kissed the top of her head. As much as he might wish it otherwise, he needed to get them on the road soon if they had any hopes of getting her back to the office before daybreak. And although he'd like nothing better than a round two, he knew she'd need to rest before making the three-hour trek north.

"Get some shut-eye. We'll need to leave in a few hours if we hope to get you to work on time."

Cara groaned. "You had to go and ruin the moment."

"I thought you liked your job?"

"I do when it doesn't include trying to pin a murder on you."

Kane tipped her chin so she looked him in the eye. "Still believe I did it?"

She shook her head. "But now that the state is involved..."

"The pencil-pusher."

"Robbie?"

"You know the captain personally?"

Cara lay there for long moments, not saying a word. Finally, she said, "We dated."

Kane drew his brows together. So Cara had fucked the captain? A fire began in his gut. Now he had more reasons not to like the man. "It better stay past tense."

"You have no worries. Trust me, I'd rather not be anywhere near the ass. But without telling everyone about our past, I'm stuck working this case with him." Cara glanced up at him. "He seems bent on laying this on your doorstep."

"Doesn't surprise me. You let me worry about Captain Melchor. You want to tell me what happened?"

Cara sat up, pulling the sheet around her nakedness. Kane wanted to pull the cotton barrier from between them and wrap her naked frame back around his. But because she seemed bothered by whatever had happened between her and the captain, he allowed her the space.

Her gaze left his and trained on the outdated, gold striped wallpaper. "He's the reason I left Eugene and came back to Pleasant. That and being closer to my grandfather, of course."

"Then maybe I should thank him."

Cara clenched her jaw and further closed herself off. Kane hated the emotional distance. He needed to hear what happened and she needed to let it go. "Tell me about him."

Cara glanced at him and smiled. "It's not pretty. You sure you want the ugly truth?"

Kane nodded.

"I've never been good at relationships. Blame the lack of great parenting. The best I had was my grandfather. My father was overworked and my mother only cared about reaching the bottom of a bottle. Seems being drunk was much better than spending time with the daughter she never wanted."

"I'm sorry, Mia Bella."

Cara shrugged. "I guess because of my past, I never really believed in love-ever-after anyway, maybe like-for-the-moment. And truthfully, I'm probably still no better at it. Anyway, Robbie was my superior at the PD in Eugene. Dating him was against department rules.

"He didn't care, so why should I. He was cute, paid attention to me. Eventually, we started meeting secretly. Back roads, back rooms, back seats. Wherever we could find a few minutes of privacy. It was fun for the time being ... exciting even as we tried to keep it covert. Then something changed ... Robbie changed."

"How so?"

"He became possessive. Not that I was dating anyone other than him. But he started having some of my fellow officers follow me when I was off the clock."

Cara paused, absently tracing the veins running along the back of Kane's hand that now rested on her knee.

"I confronted him with it. He didn't even deny it. He called me a slut, said I was seen having drinks with one of the third-shifters. That much was true, but we were just friends. He told me I was his whore and that if I took my pants off for anyone else, he'd make sure they had an accident, cop or no cop."

Cara glanced up at Kane, pain lacing her gaze. "I knew he would carry through with his threat. If I even looked at another guy, he'd take him out. I couldn't risk it. So I called off the affair. Told him we were over and if he even so much as looked at me cross-eyed, I'd tell the police chief."

Kane turned his hand over and intertwined his fingers with hers, giving her hand a light squeeze.

"As you can imagine, he didn't take it well." Cara's laugh rang false. "Hell, he didn't take it at all. Acted as though we were still together. One night, he showed up at my place. I tried slamming the door in his face, but he was too quick. He stuck his boot in the door and wrestled his way into my apartment. I don't need to go into

310 | PATRICIA A. RASEY

details. He raped me. Slapped me around. I wound up with several lacerations about my face and a broken nose, earning me two black eyes."

Kane growled as his hatred for the pencil pusher just skyrocketed. "I'll kill the son of a bitch."

Cara shook her head slowly, looking away as her eyes filled with unshed tears. "I came to terms with it, Kane. But I couldn't tell anyone what had happened or Robbie would see that I was the one on the wrong side of the dirt if I ever told soul. So I kept my mouth shut."

She looked back at him, a tear slipping down her cheek. Kane used the pad of his thumb on his free hand to swipe it away.

"That's when I moved here. I was able to put it behind me. That is, until yesterday."

Cara placed her palm against Kane's cheek as if she meant to comfort him. Jesus, what she had gone through. "He's set on solving this case, and I'm afraid he won't stop until he finds something to convict you with, even if he has to plant evidence. He'll play dirty. He wants all the glory. Always has. I'm sure that's how he got his promotion. He doesn't play fair."

Kane grinned, a grin laced with malice. "That's okay, Mia Bella, because I don't play fair either.

"I'LL BE JUST A FEW MINUTES," Cara said as she entered the clubhouse in front of Kane. "I need to change clothes, then you can run me to the office."

"You sure you have to go in today?"

Cara could hear the smile in his voice, but she knew better than to look at him or she'd never make to work. No doubt he'd succeed in seducing her right back into bed.

"How about meeting me at my house later this evening?" She didn't miss a beat, not giving his suggestion an answer. "I need to stop by the nursing home and visit my grandfather after work. Say maybe around eight?"

Kane's boots sounded off the scarred flooring behind her, kicking her heart rate up a notch knowing he was so close. She swore, as long as she lived, she'd always have a thing for this biker. Cara wasn't sure she believed in love, but what she felt for this man ... vampire, she mentally corrected with a smile, had to be damn close to it.

"You wanting to try out that big bed of yours?"

His deep voice washed over her, making her shiver. Lord, he could beguile her easily enough just by talking. Heat rose up her neck, undoubtedly reddening her cheeks, just at the reminder of how they had spent their prior evening. They had made love once more before getting back on the road. Kane had allowed her to sleep a few hours before waking her with his questing fingers and well-placed kisses before hitting the shower together. Damn, just the thought of it made her hot all over again.

The ride home from Bookings had been chilly, but Cara had used Kane's body for warmth and she hadn't minded the trip at all. There was a lot to be said for riding on the back of a motorcycle. Nothing like the freedom or the closeness. Maybe she'd start taking more trips with him. Cara almost chuckled, wondering what Kane would have to say about that. After all, he normally traveled solo.

She turned, walking backwards toward his room, unbuttoning her blouse as she went, earning her a low growl. The look in his now obsidian gaze, told her she had as much effect on him as he did she.

"Keep that up and you won't be making it to work today at all," he said, catching her by the wrist and pulling her flush against him. He kissed her soundly, probably in hopes of changing her mind. Cara melded into him, loving the feel of his heated skin against hers. If only they had time to indulge themselves. Instead, she had to hit the S.O. and contend with Robbie Melchor.

"Sorry, fang boy. No time," she said, pulling reluctantly away.

"So why do we need to go to your place?"

"Because I need another change of clothes if I'm to stay here tonight."

"You aren't going to need clothes, Mia Bella." One large palm encased one of her breasts, pebbling the nipple. "I plan to keep you out of them."

"Am I missing something?" came from the side of the clubhouse, startling her.

If her cheeks hadn't been red before, they certainly were now. She had thought the two of them alone. *Oh Lord, please open the floor and let it swallow me whole.* Kane's senses were far too acute not to have known that his brother was in the shadows of the room. She'd kill him later for not letting her in on the fact they had a witness. The amused look on Kane's face told her he didn't even feel guilty for playing her. Cara quickly slipped the buttons back into their moorings while sticking out her tongue at him.

Kaleb stepped from the darkened corner, his face heavily shadowed from whiskers, appearing as though he hadn't slept in days. He also didn't appear too impressed by their provocative play. Quite the opposite, in fact. His lips turned down and a muscle ticked in the hollow of his cheeks.

Bare to the waist, his build was muscular like Kane's, though not overly so. Tattoos covered more expanse of his bare skin than his brother's, giving him the edgier appearance. Kane sported two tattoos: the tribal covering his shoulder to his elbow and the Sons of Sangue skull, with two red-tipped fangs, taking up most of the real estate on his back, mimicking the skull on the back of the club's motorcycle vests. Though not opposed to a little skin art, she preferred Kane's cleaner look.

Kaleb glared at Cara, not hiding the animosity he held for her. His nearly black eyes brimmed with dislike. "Last I checked, Detective Brahnam was hell bent on arresting you, Viper. Something happen to change that?"

Having had enough of his censure, Cara placed her hands on her hips and faced him head on. "I was never hell bent on finding him guilty. I only suspected the Sons. It's my job to follow all leads when it comes to solving a case. This one being no different."

"And now?"

"He's not my pick of suspects, though at the moment, we don't have any others. Now that the state has arrived, I'll need to find a way to convince them he's innocent. Not like I can let them in on this ancient vampire creating havoc in Pleasant."

"Would you two stop talking about me as though I'm not in the room."

Kaleb continued to stare at Cara, as though weighing her admission. He steeled his jaw, then turned to Kane without giving her reply the courtesy of a response.

"Suzi's missing."

"What? Weren't you supposed to be watching her?" Kane roared.

"Don't pin this on me, brother. You're the one who didn't come home. And last I checked, I didn't sign up to be a babysitter to your women, nor did you ask me to."

"I assumed you'd keep her safe, knowing full well she could be in danger. Why the hell didn't you call me?"

"I thought I could find her," Kaleb's voice rose to match his brother's. "I didn't."

The two stood toe-to-toe, each face could have been carved in stone. Cara would have stood between them if worried they might come to blows, but she doubted Kane would raise a hand to his brother over a missing donor. Besides, by the look of things, Kaleb was more worried about the missing Suzi than Kane was. As a matter of fact, he looked damn near sick with it. Cara realized his anger was nothing more than a front to hide his fears.

Kane cursed beneath his breath then turned to Cara. "Get changed. We'll drop you at the sheriff's office. I take it that the captain won't need me today since he had his fun yesterday?"

"I'll see that he doesn't."

"Good." He turned back to Kaleb. "We'll drop off Cara then go look for Suzi. First stop, K & K. We'll enlist a few of the Sons to help. We'll find her."

CHAPTER TWENTY-FOUR

CARA STOPPED JUST OUTSIDE THE FRONT OFFICE DOORWAY, near the bank of computers lining the inner wall. Jeff Reeves was bent over, speaking with the daytime dispatch who had come in at seven, likely filling her in on the night's events before he called it a day. He laid his hand on her shoulder and smiled, saying something that made her giggle, then stood and turned his warm, show stopping smile in her direction.

He paused in the doorway, crossing his arms over his chest, his stance wide, his grin even more so. "Captain Melchor is waiting in your office," he informed her. "The man doesn't believe in getting sleep. He's been here since five."

"Hernandez in there with him?"

"He called, said he'd be a few minutes late. The sheriff hasn't come in yet either." His face sobered. "I hope it's okay I allowed the captain into your office."

"No, that's fine. He needs access to the files. He has a right to look over them." Cara sighed heavily. Robbie wouldn't be out of her life fast enough for her liking. "I just hope we solve this and quick so we can get Captain Melchor back to Salem."

"I can tell by your reaction you aren't too happy he's here taking over your cases."

315

316 | PATRICIA A. RASEY

"It's not a problem. We're lucky to have the state's assistance on this one." Cara blew off his assumption, though Jeff had hit the nail on the head. She'd have to be more careful to mask her feelings where Robbie was concerned until she could put this case behind them. She certainly didn't want to have to offer up explanations. "I want this case solved as much as he does. What are you still doing here, anyway? I thought you had evenings yesterday, not the night shift."

"I pulled a double." Jeff shrugged, his smile easy.

He always seemed to be in a good mood, even if he had gotten stuck working sixteen hours. Cara thought they could all benefit from his laid-back attitude.

"Third shift called off. No big deal. I can use the money and I don't have to work the next couple of days anyway. Now, though, it's time to get some shut eye. Got a date tonight."

"The redhead from the bar again?"

His grin turned lit up his blue eyes. Cara could tell that the dispatch had it bad for the girl. She hoped the girl knew what a great catch she was getting in Jeff.

"Pretty girl."

"And she happens to think I'm hot, too. Don't you go telling her any different, Detective."

Cara laughed, holding her hands up. "I wouldn't dream of it. Now get out of here, Romeo, and go get your beauty rest."

Jeff moved past Cara, calling back, "See you around, Brahnam."

Cara closed the distance between her and her office, her legs leaden and slow moving as she inched her way toward Robbie. She hoped like hell Joe moved his ass, as the less time spent alone in

Robbie's company, the better off she'd be. He glanced up as she entered the room, barely giving her any consideration as he looked back to the files he was flipping through.

"Find anything of use?"

"You mean other than the obvious, that those bikers are lying through their teeth?"

"It's our job to prove they're lying. Last I checked, we didn't." Cara couldn't keep the censure from her tone. She despised the air space the man took up. "Everything we have is circumstantial and a whole lot of conjecture. You find something in there I didn't?"

Robbie stood, walked to the window and looked out at the grey sky, giving Cara his back. His dress shirt stretched across his broad shoulders. Cara knew all too well that the captain kept himself in excellent shape and that the man didn't sport an ounce of fat. He hadn't gone soft with his promotion. Robbie was far too vain to let his physical appearance slip.

"You want to tell me where you were last night?" he asked.

Heat itched up her spine, her ire rising. He had no right keeping tabs on her, unless he seen her getting onto the back of Kane's Fat Bob. If that were the case, she'd have a lot of explaining to do.

"That's not any of your business, Captain."

"Your car was in the parking lot all night."

"Last I knew, that wasn't a crime."

He turned, leveling her with a look of pure malice. Lord, how the hell had she ever found him attractive? His icy blue gaze held no warmth or compassion, his lips but a hard line. Robbie Melchor could turn on the charm and was as handsome as any runway model. But beneath the surface, Cara knew the ugliness first hand.

"Who are you fucking these days, Cara? Your partner?"

"What?" Her brows knit together. "You disgusting pig. Joe is happily married."

"Who seems to think a lot of you."

"We're partners. That's what partners do. We have each other's back. Not to mention, he's a co-worker."

"Didn't stop you before."

"You cured me of that."

"I'm no longer your superior. So what's your evening—"

"Oh, hell no! Not in this lifetime, Melchor," she said before he winked at her, letting her know it was a jest she had stupidly bought into. He had always loved to get beneath her skin.

"Did I miss something?" Joe asked as he walked through the office door, perfect timing.

Cara wanted to kiss him for saving her from continuing that line of conversation. "Nothing, we were just discussing the case."

The look on Joe's face as he glanced at them both said he didn't believe her, but thankfully he let it drop. "So what's on today's agenda?"

Robbie clenched his jaw, clearly not as happy at Joe's arrival as she had been. He grabbed a thin file on the table and held it out to her partner.

"This is all we have on the rest of the Sons? You think you two might have thought to bring them each in for an interview."

Joe took the file from him and leafed quickly through it. It held very little. Cara hadn't wanted to believe any of the Sons were involved. Besides, the sheriff frowned on accusing them of anything without substantial evidence. And until now Cara didn't have enough to bring them in and potentially damage that relationship with the sheriff.

"I think it's about time we bring them in, one-by-one. Call them, Hernandez. Invite them in for a chit chat. I want to see every one of them this afternoon."

"And Kane Tepes?" Joe asked.

"No, I believe I heard enough from him yesterday."

CARA EXITED HER CHARGER, AND pointed the key fob at the doors. The lights blinked and the horn beeped twice. She pocketed the remote, then pulled her coat more closely about her, warding off the evening chill. Funny how she hadn't minded the cold at three in the morning on her way into work, not when she had been huddled behind Kane on his Harley. She picked up the pace, in a hurry to get inside and away from the brisk wind.

Spending the day interviewing several of the Sons of Sangue certainly hadn't earned her any brownie points with the MC. Robbie had made sure they talked to each and every one of them, with the exception of Kaleb whom they hadn't been able to reach. Cara had a strong feeling Kaleb was ignoring their request out of spite and they couldn't force him to come in for the interview. But Kane had been correct. The Sons would never give him the okay to turn her or to allow them to mate. The club members had made themselves perfectly clear how they felt about her. She might as well have had leprosy.

With a heavy sigh she huddled farther into her coat. What the hell had she been thinking anyway? Just the thought of ingesting blood sent her stomach roiling. She certainly wouldn't make an exemplary vampire. Spending time with Kane would have to be enough ... at least for the time being. Who knew how long before he tired of her. Too late to tell her heart to stay the hell out of it. Just the thought of letting go of him stole the breath from her chest. No, when Kane walked away, she'd be crushed and left broken-hearted. Funny how she had tried her best to avoid relationships at all costs, only to stumble head first into the first hot as sin vampire she met. Not to mention he certainly knew how to please a woman. Cara grew warm at the remembrance. No doubt she'd want to get him horizontal again first chance she got.

Cara ducked her head, a smile curving her cheeks, and headed for the front of the nursing home. Pulling open the outside door, Cara stepped inside the vestibule just as her phone jangled. She dug into her coat pocket, pulled out the cell, and looked at the name of the caller.

Suzi.

Cara slid the lock screen and placed the phone next to her ear. "Suzi? Are you all right? Where the hell are you?"

"Well, hello to you, too."

"I think since you pulled a disappearing act, I have a right to be a little worried."

Silence greeted her. For a second she feared Suzi might have ended the call. Cara even pulled the phone away from her ear and glanced at the screen to make sure they hadn't disconnected.

Replacing it, she asked, "You're okay, aren't you?"

"I'm fine. I needed to get away, but I felt like I owed you an explanation. I mean, you just apologized for the way you left town and now I'm the one walking away."

"Where are you? I can come get you."

"No, Cara. This time, I'm the one who needs some time. I'm going to stay with a friend for a bit."

"Here? In Pleasant?"

"No, though for now I think it's best to keep my location to myself."

"Why? Talk to me, Suzi. What happened? Did Kaleb—"

"No," Suzi said quickly and sniffled.

"Are you sure you're okay?"

"I'm fine." She cleared her throat. "Look, I didn't want you or Kane to worry with that crazy ass ancient running loose. Can you let Kane know I'm fine?"

"And Kaleb?"

"He won't care."

"I wouldn't—"

"Cara, please, just let Kane know."

"Of course. Will you stay in touch?"

"You have my number, Cara. Don't give it to anyone, not even Kane. I need some time. And the last person I want to see is Kaleb. I don't trust Kane not to give the number to his brother."

"I can respect that. After all, I know the feeling a little too well."

"Take care of yourself, Cara."

A lump formed in her throat. Who was she going to share her own turn of events with?

"Thanks, Suzi. You take care of yourself, too. And call me," she added quickly.

"Goodbye, Cara," Suzi said and the cell went silent in her hand.

Cara pocketed it as her chest tightened. At least Suzi had thought to call her instead of pulling a disappearing act as she had ten years back. She didn't deserve Suzi's consideration, but was thankful for it nonetheless. Pulling on the handle to the second entrance door, Cara headed down the tiled floor leading to her grandfather's room. Obviously, whatever had happened between Suzi and Kaleb while Kane and she were on the road led to her hasty exit. She doubted Kaleb would be forthcoming about it, so questioning him would be pointless.

Cara smiled at an older woman in a wheelchair sitting by the central desk, before turning the corner and continuing down the corridor to her grandfather's room. This late, not many roamed the hallways, as the staff busied themselves getting the residents ready for bed. Just outside the doorway, Cara pulled out her phone and tapped a quick message to Kane, telling him she would be done within the hour and that he could meet her at her house when she finished up. Leaning a shoulder against the doorjamb, she watched her grandfather.

He sat in a recliner, facing the window. His hearing wasn't what it used to be, so he hadn't even heard her arrival. Her soft soles made little noise as she crossed the distance between them. He seemed content to watch the birds and any other activity outside. His room faced Main Street, likely giving him plenty to gossip about with the nurses and aides as he watched people coming and going from several of the downtown businesses. Nothing probably went down without his knowing. Cara was looking through the field at Tom's Deli when she realized that it was possible her grandfather had seen the primordial.

"Grandfather?" She laid her hand on his shoulder, careful not to startle him. Cara leaned down and bussed his cheek. "How're you doing?"

He placed his weathered hand atop hers and smiled. "Having a great day, dear. You?"

Cara pulled a black padded folding chair beside his recliner and looked out the window with him. He had a clear view of Tom's Deli, only one street away.

"You watch the deli, Grandpa?"

"When I'm not in therapy or playing cards. Not much else going on around here."

"A few nights ago ... last Thursday, did you happen to see a man outside talking on a cell?"

"Lordy, girl, you're asking a lot of me to remember a few nights back, let alone yesterday."

"Nonsense, Grandpa. Your mind is sharp as a tack."

"What's this person supposed to look like?"

"I don't know. I was hoping you could help me with that."

He cackled. "I doubt I'm going to be much help if you don't even know who you're looking for."

"A man, or maybe a man with a woman, now that I think of it," she added, rationalizing that if Rosalee was involved then it was possible she didn't act alone. That was if she managed to get out of Italy.

"Make up your mind. You want me to remember a man talking on a cell or a woman and a man?"

Cara sighed. "That's just it, Grandpa, I'm not sure. The voice was definitely a man's. But that doesn't mean he was alone. All I know is someone called in a murder then dropped the cell from that location. We found it in the grassy field across the street from the deli."

"Well, then, why didn't you say that in the first place?"

"You remember?"

He nodded and pointed a gnarled finger to the grassy, empty lot in front of the deli. "It was a man, by himself. That much I'm sure of. Tall drink of water, he was. Wore a black wool coat. Like a dress coat for a man. Blond hair slicked back. Used too much gel. That shit gleamed, it did. He paced about, talking on the cell. Then, just like that, dropped the thing in the grass and walked away. I thought it seemed queer that he would just leave it."

"You remember anything else?"

He tilted his head, pensive, then raised his forefinger. "He seemed to wipe it, like you know when the screen of those things get dirty, then just dropped it. I remember because I told my nurse I thought the whole thing seemed strange, but I'm sure she thought it was nothing. After that, I was wheeled down to the common area. We had cards that night."

"What time do you play cards?"

"Seven. A few of us gather for a mean game of Rummy."

Cara patted his hand, now returned to the recliner arm. The timing matched. "Thanks." She kissed his sunken cheek again. "You may have helped. At least now I have a bit of a description and I know he was alone at the time he called the station."

Cara pulled out her cell, typed: *Heading out and I might have a description* onto the screen and tucked it away again. "Look, Grandpa, I have to head out."

"You meeting up with your man?"

Cara laughed, "I told you, Grandpa, I'm too busy to date."

"Bah, you take the time, girly."

"I will, Grandpa, soon. I promise." She rose and gave him a quick hug. "Don't you go giving these nurses a hard time, you hear?"

He waved her on, then went back to watching out the window. Cara hurried out the door and headed for her car. Maybe Kane would recognize the description, either that or her grandfather had just described half the population of Italy. She certainly hoped it gave them some direction, even if it was vague. One thing was for certain, the person who called it in wasn't a member of the Sons. Grandfather said a long dress coat ... not a motorcycle vest.

KANE AND KALEB HAD LITTLE LUCK finding Suzi. If anything happened to her, and it appeared this primordial was involved, he'd never forgive himself for leaving the little brunette with Kaleb. He couldn't fault his brother for her MIA. Though Kaleb had a habit of making bad judgment calls, resulting in Kane getting him out of one scuffle after another, he took total blame for this mess. He had put both women on the ancient vampire's radar. First by allowing his interest in Cara to cloud good judgment and instead thinking with his dick. And secondly showing up at Suzi's like a madman. Had he waited to retrieve Cara the following day from the Sheriff's Office, then Suzi wouldn't have been involved.

Kane sat sideways on his parked motorcycle as he took in Cara's empty house, his booted feet kicked out in front of him. He had received her text telling him about a possible description on the primordial. Hopefully, she had somehow stumbled across something that would aid him in finding this son of a bitch. Too many women had already died and Kane couldn't bear to think of losing Cara to the same fate. The piece of shit would have to kill him first.

Twin headlights cut through the black night, illuminating the single lane back road as a car headed in his direction. Instinct told him it was Cara, even before the car slowed at the beginning of the narrow gravel driveway. Kane stood, walked to the car as it stopped and opened the door, happy as hell to see for himself that she was all right. With this nut bent on taking her life, Kane hated the idea of her being out of his sight, even if it couldn't be helped. Kane reached out his hand, which she took, and helped her alight.

"You have a description?"

"Hello to you, too," she said with a saucy smile. The look on her face told him she was just as happy to see him, if not the jest in her tone. "Is it always business with you?"

His skin heated and his groin hardened. The scent of her desire wafted to his flared nostrils. If she only knew how badly he wanted to forget the world existed and jump her bones right now, to sink deeply into her and never let her go. Nothing compared to having his cock sheathed within her. If indeed there were a heaven, then he'd live every moment of it making love to her. Just the thought of laying her across the hood of her car and slaking the hunger she began just by her arrival had his dick standing at attention. But instead of ripping off every last shred of her clothing, he palmed the back of her head, and brought his lips to hers. Kane nipped her lower lip, then drew it between his lips before tangling his tongue with hers, thrusting deeply. She responded in kind, fisting the front of his black Henley shirt and anchoring him to her. Her body aligned with his, her abdomen resting against the thick bulge in his jeans. No hiding his erection or the direction of his thoughts.

Cara ran a hand down his trembling abs to the front of his jeans and over his cock. Kane released her and backed up, hands up in surrender. If they didn't slow down, he'd have her naked and atop her Charger before either had time to think about it. This far out, no one would likely see them, but Kane wasn't willing to risk it as long as the ancient vampire was still out there. There was too real a possibility he watched their every move and Kane would be damned if he'd allow the piece of shit to see him lose control. And he did, every time he made love to Cara.

"Now that I call a proper greeting," she said, her grin promising much, much more.

He quirked one eyebrow heavenward. "And I haven't even begun to play, Mia Bella. Now, the description?"

Cara's eyes danced in excitement. She told him about her grandfather's view from the nursing home and how he had seen the man who had tossed away the phone. She described him as best she could, right down to the long black dress coat. "Does any of that ring a bell?"

"Over six-foot, long black coat and slicked back hair? I'm afraid you've described half of our race. Likely not a Sons since he wore a dress coat and not a motorcycle cut, but still a pretty broad description. Though, we now know it's a male, which leaves out Rosalee."

"Unless she's working with him."

"It's possible, but I still highly doubt she'd be in the States. She's not stupid enough to go against Mircea's wishes. Her stepfather would not allow her actions to go without severe punishment. To

328 | PATRICIA A. RASEY

do so would speak of weakness, which is not a good trait for a ruler."

Cara placed a quick peck on his lips before straightened the neckline of his shirt. "Where's your chain?"

Kane's hand went to his throat. "I must have lost it. Hell, Kaleb and I have been all over the county. No telling where it might have fallen."

"I hope it wasn't costly."

"Ion gave it to me."

"I'm so sorry. It must have been precious to you. Maybe I can help you find it."

"I'm afraid that's a lost cause, Mia Bella." Kane had not been without that chain since Ion had gifted it years ago. The clasp had doubtlessly weakened. "But Suzi? I have no idea where the hell she went off to."

Cara grimaced. "I'm sorry, Kane. I forgot to mention she called me."

"Kaleb and I spent the day looking for her, and you forgot to mention it?" He shook his head and chuckled, unable to be mad at her for a second...especially with her sheepish grin. "Unbelievable."

"I'm sorry." She placed her palm over his heart. "In my excitement over getting a description of my suspect, I guess I forgot to tell you. She called to say she is staying with a friend."

"Where?"

"She wouldn't tell me. I think she wants space from your brother. What happened between them anyway?"

Kane rolled his eyes. "I haven't a clue. What Kaleb does in his personal life is no concern of mine. Though we should probably tell him so he doesn't worry. I'll give him a call."

"Make it quick. I've got something I want to share with you," she said, using her forefinger to dip the neckline of her blouse between her breasts.

Kane swallowed, his Adam's apple bobbing in his throat. Shit, he'd make this the fastest call ever to Kaleb. "You best make good on your promises."

"Oh, I intend do. I could use a little stress relief."

He certainly hoped to hell they were of the same mind. Blood rushed to his cock. Damn, as if he wasn't rock hard enough already. Much more and he'd be needing a new zipper for his jeans. Kane pulled his cell from his jeans pocket and selected Kaleb's name from his quick dial list. Kaleb picked up after the second ring.

"I've got news, bro."

"You find her?"

Kane nearly laughed at the urgency in his brother's inquisition. Maybe there was something between the two Kane hadn't been aware of, causing him to wonder what Suzi's motives were when she had come on to him at the Rave.

"She's with a friend."

"Where?"

"Didn't say. She called Cara to let her know she was all right. Apparently, she needs to cool off. You know anything about that?"

Silence greeted him.

"What aren't you telling me, Hawk?"

"Look, it's nothing. As long as she's okay, then she's free to do whatever the hell she wants. See you back at the clubhouse," he said, and ended the call.

Kane pulled his cell away from his ear, looked at it queerly, then shoved it back into his pocket. Suzi could gladly be Kaleb's problem, not his.

"Everything okay?"

"Nothing to worry ourselves over," Kane said, his gaze traveling her length. He quirked one eyebrow upward. "Now, about getting inside?"

Cara laughed, turned and jogged for her back door, Kane fast on her heels. If he had his way, she'd never make it up those stairs. He wanted her fiercely. Stepping inside the back door and into the kitchen, Kane gripped her wrist and yanked her against him. Using one hand to trap her wrists overhead, he backed her against the wall. The other hand grabbed her thigh and wrapped her leg about his waist, bringing her center flush against his cock.

Kane breathed in her desire. His fangs grew, his eyes blackened, and that's when the smell of freshly spilled blood caught his attention. He dropped his hold on her, taking a quick look about. His nostrils flared as he inhaled deeply again.

Shit!

Kane headed for the stairs. Cara stayed her position. Her limbs trembled.

Finally, taking a quick breath, she followed him up narrow stairwell.

"Kane? What is it?"

He stopped just inside her room. Cara bumped into him, tried to step around him. Kane help out his hand, though too late to keep her from viewing the scene. Her gaze widened, and she drew in a sharp breath. Blood was everywhere: the walls, her bed, the carpeting. The fucking room was bathed in it. In the middle of her bed lay a young man, legs and arms askew, eyes wide in horror, neck sliced ear to ear.

"My God! Jeff," Cara whispered, before dropping to her knees.

CHAPTER TWENTY-FIVE

CARA SENT KANE PACKING THE MINUTE SHE HAD COLLECTED herself and dialed the S.O. Finding Jeff Reeves dead in her bed had been a huge shock, not to mention the gruesomeness of the crime scene. Out of all the years she had spent on the force, here or in Eugene, never had she seen anything quite like it. Kane hadn't wanted to leave, but he had little choice in the matter. His features wouldn't return to their human state with the scent of fresh blood painting her room. Not to mention having him found anywhere near the crime scene would surely only spell trouble. She promised to call as soon as she was able to get away.

The killer's preference, until now, had been women with pale-blonde hair which made sense why she herself had been targeted. That and her relationship, whatever it might be, with Kane. The victims all shared a similar appearance, but she had yet to determine if Kane was indeed a common denominator as well, since she could only positively link him to Tabitha and her at this point.

But Jeff?

He didn't fit the MO at all. His death made no sense. She had last seen him leaving the office early this morning, excited about an upcoming date. Cara drew her lower lip between her teeth to still its quivering. He wouldn't be meeting the redhead from the bar after all. Cara blew out an unsteady stream of air. She needed to suck it up. After all, she had a job to do, and falling apart wouldn't be of help to anyone. Once her partner arrived, they could process the scene and pray their perp had gotten sloppy and offered them some sort of evidence.

Kane had detected the primordial's scent, so she highly doubted they'd find anything of use this time either. Could it be possible this ancient vampire had sent her yet another warning? Jesus! Jeff didn't deserve to be a pawn in this sick game. Three times this piece of work had been inside her home, once standing over her while she had slept, and yet she'd lived to tell Kane about it. Why not kill her when he had the opportunity? Tears leaked from the corners of her eyes. She swatted them away.

Son of a bitch!

Cara wanted to strike something at the injustice. Jeff Reeves was a good-hearted, innocent young man who had just begun to live his life. His smile and easy-going attitude was a beacon of light that would be sorely missed at the office. And all because of some damned vendetta against Kane? She couldn't allow this piece of shit to take anyone else's life because of her. If need be, she'd personally hand herself over to the bastard.

"Cara?"

Her heart leapt to her throat at the sound of her partner's voice. Not that she wasn't glad to have him there, but she knew Robbie probably followed close behind. No way would he want to be left out of something of this magnitude, especially not when it had happened on Cara's doorstep. The sheriff would also want answers as to how this linked to her. The breaking and entering she had been able to blow off as a random crime, even if the killer had left a threat on her mirror. But this time her room was bathed in the dispatch's blood as he lay sightless in her bed. Cara approached the blood-soaked mattress, fighting to draw breath as she looked down on her co-worker, legs and arms askew. The lump in her throat threatened to choke the very life from her as more tears trekked down her cheeks.

Her ears buzzed, nearly drowning out the two sets of footfalls pounding up her stairs as she fought to stay upright. Blackness rimmed her vision. She didn't even turn around when her co-workers stopped on the landing, not until a "What the hell?" came from Robbie behind her.

Cara turned in time to see Joe Hernandez crossing himself while Robbie Melchor stood to his left, mouth slightly agape.

"You found him this way?" Joe asked, though Cara didn't think he expected an answer. Moisture pooled in his eyes. "Jesus, Cara."

Robbie skirted Joe and approached the bed. "Have you touched anything?"

Numbly, Cara shook her head. She didn't respond for fear of falling to pieces.

Placing a hand on her shoulder, Robbie said, "Why don't you sit this one out, Detective?"

Cara started to object, but he stopped her. "Cara, you're in shock. You aren't going to do us any good. A few uniforms are on the way, as well as Sheriff Ducat. We'll turn this place upside down. Why don't you have a seat downstairs and let us process the scene?"

"I'll be fine," she whispered, knowing she was anything but.

"It's not a suggestion, Cara. It's an order. The state has precedence over this case."

Panic rose in her chest. She owed it to Jeff to find his killer. "You can't cut me out!"

"I can, and I just did. You can either remove yourself from the scene, or I'll have Hernandez escort you back to the S.O. for evaluation."

Cara looked at her partner, who glanced down at the floor. She'd get no help from Joe. And maybe rightly so. She was an emotional mess and wouldn't do anyone any justice.

"You win, Captain," she said, hating giving him that kind of power over her.

But in truth she wanted to bury herself in Kane's comfort, and would, once this latest nightmare was over and she found her way back to the clubhouse. Cara wasn't sure she'd ever be able to sleep in this room again. She took one final look around the bloody room, then headed for the stairs.

THE SUN HAD LONG AGO SET, the outside safety light casting long shadows across her wood floor. Cara scrubbed a palm down her face. She had cried her last tear, or at least it felt as though she had nothing left to give. Several hours had dragged by. Her fellow officers passed by as they collected evidence. The ME had come and gone long ago, wheeling Jeff out on a stretcher, sealed in a black body bag. Cara had barely been able to watch as the metal cart with squeaky wheels rolled by her, leaving her drained.

Long moments following, she had finally drifted off to sleep, even though images of elongated teeth, sharp blades, and blood flying about haunted her every time she dare to close her eyes. Sheriff Ducat had even sat with her on the sofa for a time, one arm about her shoulders, his free hand holding her. But Cara couldn't remember one damn reassuring word anyone said to her. Her mind had numbed, and in between drifting off to sleep, it seemed as if the world had morphed into some weird sort of slow motion.

All she could think about was getting back into Kane's comforting arms. Only he could understand the magnitude of what had happened, knowing what sort of monster was responsible. Cara finally got it. Kane had been trying to tell her that the S.O. would be no match for this perp, that only he and his brethren would be able to take this piece of shit down.

She swiped at a lone tear as she attempted to swallow the lump that had taken residence in her throat. If she could find this fuck, she'd hand him over to Kane and the Sons personally, screw the law enforcement looking for him. They had no idea what they were up against. Truth be told, they would be much better off allowing the Sons of Sangue to take care of their own. Cara leaned her head against the back of the sofa, wishing everyone would just depart. Not like they were going to find anything on this fuck. Only what he wanted them to find. It had to be well past midnight. Cara didn't have a clock in the living room and the last she'd looked, the kitchen clock's hands had just passed eleven-thirty.

"Cara?"

She opened her eyes and glanced at Joe Hernandez, not liking the look in his gaze. "Did you find something?"

His jaw tightened, holding out his arm, a paper bag clutched in his fist. Cara grabbed it from his outstretched hand and opened it, looking in, careful not to disturb the contents. A red and white shop rag lay at the bottom. She didn't have to touch it to know its origin.

K & K was printed on the top right corner. She recognized it instantly as one from Kane and Kaleb's motorcycle shop.

Cara glanced up at Joe. "You found this upstairs?" she asked, wondering if Kane had possibly dropped it at some point. "Maybe Kane—"

"It was beneath Jeff, Cara. Trapped between him and the mattress. And unless you've taken to sleeping with the dirtbag biker, it's hard to dispute the evidence."

She shook her head. "It's not possible. Kane was with me."

"You were with Robbie and me all day. The ME said T.O.D. was four to six hours tops before you found him. Where was Viper today?"

"With Kaleb," she barely whispered, looking back into the bag. "That doesn't mean the rag belonged to him."

"That's not all."

Her gaze snapped back up as he handed her an envelope she hadn't noticed him holding earlier. Cara took it and opened the flap. Her breath stuck in her chest as her world tilted on its axis. Her ears buzzed, her heart ached.

"I take it you've seen that before?"

I must have lost it.

She nodded slowly, remembering Kane walking toward her in the hotel room, bare from the waist up ... save for the silver chain that encircled his neck.

Ion gave it to me.

"It looks like the one Kane wears."

"Then if we find him, we'll be able to verify if he still has his."

A sob tore through her, before she managed to shake her head. "He lost his."

Joe's gaze hardened. "When, Cara?"

"I don't know. I saw him after work and he wasn't wearing it."

Cara looked beyond her partner to see Robbie standing at the bottom of the stairwell. She placed a hand over her quivering lips. Before she could think of one thing to say in Kane's defense, Robbie approached Joe and cleared his throat. Joe faced the captain.

"Put an APB out on Kane Tepes, Detective. I'll meet you at the S.O. We'll have a warrant for his arrest ready within the hour."

"I'll get dressed," Cara said. She needed to be there for Kane.

Robbie turned his darkened gaze on her. "From what I've been hearing, you're too fucking close to this whole mess, Brahnam. As of now, you're off the case."

Not giving her a chance to reply, he headed for her back door and into the black of night. She returned her attention to Joe.

"You can't think Kane is guilty."

"Christ, Cara. Wake up. The chain was gripped in Reeves' left hand. I have to head to the S.O. I'll leave a uniform here with you. You shouldn't be alone."

"I'll be fine."

"No, Cara, you won't. Besides, I can't chance you'll call Kane to warn him." He placed a warm hand on her shoulder, his look pitying. "Get some rest."

Joe walked out, leaving Deputy Higgins standing by the door watching her. Cara curled up on the couch, wrapped her arms about herself and cried the tears she thought she no longer had. Surely, she hadn't been that much of a fool. Kane couldn't possibly be guilty of killing Dispatcher Reeves or ransacking her house and threatening her life.

"WHAT THE FUCK IS THIS ABOUT?" Kane asked, barely containing the desire to wrap his fingers around the pencil-pusher's throat as he stood on the stoop of the clubhouse. Kane's hands fisted at his side. Now was not the time to teach this ass a lesson in manners.

The captain's condescending smile caused his ire to inch up his spine. "Kane Tepes," he began and flipped open his badge, "we're here on official business, I'm afraid. You'll need to come with us."

Kane looked to the three black and whites that sat in the gravel parking lot, red and blue LEDs lighting up the dark night. Six deputies stood, guns drawn, with Detective Hernandez just a few feet behind the captain.

"Where's Cara? Is she all right?"

He'd never forgive himself if something happened to her after leaving her alone at the house with the dead body. He had stood close by until the uniforms arrived, but that didn't mean the primordial couldn't have slipped past his notice.

"She's home, resting. But she's of no concern to you."

"Then what's this about?"

"Kane Tepes, we have a warrant here for your arrest."

His brows knit together. "On what grounds?"

"For murder, four of them to be exact."

"You can't be fucking serious?"

"Where were you today between the hours of ten and two?"

He rubbed his brow. Why the hell was Kaleb always MIA when he needed him most? Even Grayson had taken off about two hours earlier, leaving Kane alone to deal with these fucks. He had no choice but to follow their direction to keep from creating an even bigger mess. Once at the Sheriff's Office, he could talk to Ducat.

"I was with my brother Kaleb," he said. "All day."

"Is your brother here so we can speak to him?"

"No."

"Then you'll get your phone call. Turn around, hands on the door, legs spread."

Kane did as the captain asked, though he felt more like draining him of every last ounce of blood. At least he'd be deserving of Kane's wrath. One of the deputies stepped up and patted him down. Thankfully, Kane had removed his hunting knife when he had arrived home earlier, and he carried no other weapons. Detective Hernandez read Kane his Miranda rights as he slapped one cuff on Kane's wrist, then pulled his arm behind his back before yanking on the other and securing both wrists. Hernandez led him to the unmarked car, placed his hand on the top of Kane's head and assisted him into the back of the cruiser.

These clowns were fooling themselves if they thought simple cuffs and the backseat of a secured cop car could contain him. But for now he'd humor them. Kane needed to talk to Cara. Why hadn't she called to warn him about what the hell was going down?

Gritting his teeth, feeling the ache clear to his ears, he leaned his head against the backseat of the cruiser.

Fuck.

He needed to get hold of Kaleb and fast. If Cara was indeed at home resting, that meant she was easy pickings for the primordial. Maybe that had been the ancient vampire's plan all along. Once they reached the Sheriff's Office, he'd make sure Ducat found Kaleb and delivered his brother a message to get Cara out of that house, out of town, and under the Sons' protection, stat.

CHAPTER TWENTY-SIX

S OMETHING WAKENED CARA. SHE COULDN'T BE SURE OF THE cause as she'd been out like a light. No dreams, just a deep sleep. Shaking her head, she tried to dislodge the groggy remnants. When she first laid her head on the arm of the sofa, she thought she had no hope of catching any shut-eye. Every time she closed her eyes, the bloody mess of her room painted the back of her eyelids, that and her fellow officer wide-eyed and unseeing in her bed. Cara must have been more tired than she imagined or the shock of the day had totally drained her, for she had fallen easily to sleep once she allowed her eyes to close. She couldn't be sure how much time had lapsed.

Sitting up, Cara peered into the darkness. Hadn't she left on the kitchen fluorescent light over her sink? Even the safety light outside didn't seem to add illumination through the windows. Total blackness hung thick in the room, with visibility being somewhere close to a foot. Maybe Higgins had turned off the lighting so he could catch a little nap himself. Slacker. The deputy's feet were kicked out in front of him as he reclined in the chair sitting adjacent to the couch. Sure enough, he didn't move a muscle as she stood.

Some watch dog they left in charge.

Cara made a mental note not to put Higgins on nighttime surveillance in the future. Using the arm of the sofa to steady herself, she stood and stretched her cramped muscles. The previous day's images flooded her thoughts like a damn breaking loose: the blood staining her room, Jeff sightlessly staring at the ceiling, Kane by her side.

Kane.

Now that she didn't have anyone from the S.O. watching over her shoulder, she needed to warn Kane that Robbie would no doubt have a warrant out for his arrest. Though Robbie had presented her with the evidence of Kane's chain clutched in the dead dispatch's hand, she knew without a doubt Kane had not murdered those women and that the primordial had somehow gotten hold of the choker and planted it on the body.

Her breathing hitched and she strangled back a sob.

Poor Jeff. He hadn't deserved to be caught in the middle of the nightmare that had become her life. Tears pricked her eyes, but didn't fall. She needed to suck it up. The living still needed her, and getting caught up in emotion now would do no one any good, especially Kane. She needed to get to Kane before Robbie did.

And Higgins untimely nap had just given her the opportunity.

Cara did a quick sweep of the living room, looking on the end tables for her cell. Three end tables and the kitchen table behind her, she had come up empty handed. If Higgins had planned a little power nap, then possibly he had pocketed the phone. Approaching the deputy, she ran her hand across the surface of the end table next to his chair, finding nothing more than her black, wrought iron lamp. At this point, she doubted that if she turned it on, Higgins would even notice. She could have left the house and been long gone without him the wiser.

Reaching for his pockets, thinking maybe he had thought best to keep her cell where she might not dare search, she noted the deputy's eyes weren't closed after all, but staring right at her ... or rather sightlessly through her.

Her scream cut short as a hand covered her mouth and a strong forearm wrapped her windpipe. Cara fought the hold, as she tried desperately to draw breath. Losing consciousness was inevitable if she didn't break the iron hold on her throat. Dear Lord, she hoped Kane wasn't sitting the night in county lockup. If she was unable to get word to him, he'd be too late to save her. Her limbs numbed, her ears buzzed. She couldn't suck in oxygen.

"Nighty night," her attacker whispered, warm breath feathering across her ear just before her world blackened.

KANE PACED THE CEMENT FLOORING, waiting to hear back from Kaleb. It didn't take much to reach each side of the six-by-eight foot cell with his long gait. Old iron, prison bars closed off one end, making him feel much like a caged animal. And truth of it, he wasn't far from being one. He could easily jerk the old iron from the cinder block walls had he wanted and been on the street looking for Cara in the blink of an eye. But Kaleb had convinced him to hold tight, to not draw unnecessary attention to the Sons.

"This is non-negotiable, Viper. Stay put," he had said. "I'll find her."

His brother had given him a direct order. And with Kaleb acting as club pres while he sat incapacitated, Kane was expected to follow the directive without question. He needed to keep the Sons' best interest in mind. Breaking out of jail would only cause them more problems and draw questions the club wasn't equipped to answer.

Thankfully, he had been able to get hold of his twin upon arrival at county lockup. Kaleb had been pretty pissed at having to prioritize finding Cara. After all, the detective wasn't high on his brother's list of favorite people. To Kaleb, she had done nothing but cause trouble from the minute she entered their lives, not to mention she fronted the team trying to convict Kane of murder. Now here he stood, in the very cell she had first tried hard to put him in, but hopefully didn't believe in his guilt, no matter the evidence presented her.

Kane sat heavily on the thin mattress covering the molded cement bed and ran his cool hands down his tired face. He probably looked like death warmed over. The last time he had taken communion was three nights back when he drank from Cara. And the truth of it, he had been careful to draw very little. He held out his hands, noting the map of blue veins beneath the surface. His skin had taken on the translucent look and his body felt the stirrings of the death chill. He needed to feed soon if he hoped to keep his strength, or getting out of this cell on his own wouldn't even be an option.

With no windows in this part of the Sheriff's Office, Kane had no idea if the sun had even begun to rise, though his senses told him morning had not yet come. Every minute that passed put Cara closer to danger of being bled dry by this son of a bitch. Whoever the fuck he was, he had managed to take Kane out of the equation, though he had to know no jail cell would ever hold him. The ancient vampire had to know he operated on a tight time schedule.

Kane couldn't leave another moment to chance.

Waiting for Kaleb might mean the difference between life and death for Cara. He needed to find her, the consequences of breaking yet another rule and not following Kaleb's order be damned. Approaching the door barring his freedom, Kane gripped the bars tightly in his fists at chest level. He braced his booted heels against the cement pedestal of the bed and pushed steadily outward. Cement crumbled; chunks fell to the floor. With one last push and an inhuman-like growl, the bars separated from the walls. Thankfully, he had managed to do so with a minimal amount of noise.

Kane leaned the bars against the adjacent wall and headed down the long hallway to the locked door with the window looking out at the dispatch area of the Sheriff's Office. He hoped the night shift deputies were still making rounds. The fewer he had to hypnotize, the quicker he was outside the office.

The cylinder in the lock crunched, steel scraping steel, as he twisted the knob and easily broke the fixture. Kane's gaze locked with the dispatch's through the door's window—her mouth hung agape. No ordinary man could have broken the fixture.

"Don't move," Kane ordered as he stepped through the doorway and into the adjacent room.

The young woman's fear was evident in her scent. Other than the tremble of her hands, she did as Kane asked.

"Are you alone?"

She shook her head, her forefinger pointing toward the back of the station. "Just one."

"Good. Look at me," he said, his eyes heating, becoming obsidian.

She couldn't have looked away from him if she tried.

"Erase the surveillance tapes for the last hour, then turn them off."

"I can't do that."

"You can," he leaned in, "and you will."

The woman messed with the computer, typed in a series of numbers, then hit the delete key.

"Done."

"You didn't see me and you don't know what happened. You will not call for backup and you'll sleep until someone finds you."

"I'll sleep," she repeated, then yawned. "I'm suddenly tired. I can't hold my head up."

The woman laid her head on her crossed arms atop the desk and promptly fell asleep. Kane pushed a button on the desk near her elbow, causing the exit door to buzz, giving him five seconds to exit. He headed out the door, thankfully unseen by the second party in the Sheriff's Office. Hitting the pavement running, he knew he'd reach the clubhouse in less time than it would take to drive. Kane needed every spare second he could get.

"WHAT THE FUCK ARE YOU DOING?" Kaleb roared, his gaze zeroing in on Kane as he entered the clubhouse.

Grayson, Alexander, Nicholas and Joseph all turned in unison, their look no more approving than his twin's. Kane got it. He had just broken another rule by not following Kaleb's order as acting president. But what the hell did they expect? He wasn't about to sit around while Cara got her throat slit from ear to ear. Kane slammed the heavy entrance door.

"Are you fucking insane?" Kaleb continued. "The cops will be swarming this place before we even have a chance to get out there and look for Cara, and we'll have you to thank for that. Don't you know how to follow rules any more, Viper?"

Kane took a deep breath, slightly winded from his sprint. "Look, I don't have time to explain my actions. You can dole out my punishment later. Right now I need to find Cara."

"What the hell do you think we're doing here? Throwing a fucking party?"

Kaleb was angry. That Kane understood. Acting as president, he had every right to be pissed that Kane had not followed his order to stay put. He'd lost Ion; he wasn't about to lose Cara, too.

"Did you try her house?"

Kaleb scratched a spot just above his left ear, telling Kane that he tested his twin's patience. He blew out a stream of air through pursed lips, then skirted the four other Sons and approached Kaleb.

"Well, you're here now. Might as well give us a hand. I was about to split the territory among us. We'll travel in twos."

"Where's Blondy?" Kane asked.

"Don't know. Not answering his cell. Likely got piss drunk last night and is sleeping it off in some bitch's bed."

"Let's hit the streets then," Kane said. "You and I can check her house first."

"Already been there, Viper. It's not good." Kaleb laid a hand on Kane's shoulder. "The deputy they put there to watch her got his throat slit and Cara's nowhere to be found."

"Jesus!" Kane's pulse kicked up, his anxiety hitting a high note. "Any ideas?"

"The primordial's scent was all over the fucking house. I'm betting he took Cara, though I doubt they went far."

"What makes you think that, Hawk?"

Even thinking of Cara in the hands of that psycho made him want to kill something and this piece of shit was number one on his hit list. "Why not kill Cara and get the hell out of the States, head back to Italy?"

"Because she's never been his target. Think about it, Viper. It's always been you. If he took her, it's only to lure you to him. These murders started before Cara became your obsession of the moment."

He bit back a retort to the reference. Getting angry would serve no purpose. "She's not an obsession."

"Whatever you want to call her. I see it differently."

Kane didn't have time to argue with his brother. "I hope to hell you're right that his target is me, because that means we still have time."

Not wanting to undermine his brother's authority in front of the men, even though his no longer being incarcerated meant the role of pres returned to him, he asked Kaleb, "So what's your plan?"

CHAPTER TWENTY-SEVEN

"SOMEONE WANT TO TELL ME WHAT THE HELL JUST HAPpened back there?" Robbie growled.

His thumb pointed behind him, indicating the long hallway where a set of bars leaned against the cement block wall. The blocks were crumbled where the door had been bolted, littering the floor with dust and debris.

Sheriff Ducat didn't like the captain one bit. Smug bastard and self-important is what he was. Walking into the office this morning, he felt like he was stepping into a gigantic pile of shit. He just wished he could rid himself of the dung that was Robbie Melchor as easily as scraping the bottom of his boot. Instead, because Major Thomas of the Police Services Bureau of the Oregon State Police said they had to follow orders from this ass wipe, he had to play nice.

He had no idea how Kane managed to break out of that cell block without being seen or heard, but he was pretty sure how he managed to yank the bars from the walls holding them. These jerk-offs were foolish to think they could lock up one of the Sons. They had no clue what those boys were capable of. But Sheriff Ducat did. It was better to work with them, than against them. Oh, he had known they were vampires for some time, but their secret was safe enough with him.

Truth of it, he liked having them as part of his community. Anytime the law failed the county and some criminal went free on a technicality, he'd pass along that information to Viper and his boys to be sure justice always prevailed. The Sons of Sangue and the S.O. had a nice little understanding going. He wasn't about to let this fuck come here and mess that up.

"I swear heads will roll."

Melchor fisted his hands and leaned on his knuckles, coming nose to nose with the crying dispatch.

"If she says she doesn't know anything, Captain Melchor, then she doesn't. Bullying her isn't going to change that fact," Sheriff Ducat said, using his thumbs to hook the belt loops and hike up his pants. "I don't suppose making her piss herself will work either."

The captain turned on him, his cheeks mottled red in his agitation. "All I know is there were two people working last night's shift when this all went down. Deputy Miller was in the restroom taking a shit. His words, not mine. And this one"—his forefinger jabbed in the dispatch's direction, narrowly missing her face—"had her head down on the desk, asleep. You always let your employees sleep on the job, Sheriff?"

"My employees are not your concern, Captain, nor is their insubordination. You're overstepping your bounds here."

"The state has jurisdiction. That gives me the right."

"Maybe on this case, but not over my office."

"Your lackadaisical employee cost me my prisoner!"

Sheriff Ducat squared his shoulders. "Then maybe you should have transported him last night to the regional jail instead of leaving him in my county lockup. Don't blame my office for your lack of attention to detail. The entire reason we have a regional jail is because most of the county lockups are in disrepair. Case in point."

Melchor hardened his jaw. "You're damn right I shouldn't have trusted you with such a high profile prisoner. But it's too late for that now, isn't it? Where's Hernandez?"

"Due in within the half hour."

"Good. I want an APB put out on Tepes and his band of misfits." He looked at the dispatch. "Call Deputy Superintendent Wiles of the State Police, make sure he's apprised of the situation and they have every available car out there looking for the escaped prisoner. Tell them Tepes should be approached with extreme caution. He is thought to be armed and dangerous. If they come across any of the Sons, they are to be apprehended as well."

"What's the Sons got to do with this?"

"Come on, Sheriff, you and I both know Kane did not walk out of that cell by himself. I'm still not sure how the hell they waltzed right in here sight unseen but we'll surely discover that when I get a look at the surveillance tapes. In the meantime, I think you should get every one of your deputies on the road looking for them."

Melchor dismissed the sheriff and looked at the dispatch. "Can you pull up the last few hours of feed?"

She sniffled, then swiped away a few stray tears. Turning to her bank of computers, she typed on the keyboard, then sat back and glanced queerly at the monitor.

"That's odd."

"What is it?"

"The cameras weren't running. As of six-o-five this morning, the feed just ended. Those cameras are never turned off. They run twenty-four-seven."

"What the hell do you mean?" Robbie's brow furrowed as he slapped the desktop. "What kind of rinky dink operation is this?"

The sheriff approached the monitor and stared at an image of Kane sitting in his cell on the mattress, hands running down his face, then the screen went static. Sheriff Ducat hid the smile itching at his lips. He didn't know how the hell Kane had managed to stop the live feed without his dispatch's knowledge, but everything beyond that point was useless.

He cleared his throat, fist covering his mouth to hide his amusement. The captain whirled on his heel and glared at him. If a man's gaze could strike you dead, he'd be lying on the wrong side of the dirt for sure.

"What kind of equipment do you have, Sheriff? This is useless!"

"It's always worked."

"You want to tell me how it conveniently quit last night, right about the time Kane Tepes walked out of here?"

The sheriff shrugged. "I don't have a clue."

"I do! It's obvious," he pointed a finger again at the poor girl. "She's working for them."

The dispatch's mouth dropped and she sputtered. "Honestly, I have no idea."

Melchor let out a curse not fit for anyone's ears as he raised his hands in the air and stormed from the room. The sheriff could no longer hide his smile as he patted the poor dear on her shoulder.

"Why don't you head out, get some rest. I'll keep an eye on it until day shift gets here."

CARA AWOKE, A MIGRAINE STEALING her breath, making her wish she stayed unconscious instead. Sitting up slowly, she rubbed her forehead, trying to alleviate some of the pain shooting through her head. On a pain scale of one-to-ten, she'd give it a solid eight. The damn ache packed one hell of a wallop.

Deputy Higgins' sightless gaze filtered through her fog-filled brain. *Jesus!* Her body quaked. A hand had covered her mouth, a forearm across her throat kept her from drawing breath. She'd struggled to stay conscious, but had lost the fight, her world going black. Evidently her attacker had only cut off the oxygen until she passed out. The headache came from a sizable knot on the back of the head, which she now rubbed. The son of a bitch must have dropped her to the floor and bounced her head off the wood decking.

Cara groaned, nausea gripping her gut and making her head swim. Standing on shaken limbs, she stumbled to the corner of the room and dry heaved, one hand bracing herself on the rough-hewn wooden walls. She had eaten little in the last twenty-four hours, and her stomach had nothing to give but bile. A likely concussion caused her nausea. Leaning against the empty shelving behind her, Cara took a look around. The fuzziness holding her brain captive slowly started to lift, leaving only the massive headache.

Tiny, dust-filled rays of light filtered through the slats of the boarded windows. Where the hell was she? Swiping her sleeve across the back of her mouth, she approached one of the windows and peered through the cracks. Large evergreens stretched as far as she could see, giving her no clue as to her whereabouts. She could have been in any one of the numerous woods around Lane County. Somehow Cara doubted they'd gone far, not if this psycho hoped to lure Kane.

Taking a look around the dirt-littered shed, Cara hoped to find something, anything, to use as a weapon. But everything had been removed. Not as much as a stray nail remained. The son of a bitch had the foresight to make sure nothing could be used against him, that or the shed had been empty to begin with. Cara couldn't tell how much time had passed or what time she had awakened. For as much as she knew, an entire day could have passed. She needed to break free, to find Kane, before the primordial returned. Maybe her sketchy description would aide him in finding the ancient vampire murdering Pleasant's residents. With any luck, her captor had left her alone.

Approaching the rickety door, Cara gripped the metal handle and pushed. Something held the latch fast on the opposite side. Not that she expected to just waltz out the door, but it would have been nice. Cara stepped back, then slammed her shoulder into the door. The old wood held fast, surely giving her a bruise for her efforts. Her energy waned. Her limbs hung like limp noodles.

Not one to give up, she lifted her leg and thrust-kicked the door, even if it was a half-assed attempt. The dry wood creaked and the door shook. She didn't think she had the energy to give it a second try. But running on pure adrenalin, she gave it another. To no avail. Cara leaned back against the built-in bench, on the verge of collapsing, her head ready to split it two.

Just as she took a deep breath and was about to give it another try, the lock on the outside scraped against the wood and slid free. Her heart damn near stopped beating as fear immobilized her.

The door swung outward.

The obsidian-eyed blond vampire stood before her, fangs pressing against his upper lip, his prominent brow and sunken cheeks much more pronounced than Kane's. Cara had no doubt this was the primordial they had been seeking and that he would kill her without conscience. Unless Kane found her soon, he'd slice her throat, drain her, and bury her in a shallow grave like the others.

"Going somewhere?" he asked with a smile so evil he could give Hannibal Lecter a run for his money.

"I hoped. I don't suppose you'd point me in the direction of home."

"You have a sense of humor. I like that." He held out a white sack. "I brought you food."

Cara harrumphed. "What did you lace it with? Arsenic?"

"I have no need of poisons, Detective. If I wanted you dead, you would be."

"You threatened me if, I recall right. That lipstick was hell to get off my mirror."

This time, the primordial did chuckle. "Sorry to inconvenience you. But I needed to get Viper's attention."

"You could have done so by using *his* mirror."

He shoved the sack into her hands. Cara didn't think she'd be able to stomach whatever he had brought.

"The dear boy is a bit hard-headed. I fear merely threatening his life wouldn't have produced the same results. Go ahead." He pointed at her lunch. "Eat."

"If you meant to give me my last supper, it would have been polite to ask what I wanted." Cara opened the bag and peered in, the smell of rye bread greeting her. "Death row inmates get treated better."

He shrugged. "You were still out cold when I left. I took the liberty of ordering you a turkey on rye."

Cara did have a weak spot for turkey, but she couldn't keep the sarcasm from her tone. "How did you guess I have a soft spot for turkey? Next, you'll be picking the movie, too."

"No wonder Viper fancies you. I have to admit, your sense of humor appeals to me. Too bad beyond getting revenge on him, you serve no purpose. Pity."

She held out the sack and shook it in his face. "If you plan to kill me, then why the hell bother feeding me?"

He didn't take it. Drawing his brows together over the bridge of his nose, he said, "Because I'm not cruel. I wouldn't want you to suffer. It could be a while before your boy finds you."

"You don't want me to suffer, and yet you plan to kill me. What the hell do you call that?"

His smile turned wicked. "Trust me, dear, you won't feel a thing. There will be no suffering involved."

Before she could form a response, the door shut and the lock slid in place. Cara kicked at the door again, the wood rattling on its old hinges.

"Tsk, tsk, my dear," he called with a chuckle. "You might as well save your energy. Should you break through the door, I'm right on the other side. You won't make it a foot, forcing my hand to expedite your end. After all, I really don't need you alive to flush out Viper. He'll come either way."

And Cara knew the truth of it. If Kane didn't come to rescue her, he'd come to avenge her death. She slid to the floor in a cross-legged sitting position, the white bag of turkey and rye still in her hand.

KANE BALANCED HIS FAT BOB WITH his thighs, the heavy machinery rumbling beneath him, as Kaleb and he sat at a crossroads. The woods surrounding Cara's house had been his obvious first choice. But an hour later, they had come out empty handed. His chances of finding Cara alive diminished by the hour. Hopelessness washed over him at the thought of her life depending wholly on him. He had been too late to help Ion. God help him, he couldn't survive it a second time.

He adjusted his sunglasses, the mid-morning sun too bright to his UV-sensitive eyes, one of the disadvantages of his kind. Where his night vision enhanced as a vampire, the sun diminished it. Relying on his other senses, Kaleb sniffed the air, hoping to detect the primordial or the scent unique to Cara. He had a feeling that this shit hadn't gone too far, that his ultimate goal was to flush out Kane.

So why not hang a big red flag?

Kane would be more than happy to answer that call.

His thoughts drifted to Cara and the night she had spent in his arms at Bookings. She had taken everything he had to give, matched his appetite, and given back in spades. Not only that, but she had touched a part of him he thought long dead. For the first time in years, something akin to love squeezed that life-pumping muscle in his chest. That same muscle now ached at the thought of losing her.

Jesus! He hung his head, and shook it. He had fallen ... hard. And now, because of it, he'd gladly lay down his life. Finding her dead was not an option.

He looked at his brother. "Anything?"

Kaleb pulled out his cell and checked for messages. "Nothing. Sorry, Viper. Without direction, no one knows where to begin. We don't have the manpower to cover the entire state. I'm afraid we won't find her unless this primordial wants us to."

Kane knew the truth to Kaleb's words. Just as when Ion had been staked, they had been clueless until the cartel gave up the location of Rosalee and his son. By the time the Sons had arrived, it had been too late. Although Rosalee and Ion had both suffered at the hands of drug lords, Ion had been the one to pay with his life. Kane couldn't allow that to happen again. Cara's only crime had been her weakness where he was concerned, and he had selfishly taken advantage of that. She didn't deserve to be in the middle of a pissing match with this ancient vampire, one who meant to teach him a lesson.

Kaleb was right, they needed manpower if he hoped to have even a half-ass chance at finding her. Pulling out his cell, Kane slid the lock screen free and tapped Red's name. The president answered on the third ring.

"Red," Kane greeted.

"What can I do for you, Viper?" His smoke-roughened voice came through the phone's speaker.

"Detective Cara Brahnam ... you know her?"

"I've had a run-in with her in the past. What do you need?"

"She's missing and I need her found. Like yesterday."

"Any idea where?"

"Somewhere near Lane County. How soon can you and the Knights be here?"

"Couple of hours."

"Good. Be looking for anything on the way, a cabin in the woods that seems uninhabited, an abandoned shed or building. Someplace that wouldn't normally draw attention. Leave no stone unturned."

"You want her alive?"

"Yes, no one touches her. If you run across the detective—she won't be alone. Don't play the hero. The man who took her is extremely dangerous. Call me. Hawk and I will deal with him."

"Any idea what he looks like?"

"Not much of a description. Tall, blond hair."

Red chuckled. "Well, if this isn't going to be like looking for a needle in a haystack."

"Not finding her isn't an option, Red."

Kane hit End and pocketed his phone, waiting for Kaleb's disapproval, which was sure to come. "Have at it, Hawk. You know you want to say it. I can see it in your face."

"What the hell has gotten into you, Viper? What's so special about this piece of ass that you would forsake your commitment to this club? You know they'll never vote to allow you to turn her."

Kane's gaze snapped to his brother's. Anger coursed through him and he snarled, "I'd never subject her to our lifestyle."

"Then what the hell are you doing? If she doesn't become one of us, you can't mate with her. There's no future."

"You think I don't know that, Hawk? All I know is I'd gladly die for her."

"Man, you got it bad, bro." He shook his head in disgust. "Ain't no woman worth dying for. We find her ... we get you out of this fucking mess, then you need to cut her loose."

One of Kane's brows rose. "Is that an order? You realize I'm still pres."

"Not an order from me acting as pres. Call it a stern nudge from your concerned brother. Now let's get the fuck back out there and find her so you can get on with your life."

Kane should have responded, let his twin know he had no say in his life. Instead, he kicked off with his feet as he gave the bike gas and sped down the winding back road, Kaleb following on his heels. He couldn't argue with his brother, not when he knew Kaleb was correct. He needed to cut Cara loose, for her own good.

CHAPTER TWENTY-EIGHT

Huddled on the dirt-littered floor, Cara sat cross-legged, turkey and rye crumpled in the corner behind her. She wasn't about to eat anything that psycho had given her. The sandwich could've been laced with poison or sedatives, and she needed her wits about her. The primordial hadn't shown his face since he had presented her with food, which was just as well. Hard telling how far he had gone or where to. No doubt on a mission to snare Kane.

Her knuckles and fingers sported splinters and abrasions from trying to break the boards from the windows to no avail. Those damn things must have been screwed in because they hadn't budged. Several kicks to the door hadn't produced the desired effect either. Cara had finally sunk to the floor in defeat. She wasn't getting out of here any sooner than the psychopath vampire was ready to let her out.

The noon hour had long passed, if the position of the sun was any indicator. This deep in the woods, not much light passed through, so even that was a haphazard guess at best. By now, the entire Sheriff's Office was probably combing the woods and hillsides looking for her. She had a feeling, though, unless the piece of paranormal crap wanted her to be found, no rescue crew stood a chance.

363

The ancient vampire wanted her alive for a reason. Because had he wanted her dead, she already would be.

Kane came to mind.

Cara had no idea what had happened with him and the Sheriff's Office. Kane's chain had been found in Jeff Reeve's hand. Something she couldn't explain away, even though she knew Kane hadn't been the one to cut the dispatch's throat. With her stuck here, Cara wondered if Kane had been detained in a jail cell at the S.O., or if he headed a search and rescue with the OMC. Cara knew, though, that without Kane's lead the rest of the Sons had no reason to want her found.

If this primordial waited on Kane, then the joke was on him. Kane might very well be in custody, while the primordial did his damnedest to lure him into rescuing Cara. The Sons didn't give a damn one way or the other what happened. After all, they thought she had tried her best to pin these murders on one of them. A heavy sigh escaped her. Wrong vampire. Something told her this psycho wasn't about to answer for any of his crimes. How did one go about arresting an ancient vampire anyway?

White straightjacket, here I come.

She could imagine how that conversation with Robbie would go. He'd likely offer to personally drive her to the state hospital while the primordial high-tailed it back to Italy and Kane fried for crimes he wasn't responsible for.

The door to the shed suddenly opened and light filtered in. Cara looked at the blond haired, blue-eyed vampire as his large frame filled the doorway. His gaze traveled to the crumpled sack.

"Not hungry? I'd hate to have Kane think I starved his favorite human."

"I wouldn't eat anything you brought me."

A wicked smile curved his lips. "I would gain nothing from poisoning you, my dear. I want you fully alive when Kane gets here. What fun would it be for me if he didn't get to participate in the festivities?"

"You're going to kill me like the others?"

"Eventually."

"Why?"

"I'm not totally heartless."

"Why are you bent on punishing Kane?"

"Because he needs to be taught a lesson. I have yet to decide if I will be merciful and kill him, or whether it would be best to allow him to suffer, knowing his actions caused your death. To know that he has found a soft spot in his heart for you makes this all the more rewarding. If it were totally up to me, I'd kill you both, as I've tired of this cat and mouse game."

"If it isn't just up to you, then who is calling the shots? Who wants Kane to ... Rosalee," she whispered.

"Good, girl. You're smarter than I gave you credit for. For some reason, she fancies the idiot and wants him to suffer as she has. Though she hasn't ordered his death." The primordial sighed dramatically, waving a hand in the air as he paced the small shed. "I'm of the mind the world would be a better place without him. You're just a casualty."

"What about the Sheriff's Office? You plan to elude them as well? You've murdered innocent people. You have to pay for that.

And if you kill me, they won't stop until they find you. The law doesn't go easy on cop killers."

Cara knew it was weak, but she had nothing better to offer. If Kane had been arrested—

"You think your justice system can hold one of us?" He laughed, the sinister sound raising goose flesh along her flesh. "We hold our own accountable. We have no need for your laws."

Cara narrowed her gaze. "So it's perfectly okay for you to kill innocent women?"

"If it's for the greater good."

"And what might that be?"

"Kane needs to know his place. He may be a descendant of Vlad, but he's no primordial. There are consequences for his actions."

"And you're one of Rosalee's lackeys?"

His brow knit and his lips turned down in a scowl. "I am a primordial. I am no one's lackey."

"So if you're here of your own free will, what has Kane done to you?"

"Viper oversteps his boundaries. I am here to make him see that."

"And if he doesn't come to my rescue?"

"He will."

"How are you so sure? Because of you, he's probably sitting in a jail cell."

"If Viper wishes to save you, then he's sitting in no cell. You haven't built a jail strong enough to hold him."

Cara sure as hell hoped he spoke the truth, because Kane was her sole chance at getting out of here alive.

"And knowing that, I also placed a call to the Sheriff's Office so they, too, will know where to find you."

"Why?"

"In hopes that by the time Kane gets here, your fellow officers show up to save the day. It will be too late for you, however," he said, looking as if he had no soul. "And Kane will be left with saving your life, following me, or skipping town. If he chooses you, your fellow deputies will no doubt put a bullet straight through his heart, ending his life and too late to save yours. It's all in the timing."

"You're crazy!"

"No, my dear, I am quite sane, I assure you."

PANIC FLUTTERED IN KANE'S CHEST. He hadn't felt this level of anxiety since racing to Ion's aid so many years ago. And just like then, he feared arriving too late. He had every possible man out looking for this primordial, and not one of them had a clue where he had sequestered Cara away. Hell, even Kaleb had started looking at him with pity in his eyes.

The sun had begun to set and daylight was beginning to wane. Though his brothers could see well enough at night, the Knights wouldn't be of much help. He had heard from Red throughout the day, but they hadn't had much luck either.

Kane took in a deep breath as he leaned into a corner, Kaleb's Harley following the curve behind him. The cool, damp air caressed his face, and normally the open road would have given him a sense of peace.

Not today.

He couldn't believe that in less than a week's time she'd come to mean as much to him as drawing his next breath. The alternative was unthinkable. He had lived a hundred-plus years, but the thought of losing Cara had him questioning if he even wanted to live another hundred. Bottom line, for the first time in his godforsaken life, he knew what truly loving someone felt like. And not the parental kind of love he had for Ion.

Just as Kaleb and he rolled up to another crossroads, his pocket vibrated. He pulled out his cell, saw Red was on the other end and slid the lock free to answer the call.

"What news do you have for me?"

"We're out here by North Fork Road, sitting in the gravel parking area of Bender Landing County Park. It's getting pretty dark out here, Viper."

"I know. Not good news."

"Except this time it might work in our favor. I spotted a small light coming from back in the woods just as we pulled in and killed the motors on our bikes. Saw some sort of illumination peeking from the trees."

"Did you get any closer? See what the cause might be?"

"I was about to head down one of the hiking paths when the light extinguished. I heard several thumps, followed by a lot of cursing and a woman's scream. That's when I saw a man ... couldn't really see much of anything, just that someone was out there. He turned toward me. And though I couldn't see his eyes, it felt as if he looked right at me. I wanted to head down that path, check things out, but it was as if my feet would not move in that direction.

Damnedest thing. That's when I headed back to the bike and called you."

"Get the hell out of there, Red."

Kane knew exactly why Red seemed frozen in place. The primordial manipulated Red's thoughts, something only a very old vampire could master. The power of suggestion only worked on humans, not on his kind. The vampire could have easily hypnotized Red into forgetting what he saw, but for some reason didn't. The ancient vampire no doubt hoped the biker would lure Kane to that exact spot. Kane intended on complying.

"Hawk and I are a mile down the road. You and your boys head out. We'll take it from here."

"You don't want us to stick around, be your back-up?"

"No. This man we're looking for? It's personal. Between him and the Sons. I owe you one, though. I appreciate you having our backs."

"No problem, Viper. You need us ... call."

Kane ended the call and glanced at his twin. "Looks like our boy isn't far from where we found Tab. Good news: looks like Cara's still alive."

"What's the plan?"

"He isn't counting on you being with me. You come in on foot while I have him preoccupied. If need be, you get Cara out of there and to safety. I'll take care of this piece of shit. After all, it's me he wants."

"You want me to call in the rest of the Sons?"

Kane shook his head. "No time. Give me ten minutes, then get over there as fast as you can."

Using his booted feet, Kane pushed off and headed his Fat Bob in the direction of the park. Looks like the primordial was finally going to get what he was after in the first place.

Him.

CARA HEARD THE RUMBLE OF motorcycles, right before this psycho-ass vamp shut the lights off on her. Her hands hurt, but that didn't stop her from pounding furiously on the door and yelling at the top of her lungs. But in the end it hadn't done her a damn bit of good. The sound of the bikes started up again and faded into the distance.

Sinking to the floor and sitting back on her haunches, she covered her face, despair washing over her as she growled in frustration. Kane and the rest of the Sons had been so close, only to have them drive away. Now what would this vamp do? Kill her because he, too, hadn't gotten what he wanted? Tears filled her eyes. She likely wasn't far from having her life cut short.

Her grandfather came to mind. Who would take care of him, visit him, take him peanut butter pies? She was the only family he had left and Cara worried he wouldn't survive the news that his granddaughter had been murdered.

And what of Kane? She couldn't help wondering how he would react. Cara thought back to his cavalier attitude when he had been interviewed about Tab's murder. He acted as though the news hadn't bothered him. Tab wasn't his girlfriend, he'd said. Fucking did not equate to a relationship.

Is that all she meant to Kane? Just a fuck buddy?

Her chest ached. Why it suddenly mattered how Kane viewed her she didn't know. But something had changed between them the night they'd spent in Bookings and Cara had given him her heart. Foolish as it was, she had fallen in love.

"Know that I claim you."

Claiming her was likely as close to him loving her as she'd ever get. Cara didn't know if Kane was even capable of loving another after what he had gone through with Rosalee. Though, now, she'd never know. Her time had just about run out and she'd never get the chance to tell Kane that she loved him.

She allowed the tears to fall, seconds before the sound of an approaching Harley reached her ears. It was singular this time. Not a group of them. Her heart beat heavy with dread. Surely, Kane wouldn't be stupid enough to come alone. He had said this centuries-older vampire was superior in strength. He would be no match and they'd both be doomed. Just about the time the engine rumbled to a stop, the door to the shed flew open. Before her stood a smiling primordial.

"Your boyfriend has arrived," he said, his obsidian gaze instilled terror in her heart.

Her stomach clenched and her breath hitched as her heart damn near stopped beating. Begging for Kane's life would do her no good. Cara made a break for the door, but the primordial was much too quick as his powerful grip closed over her bicep.

"Kane," Cara screamed at the top of her lungs. "Run!"

CHAPTER TWENTY-NINE

KANE PULLED INTO THE GRAVEL PARKING LOT, FLIPPED THE centerstand down on the bike and hit the ground running.

"Kane! Run!" Cara's warning traveled to his acute hearing.

Blood roared through his veins. He knew he should be more cautious, but there was no way he'd sneak up on the primordial. Not when the vampire expected him. The moment Kane arrived, the vamp felt his presence. Kane's best hope lay in him not expecting Kaleb. If he could hold the primordial's attention captive while his twin snuck in and ambushed him, it would be their best hope at surviving this thing. Without the element of surprise, neither Kane nor Cara had a prayer against this psycho. The ancient vampire was far superior in strength and mind.

Running down the path, the forest but a blur, Kane quickly closed in on the small abandoned shed. Nighttime forest creatures scurried at his approach, detecting impending doom. A dog growled from his hiding place by a downed tree. His glassy eyes reflected the moonlight peeking through the evergreens.

The light coming from the wooden shack cast a glow just beyond the door illuminating a small area of the forest beyond. Kane could smell the primordial, knew he was close. Just beyond the door, Kane paused, listening to the rustle of clothing, the shuffling of feet, detecting more than one person inside the shed. And unless the primordial stole more than Cara, he had pinpointed the location of both.

Kane steeled his jaw and stepped across the threshold, his form filling the small doorway. What he saw turned his blood cold. Cara stood just out of arm's reach, her back against the blond vampire, one of his pale forearms wrapping her waist, while the other hand held the sharp edge of a hunting knife against her throat. Kane had to give her credit. She masked her fear quite well, holding her composure. One swipe of that knife and it would be all over. Even with Kane's quick reflexes, he wouldn't be able to stop the son of a bitch. She'd bleed out well before he had time to get her help.

"You took your sweet-ass time getting here," the smarmy vampire said. "I was slowly losing my patience."

"Let her go." Kane held out a palm. "It's me you want."

The man smiled, chilling Kane to the bone. "Oh, but it's so much more fun to watch you squirm."

Kane dropped his hand. "What do you want with me?"

"I believe we share a lover. But when this is finished, she'll only have one."

"Rosalee," he barely breathed, his heart icing over. He had guessed as much. The bitch needed to be stopped.

The man's smile grew.

"Who are you? I'd like to know the name of the man who thinks to take me out."

"Alec Funar," he said, his smile condescending. "Not that it will do you any good. But there is no thinking about it. You will die at my hand."

Alec tightened his hold on Cara, causing her to wince as the sharp edge of the knife pressed farther into her throat. Kane held her gaze but a moment before returning his gaze to Alec's.

"I met Rosalee after you so coldly sent her back to Italy," he continued. "I was living under her father's household. I should thank you for releasing her."

"You're from Mircea's clan?"

"Not Mircea's. I'm a guest in his home."

Kane needed to keep this piece of shit talking. Give Kaleb time to arrive. Hopefully Kaleb's scent was similar enough to Kane's that the primordial wouldn't be able to detect his arrival.

Cara swallowed, drawing his attention again, her gaze wide and hopeful. Though her bravado held strong, he could still smell her fear. He wished he could tell her all would be okay, but he couldn't promise her something he might not be able to deliver.

"Actually, I come from Vlad's clan. Where you're a great grandson of Vlad's loins, I'm merely the son to one of his concubines, having no relation to the Romanian ruler at all. Old enough to be a primordial, but not a member of any royal bloodlines. Taking Rosalee as a mate would seal my place with Mircea's clan."

"Rosalee is already mated."

"To you."

"Nothing breaks the mating bond and you know it."

"Your death will."

"She would never wish me dead."

Kane heard the catch in Cara's breath, saw the hurt in her eyes. She, no doubt, thought herself just a passing piece of ass as Tab had been. Nothing could be farther from the truth. If they ever got out of this alive, he'd make sure she knew exactly how important she was to him. The hell with his bond to Rosalee. Cara would be his choice for life. He'd hunt down Mircea himself to get the ancient's blessing.

"It won't matter," Alec said, his self-important tone grating Kane's last nerve.

Kane wanted to take the blade pressing into Cara's throat and sever his fucking head from his body.

"Regardless of Rosalee's desire, you won't make it out of here alive."

"She's behind the murders?"

"She wanted you to suffer, to drain the women you slept with."

Kane raised a brow. "I don't even remember all of the women who were murdered. That makes this whole debacle pointless. Those women died for nothing."

Alec made a tsking sound. "For nothing? What about the last one? Surely after three years you remember her quite well."

"An inconvenience to be sure as I'm still in need of another donor. But mourn her loss? No."

"There had to be casualties to get your attention."

"So now you have my attention. But I promise you, if you think to kill Cara and allow me to walk as Rosalee wishes, I won't stop until I see you dead."

"Rosalee may want you alive, but it's not in my plan."

"If my death comes at your hand, you know she'll never forgive you."

"You let me worry about Rosalee. With you in the way, she never will be mine."

Kane felt his twin's connection the minute he arrived. Kaleb wasn't far beyond the doorway and it didn't appear Alec had yet detected him. Kane needed to keep Alec's focus, so he took a step in the primordial's direction. The knife bit into Cara's flesh and a drop of crimson blood trickled down her throat. The scent caused his gums to ache and his fangs began to fill his mouth. He wasn't far from becoming the frightening animal Cara thought she had witnessed ten years back. That man had sex and satisfaction on his mind. This man, the one before her now, wanted to rip out Alec's throat with his teeth.

Kane wanted blood all right. He wanted primordial blood.

KANE HAD FOUND HER, BUT LITTLE good it would do as she stood no chance of getting out alive. It was but a matter of seconds before the cold steel blade cut through arteries and veins, nearly decapitating her. She couldn't die without letting him know how she felt, selfish as it might be. Because if he lived, and her instincts were correct, he'd have to deal with losing someone else he deeply cared about.

She held his gaze. Tears filled her eyes and slipped down her cheeks, making watery treks. The salty taste reached her lips as she opened her mouth to speak. It was now or never.

"I love you."

Kane lunged for them, whether it was her admission or his desire to kill the vampire holding her, she was unsure. Time slowed to a snail's pace as the sharp blade slid across her throat, the sting of the bite traveling to her brain. Her hands covered the wound, blood splaying out as the ancient vampire released her and shoved her in Kane's direction.

"I'm not done with you, biker," he hissed, "but follow me and she dies. It's your decision to make."

Alec could have left the shed for all she knew for her gaze stayed on Kane, wanting his face to be the last she saw before bowing to death. He pulled her into his arms as he carried her to the floor, cradling her in his strong embrace. Her blood covered his face, throat, and chest. My god but it was everywhere. His obsidian gaze glassed over like the Black Sea as he leaned down and placed a tender kiss upon her forehead.

"Forgive me, Mia Bella," he whispered, barely audible over the buzzing in her ears.

Kane sank his fangs into the flesh of his forearm tearing open an artery and carried the bleeding wrist to her lips. Cara couldn't speak, her mouth gaped for oxygen of which she seemed incapable of drawing. The knife had probably sliced through her trachea as well. Unable to question his actions, she watched as he placed the bleeding wound over her mouth and laid it against her lips. The first drop of his sweet blood passed over her tongue, nearly causing her to choke.

"Drink."

Cara latched onto his jagged cut as if it were the most natural thing in the world, the warm metallic tang a balm to her dying soul. Her gaze fixed on his. She wasn't ready to die. Her soul cried out and bright lights beckoned to her just beyond the black shadows clouding her vision.

The last thing she heard before succumbing was Kane's watery admission, "I love you too, Mia Bella," he said, then placed another warm kiss upon her temple.

Weightlessness settled over Cara. Her last thought before yielding to the darkness was that Kane had loved her.

THE STRONG SCENT OF HUMAN blood wafted to his nose. *Son of a bitch!* Kaleb stood just beyond the door, waiting for the perfect timing, praying to any god who might hear. They needed the fates to be on their side if they were to get out of this alive. Time sure as the hell wasn't, if the scent of Cara's blood was any indication. If the primordial even suspected he stood just beyond the door, they'd all be dead. No way could Kane and Kaleb's combined strength match that of the ancient vampire's. The best they could hope for would be blind-siding the bastard.

Taking a deep breath, crouching just beyond the entrance, Kaleb readied to pounce on the son of a bitch as he heard footfalls heading for the door. Just as he made his move, he leapt into the oncoming path of Alec Funar. Kaleb rolled backwards from the force and Alec flew head first into the dirt. Before Alec could get his footing, Kaleb jumped to his feet and dove on top of the vampire.

He grabbed a fistful of blond hair and yanked back his head, Alec hissing in response. Kaleb had all of two seconds to act before this shit tossed him like a rag doll and ripped his limbs from his body. Snatching the large hunting knife from the dirt that the vamp had dropped when colliding into Kaleb, he drew it across the ancient's throat with all his might and separated his head from his shoulders, drenching himself in the primordial's blood.

Kaleb shuddered at the dying wail. After a few violent thrashes, the body beneath him stilled. He tossed the blond head a few feet away, just in case the damn thing had the ability to bite by reflex. Kaleb stood up from the headless corpse, watching as the flesh quickly fossilized before his eyes.

Not wanting to waste another moment on the fuck, he turned and headed for the door of the shed, hoping Kane hadn't been too late. Inside, he saw Cara's pale lifeless form in his brother's arms. He couldn't help but ache at the loss.

"Is she gone?" he asked.

Kane's obsidian gaze turned on him and he shook his head. "Her heart beats."

Kaleb cursed a colorful stream. "Jesus, Viper! What the hell did you do?"

His brother looked back at the woman lying in his arms, her limbs now twitching and the gaping wound on her neck closing miraculously. No divine healing here.

"She's one of us."

Kaleb ran a grimy hand through the overlong curls on his head. "Ah, hell! What the fuck am I supposed to tell the Sons?"

"Tell them the truth." Kane reached to his breast and pulled the president patch from his cut and handed it to Kaleb. "I know what I did was against club rules. But given the option, I'd do the same. Take them the facts, let them judge me."

"And if they decide to take your rockers?"

"As long as it's not a death sentence, I can live with it." Kane turned from him and looked down on Cara. "Living without her wasn't an option."

"I know," Kaleb said.

And he did. The look in his brother's eyes told him as much, as if the bond they shared as twins wouldn't have. But that wasn't going to be reason enough for the MC not to hand out punishment for his actions. Turning another into a vampire was forbidden, unless first voted and agreed to by every voting member.

Kane glanced back at his twin. "And Alec? Did he get away?"

"No. I wasted that fuck." Kaleb grinned. "Guess I'll have my own actions to answer for. You know as well as I do, killing a primordial is forbidden. If convicted of such, you and I both know the judgment is death. Looks like we better bury this fuck and pray that no one finds him."

A cell phone rang, drawing their attention to the door where one lay in the dirt just beyond the opening. Alec must have dropped it in his hurry to flee. Walking over to the downed phone, Kaleb smiled at the name staring back at him.

"It's Rosalee. You want to speak to her?"

His smile grew as Kane's laughter filled the small building.

CARA LEANED DOWN AND KISSED the old man's balding pate. Knowing that her grandfather wouldn't have to learn his last living relative had nearly died made the scorching pain of the last few days worth it. There had been times she felt as though she wished for death. To say the transformation had been painful was an understatement. Liquid fire coursed through her veins and arteries.

"You best eat that peanut butter pie after supper, Grandpa. Otherwise, you'll spoil your supper."

"Bah! Nonsense. You can't spoil the meals they serve here. Anything would be an improvement."

Cara laughed, her fingers going to the scarf wrapping her throat. The deep wound had healed for the most part, leaving behind nothing more than an angry scar and a sore throat.

"Now I know you jest. You forget I've eaten meals here with you, old man."

She patted his arm and stood, clearing her throat. The gesture had Kane reaching for her hand and squeezing her fingers. The simple gesture warmed her heart. Cara glanced at him, holding his gaze and offering him a tender smile. He winked at her and mouthed the words, "I love you."

Cara's smile grew. She'd never tire of hearing it. Turning back to her grandfather, she leaned down and kissed his weathered cheek. "We have to go, Grandpa. But we'll be back soon."

The old man turned his watery gaze on Kane and pointed a gnarled finger in his direction. "You take care of my granddaughter. Otherwise, you'll be answering to me."

"I wouldn't allow anyone to harm her, sir. Death to anyone who tries."

He nodded in acknowledgement. "She ain't got anyone else in this world but me."

"If you don't mind me saying so, sir, she now also has me."

Her grandfather held Kane's stare for a long moment, then turned to Cara and grabbed her free hand, taking it to his lips, placing a kiss on the back, then whispered, "He's a keeper."

"You don't have to tell me that, Grandpa. I'm not letting this one out of my sight for a minute."

He smiled, then touched his throat. "You take care of the cold."

Cara almost denied the fact she was ill when she realized he referred to the hoarseness of her voice and the scarf draping her neck.

"You worry too much."

"Get on out of here. I'm sure you two have something better to do than spend your evening entertaining an old fool."

Twenty minutes later, Cara lay stretched out, naked in Kane's king size bed, reveling in the feel of the sheets against her highly sensitized skin. They had the clubhouse to themselves for the time being, and Cara planned to take advantage of every second of it. Relocating Kane to her house seemed the better option, and maybe she'd even talk him into it, but for now she just wanted to be wrapped within his strong arms, with him buried deep inside her.

Kane pulled his shirt over his head; his black jeans hung low on his muscular hips. His tee hung from his slack fingers as he advanced upon the bed and dropped it at the foot. Cara's mouth watered. His six-pack abs and the muscles at his hips arrowing into the Levis had her fairly salivating.

"You ready for this?"

Her gaze widened and he laughed. "You have no idea what you're in for, Mia Bella."

Cara laid her hand on his chest, feeling his heart beat mightily beneath her palm. "This isn't our first time."

"No," he kissed her brow, "But it's your first time as a vampire. Take your last orgasm and times it by ten."

Her brows rose. "Seriously?"

What a perk!

Kane ran a hand from her shoulder, down the soft flesh of her chest to her breast and covered it with his palm. Heat like she had never felt before pooled between her legs and spanned out along the rest of her body. The ache between her thighs grew nearly unbearable.

Cara could hardly speak as she shifted on the sheets. "Please, Kane."

"Oh, I plan to please. You have no idea."

He lowered his head and covered her other nipple with his mouth, suckling it, teasing it, then nipping it with his growing fangs before soothing the ache with his tongue. Cara cried out, her back arched off the mattress and her gaze heated and her vision sharpened. Fangs filled her mouth and suddenly, not only was her libido at an all-time high, she was ravenous. Instead of waiting for permission, she sank them into Kane's shoulder, tasting his blood, drawing it into her mouth. He tipped his head back, cords in his neck standing out as he roared from the pleasure.

Kane allowed her to suckle for few minutes longer then pulled her head from his shoulder and chuckled. "Careful, Mia Bella. My blood offers you no nourishment. Save it for a donor."

She wiped her hand across her mouth, seeing the rich blood now on her palm. "Then why do I have this insane desire to feed from you?"

"You're mistaking passion and hunger. Biting and drinking from me during sex will give you pleasure you've never known, but nourishment can only come from blood untainted with our DNA." His smile washed over her, increasing the ache between her thighs.

"We'll go to the Rave later, see that you're nourished. But for now, let's satisfy another hunger."

Kane reached for the bedside table and pulled out a condom. Cara looked at him queerly as he tore open the little foil packet with his teeth.

"I thought you couldn't get me pregnant and diseases weren't an issue?"

"Diseases will never be a problem for our kind, that is true. But now you're a vampire, procreation is definitely a possibility. That's why we only have sex with humans unless we are mated."

"But we aren't mated."

"Yet."

"You're still mated to Rosalee." It shouldn't bother her and she hated herself for allowing it to.

"Until I visit Mircea. Once he hears of his stepdaughter's actions, he'll abrogate the joining and I'll be free to mate again."

"Is that so?" She cocked one brow. "And who do you plan to mate yourself with, vamp boy?"

"Need you even ask?" Kane leaned down and kissed her, one full of possession, leaving her no doubt as to who he intended to mate with. "Any other questions?"

"Yeah. How about you get out of those jeans?"

"You don't have to ask me twice, Mia Bella." He quickly did as she asked, rolled on the condom then situated himself between her spread thighs. "Now ... where were we?"

She framed his handsome face in her hands, loving the features that once had caused her nightmares. "You were about to show me how much you love me."

"That I was," he said, then leaned down and kissed her, proving to her just how much.

EPILOGUE

KALEB TOSSED THE VICE PRESIDENT PATCH ON THE TABLE, THE President one now sewn to his cut. Conversation came to a halt as every pair of eyes focused on the telling patch. All voting members sat in a semi-circle around the large oak table in the center of the room. Kane and Ion's chairs remained empty.

Grayson was the first to speak. "What happened to Viper?"

"Viper's relinquished his role as head of the Sons of Sangue. That makes me club Pres. This church meeting has been called for a couple of reasons. First, we need to vote on a new VP. I vote Gypsy as the successor. Anyone care to second that?"

Grigore Lupie was the first to raise his hand. "Aye."

"Let's take it to a vote."

One-by-one the voting members concurred, making Grayson 'Gypsy' Gabore the new VP of the Sons.

"First order of business," Kaleb continued, "is what to do about Viper's actions."

The members looked from one to another, though no one spoke up. Kane had been the rule follower, the straight shooter. To him everything was black or white, no grey in-betweens, that is until Cara Brahman entered the picture and set out to take him down. Since the interruption in their lives, he had been breaking rules right and left. The Sons had chosen to look the other way for his

387

previous disregard of the rules. Kaleb doubted Kane would be given the same exemption this time.

"What's he done?" Grayson asked. "Don't tell me this has something to do with that detective bitch? I take it she's been found."

"The primordial, Alec Funar," Kaleb began, "acting on orders from Rosalee, sliced her throat clean through. She was bleeding out, and there was no time to get her to help."

"So she's dead? Good riddance," said Grigore.

"She's not dead, Wolf."

"I thought you said—" he began, then went silent in understanding.

"Kane turned her."

Everyone started talking at once. Kaleb had to bang the gavel against the wooden block to restore order. Silence once again filled the room.

"Before we vote on the consequences for his actions, I'd like a moment to tell the story."

"I'm not sure he deserves the right," Joseph spoke up. "He's been sniffing that tail and causing this club problems. And yet he continued when he knew it wasn't in our best interest."

"I can't say I disagree, Kinky. However, as club Pres and as my brother, I would like the right to speak on his behalf." When no one argued, he continued, "My brother loves Cara ... deeply. That much is apparent. He was left with the decision to watch another person he loves die," Kaleb did not have to mention Ion's name, "or give her ... himself a second chance. He didn't have time to ask for a vote. He acted out of love and gave her his blood."

"They cannot be mated," Grayson pointed out.

"Not as long as Rosalee lives, Gypsy. You're correct. We all know to mate with someone is for life. Unfortunately, unless Kane can get Mircea's blessing, he's stuck with that bitch. Cara knows that, and yet she is willing to be with my brother."

"And the primordial?"

Kaleb took a deep breath, bracing his hands on the table. "Is dead by my hand."

Blasphemes filled the room before angry talk begun amongst the members, knowing the consequences for killing a primordial. Kaleb would deal with the fallout, without repercussions to the Sons. He had acted alone and made the decision to behead the bastard.

"He's been ashed."

"And the pigs?" Nicolas asked.

"They arrived shortly after the shed where Alec held Cara went up in flames. His skeletal remains will be found inside. Cara sported the knife wound to her neck to prove Alec's misdeeds, though it had already begun healing. What they saw was an attempt made on her life and her testimony that Alec had confessed to her all previous crimes before trying to take hers. Those cases are now closed.

"And although Captain Melchor insisted on taking Kane back to the S.O., the sheriff denied his request." Kaleb chuckled. "Let's just say Captain Melchor is returning to Salem sporting a couple of black eyes to compliment his broken nose. Kane said he owed him that. And unless the captain wanted to explain Kane's reason to the sheriff—that he once raped Cara—then he was to get back in his vehicle and never step foot in Pleasant again. To do so would be disrespecting the Sons of Sangue."

"And Kane?" Grigore asked. "What do you suggest his penalty be for turning a human?"

"I ask for leniency for what he's endured already and allow him to live in peace with Cara. I'll leave the room for you to come to a decision."

Kaleb walked out, shutting the heavy meeting doors behind him. He prayed his brothers would see reason, because whether they approved Kane's actions or not, he was still his brother and he'd always have his back. Walking over to the bar, Kaleb pulled down the bottle of Jack and poured himself a shot. He knocked it back, welcoming the burn.

What the hell was wrong with his twin? No woman could possibly be worth turning your back on your brothers and the MC. This had been their life, their family, for as long as he could remember. A woman's worth was measured by the quality of the piece of ass you got. Why the hell waste your life on just one?

Suzi flashed through his mind and that kiss they shared in the parking lot a couple of days ago. That had been one hell of a knock-your-socks-off kiss. No wonder she had run. Hell, he should be thanking her for putting the distance between them and slapping him with reality. Only once had he allowed himself to tap that. And yet, he hadn't forgotten one damn second of how sweet it had been to slide between her thighs. And just like that, with one kiss all those old feelings started sliding back in. Yep, he needed to steer far away from that one. Let the rest of the Sons tap that.

Kaleb clenched his teeth, causing an ache to travel up his jaw and end with a ring in his ears. He quickly shook off the jealousy trying to take up residence in his gut. Suzi could fuck anyone she chose as far as he was concerned.

"Hawk?" Grayson said through the now opened door. "We've come to a decision."

Kaleb shook off his thoughts of Suzi, took another quick shot of the whisky, then followed Grayson back into the church meeting.

Once inside, Grayson gave him the verdict. "Kane can keep his rockers, effectively staying a member of the Sons. Hell, it doesn't seem right him not being a member. But he shall have no voting rights."

"Is this unanimous?"

"Aye," Grayson said, and the members around the table nodded in agreement.

Kaleb picked up the gavel and struck the block of wood, pleased the Sons of Sangue had granted Kane the leniency Kaleb had asked for. "Then let it be known, Kane Tepes is to remain a member of the Sons of Sangue and this meeting is adjourned. Now let's go get us some whiskey and women ... I've had about all I can take of this day."

ABOUT THE AUTHOR

A daydreamer at heart, Patricia A. Rasey, resides in her native town in Northwest Ohio with her husband, Mark, and her lovable Cavalier King Charles Spaniel, Todd. A graduate of Long Ridge Writer's School, Patricia has seen publication of some her short stories in magazines as well as several of her novels.

When not behind her computer, you can find Patricia working, reading, watching movies or MMA. She also enjoys spending her free time at the river camping and boating with her husband and two sons. Ms. Rasey is currently a third degree Black Belt in American Freestyle Karate.

Made in the USA
Lexington, KY
14 July 2014